Beside & Other Stories

Uri Nissan Gnessin

BESIDE
& OTHER STORIES

WITH AN INTRODUCTION BY
Rachel Albeck-Gidron

The Toby Press

First Edition, 2005

The Toby Press LLC, 2005
POB 8531, New Milford, CT 06776-8531, USA
& POB 2455, London WIA 5WY, England
www.tobypress.com

Introduction Copyright © 2005 by Rachel Albeck-Gidron

The Toby Press thanks The Institute for the Translation of
Hebrew Literature for their kind assistance in the preparation of
this revised edition. All translations are © The Institute for the
Translation of Hebrew Literature, except as noted below.

Sideways was first published in Hebrew as *Atzida* in *ha-Z'man,* 1905.
English translation by Hillel Halkin, copyright © 1983

Meanwhile was first published in Hebrew as *Benatiyim* in 1906.
English translation by Jeffrey Green, copyright © 2005, The Toby Press

In the Gardens was first published in Hebrew as *BeGanim* in 1909.
English translation by David Segal

Uproar was first published in Hebrew as *Ketatah* in 1912.
English translation by Yael Lotan

The Time Before was first published in Hebrew as *Be'terem* in 1909/10.
English translation by Yehuda Hanegbi

Beside was first published as *Etsel* in 1913.
English translation by Reuven and Judith Ben-Yosef

ISBN 1 59264 093 1, *paperback*

A CIP catalogue record for this title is available from the British Library

Typeset in Garamond by Jerusalem Typesetting

Printed and bound in the United States by Thomson-Shore Inc., Michigan

Contents

Rachel Albeck-Gidron

Introduction

Uri Nissan Gnessin, the greatest writer of modern Hebrew prose and the brilliant creator of its introspective fiction,[1] was born in the winter of 1879, in the small town of Starodub in the Ukraine. The second son in a Jewish family, Gnessin grew up surrounded by the warmth of a typical provincial community of the old Jewish world.

His father and teacher, Rabbi Yehoshua Natan (in Yiddish: Rabbi Heschel Neta), was an unusual man. As a Chabad *hasid* and an outstanding scholar, he was well versed in the Talmud and the halakhic rulings of the Jewish codifiers as well as in the Midrash and the Aggadah. Moreover, he was learned in the writings of Kabbalah and the Jewish mystical works so venerated in the Hasidic world. At the same time, as was customary among Jewish scholars even in remote Russian villages, Gnessin's father was steeped in the Hebrew language in all its various historical layers, spanning from biblical times, through the Mishnaic period, the early prayers, and the medieval liturgy up to the Responsa literature composed by the contemporary halakhic decisors.

During his lifetime, at the close of the nineteenth century, Hebrew was a liturgical and textual language. It was the language of the daily cycle of Jewish rituals that preoccupied most of a person's waking hours, from the moment of rising in the morning, blessing the Creator for returning the soul to one's body, until climbing into bed at night and reciting the *Shema* before closing one's eyes.

In addition to his expertise in the Hebrew language, as a rabbi, a Talmud scholar, and a *hasid*, Uri Nissan's father was also versed in the Aramaic of the Babylonian Talmud and in the later-day Aramaic of the Jewish mystics. Furthermore, along with these textual and liturgical languages, he was conversant in Yiddish, as were his contemporaries. In the small Jewish towns and shtetls, on the street, and in the home, a secular, friendly Yiddish was the spoken language. Handed down from generation to generation for some five hundred years in Eastern Europe, it was a language full of poetic and naturalistic expressions, picturesque blessings, and colorful euphemisms.

This rather absent-minded, learned, and generous man brought up his four children, Eliyahu Pinchas, Uri Nissan, Menachem and Hiyyah to be extremely knowledgeable in their rich Jewish tradition and its languages. In addition, he hired Russian tutors to teach his children the Russian language and its literature. In this respect, he differed from the separatist Jews of his milieu, all the more so since this openness to foreign culture was incompatible with his position as a rabbi and as the head of the yeshivah in his small town.

Later, Uri Nissan continued to study on his own, and eventually was conversant not only in Russian but also in German and French. From his youth he would read books in these three languages, and he even translated from them into Hebrew. Simultaneously, he studied Greek and Latin, and later, in his twenties, he learned English. This wealth of language and culture was deeply ingrained in his consciousness, alongside the Hebrew and Aramaic taught by his father—while he continued to think and express himself exclusively in Yiddish.

By the time Uri Nissan had reached the age of nine, his father had already moved the family twice. In 1881, they moved from Starodub with the eldest son, Eliyahu Pinchas, and with Uri Nissan, who was two years old at the time, to the small town of Krichev in the province of Mogilev, to which the father had been invited to serve as a rabbi, and there his third son Menachem was born. Menachem would grow up to become Uri Nissan's bosom friend and closest ally. In 1888, when Uri Nissan was nine years old, Rabbi Yehoshua Natan was invited by his father-in-law to serve together with him in the rabbinate of Pochep, a small town in the province of Orel, in Belorussia. Uri Nissan's grandfather, the father of his mother, Esther, was the scion of generations of rabbis. Highly devoted to Jewish tradition and wishing to protect it from foreign influences, he opposed the liberal, European education that his son-in-law introduced into his home, even though he otherwise held him in great regard.

Pochep became Uri Nissan's psychic homeland and an expansion of his soul that persisted throughout his entire life, which, however brief, was replete with suffering and longing. His wanderlust may have begun on the two occasions in which his father relocated the family in his early childhood. However, Uri Nissan would always return home to his parents from his wanderings. These two intense impulses of Uri Nissan's, to wander to the large and distant cities and to return to the small home in the provinces, intermingled and created for him a tragic confusion. His travels led him throughout the stormy, pre-revolutionary cities of Russia and Poland, brought him a life of poverty and hunger in the East End of London, sent him via Genoa to the Land of Israel, then under the Ottoman rule, and back to the metropolitan cities of Eastern Europe, until his early death in Warsaw in 1913. But time and again, he would return home to the remote shtetl of Pochep, "to the warm bed of Mama," as he coined it, and to the pines of his native land, where he would seek—in vain—rest for his soul among the family who awaited him: his parents, his young nieces, whose tutor and guide he became, and his nephew, who died while still in his youth. Pochep stimulated Gnessin's artistic soul; he would gaze at the beautiful forests, at its surrounding hills, and at the wonderful river.

Gnessin's parental home emerges as an enigma. Apparently, the two brothers, Uri Nissan, the author, and Menachem, the actor, led there double lives, in which they were simultaneously forbidden and allowed to be secular Jews with Russian-European orientations. A strong love, spiritual and sensitive, bound the family together, but there was also room for secretive privacy, for leading a meaningful life unknown to the members of the family. It is otherwise impossible to account for the fact that Gnessin's parents were unaware of their son's illness until the day he died. A heart disease that developed toward the end of his adolescence became more and more severe during the terrible years of hunger in Warsaw, Kiev, and London. When he was already in the hospital, approaching his own death, Uri Nissan wrote to his friend M. Hoffenstein, urging him not to let his parents know of his condition. As indicated in the memoirs of his brother and of one of the women who loved him "to distraction,"[2] all of those who saw Gnessin were aware of his physical suffering and his prolonged dying; however, when he stayed at home, that aspect of his life was always repressed, hidden from his parents.

The mixture of the permitted and the prohibited, this interweaving of tradition with strands of modern cultural life, is well-illustrated in an anecdote that appears in the autobiography of Menachem Gnessin, who was an actor and a founder of Habimah,[3] the first Hebrew theater. Menachem relates that once before the Jewish New Year, which is a time of intensified public prayers and moral accounting, posters advertising Henrik Ibsen's *Nora* appeared on the walls of the houses in the small provincial town of Pochep. The single performance of the play was to take place in "the Castle of the Prince in the City Garden." On the evening of the performance, a beautiful young Russian woman, with a small golden cross "hanging on her bare, marble white neck," suddenly showed up at the door of the Rabbi's house and asked to speak with the bewildered son of the Rabbi. Menachem went outside with her, "fearing his parents would hear them," and there she told him she had heard that he had Ibsen's writings, and that she would like to borrow them from him for a few days. In exchange, she said, she would give him a ticket to the performance.

Still agitated, as he relates in his memoir, that evening he went to the theater, and there, to his boundless embarrassment, a loud voice was heard from the direction of the box-office, asking him to come and pick up the ticket left for him by one of the actresses in the play. The Jews of the town among the audience looked on in disapproval at the Rabbi's son, who had some affair with a gentile stage actress.

Thus, his first, hypnotic encounter with the theater, an experience that determined the course of his life, was inseparably mingled with the deep shame he felt under those glances and with guilt for having "succumbed to the evil urge" just before the Jewish New Year.

How extraordinary that an actress who had chanced to be in this remote provincial town and asked if there was someone who could lend her the plays of a Norwegian playwright, in whose play she was about to perform, should have been directed, of all the houses in the town, precisely to the Rabbi's house, to the library of that young man, his son!

Gnessin's brother further testifies that Pochep's young Jews used to follow contemporary Russian literature with great interest; they read the works of Tolstoy, Gorky, Chekhov, and Turgenev and compared them to contemporary Scandinavian literature, to the plays of Ibsen and Strindberg and to the prose works of Knut Hamsun. According to Menachem's memoir, they would take patriotic pride in the superiority of Russian literature, no less than the pride they felt when reading the Hebrew writers of their generation, or contemporary Yiddish literature, such as that of Y.L. Peretz, which at that time was being translated into Hebrew.[4] These youths were part of a new generation of Jewish modernism. Living a modern nationalistic life, they were just beginning to address the question of their identity and its future as an ethnic minority, while identifying with the artistic works of the host culture. Intermittently they were repressing and acknowledging the fact that they were being literally persecuted to death by the very culture they adored.

Moreover, since Hebrew wasn't a spoken language at the time, the project of turning it into a modern, living language was an overwhelming task, which had been going on since the emergence of the *Haskalah,* the Hebrew Enlightenment movement, in the eighteenth century, though it was almost entirely focused on the written language. Only in the late 1920s, in Eretz Yisrael, far from Europe, had Jews made a hesitant beginning, not without struggle, of speaking Hebrew in their daily life. Surprisingly, the modern Hebrew literature composed by those Jewish youths, who deserted the Talmudic academies, managed to represent the life that had been conducted in Yiddish, but it did so with continued difficulties and distress. Not only were Hebrew readers scarce, but an immense amount of social commitment and political vision was required to maintain momentum to keep reading this "dead language" that was undergoing a renaissance. One can see how the sentences of the early Hebrew fiction were more than once drafted awkwardly and inadequately, for lack of words to convey the personal and the modern, secular spheres of life. The Hebrew language had to break out from the liturgical scripts into common everyday life, life of business and productivity, of love and sex, and especially the inner life that literature normally describes. As they created their narratives, rhymes, and metaphors, these writers of the revived Hebrew were somehow chiseling the Hebrew language itself, just like the mountain climbers who cut steps in the ice underneath their feet.

Apparently, in the small yeshiva in Pochep, under the leadership of Uri Nissan's father, the semi-forbidden spiritual life of the *Haskalah* movement of modern times was as flourishing as the religious life of Torah learning and piety, which attracted youths from all the surrounding towns.

It can hardly be a coincidence, then, that two of the most significant writers on secular Jewish life in their day had attended this small yeshiva. Yosef Haim Brenner (1881–1921) arrived at Pochep when he was around fifteen years old, and so began his enduring friendship with Uri Nissan. This was a painful friendship of love, zealous rivalry, and hard labor in the service of the developing national culture. It is difficult to imagine these two youths, so different from one another, developing side by side to become outstanding authors: Uri Nissan, tall, light-haired, broad shouldered,[5] distant and secretive, aesthetic and refined, introverted and with a melancholic irony, at home in the open spaces of nature; and opposite him Yosef Haim, rough, unruly, feverish, common, whose black curls were wild and his eyes glowing, whose irony was social, communal and naturalistic, so much so that nothing repulsed him, and whose great dedication can be compared only to that of the great martyrs of tradition. The two of them may have begun their work as authors and editors of journals in those days in Pochep, since even then, during the years 1897–1898, they published three journals: *Ha-Perah* ["The Flower"], *Ha-Kof* ["The Monkey"], and Ha-Kayits ["The Summer"][6]—journals which were to showcase Gnessin's first poems and the early works of Brenner.

Soon enough, Gnessin's storage box became filled with notebooks piled upon notebooks, of his poems and his translations of Russian and German poetry,[7] including his first story (one that he rejected), all of them written in a beautiful pearl-like handwriting. When Uri Nissan was eighteen, one of these notebooks found its way into the hands of Nahum Sokolov, the editor of *Ha-Tsefirah*. This illustrious Hebrew journal was published in Warsaw, which at the beginning of the twentieth century was an important metropolitan center and one of the large urban focal points of Hebrew and Zionist activity. When Sokolov saw the jottings of Gnessin's poems, he invited the unknown young man to work with him on the staff of his journal, and thus in 1899, Gnessin's wanderings began. He accepted Sokolov's offer and left for Warsaw, where he began to publish in 1900, initially his first poem and then several critical reviews. That same year, he wrote and published in two other forums: *Ha-Shavua*, which was printed in Krakow, and a yearbook edited by Sokolov. Uri Nissan also began to write for *Tushiyyah* and through that publishing firm he was first introduced to Warsaw's Hebrew authors. As a result of his selective taste and perhaps also because of his tendency to react to urgent inner imperatives, in less than a year he was fed up with Warsaw, particularly with its group of young authors. Gnessin left without saying good-bye to anyone and returned to his familiar Pochep and to his parents' home.

In Warsaw, as in all the other cities he was to visit in the future, he left a deep and enduring imprint on the intellectuals and the literary milieu—an impression that was at once mysterious, evasive, poetic, amazingly quiet but also disturbing and penetrating. An aura of intriguing strangeness surrounded him, as in the future the different eulogies articulated by this group were to affirm. In the women who happened to meet him, he awakened a magnetic and often tragic love. They felt that he deeply influenced their inner life and spirituality, so much so that one of them was moved to write: "Women who do not know Gnessin have no idea of what a human being should be."[8]

In the years of 1902–1904, Gnessin wandered intermittently through the cities of czarist Russia and Poland, among them Kiev and Warsaw. During this period, he continued writing his early short stories, on which he had begun working two years earlier. In 1902, he finished writing his first big story, *Genia*, about a young Jewish woman with a turbulent soul, who joins a group of Hebrew Zionist activists. This realistic work portrays the emotional and political Zionist state of affairs, along with the psychological, erotic, and idealistic aspects of this representative group of youth. In 1903, Gnessin wrote the story *Ma'aseh be-Otelo* ["A Story of Othello"], about a love affair between a tutor and his married student that ended in a minor scandal. In the same year, he also wrote *Shmuel Ben-Shmuel*, a story about a ridiculous and detestable family man, who commits adultery with a young farm girl at the moment his wife is giving birth. Gnessin compiled the three stories into one book and called it *Tsilelei Hayyim* ["Shadows of Life"]. He sent the manuscript to the Tushiyyah publishing house in Warsaw, for its Hebrew Library series, which was in the hands of the naturalistic author well known in his time, Ben-Avigdor (A.I. Shelkovitz). In the winter of 1904, *Shadows of Life* was published as a book.

Summing up Gnessin's literary activity so far, one can only say of him, along with his first critics and most of the later ones, that all of this first writing was no more than mediocre, or "epigonic," as some of them suggested; it left no striking impression and inspired only a few critical reviews. In fact, in those early works there was no indication that a few years later Gnessin, would be writing the most excellent and refined of Hebrew prose since the eighteenth century and until this day, and without a doubt the most innovative among the community of modern European authors—the French, the English, the German, and the Russian of that time. Therefore it is customary to speak of the "early" Gnessin (till 1905) and the "late" Gnessin (from 1905 on); the former absorbed in the corpus of realistic Hebrew literature, which was influenced by the Yiddish Mendele Mokher Seforim (Shalom Abramovitz) and afterward by Berdichevsky, Feierberg, Bershadsky, Ben-Avigdor, and others, whereas the latter glows as a unique, unparalleled phenomenon, so that to this day no one has attained the subtle qualities of his works.

His story "The Guest," or "In Grandfather's House," which was written at the end of the first period and sent that same year to the editors of *Ha-Shilo'ah,* was returned to its sender by Bialik, then the editor, after being found not worthy of printing.[9] It was published posthumously years later, with the publication of Gnessin's literary remains. This fact is rather puzzling because although the story was written in the "early Gnessin" style, it is the most beautiful of all the stories he wrote during that period, displaying an epigrammatic quality, romantic and charismatic, that by no means can be labeled as mediocre. The following quotation from the story illustrates this quality. It reflects an unresolved paradox in the metaphysical climate of those that deserted the Talmudic academies, and is both sad and witty:

> Man is as weak as a fly, but the great God is in his heart, so to speak. As long as he climbs—he climbs...Perhaps he even manages to transcend. But once he pauses, however briefly, his God instantly pulls him down.[10]

Atheism mingled with the ghostly shadow of belief is discernible in the description of the greatness of God as a weight that actually pulls the believer down to the depths, apparently toward the Devil's abode. The phrase "so to speak" in the second line is habitually used by the devout to stress the theological fact that God cannot be described. A Nietzschean spirit permeates this epigram, just as it ran through many aspects of the Hebrew ideology of that period. Also Nietzschean perhaps is the enchanting character in the story, R. Asher, the guest, who is a kind of mixture of Cain of the European romantics and the false Messiah Shabbetai Tsvi, albeit placed in a truly realistic context, in a manner that aptly captures the opposing forces of the Zeitgeist that prevailed in the Jewish towns at the turn of the century. Along with this story, Gnessin published an additional story, *Se'udah Mafseket* ["The Meal before the Fast"], which should be associated with the first period, even though chronologically it was written and published along with the first story of the other period.

The year of 1905 marks the beginning of an entirely different chapter in Gnessin's literary biography, which opens with his great work *Hatsidah* ["Sideways"], the first of a collection of stories of the same title. This year, when he was twenty-six, his traveling desire brought him to Vilna, where he stayed with a group of young authors that worked for the Journal *Ha-Zeman*. He submitted the work to that journal and it lay there unwanted for days, weeks, and months. And then, suddenly, it all changed. David Frischmann, the powerful and authoritative editor of *Ha-Zeman*, "discovered" the story and immediately recognized its unparalleled merits. Frischmann, who was famous for seldom giving compliments and always understating them, went out of his way, warmly praising the work before his acquaintances, and published it without delay on the pages of his journal. When it came out, it was applauded with a sense of wonder and excitement, as affirmed—for the benefit of future generations—by the eulogies of the greatest authors of the time. Eight years later, while the critics were still overwhelmed with shock and grief over Gnessin's sudden death, their eulogies were compiled into a book published in his memory. This book was called *Hatsidah*, after the title of his first masterpiece.

In 1906, Gnessin was once again in Pochep, from where he left for Vilna, and afterward for Kiev. He started a literary publishing house called *Nisyonot*, "Attempts," where he published his latest story *Beinatayyim* ["Meanwhile"]. He also translated and published three of Chekhov's stories: *Talant*, ["Talent"], *Ishah Mesaperet* ["A Woman Tells"], and *Ba-Aviv* ["In the Spring"]. At his publishing house, Uri Nissan gave the same prominence to his translations as to his original works. This was no coincidence. From his early youth and until the time he died, he was translating the works of Lermontov, Nadson, Nikitin, Shestov, Heine, Byron, Nomberg, Wasserman, Baudelaire, and others. To understand Gnessin's prose in depth one must view it in the context of its wonderful and unique cultural crossroads. This was a precious artistic moment in the history of national literatures—a moment that also made possible the birth of a phenomenon like Freud, and for exactly the same reason. At this very moment, the Jewish traditions, with their profound oriental and primordial spiritual moulds, met with the intellectual and artistic sensibilities of European culture, with its diversity of national temperaments and heritages.

Gnessin, the translator of Chekhov and of the prose poems of Baudelaire, imported into his works a mixture of Chekhov's talent of placing atmosphere and mood in the center and relegating the action to the sidelines of the narrative. The protagonist's vague longings and sorrows are the deep subject of the story, as in Chekhov's play *The Seagull.* In addition, Gnessin imported the absolute polishing, the opposite of vagueness, as it appears in Baudelaire's prose poems, which are distinguished by preciseness and clarity of language as best manifested in the French literary tradition. One can also discern in Gnessin's writing a blend of the Russian soul—as it is embodied in Dostoyevsky's works, which deal obsessively with fervent and accelerated states of consciousness—and the pessimistic compliance evident in Schopenhauer. For both of these writers deeply influenced Gnessin and his literary circle, even though he did not translate any of their works.[11]

Only by acknowledging the impact of these diverse influences is it possible to understand how this youth from the provincial town of Pochep succeeded in producing a Proustian tone some seven years before Proust himself began to publish his *Remembrance of Things Past* (1913) and a stream of consciousness prose about eleven years before Joyce wrote his early work, *A Portrait of the Artist as a Young Man* (1916). These two works were published when Uri Nissan Gnessin was already long dead. He managed to attain these accomplishments while writing in the ancient Hebrew of his period, in which every single word was liturgical, yet in his hands this language became flexible and flowing, personal, bubbling and poetical, until his early critics justifiably called him a "lyricist of prose" and a "violinist" of narrative textuality.

Two great tragedies affected the unique prose of Gnessin in the historical course of its reception. Miraculously, the first did not destroy it in the slightest way; unfortunately, the second sadly turned Gnessin's work into the exotic literature of foreign peoples.

The first disastrous event relates to the development of the pronunciation of Hebrew prose and its transformation from the Ashkenazi pronunciation, as it had been spoken in Europe, into the Sephardic pronunciation, as articulated by the Sephardic Jews and then, beginning in the late 1920s, also by the Ashkenazi Jews that settled down in the land of Israel. Hence the intonation of contemporary Hebrew in Israel and its phonetic pronunciation are almost unrecognizable from the ritualistic Hebrew of Jewish towns in Europe. So much so that when a modern Israeli hears a reproduction of the original Ashkenazi pronunciation of Gnessin's work, he may not be able to understand it. Thus, Gnessin's work is read today in a melody and intonation that are completely different from the original, yet the heart-catching beauty of his prose remains the same, and it still thrills the sensitive reader.

The second tragedy happened because of Gnessin. In a letter to his nephew, Israel Noah Sprintz, dated May 1906, he wrote:

> If I had a little more sympathy in my heart for our Ivan,[12] I would set aside some time now to translate, together with him, "Sideways" and "Meanwhile" into Russian. It's possible I could get a few roubles from this, but first of all, my sympathy for him is not so great and secondly, even though we succeeded in translating the story *Aggadah* by Peretz, I don't know if his non-Jewish soul will be able to translate such things. It's true that I'll be the translator, but you know the Yiddish saying: "Even the cat can mess things up," particularly with regard to literature, and especially literature like this, built completely on half-words that, when they aren't in the right place, don't say anything. However, I will try to settle this matter, for after all, I do like his robust and lively Russian style.[13]

It follows that for various apparently valid reasons, Gnessin decided not to have his stories translated into Russian, even though he had the opportunity to do so. The history of modern Hebrew literature and perhaps of Russian literature as well, might have been different if this new prose had been translated into Russian. As it stands, to this day Uri Nissan Gnessin has remained anonymous to readers who do not know Hebrew—or Yiddish. Gnessin himself translated one of his Hebrew stories, *Ba-Ganim* ["In the Gardens"] into Yiddish, under the title *Tsvishen Gertner*—or perhaps it was the other way round, as one scholar speculated.[14] Perhaps this is why very few Hebrew writers followed in his footsteps.

Gnessin's life of wandering and his brief visits home continued until 1907, when he decided to join his friend Yosef Haim Brenner, who was living in London. There, in abject poverty, laboring beyond the reserves of his strength, Brenner published the journal *Ha-Me'orer*. Gnessin, haunted by the persistent inner voice that constantly urged him to travel somewhere—anywhere, arrived in London, and there, as always, he was unable to find tranquility. Nevertheless, it was during that year that he collaborated with Brenner, even as their relationship became increasingly tempestuous. Eventually, Gnessin decided to leave the apartment he was sharing with Brenner in the seedy neighborhood of the East End and to immigrate to Eretz Israel, where his brother Menachem was living. During this period, Menachem was deeply involved in founding the first Hebrew theater in the land of Israel, on the sands of Jaffa.

Yet here, too, the same restlessness characterized his life. Gnessin was disappointed and sick, but he continued to write, and between 1909–1910, he published his story *Be-Terem* ["The Time Before"], which appeared in installments in the literary journal *Reshafim*, edited by David Frischmann (in collaboration with F. Lachover)—by which time Gnessin had once again returned home to Pochep.

Something odd must be said about Gnessin, the man and writer. Although he crossed lands and seas, wandering for years across noisy Europe at the beginning of the century, staying in gloomy Jewish villages; although he lived through the riots of the abortive Russian uprising of 1905 and experienced the czarist reign of terror on the eve of its collapse—terror that took the form of government censure of letters, journals, and books, in a period when youths were arrested as revolutionaries, among them young intellectual Jews, acquaintances of Gnessin; and although his was a life in which one was forced to get a permit to go from one city to the next and in which travelers were arrested for not having a permit, as once happened to Gnessin himself—in spite of all this, there is no hint of any of these events in his writing. Furthermore, these were the years of pogroms against the Jews of Eastern Europe, in which whole families were murdered and died violent deaths even in the villages next to his Pochep. And in addition, it was the young Gnessin himself who initiated and organized the self-defense of his small town in the event that the pogroms reach them too. Still, these events escape mention in his introverted writing. Only the atmosphere of grief on the edge of a catastrophe, which is mirrored in the state of mind of his protagonists, as suggested by the voice of the implicit narrator, gives any hint of the frightful events that were taking place during this time.

Even the death of his nephew, whom Gnessin had loved profoundly and had not ceased to worry about, received notice in just one paragraph, as an answer to a friend who had mentioned him in a letter:

> That fellow Noah you ask about…my sister's son, was the love of my heart; but don't ask about him any more…"We will go to him but he will not come to us." Excuse me for this tone, for he was very dear to me.[15]

Nevertheless, despite the fact that the great historical events that had caught up the Jewish people were not explicitly mentioned in his stories (as opposed to the stories of his friend Yosef Haim Brenner), there is no doubt that Gnessin was documenting the life about him in a very tangible and realistic way, through the impact it had on his characters' consciousness, with its idiosyncratic twists and turns.

Gnessin was to embark upon just one more journey. During the next three years he wrote his last great story, *Etsel* ["Beside"], as his health slowly began to fail him completely in his parents' home. In this period, he remained strangely charismatic, and finally he went to Warsaw, hoping desperately that he would still be able to find a cure at its hospital. It was there that he died, in 1913, when he was just thirty-three years and four months old.

In his last documented letter, Gnessin wrote to one of his friends: "Will the day yet come when together we will laugh our sad laugh of the dead? You see, days have come that even such a laugh you renounce."

ᴈᴇ

Critical opinion has revolved around four basic widely accepted conclusions emerging from the body of Gnessin's writing, and even the detractors have first addressed these propositions before proving their own readings.

The first conclusion divides Gnessin's work into two different periods, the early period and the late. This evaluation was established immediately after Gnessin's death, when the critics began to define the distinguishing features of Gnessin's work in its entirety. Following Gnessin's death, David Frischmann and the poet Zalman Shneour described the surprise they felt upon discovering the emergence of Gnessin's new and innovative style in his story *Hatsidah* ["Sideways"], as compared to the character of the poems he had published until that time and to his early prose works. Shneour wrote as follows:

> At once, Gnessin left behind all the accepted forms in Hebrew literature, all accepted styles, all the accepted techniques of description and of phrase concentration, and he did so holding his head high and with the confidence of a mature talent on its own path. We were amazed. This man began with poor imitations of the stories of M. Spektor, moved to the weak stories in the collection *Tsilelei ha-Hayyim* ["The Shadows of Life"] (1904), and then wrote some lean poems in *Ha-Dor*. Then, suddenly, in one grandiose leap, he rose up and placed himself to rule as a king over his great talent by virtue of the faculties of his soul. We read his story

"Sideways" over and over again, reading it and rising up, and then we looked through his translations and his old stories and articles, and it was as if we were looking down from the giddy heights of a tower, as if some sweet dizziness seized upon us with some intense emotion. Suddenly we had an overwhelming desire to shake this fellow's hand, to look into his eyes, to hear his silence, to walk with him from one coffee house to another, to pat him on the back; to thank him in words and to speak with him...[16]

Some might have been able to discern a foreshadowing of his later stories in his 1904 collection, *The Shadows of Life*, while others may even address questions about the discrepancies in quality between the two periods. Both groups, however, would not fail to perceive the essential differences in genre, style, and theme between this first collection and Gnessin's later stories. The former, modeled on the narrative conventions of realism, describe events that were happening inside buildings and houses, public halls and rooms, in a (narrow or broad) social context, in clear reference to contemporary idealistic and collective issues. The latter, on the other hand, illustrate—in a manner that was initially labeled "impressionistic," for lack of a more suitable term—occurrences on the streets, in trains, in the fields, in the forests, and on the banks of the river beside which a solitary soul wanders. The stories deal with thoughts and meditations of the private individual and are clearly very much removed from the burning issues of the day. While the early stories express an action-oriented state of mind, described from an external viewpoint, the later ones evoke a passive and sinking atmosphere, perceived from an introspective point of view and filtered through the feelings and mindset of the protagonists. While the style of the early stories was referential and almost resolute, the style of the later ones, which were examined extensively by Gnessin's critics and are still being explored, tends more toward a lyrical discourse, an inner monologue, and the technique that later came to be known as the "stream of consciousness," and is distinguished by its linguistic and poetic innovations.

In fact, in the work neglected by Gnessin's critics, namely his poems, one can see a great difference between the early poetry, written in the style of Bialik and the Russian romantics of that period, and the one poem in "Sideways," which some critics defined as modernist. It is worth mentioning here that an early version of this poem, in Russian, was in fact written by the poetess Celia Levin-Dropkin, and given to Gnessin. As she relates in her memoirs, Gnessin put these words in the mouth of one of the female characters in his story, whose obsessive love for the hero of the story in fact resembled her own love for Gnessin. In her memoirs, the poetess writes of her anger that he has "stolen" her poem, even though he translated it and adapted it for his own use. This question is interesting from other points of view, as suggested subsequently.

The second consensus that has been reached and accepted by researchers of Gnessin is that the critical history of his works can also be divided into two different periods, the first beginning directly after his death, and the second continuing until this day. The first period was called by Lily Rattok the period of "the Gnessin myth." In her introduction to the collection of critical essays on Gnessin that she edited, Rattok explains that during this period, the critics were strongly impacted by the writer's personality and his sudden death, and by their own guilt feelings at having ignored his writing when he was alive.[17] During this time, critics tended to confuse Gnessin's personality with his writing; thus there would be judgments about his dreamy and lyrical personality and its relation to the melodic and meditative character of his writings, or to "the cold impressionism" of his style—as Brenner qualified it—alongside the unassertive elitism of his personality.

Only afterward, and only in Israel, where the Hebrew literature originating in Europe immigrated, along with its followers and critics, who had not known Gnessin personally, did the criticism of Gnessin begin to be concerned directly with his works. Rattok points to Rachel Katznelson-Shazar as the critic who began that trend in her essay on Gnessin, which was written in 1966. Fishel Lachover is the one exception. He wrote an excellent comprehensive introduction to Gnessin's late stories about a year after the author's death.

Though he had known Gnessin during his lifetime, he succeeded in writing a penetrating work of criticism in two separate parts: an in-depth criticism of his writings, and a biographical description of the author. Since the 1960s, numerous studies have been published about Gnessin's works, among them Hamutal Bar-Yosef's significant book (1987), which explores Gnessin's unique style and subjects it to a literary and linguistic analysis, and Dan Miron's authoritative book (1997), which analyzes Gnessin's various works. Yitzhak Bakon, in his book on Brenner and Gnessin (1986), researched Gnessin's bilingualism as a Yiddish-speaking author writing in Hebrew. Lily Rattok's anthology (1977) includes a collection of classic articles on Gnessin's works.

The third proposition in the accepted criticism of the work of Uri Nissan Gnessin claims that his last four stories are actually one long story containing four chapters, all of which concern one single protagonist, despite the four different names he assumes.

The basis for this claim, which various critics have made, and which others have devoted entire pages to moderate or challenge, was first established by Z. Shneour in 1913, when he wrote: "*Hatsidah* ['Sideways']. This was the beginning of a poem of a great loneliness, which persisted until the last line of *Etsel* ['Beside'], his last story."[18] This impression of the continuity of Gnessin's stories is related first of all to an awareness of the specific structure of these stories, which more than anything else marks them as modernistic and innovative par excellence. Later on, precisely this feature was to be considered as the precursor of a new, innovative literary school, which developed in European and Anglo-Saxon prose during the 1920s and 1930s. This structure does not follow the narrative sequence of events recommended by the Aristotelean poetic tradition. According to this convention, a narrative consists of an introduction, which provides the necessary and sufficient causal basis; a middle, in which the action progresses according to a purposeful chain of events; and an ending that locks the sequence with a convincing click. Gnessin's deviation from this conventional structure can be defined with the help of his own wording. In one of his letters, which concerns a totally different matter, he states: "A middle. It all begins in the middle, and it all ends in the middle, and all that you see is nothing but the middle."[19]

What is apparent here, perhaps, is the influence of Baudelaire, who in his accompanying letter about the manuscript of "The Spleen of Paris" (some of these prose poems were translated by Gnessin into Hebrew), wrote to his editor:

> My Dear Friend:
> I send you a little work, of which it cannot be said, without injustice, that it has neither head nor tail; since all of it, on the contrary, is at once head and tail, alternately and reciprocally. Consider, I pray you, what convenience this arrangement offers to all of us [...]. Remove the vertebra, and the two parts of this tortuous fantasy rejoin painlessly. Chop it into particles, and you will see that each part can exist by itself. In the hope that some of these segments will be lively enough to please and to amuse you, I venture to dedicate to you the entire serpent.

And then he added:

> Which of us has not, in his moments of ambition, dreamed the miracle of a poetic prose, musical, without rhythm or rhyme, sufficiently supple, sufficiently abrupt, to adapt itself to the lyrical moments of the soul, to the winding and turnings of the fancy, to the sudden starts of the conscience...[20]

In Baudelaire's writings, which were close to his heart, Gnessin found not only the "Spleen" ambience, which prevailed in his own urban descriptions, and perhaps also in those of the province and its landscape. Gnessin also found in Baudelaire's works the theory and the permission to treat the classical demands of the plot with great license and to give expression to the spontaneous flickering of the eclectic poetic drive. He took the license that Baudelaire had applied to his short prose poems about Paris and turned it into something much more radical—a poetics of a long novella in prose, or of a long novel in four chapters.

It is hardly surprising, then, that precisely this fiction—whose narrative structure is non-organic, in the sense that it does not follow the full cycle of human life through birth, growing up, and death, but instead offers a fragmented and seemingly accidental portion of it—encourages the reader to look for a sequel that will satisfy the aesthetic urge for totality and completion in the textual regions outside the single story.

This doesn't mean that these stories are lacking structure in other senses: a reader whose holding power is good enough to grasp each and every one of those stories comprehensively and all at once—an abstraction that is necessary for understanding the structure of any mechanism—can also discover qualities complete in themselves in each one of the stories. "*Sideways*" is a story that follows the psychological course of a young Hebrew intellectual, Nachum Hagezer, during the yearly seasons of about two years, according to the way in which those seasons impact his interaction with the social and human context that surrounds him and the decisions he makes in his life. "Meanwhile" [*Beinatayyim*], which does not appear in this collection, tells the story of Naftali Berger, a young tutor of two children, who is worn down by his experiences in the city—itself a muted entity in the story. The urban setting is almost abstract, and its decadent and dreary features threaten to push sensitive young people to the brink of suicide and beyond it (as happens to one of the protagonist's acquaintances). Even though middle-class bourgeois life is depicted well, almost realistically, it serves as nothing more than a background for the foul mood of depression that overcomes the youth, and it is this mood that becomes the focal point of the story. *Be-Terem* ["The Time Before"] is about the attempts of Uriel Ephrat, a young adult, to return to his parental home. As Uriel discovers, time is irreversible and the wish to go back is unreal. "Beside" [*Etsel*] is about Ephraim Margalit, a young poetic youth who has been trampled by the strong forces of life, by the ironic melancholy of his soul, and by the weakness of his body. Ephraim manages the household of his close and distant memories, which flood him with tremendous vitality. The phenomenology of the remembrance process is the focal point of this story.

All of the stories are written in a mood of quasi-nostalgia oriented toward the present. Every single moment of life already involves the yearning for it, as it contains the ache of awareness that this moment will be lost in the immediate future. There is the same sensation of deja vu that we know only from rare experiences, infinitely charged and highly inexplicable, that last only a second in our consciousness; this atmosphere perseveres throughout these novellas and floods the reader with a sense of intensified and suspended sentimentality. Perhaps it was this atmosphere that made Yosef Haim Brenner call his friend "a cold impressionist"—meaning someone whose perception of the senses is held in check by a mechanism of suspension and contemplation.

It is easy to conclude that those four young men in Gnessin's stories are in fact one man held in the grips of his soul and subjected to psychic processes as an artist, an intellectual, an onlooker, and a witness, while these inner processes, in turn, are nourished by his social, architectural, and natural surrounding. This is what gave rise to the critical notion that these four different stories are actually a continuous chronicle of the mental life of a single person.

From here we reach the fourth accepted critical conclusion emerging out of the last stories of Gnessin: that all the heroes are actually reflections of his own soul.

David Frischmann, who published "Sideways" [*Hatsidah*], the first story of Gnessin's last period, and who was also the first person to discover the "late Gnessin"; that self-same Frischmann to whom Gnessin dedicated his last story (which was published posthumously) with the words "for David Frischmann on his Jubilee," explained, in referencing the comparison of Gnessin's heroes with the author, the writer's puzzling leap from the early period of realistic writing into the later period:

I cannot picture him as a writer who was capable of

writing about the life of someone else. And truly, each time Gnessin tried to write about the psychic life of others, he immediately became a third- or even fourth-rate author, despite the fact that he had a very keen eye and that he saw so very much and understood so very much and explored so very much.

Then Frischmann continues:

But whoever reads "Sideways," "Meanwhile," "The Time Before," and so forth, will find them forever imprinted in his heart.[21]

Notes

1. Alongside Uri Nissan Gnessin, S.Y. Agnon is considered the outstanding artist/creator of Hebrew prose. Their styles and their mindsets were extremely different, and represent the two main directions taken by a fiction that reflects the Jewish world in the twentieth century and the world of the individual within it.

2. Celia Levin-Dropkin, "*Zikhronot:* Memories of U.N. Gnessin," in *U.N. Gnessin: Studies and Documents*, ed. Dan Miron and Dan Laor (Jerusalem: Mossad Bialik, 1986), p. 419.

3. Menachem Gnessin, *My Way in the Hebrew Theater: 1905–1926* (Tel Aviv: Hakibbutz Hameuhad, 1946), pp. 18–19.

4. Ibid., pp. 16–17.

5. Celia Levin-Dropkin (supra, note 2), pp. 403–407.

6. S. Bicovsky, ed., *Hatsidah: A Memorial Collection to U.N. Gnessin*, ed. S. Bicovsky (Jerusalem: Ahdut, 1914), p. 88; Shena Nashkes, "Bibliographia and Dates," *The Collected Works of U.N. Gnessin*, vol. 3 (Merhavia: Sifriyat Po'alim, 1946), p. 236.

7. F. Lachover, Introduction: "U.N. Gnessin: His Life and Works," in *The Complete Writings of U.N. Gnessin* Vol. 1 (Warsaw, 1914), p. XXII.

8. C. Levin-Dropkin (supra, note 2), p. 403.

9. See Letter 25, sent to H. Brenner, the end of May 1904. From a collection of the author's letters included in U.N. Gnessin, *The Collected Works of Uri Nissan Gnessin*, vol. 3 (henceforward: *Letters*), (Merhavia: Sifriyat Po'alim, 1946), pp. 51–2.

10. U.N. Gnessin, "In Grandfather's House," in ibid., vol. 2, p. 93.

11. He wrote to Brenner concerning the translations of Dostoyevsky's *Notes from*

Underground; see Letter 45 in *Letters* (supra, note 9), p. 81. Lea Goldberg wrote in her article on Gnessin: "They say—he walks around Kiev hungry and in his pocket a volume of Schopenhauer." See L. Goldberg, "Around 'Sideways,'" in *Uri Nissan Gnessin: A Selection of Critical Essays on His Literary Prose*, ed. L. Rattok, selected with an introduction (Tel Aviv: Am Oved, 1977), p. 97.

12. This man, Ivan, who is always mentioned only by his first name, was a Russian-Christian acquaintance of Gnessin from Pochep, and together with him he translated a story by Y.L. Peretz, and published it in a Russian monthly in Petersburg, in 1905. See Letter 35, in *Letters* (supra, note 9), p. 67, footnote 4.

13. Ibid., Letter 71, p. 109.

14. Yitzhak Bakon, *Brenner and Gnessin as Bilingual Writers* (Be'er Sheva: The Yiddish Chair, University of Ben-Gurion, 1986), pp. 47–48.

15. Letter 145, in *Letters* (supra, note 9), pp. 168–169.

16. *Hatsidah* (supra, note 6), p. 105.

17. A wonderful and surprising aspect concerning the "Gnessin Myth" is suggested by the fact that even though the chronicles of Gnessin's life were written and dated exactly by several scholars of well-known and respected authority, some of whom knew him personally while the others knew him from careful research of written documents, and even though an exact and detailed table of dates indicating his personal and literary biography was published more than once, and, finally, even though he lived and wrote in the last century, oddly enough the different scholars set his age at the time of his death differently, as though they were dealing with a writer of ancient times, or with a mythical imaginary figure; B. Harshav, in his *Hebrew Renaissance Poetry* (Tel Aviv: Open University of Israel, 2000), attached his death to the age of thirty-four; Dan Miron at the end of the date table on Gnessin's life, which he introduced in the introduction to "Sideways," indicated the age of Gnessin's death as thirty-two, as opposed to what could be understood from the very same date table; while Uri Zvi Greenberg, in an article in his memory on the eleventh year after his death, wrote as follows: "Uri Nissan Gnessin. Thirty-one to the dust," namely, buried at the age of thirty-one.

18. *Hatsidah* (supra, note 6), p. 105.

19. Letter 41, in *Letters* (supra, note 9), p. 75.

20. T.R. Smith (ed.), *Baudelaire: His Prose and Poetry* (New York: The Modern Library, 1919), pp. 61–62.

21. *Hatsidah* (supra, note 6), p. 97.

Selected Bibliography in Hebrew

Bakon, Yitzhak. *Brenner and Gnessin as Bilingual Writers*. Be'er Sheva: The Yiddish Chair, University of Ben-Gurion, 1986; *The Lone Youth of Hebrew Literature, 1899–1908*. Tel Aviv: The Students' Association, University of Tel Aviv, 1978.

Bar-Yosef, Hamutal. *Metaphors and Symbols in the Writings of Uri Nissan Gnessin*. Tel Aviv: Hakibbutz Hameuhad, 1987.

Bicovsky, S. (ed.). *Hastidah: A Memorial Collection to U.N. Gnessin*. Jerusalem: Ahdut, 1914.

Gnessin, Menachem. *My Way in the Hebrew Theater: 1905–1926*. Tel Aviv: Hakibbutz Hameuhad, 1946.

Gnessin, U.N. *The Collected Works of Uri Nissan Gnessin*, 3 vols. Merhavia: Sifriyat Po'alim, 1946.

Lachover, Fishel. "U.N. Gnessin: His Life and Works" (introduction). In U.N. Gnessin, *The Complete Writings of U.N. Gnessin*, vol. 1: Stories. Warsaw, 1914.

Levin-Dropkin, Celia. "*Zikhronot*: Memories of U.N. Gnessin." In *U.N. Gnessin: Studies and Documents*, edited by Dan Miron and Dan Laor. Jerusalem: Mossad Bialik, 1986.

Miron, Dan. *Posterity Hooked: The Travail and Achievements of Uri Nisan Gnessin; A Study in Five Cycles*. Jerusalem: Mossad Bialik, 1997.

Miron, Dan and Dan Laor (eds.). *U.N. Gnessin: Studies and Documents*. Jerusalem: Mossad Bialik, 1986.

Rattok, Lily (ed.). *Uri Nissan Gnessin: A Selection of Critical Essays on His Literary Prose* (selected with an introduction). Tel Aviv: Am Oved, 1977.

Sideways

Lhe first time that Nachum Hagzar set foot in that pleasant house at the far end of the quiet street was due to some trivial reason that was forgotten by him no sooner than it had occurred. Much to his surprise, he met there his stout neighbor, young Hanna Heler, with her unnaturally loud staccato laugh, and conversed with her for the first time, too. Yet he didn't stay long on that occasion, for he was dreaming of other things; feverishly, his coattails flapping behind him, he hurried home to await the new job and the challenging life that would begin the next day, here in this provincial town to which he had chosen to move from Vilna.

The next morning, however, turned out to be leaden and dull. The walls were cheerless, the ceiling was low, and the windowpanes were streaked as though with sweat. He sat chin in hand for a long while, biting his lips; then suddenly he roused himself, found some excuse to call on his neighbor, and went together with her to that house at the end of the street. Inside were new faces. Sitting back a bit from the round table was a lively young man in a semi-Oriental position, his two arms hugging his outthrust knee while he rocked back and forth and made everyone laugh at his jokes. This time

Hagzar stayed longer. Indeed, as he passed through the entrance hall on his way out, a new peal of laughter from the room he had left so intrigued him that, after briefly regarding the gray windows, he turned around and rejoined the company inside.

His third visit to the house was prompted by the same young man. One morning the latter dropped in on him for a while, and after a friendly chat suggested that they pay a call on Rosa. By then Hagzar knew that his new friend was the only son of one of the town's leading citizens; donning his coat while thinking of Rosa's pretty face and her pale, pure smile in the misty glow of the shade-spreading lamp, he reflected, not for the first time, what strangers all these people still were to him.

Subsequently he stopped by several more times. He often saw Ida, the pale lycée student, and her older sister Manya, who planned to resume her studies soon as well and was forever wandering in and out and looking for something while humming jerkily under her breath. Rosa was rarely there, except when once or twice he found her laughing prettily and with infectious gaiety at the jokes of the lively young man.

The mother of these three sisters had passed away early in the spring of that year, and their father, Simha Baer, was away on an extended business trip in the Ukraine. At the time Hagzar's large wicker trunk, which was filled with books and manuscripts, still stood unopened by the door, exactly as it had arrived from Vilna two weeks before, for he had not yet finished arranging his room. He had come to the provinces hoping to find the leisure to carry out his many literary projects, and afterward to travel in Europe, as had always been his dream.

Before long the trunk was opened and he had set to work. He had four pupils to tutor every morning, the hours of which were divided among their houses; afternoons were free for his own pursuits. That summer a Hebrew journal published a long article of his on Hebrew literature, replete with copious citations. Much of the summer was taken up with founding a local literary society, a long-standing ambition of his; in addition, he was hard at work on a second article, upon completion of which he expected to be paid for both contributions together. In fact, he was already making plans for studying abroad the following year; yet after some brief financial negotiations with the editors of the journal, he was forced to admit that he had made a slight but regrettable miscalculation—and so he turned his attentions instead to the composition of an outline for a major series of essays on the modern Hebrew novel, which boded no end of work.

Afterward, when autumn came and—buttoned up in his bulky overcoat and wearing his high boots—he had to knead with his feet several times each day the thick batter of mud into which the town square was transformed, he occasionally passed Rosa in the street, acknowledging her when he did with a brief nod of his head. Once, however, when they chanced to be going in the same direction, he learned from her that they had a mutual…well, not exactly a friend, but an acquaintance: Gavriel Carmel, who had himself been a teacher in the same town several years before. In those days Rosa had been staying with an aunt in the country and had come home only infrequently, so that she and Carmel did not meet more than a few times. Hagzar, for his part, told her that his friend had been abroad for at least two years now, and that he himself had lost all track of him, having last seen him in Vilna before his departure.

On the same occasion he was also informed that Ida had been his friend's pupil. And so that evening found him sitting at the round table in the pleasant room, where he had not been for many days, while Rosa stood beside him, one hand on the back of his chair and the other on the red tablecloth. By the misty glow of the shade-spreading lamp the two of them studied the brave, youthfully chaste face that looked up at them from a page of the handsome album. Hagzar's own face, which had worn a slight smile before Rosa opened the album, was now an image of excitement concentrated on the two large, innocently self-assured eyes that stared back at him from the picture. How distant this face seemed to him—yet how it drained the blood from his own. The trace of laughing mockery upon it, which seemed reminiscent of something and cut to the heart's quick—that subtle trace that kept reappearing and vanishing into the mystery of those unsullied lips, reappearing with triumphant insolence and vanishing, as though tauntingly, with the cunning of a cat—that laughter haunted him, like the forgotten end of a dream.

Later, while calculating that the photograph must be at least eight years old, he listened to Rosa chatter on about Carmel: how fond he had been of her little sister Ida, whom he had helped prepare for the lycée; how unrecognizable he was in the picture; and how her middle sister Manya, who was two years older than Ida, always used to hide from him…ha, ha…There followed a melancholy silence in which the oil lamp burned and the samovar boiled on its yellow stand and was poured bubbling out into glasses, while Hagzar sat quietly staring at the other lamp, the one reflected in the dark glitter of the window by the night outside. By ten o'clock his boots were sinking one by one into the mud of the strange, dark street, his body bent slightly forward as he thought of the warm room and its misty, penumbral glow, of his distant friend Carmel, of Rosa with her kind, intelligent eyes, and of life as a scroll that was pleasantly being unrolled. For a moment, too, he recalled the weak, suffering groan that had reached him as he stood in the dark hallway at twilight—that groan that had seemed, as it were, to solve some problem in arithmetic—and the vexed, secretive whisper that had followed it. He thought of plump, dark-eyed Manya, and of Ida, weak and pale; and upon arriving home he went straight to work, humming a mischievous tune.

After that he began coming often, as a rule in the evenings when Rosa was alone in the room. Jumping up from her dimly lit corner to greet him, she would silently hold out her small, kind hand to him and heighten the penumbra of the lamp. The corners of the room became dimmer, the tall flowers grew indistinct, and the windowpanes gleamed blackly through the parted curtains. Their harmless chatter flowed quietly between them, although by the time he had to leave, the sound of his laughter might often be ringing out loud.

The lively young man was seldom seen anymore. Once or twice he dropped by with an older sister; they sat, joked for a while, and departed. Hagzar no longer felt that these jests were malicious. On the contrary: the young man was careful to hurt no one's feelings and was certainly no worse than most youths his age. If one compared him to Rosa, who took part in these contests of wit, Hagzar pleasurably observed, with an almost feverish passion, she was far the more venomous of the two: her barbs were so nimble and never failed to strike home. Yet such evenings left him ill at ease, and having walked the guests to the door he gladly forgot them at once.

As soon as they were gone Rosa would begin to talk volubly about herself, Manya, Ida, her father, or whatever else was on her mind. Her speech had a feverish intensity, which she broke now and then with a softly enigmatic laugh while regarding him with confident affection. Hagzar rose at such times to his feet, tucked his hands behind his back beneath the skirts of his frock coat, and paced step by step across the soft carpet, absentmindedly enjoying each squeak of his shoes as they sank into the pliant fabric. When Rosa had finished, it was his turn to confide his thoughts to her, and so they chatted and laughed, or perhaps even sang quietly to themselves or went out for an evening stroll.

Occasionally they were joined in the room by plump, virtuous Manya, whose small, dark eyes had a look in them of mocking suspicion. Placing her open book before her on the table and slipping her hands beneath her black smock, she sat wordlessly on the edge of the couch as if proudly waiting for something. The conversation ignored her, except that now Hagzar fingered the ends of his lead-colored mustache and wrinkled his high forehead repeatedly. The first few times that this happened Manya soon rose again and returned to her room with a bitter air of injured pride, while Hagzar continued to pace back and forth and hum snatches of old melodies to himself, unconsciously biting his bottom lip.

Gradually, however, Manya's visits grew longer; as though out of spite she sat silently facing him, while he slowly took on the look of a man struggling with a toothache. He was aware by then that neither Ida nor Manya had been in good nervous health since their mother's death; yet whereas Ida had taken a leave of absence from the lycée on doctor's orders, Manya had insisted on continuing her preparations for acceptance to the school's fifth form, which had already ended unproductively several times in the past. More than once Hagzar tried talking in her presence of the unhealthy effects of too much study, which could waste the best years of one's life and "nip in the bud" the "springtime of one's youth." At first glancing obliquely up at him with half-lifted eyes, then slowly revolving toward him her full, spiteful face, whose look neatly dissected him in two, Manya casually jiggled one leg on its toes and coughed deliberately to announce that none of this concerned her in the least. As soon as Hagzar paused for breath she rose and returned to her room, while the conversation went on as before.

That winter Hagzar's literary work proceeded slowly. There were several reasons for this. The outline that he had begun for the series of essays was interrupted in the middle by a long, critical article that he had decided to write on a novel that had recently appeared, in which he hoped to focus on certain issues that, although the best of Jewish youth was concerned with them, Hebrew literature had unaccountably overlooked. Yet the literary society that he had started, which had fallen on difficult times, and a fifth pupil whom he was forced to take on, consumed nearly all his free time, so that he could only jot down some preliminary notes regarding the article's content. In addition he was busy making entries in his journal, which he hoped one day to transform into a new set of essays that he was already at work on.

That spring the brother of the three sisters, a bookkeeper for a trading firm in the south, came home for several weeks of vacation. More than ever Hagzar was a visitor in the house, which now had a different ambiance. Manya, though still as spiteful as ever, began appearing more often and at times even joined the conversation, addressing her remarks at first exclusively to her brother, and then, little by little, to the rest of the company as well. Soon Ida, an open book in one hand and a white pillow in the other, began to join them too, half-sitting and half-reclining on the couch. Friends of both sexes dropped by to talk, joke, drink tea, and toss nutshells at each other. Each time they had left, Rosa, her fastidious features and gestures prettily graced by fatigue, would complain of what bores they had all become and of how she had nothing to say to them anymore. What a wit her brother Shmuel could be, though! He had been the evening's saving grace.

Shmuel, a dandyish young man of about twenty-five with a

sallow, bloodless face that could have enabled him to pass for sixteen, would regard the pince-nez that his thin, petite hands were wiping with a snowy-white handkerchief, and exclaim with open disdain, "Small-town intellectuals!"

And Manya would look at him, curling her lips with forceful assurance, and repeat, "Small-town!"

After which Shmuel would replace his glasses on his nose, tilt his head slightly backward, and recall with a gleeful guffaw how he had "really put" that "dumb blond" or that "fat tub" in "her place." Had anyone noticed how she had turned up that trumpet that served as her nose? Then Rosa would make a crack of her own, Manya would cast all caution to the winds, and Shmuel would interrupt them again with more of his recollected repartee. And so, in giggles, gossip, jesting, and song the time went by.

Within a few weeks the season arrived for merry walks in the marvelous woods, gay boat rides on the river, poetic campfires beneath dark, satiny skies, boisterous breachings of the silence of the before-dawn-and-after-midnight sleeping streets. Now they were joined by a newcomer, another former acquaintance of Hagzar's, who had come to look for pupils in the provinces, too, although only for a few months. This was a devil of a fellow with pointy brown eyes, black Gogolesque hair, and a repertoire of comically rendered folk songs, itinerant synagogue sermons, monologues of peasants called to testify in court, and soliloquies of drunkards cadging drinks from Jewish innkeepers that reduced them to helpless laughter in the end. That summer was an unforgettable time for all of them, the memory of which lingered on for many a long month after.

And so when one day long, slender cobwebs spiraled down through the air and yellow leaves dropped from the trees and littered the paths in the parks, Hagzar trampled on them with a joyous burst of savage energy unleashed. He stood straighter now, his chest more expanded and his face more alert. In another week or two the skies would cloud over; the wind would howl; windowpanes and tin roofs would rattle once more in the gloom: hurrah! His mood would be defiant then; his mind free of fetters; his heart brimful; his cork crowded with satisfying new discoveries…Yes, a week or two would bring black nights pierced by a few quivering streetlights, torrents of rain, mud up to the ankles…but that dear, pleasant house would be warm and well lit. Beneath its spread of red velvet the couch would be spacious and soft; the lively eyes of the three pretty sisters would glow with a tender light; Rosa's pleasing chatter would flow self-indulgently on; Manya's deliberately spiteful outbursts would interrupt him as usual, break off in the middle as they always did, and resume again; and pale little Ida—Ida with her wondering look and her soft, lovely braid, who stubbornly refused to sit in his lap or rest her dear head against him until he grabbed her by her soft, warm underarms, which were no longer the arms of a child, and placed her there forcefully—would docilely cling to his chest like a newborn lamb, her dear, rich, smooth hair his to play with as he pleased.

One autumn day Hagzar went to the public library and borrowed an absorbing new book which he took that same night to the pleasant house and read aloud there in a single sitting. When he went the next day to return it, Rosa accompanied him in the hope of finding "something else just as nice" which they might read the following night. The sky was covered with clouds. The wind raged, the mud reached their ankles, and raindrops spattered down.

At first they formed a trio for these readings. Gradually, though, Ida joined their little group too. Palely holding her white pillow, she would enter the room and sit listening silently in one of the corners with her arms crossed before her. Manya sat on the couch's edge, one arm draped over the windowsill, while Rosa leaned against the back of the rocking chair, swaying slowly with it back and forth. Ensconced in red velvet, Hagzar read clearly and with controlled emotion from the volume that he held in his hands.

Sometimes Manya asked a spiteful, disjointed question, which he did his best to answer without showing his distress. Sometimes Rosa challenged him too. In the beginning he deferred to her by blithely, almost shyly agreeing, yet soon he took to arguing back. And when she refused to back down—not with any great show of logic, to be sure, but with an adamancy that spoke for itself—he concluded that she was a person with a mind of her own and rare properties of soul such as belonged only to those who have been through a great deal in life. If then he thought of that lively young man and of Rosa's venomous barbs, he had to admit that she was deucedly attractive. If only, he mused bitterly, women's souls were not such closed books to him, and this were not always fated to be the case, since his relations with the opposite sex were one irreparable mistake from the start.

For a moment he thought of his stout neighbor, whose buxom arms collided with his own whenever they walked side by side. Like the shadows of owls on frozen, moonlit nights, fleeting images arose and vanished in his mind. Though it made no sense at all, when he looked at Rosa's pure, noble face her eyes reminded him for some reason of his own gray cat, which liked to sit perched on the red commode in his bedroom. Curiously, the thought of this amused him. Rosa had stopped rocking with the chair; her eyes shone and her cheeks were slightly flushed. Her voice, which trembled when she spoke with the excitement of the pleasures of the mind, brought him back to himself. At once he began to refute her, none too logically himself, stopping repeatedly to ask, "Do you follow me? Well, do you?"

And when she did not he turned to face Manya, who sought at first to return his direct gaze. Soon, however, she had to lower her eyes; yet immediately this annoyed her; so that spitefully she stared back at him again until he began to falter and felt suddenly so stupid that he forgot what he was saying and turned back to Rosa once more, who still refused to concede the point, which compelled him to start all over again from the beginning.

Upon returning home late that night he climbed into bed and lay there reviewing the day's thoughts and feelings and his hopes for the months ahead. He wished the winter would come. He was eager to get back to his work again, which had lately been neglected—although the fault was not his own but that of the circumstances in which he lived. As soon as the month was out he would rent a larger room in which it would be easier for him to concentrate, and everything would fall into place.

Thus the autumn went by. And one morning when the first gleaming coat of new snow lay upon the broad, empty streets and the gleeful caw of the crows sounded over the low, whitened roofs,

Hagzar and Rosa, wrapped in a long woolen shawl, walked down the long street together until they came to a farmyard. A large, chained dog began to bark at them, while a fat sow squealed from beneath a summer cart that lay lamely in the middle of the white yard. A tall, sun-bronzed peasant woman came out to greet them. Her sleeves were rolled back and the edge of her apron, which was slick with grease, was tucked into her waist. With her tongue she kept searching for something in her gums or between her teeth, while burping repeatedly with a harsh, ringing sound that was accompanied by a smell of half-digested herring and onion. Rosa addressed her by her patronymic. She spoke to her briefly, and they followed her to a large, low-ceilinged room with simple but ample furnishings, a clean white floor, lots of flowers, and a high bed standing in one corner beneath a mountain of pillows. Numerous pictures of generals on horseback galloped over the walls, and a few gloomy icons hung darkly in the corners.

That same day Hagzar moved in. In the evening Rosa and the girls came to visit. They praised the room and joked with the peasant landlady, laughing especially when she paused on her way out, pointed with a finger to the pillowy mountain, and declared, "I do believe you'll sleep well here…"

Then they took Hagzar back with them to their house. They read, talked, sang, and went out for a stroll again until it was well past midnight. The next morning was overcast. Yesterday's snow had turned into a gray gruel on the ground. The winds pounded on the shutters. Hagzar felt as though his soul were incubating within him. For a long time he sat on his new bed with his feet tucked beneath him and one hand supporting his head. Then he rose, turned up the collar of his buttoned frock coat, and paced slowly back and forth in the room, his left hand holding the collar in place while his right hand braced his left against his chest.

After a while he sat down at his desk and remained immobile there with his pen aimed at a blank sheet of paper. Yet when he began to write, the round, curlicued, carefully formed letters raced handsomely across the page. His face grew intense and excited. His breath came and went irregularly, and his movements were nervous and quick. With dizzying speed he filled lines and whole pages, and he did not stop to rest until he had finished a large and crucial section of his new article. Only when he had marked the final period with a large, black ink stain and had drawn a black line beneath the last sentence did he throw down his pen on the table with a sigh of relief. He leaned back in his chair, clasping his head from behind with both hands, and sat there with his eyes shut as though he were frozen stiff.

That evening he was hurrying home from the house of an acquaintance in order to get back to work. There was a bite to the distilled air outside. The last of the snow was turning gray on the eaves of the roofs. Far on the horizon the sky was streaked with a pale, congealed red. He strode vigorously over sharp, frozen clods of mud, thinking of how gay and relaxed spiteful Manya had been the day before. He thought of what he had written that day, and of what he planned to add to it that night, and felt heartened by the winter with its sleighs, its gleaming roofs, its raucous crows, and its snows that came from afar. When he decided to look in on the three sisters he found Rosa setting glasses out for tea. He rubbed his hands pleasurably together, stamped forcefully with his foot, and exclaimed in a triumphant voice, "So it's winter after all, Rosa!"

2.

Though the winter had barely begun, Manya was already hard at work. Having failed to gain admission to the fifth form the previous spring, and having spent the whole summer "in a perfect fit" about it, she was determined to take the examinations for the seventh form the following spring, it being senseless to try forever for the fifth. For a tutor she had engaged the same young man who was a former acquaintance of Hagzar's. To be sure, he was due to leave town soon, though no date had been announced for his departure; yet meanwhile a good deal about him was known in the pleasant house, both regarding his down-at-heel past with its tale of penury, privation, mad binges, police vans, artist friends sent to Siberia, and more yet that was shrouded in mystery, and the glorious future that lay strung out before him on a long chain of light, life, space, freedom, achievement, and renown. (In addition Manya alone knew of a certain pistol shot in a dark orchard and of a shirtsleeve with a bullet hole that he still happened to possess.) In any case he was a fine sight to behold when, his curls tumbling over his forehead, he sat perched like a drunk on the edge of his chair in the middle of the room with one hand on his knee and the other in the air, poised to fall on his second knee as soon as the Delphic mood possessed him and he began to quote from Nekrasov with a windy, excruciating sigh, *"Ekh, priyát'el! I ty, vidnó, goré vidál…"*

"What a rascal of a fellow!" someone would be sure to exclaim then.

On winter evenings, sitting by himself or together with Rosa in the drawing room, Hagzar would listen as the insistent, slightly vexed drone of study coming from Manya's room repeated for the thousandth-and-first time, so it seemed to him, some perfectly trite phrase or cumbersome but trivial formula that was frequently inter-rupted by an irritable "the-devil-take-it!" At such times Ida, who had recently been forced by her health to stop attending the lycée again, might pass before him on her way out of Manya's room. Her face pale and annoyed beneath its head of mussed hair, her faithful pillow in one hand and her heavy book open in the other, she would direct a silent, melancholy smile at him, as if to say:

—You know, and I know, that the poor child is wasting her time…but what good would it do to tell her?

Then she would slip into the other bedroom, whose half-ajar door opened onto the drawing room too, lie down diagonally across the two beds that stood there side by side, and read. Rosa would sit on the ledge of the stove, her knitting or a book in her lap, and Hagzar would sink deeper into his corner of the couch, or pace back and forth in the room, while they chatted and joked and fell silent again before beginning to hum some old tune. Sometimes, still swearing by the devil, Manya entered the room to inquire what time it was and worry why her tutor had not come yet. Hagzar would stare at her face, which warned against trespassing, and at her full, handsome shoulders beneath the blouse of soft muslin that caressed her alluring back, and would seek an excuse to converse with her; yet Manya, for some reason already on the defensive, would stare suspiciously back at him and answer as sharply as she could. Once, the Lord knew why, he asked her what her dreams were and who the lucky young man in them was. With wounded hauteur she turned her back on him, replying to him from the doorway in a harsh voice that seemed to bore upward from a hidden cavern in her chest, "He's not like the likes of you, I promise you that…"

Which made him break into an uncharacteristically loud laugh.

In the weeks before the Russian holidays Ida made a supreme effort to return to school, so as to be able to be promoted with her classmates, and succeeded so well that she even finished the term with honors. Yet soon afterward the pains in her head and chest grew worse again, and often Hagzar found himself standing by her bed with a glass of water in one hand while Rosa quietly rubbed down her bare arms and chest with pungent spirit and Manya searched for something along the windowsills and under the couch with a stifled groan. In a barely audible voice Ida chattered by fits and starts; she whimpered about her dead mother, about skies like none she had ever seen and some great storm at sea, and about something else, something terribly important, that everyone kept taking for himself and leaving nothing of for her. She went on hysterically, laughing and crying at once, until Rosa had to beg her in a frantic whisper to calm down and Manya's movements grew still more exasperated.

At such times Hagzar grunted and twitched fretfully, alternately sipping cold water from the glass in his hand and sprinkling it over the pale face that was suddenly frozen in a spasm of new distress. Such crises did not last long, however. Soon Ida dozed off and they returned to the drawing room, where everything was as before. For a while they sat there in silence, letting the tension drain; then Manya went to her room while Rosa curled up on the stove ledge again and Hagzar settled into the couch. The door to the bedroom remained half-open, so that the shade-spreading lamp cast a dim light over the end of one of the beds and caused it to gleam in the dark. From her sickroom Ida continued to groan in her sleep, while Hagzar and Rosa sat talking and laughing in quiet tones before falling silent or breaking into hushed song.

At about nine o'clock Manya's tutor would arrive. Now the intervals of silence were themselves intermittently broken by his rude oaths that drifted out of Manya's room to dissipate in the hushed space of the drawing room. Later he might appear for a while to sit and banter with them, or to challenge Hagzar to wrestle. Sometimes he asked Hagzar whether he remembered this or that friend before turning to the others and relating to them with relish some comical incident from the time that the two of them had briefly shared a room in the city of H.

"One night when we were starving," he would begin gustily, savoring his deliberately coarse speech, "I went to see a pal of mine, a real sport. He was busted himself but he offered to stake us to some sausage and a small loaf of bread. So I took the grub and brought it back to Hagzar. The professor was lying in bed when I came, licking his chops. 'On your feet,' I said, 'it's chow time.' You should have seen him jump out of bed. 'What? Did you say food? Excellent, let's have it. But…*sausage*…?'"

Everyone burst out laughing. The tutor raised his voice and concluded with brio, "And what do you think happened in the end? My vegetarian friend ate a sandwich of bread on bread and went right to sleep!" With a merry cry he turned at last to the hero of his story. "I can see that by now you've had better sense drummed into you, eh? Come, let's wrestle!"

And seizing Hagzar beneath the arms, he sought to throw him, while the latter struggled to squirm free and cried quits. Then all laughed again and talked some more and enjoyed themselves until late into the night. Even Manya grew gay and spirited, and her eyes shot sparks.

Yet when the tutor rose to go at last and Manya chose to walk him part of the way, a brooding silence descended again on the room, a silence that pressed on the heart like a soft caress, and squeezed, squeezed away at it with a mild, gently narcotic pain. Hagzar and Rosa

sat dreamily, waiting to hear the noisy creak of the front door and the
squeak of boots being hastily removed—which were sometimes followed by a low, defiant voice singing chestily from Manya's room:

> *Ekh, ló-opnul obrùch*
> *Ókolo maznítsy:*
> *Trai-trrai-ti-ra-rai...*

When it was finally time to bid Hagzar goodnight too, Rosa
put on her large woolen shawl and, shivering a bit from the cold,
accompanied him along the empty street that ran in front of the house.
Sapphire crystals winked and glittered from the pure blanket of snow
that had whitened the world. A dusky, reddish wreath festooned the
moon. The trodden snow underfoot turned to slush with a merry
squish and a light, amusing puff of smoke materialized with each
breath. Hagzar talked in muted tones while Rosa walked by his side
and thought as she listened of how kind he was and of how agitated
he grew each time he had to grope for a word; he was a person, she
felt, who lived in a splendid world, and thought splendid thoughts,
and had work that was splendid too. Guilelessly she began to tell him
about the Bible tales she had studied as a girl with her brother at some
rabbi's; about the stories of Mikhailov-Scheler that had supplanted
them as she grew older and become her constant companion; about
books in general, for which she had such a passion; about her friends,
who made fun of this; and about the strange sense of remoteness,
the missing sympathy, that she felt nowadays when she met them.
The more she talked, the more enthralled she became with her own
account, every detail of which seemed so splendid to her, so full of
life and enhancing of her own past, that she actually began to believe
with all her heart that she too had had a past without knowing it.
Not until her words began to fail, yielding to little gasps of weary,
jagged laughter, did she notice Hagzar's frequent grunts, which he
struggled ineffectually to emit in token of his interest in her tale.
Then her speech lost the last of its flow to ever longer silences, until
it trailed off completely in the end—although not before one last,

pitiable grunt on his part had prompted her to laugh weakly and to conclude as well as she could, "Yes, time certainly has flown…"

By February of that year it began to thaw. In the morning hours the sun peered out, causing the snow to soften, the rooftops to drip, and the dazzling ponds to fissure and crack; yet toward evening fingers froze once more, jaws stiffened, and tasseled icicles re-formed along the eaves. It was an hour at which Hagzar liked to visit the leafless park in the center of town. The snow lay in milky-white drifts there and the branches of the trees were stiff and bare. Crows screamed over the bright, desolate expanse. He wandered untrammeled along the winding paths, tracing sinuous lines with his stick in the virgin snow and sometimes stopping to amuse himself by scrawling words in it.

Once he went for a walk in the park with Rosa. Her face was prettily flushed and the sound of her laughter rang like a child's at play. The golden fringes at the ends of the white scarf that she had tossed back over her shoulders blew against the snug collar of her jacket. Hagzar was in a quick, gay mood that day. They laughed at everything they saw and spoke about, most hilariously of all at Rosa's account of a dream that had woken Manya from her sleep the night before. Just imagine: darkness all around her, not a person in sight, so quiet you could hear a pin drop—and all of a sudden, "This drunken rascal of a fellow appears. He chases after her with a revolver, and begins to shoot, ha ha…"

It really was so absurd…at which point Hagzar stepped to one side without warning, spread his arms wide, and flung himself with a playful cry backward into the pure snow, which collapsed beneath his weight. As soon as she recovered from her fright, Rosa burst into such gales of laughter that she scared all the crows, which filled the park with their caws and noisily shook clumps of white snow down from the treetops. Hagzar looked into her bright eyes and called from where he lay with gay pathos, "Man overboard! Why don't you save me, Rosa?"

Rosa laughed even harder. She bent until her flushed, bright face nearly touched his own and seized the hands he stretched out to her. Slowly he pulled himself up, digging his heels into a hollow of snow and muscularly gripping her small palms; yet before he could regain his footing she stumbled herself and would have pitched helplessly forward had she not quickly grabbed his waist and sunk her head with a merry shriek into his overcoat at a point beneath his chest. He seized her beneath the arms and continued to hold her there for a moment after helping her up—until a sudden shiver ran through him at the changed sound of her laugh, which had grown strangely contorted, and he released her. Then, without looking back at the "snowman" that his fall had made, the two of them walked home in silence.

On the way Rosa teased him with a strange venom, reminding him with fleet hints of things long repented and best forgotten, such as the time he had clumsily tried to undo the kerchief on her head while they had sat by the window of the drawing room looking out at a stormy night. Mockingly she mimicked his helpless cry of alarm when she had been about to fall in the park, his pointless, repetitive grunts. When he finally left her for the house of a pupil, his legs took him back to the park instead. He climbed the circular railing of the gazebo that stood at one end of the long, straight promenade running from the old castle to a view of the stream at the foot of the park and of a spreading willow tree beyond it. He leaned against the shaky grating, staring down at the round well house by the stream and at the nearby bin of frozen ashes left over from holiday pig roasts. The white willow was a blur in the thick mist. The cries of the crows assailed and stunned him, told him with a bitter vengeance that people like him could never take what life offered them, had no business living at all. *Ka-a ka-a ka-a.* He suffered from the childishness, or worse yet, from the simple blind idiocy, of the eternal student, which was why he drew a line between his own inner life and his life in the world outside. *Ka-a ka-a.* Lies, lies. A person was one and the same, forever and aye. Whoever he was in the street outside he was also within his own walls…

After a while he left the park and started back through the marketplace. Breathless men hurried by him and a tall, stocky woman wiped her nose on the back of her hand. At home he took out his notebooks, dimly aware of a throbbing lump in his chest that made him want to cry, and sat down with them at his desk. For a long while he stared at them, nibbling at the cap of his pen while grunting at odd intervals with an effetely nasal sound. And when the spindly, crooked, rat-tailed letters ran from his pen at last, their sickliness so filled him with loathing that he broke off in the middle, threw himself on his bed with a suffering noise, and lay there for hours grunting and tossing in turn.

Yet soon it was nearly spring and the days were filled with light. Patches of soft blue showed through the clash of silvery cymbals in the sky. The sun was new and warm again; golden puddles gleamed underfoot and glimmering streams bubbled gaily. The newly let-out cows rubbed against the walls of the houses, seeking their stored warmth. Hagzar cut back on his lessons. Whenever he could he went for long walks through the paths and fields, splashing pleasurably through the slick bogs from which a damp glitter arose, breathing in the soft decay of the rutting earth as it warmed, surrendering himself to the steamy mist exhaled by the fat, rank soil.

Now little Ida often dropped by. She was still pale and not yet all over her illness, but there was color in her face and she seemed prettier; her chest had filled out and she was taller too. Wrapped in her shawl she would knock on his door and announce with a fetching smile that she simply could not have stayed indoors a minute longer. It was so, *so* good to be out in the fresh air now. One might almost…*ah!* And Hagzar would sit her down by his side and stroke her hair and ask whether Rosa was free yet, and had the three of them lunched, and what was Manya doing, and was her tutor there, and would she please tell Rosa for him that he would soon come himself.

He and Rosa now went walking a great deal outside of town. Lightheartedly they leaped over the ruined snow that still lay piled in the ditches, chatting gaily as they sank into the slick mud of the dark, steaming fields. By the time they tramped home again they were pleasantly numb and their fingers were frozen to the bone; shivering they warmed themselves indoors and swore how good it had been. Sometimes they found Manya standing before the door, half-whistling, half-puffing some Russian tune, the lapels of her black jacket that she had draped over her back held with one hand at the throat.

"Whistling, eh?" Hagzar would jeer dryly.

And Rosa would smile while Manya looked spitefully back at him and puffed through her lips even more.

Yet when she was alone in the house with Ida, Manya spoke often about spiritual suffering that no words could describe; about doubts that preyed on the mind; about gifts gone to waste and dark nights of the soul; about the horrors of drink and the lower depths; about great cities; about freedom, life, and strong wings; and about the need to escape—yes, to escape in the name of all that was holy since she could not go on living like this anymore.

Sometimes her tutor still appeared. Despite the gleam in his restless eyes and his hair that was as charmingly rumpled as ever, his face was drawn and he walked with an unsteady gait. Wearily he harangued them, smelling of brandy and beating his chest with one fist. Not for the first time he declared that only a worm would spend all its days in the dirt; anyone with the breath of life in him, with a bit of pluck and independence, would leave a swamp like this as fast as he could. Where was he bound for then? For a moment a lock of loose hair tumbled gorgeously down. Ha! They needn't worry about that. Wherever he fell, he would always land on his feet…and meanwhile, was he really such a bad sort to have around?

And he would dramatically raise one hand and declaim with artistic flair:

Myórtvii v gróbe mírno spi
Zhíznyu pólzuisya, zhivói!

Who among them did not know those immortal lines of Nadson's?

At such times Hagzar would glance at Manya, who sat perfectly still while the faint reflection of her tutor's smile struggled over her face, and decide that she was not nearly so attractive as he had once thought. On the contrary: her features were on the coarse side and even annoyingly dull. One look at the rapt stare with which she regarded that chest-thumping brute was ample proof of what a dunce she was.

Later, on his evening walk with Rosa, he would murmur to

her how detestably mean he found Manya, how put off he was by her vulgarity, how depressed she left him feeling each time. Gradually he shifted to how quickly young people grew up nowadays, how nothing ever stayed the same, and how little there was in human life to hold on to. Even when you considered what still might lie ahead...to say nothing of what you had already seen, heard, and knew...even then life always seemed to slip sideways and to come to nothing in the end. Was that all there was to it? Did she understand him? Was it? And Rosa would cough a gentle cough and murmur shyly and not at all clearly, "*Mm-hmmm.*"

Which made him turn even more crimson. His breath came in spurts, one hand pawed the air, and there was unspoken anguish when he said, "Lately I...it's not just that I can't write...it's...everything. And yet it's not anything either, eh? It's just that the more you look at things, the less they are what you think. Something is wrong with them...or perhaps nothing is...and yet there you are..."

Generally he broke off at this point to add after a while in an exasperatedly tormented whisper, raising and lowering his shoulders in despair, "Unless that's simply how it's meant to be..."

At which he spat loudly and exclaimed under his breath, "Phheww...the devil knows!"

And fell silent. An evening gloom cloaked the dull fields and was woven into the cold mist that arose from them. Here and there a solitary willow still stood out. They walked without breaking the silence, treading the soft earth. Now and then he hummed through his nose a quiet, plaintive air that her thin, quavering voice took up. Once she stopped to tell him that her fingers were numb and that she had forgotten to bring her gloves. Yet when he tried putting one of her hands in his pocket, the pocket proved too small, so that his own hand was left outside, holding the sleeve of her coat. Soon they felt how unnatural this was, since it forced them to walk with a limp. After a while she pulled her hand free, and they walked on humming to themselves.

3.

Simha Baer came home before Passover. For several days Hagzar stayed away from the house. The day after her father's return Ida dropped by. Her face was pale and wistful, as in the old days. She flitted from one thing to another, did not stay long, and giggled when she left that her father was eager to meet him.

Then Manya came by. She kept glancing out the window, inquired about some book whose name she instantly forgot, whistled, promised to come back again soon, and dashed home. When she returned she sat by the window again before remembering that she had left her father by himself and must attend to him. Soon she came back a third time, yet before long she spied her tutor passing by on his way to her house. She ran out to greet him and disappeared for the rest of the day.

But Rosa did not come at all, which left Hagzar feeling as once he had felt when the mailman had delivered a letter to her and she had sat reading it silently to herself in his presence before slipping it into her pocket without comment. An injured, contrary mood settled darkly over him and spewed its bile of loneliness into his blood.

That night he paced endlessly up and down like a man with a toothache, from time to time emitting a sickly, irascible cough that sounded more like a groan. And when he went to bed at last, pulling the blanket over him, the despairing thought assailed him that his surroundings had won in the end, and that the mark they had left on him could never be removed.

The next morning he rose early, thinking of his work. The crooked, rat-tailed letters flashed before him and he stalked the room some more, trying to shake off the scaly sensation of tedium that afflicted him at such times while groggily pondering a dream he had had in which he had finished a long article and was about to set forth on a European tour. At last he picked up an old essay and leafed through it, absently searching for a certain passage that never failed to bring a modest smile to his lips. He thumbed the notebook rapidly, threw it down, picked it up again, put it down once more, and finally opened it a third time and let his glance fall on a page. Slowly his face brightened. His eyes began to glow and his steps grew quicker; feverishly he tugged with shaky fingers at his mustache while making little, resolute grunts in his chest. When his legs wearied at last from their forced march he sat down to work at his desk, humming little snatches of a tune beneath his breath; yet just then the mailman came with a postcard, whose arrival so pleased him that he read it over three times. He rose and paced some more until his head spun, then put on his coat and went out.

In the distance he saw Rosa coming toward him in the company of Hanna Heler. She greeted him like a long-lost friend, and he extended the postcard to her with a sheepish grin before turning in his dry manner to Hanna and advising her to peruse it as well, since it appeared to pertain to her too; they might look at it all, he replied, when both asked at once how much they should read of it. So Rosa read the whole card out loud, already smiling before she began, while Hanna stared at her with a wide-open mouth in whose wings a smile waited too. Then both shrieked with laughter and Hagzar joined in heartily. Now they all knew that Gavriel Carmel, who was once a tutor in this town, had written from abroad to announce that he wished to see his Naples one more time before he died, to which end Hagzar should prepare for him:

1) Attractive quarters
2) Attractive young ladies
3) Two or three pupils if possible

Still the same joker as ever!

Then Hagzar retraced his steps with them and listened to Hanna assure him that she remembered Carmel quite well: a tall, dark young man who had seemed to her rather odd but certainly clever enough. The three of them chatted until Rosa went her way, and Hanna hesitated a moment before accepting Hagzar's invitation to come back with him to his room. There she kept rising every few minutes to go and sitting down again, the tower of dark hair on her head describing a weak arc around her ample bosom with each loud, staccato laugh. And when Hagzar rose to walk her to the door the thought crossed his mind that she was in fact a dear thing and really very feminine at that. For a second he thought of Manya's dull stare, of her irritating whistle, and of her jacket draped around her back. Outside the sun was celebrating spring. Rivulets of water splashed gaily by, puddles gleamed like gold, metal shovels scraped against the ice. Roly-poly children frolicked and sang, and Hagzar cried with roguish glee, "How much light and life there is, Hanna! No, I won't allow you to go home now."

Soon they were walking in an orchard high above town. Fresh blades of grass pushed up through the earth and the sodden trees stood resurrected from their sleep. The scattered tin roofs and white churches beneath them shrank and all but vanished in the great expanse of open fields that ran in all directions as far as the dew-bright woods that ringed the broad horizon. The scent of the wakened hills in their lungs roused them too. They grew gay, and he cuffed her lightly on the nose in a giddy burst of affection and called in a whinnying voice, "Ho, Hanna!"

Which made her laugh loudly and ask if he had taken leave of his senses and would he please—but how strangely in earnest she seemed!—"act his age." Yet in the end she had to slap his hand and order him to behave. Then his face lost its shape and his eyes darted moistly.

"But a kiss, Hanna…," he lisped, cocking his head to one side. "What's wrong with one little kiss?"

Again her laugh rang out, propelling the top half of her forward: she could not, for the life of her, control herself any longer, she would simply split her sides, so help her! What kind of strange creature was he? She would give a pretty penny to know who had taught him such tricks. Was it Rosa and her brood? And to think that she had always thought…well, well!

For a moment she looked at him reproachfully; yet his flushed, sheepish face forestalled her with a guilty smile and he seized her full palm with a timorous hand and stammered out, "But what have I done to you, Hanna?" Followed more boldly by, "After all, why not?" And then in jest, "A person might think that I had bit you!"

With which he was in fine fettle again. They wandered along

the bare paths, laughing each time they collided while vigorously trampling the dead growth beneath their feet. He strode now in triumph beside her, his right arm the master of her shoulder and hair, thinking distractedly at the same time, exactly why he did not know, that with Rosa, let alone Manya, such a thing could never have happened, even though life was the same all over and all the women in the world were simply one great woman in the end.

Hanna Heler returned the squeeze of his hand and looked up at him brightly. Soon they found a fallen log to rest on…

Later that day Hagzar descended with large steps the several stairs leading up to Hanna's house and stopped at the bottom of them to regard the fair sight of the broad, empty, reposeful street, the low houses alongside it, each neatly in its place, and the tranquil, pure, untroubled sky above. He thrust out his chest and turned with slow, sure strides to go home. Before long he felt as though a thin layer of something were peeling away inside him—peeling, flaking, and breaking up into small bubbles that slid quickly upward to press against his chest and burst into his throat. With surprising ease they tumbled out and he muttered to himself with satisfaction, "So it's done then."

The words sent a rush of blood to his cheeks. He quickened his pace and clapped his hat on his head with one hand. Stubbornly he growled, "And yet what nonsense, though!"

Despite the speed with which he walked it was already evening by the time the marketplace was behind him. Coal fires gleamed redly in some of the stores. Farmers urged home their horses, shutters slammed with a metallic bang. He slowed down again, locking his hands behind his back and dragging his stick in the mud. From time to time he squeezed a stubborn cough from his chest, and when he reached home he shut the door behind him and repeated out loud to the still, dark room, "Yes, what nonsense!"

He glanced at the house across the street, whose drawn curtains were lit from within. He removed a box of matches from his pocket, cast it on the table, made his way in the dark to his bed, and sank into the mountain of pillows upon it; then he rose and walked about the room until his knees were weak and his chest began to ache. An enervating slackness spread through his limbs and his brain felt stupidly blank. Again he collapsed on the pillows and lay there a long while without moving, feebly musing how pointless was the life of self-denial and how some people were born to it nonetheless—which seemed to console him, so that he fell asleep thinking of the subtle, soapy odor given off by Hanna Heler's white breasts.

On his way home one day during the Passover holiday he passed by the pleasant house and saw Simha Baer and Rosa sitting together on the bench that stood in the front yard by their gate. He greeted her without stopping; yet she jumped quickly up from her seat and called to him to come in. Where had he disappeared to lately? She introduced him to her father, made room for him on the bench, and coughed gently all in one breath. Hagzar stammered an embarrassed apology and sat by her side, while Simha Baer proffered a hand, stared down at the ground, and said as though explaining to himself, "Aha…so this must be your Hagzar…"

Rosa laughed embarrassedly too and confessed, "Yes, Papa, it's our Hagzar."

Whereupon Simha Baer grunted contentedly and began to inquire into Hagzar's past and present life. He listened carefully to the answers with his head studiously bowed, picking mildly at his bearded chin, until something appeared to please him and he broke in, "I…just a minute there, slow down…why, you must be Leivik Hagzar's son, is that right? Whew! Why, your father and I used to play tag together when we were small boys. On Goat Street in Mogilev, where we lived."

Did he know Leivik!

"But…just a minute…tell me, wasn't Rabbi Shmulka, may he rest in peace, your uncle? Of course he was." Did Hagzar remember him? That was a fine Jew! Who could forget the funeral he was given when he died? Not an infant stayed home in its crib…

Hagzar sat on the bench for nearly an hour, answering Simha Baer's queries and listening to him reminisce. The mellower her father's mood grew, the less inhibited became Rosa's laughs and the more her eyes shone with pleasure. At last, enjoying his own joke, Simha Baer inquired which synagogue Hagzar attended and had he said his evening prayers there—adding without waiting for an answer that it would have broken Rabbi Shmulka of Mogilev's heart to have lived to see his nephew's sinful ways. What a Jew that man was, what a Jew!

Simha Baer rose, excused himself, and told Hagzar to come by more often.

Then Hagzar and Rosa strolled up and down the street, in which the mud had dried. Rosa's spirits were high. Laughingly he twitted her that God was less wicked than she, since He at least had sent him Hanna Heler for his loneliness, and when she laughed back he talked about Hanna some more. Did she know that the two of them met every day and never had a dull or cross moment? Then he discussed his friend Carmel, whom he hoped he would not disappoint. She listened keenly as he told her about Carmel's life, about the relations between them, and about his pleasure that his old friend from *heder*, and later, from Vilna, was soon about to arrive...

Besides which, nothing really was new...

Subsequently he began to visit the house again daily as once he had done; yet now he made a point of first saying hello to Simha Baer. Generally the latter could be found sitting between the table and the window with a floppy silk skullcap on his head, peering over the tops of his glasses at a book that he held away from himself at arm's length. He welcomed Hagzar warmly, laid his book on the table, carefully folded his glasses, placed them on the book, pulled out a handkerchief, blew a trumpet blast into it, and commenced by declaring "well now" in the tone of an experienced man of affairs who is adept at getting along with the "younger set." Then he would chat with Hagzar about this or that latest fashion, spoofing it with a knowing air and humorously quoting scriptural chapter and verse, or citing rabbinic texts, in proof that it was nothing new. Finally his hand crept back toward his glasses and he familiarly ended the audience by replacing them on his nose.

"Well now...I don't imagine that you came here in order to be preached to by an old man like me. If you're looking for the sisters, you'll find them in the cloister..."

And, pleased with his recondite jest, he returned to his book.

In the "cloister," the large room that had been their father's until he had recently bequeathed it to them in order to banish their "reign of terror" from the drawing room, Hagzar would find the three sisters together with Hanna Heler, who had taken to slapping him sonorously on the back when they met. Uncomfortably he tried making small talk with Rosa; yet she sat with her face twitching moodily and refused to respond. Then he sang along with the others, sprawled out with them on the beds, talked until he was hoarse, and returned home in the early hours of the morning to grunt, spit, mop his brow, and grunt some more. Only the comforting thought of the approaching spring and of the imminent arrival of his friend could induce him to go to bed in the end.

At last Carmel came. In the beginning, Hagzar spent whole days and nights with him. Carmel lay on his back amid a wreath of blue smoke that spiraled up from the fat cigarette that spluttered between his lips, while Hagzar sat by his side, or paced stammering and laughing up and down, both enjoying his own excitement and wishing that there were less of it.

Now he saw his long stay in town in a new, rewarding light that made him feel much better about it—although each time he asked Carmel to tell him about Europe, an urgent, almost physical desire arose within him to finish his work and depart for there at once. The more casually he tried listing the obstacles that had detained him so far, the more annoyed with himself he became at his inability to explain them, especially as they all had seemed so perfectly clear beforehand...

Yet afterward, when Carmel became a steady guest in Simha Baer's house, where he liked to loll on the couch puffing lazily on his cigarette while Rosa crossed her arms beside him, the lips chill-cornered on her dear, sad face, and Manya sat across from them, hardly speaking but whistling often at odd times, and Ida half lay on the edge of the bed with a wistful longing in her eyes, Hagzar could feel his skin crawl. His head and chest ached, and he talked such a streak of loathsome, incurable rot that he had to escape to Hanna Heler's in the end, cuffing her nose to make her laugh and then returning home to grunt and brood some more. Once he found Manya's tutor there, talking loudly and horsing around. He pinned Hanna's arms behind her back and taunted Hagzar, who sat behind a large newspaper reading an ad placed by a doctor in Vilna.

Later that same day he stood by Ida's bed with a glass of water in his hand. A smell of valerian had been in the room when he entered; Manya bent over her sick sister, rubbing down her chest, and told Hagzar that Rosa was not in. Ida laughed and cried, too weak to open her eyes. She gasped like an animal and made delirious sounds, until a sudden tremor seized her and she cried, "To hell with it! The ship is sinking…and I…only wanted…"

Manya was a nervous wreck. Seething with pent-up anger, she burst out, "She went traipsing off just like that…with Carmel!"

Whereupon Hagzar felt a pain like a blow in his chest. The hot blood rushed to his face and stung his eyes. What was he doing here? He stood reeling beneath the memory of Carmel's smug smile, of Hanna Heler's arms pinned behind her, of the boisterous laugh of Manya's tutor as he held them. The ad placed by the doctor in Vilna flashed before him. Then came mighty Vilna itself with its halls of learning, its bookstores, its public library in which he had worked, its long, monumental nights of writing in his room there, its companions whose dreams had resembled his own. He felt that he was going to choke. Something hummed in his ears and he could hardly see. Dazedly he laid the glass on the chair and stumbled toward the door. Not until he was out in the fresh air again did his vision clear. His temples throbbed and his heart went on pounding as he walked down the street to the end of the town and continued beyond it. He ambled slowly now, staring with melancholy detachment at the long, endless railroad track that stretched flatly out before him, quite faint and desolate in the heat of the day.

Translated by Hillel Halkin

Meanwhile

At first there was a fresh wind all around, and patches wandered in the area and darkened the twigs of the trees, and song passed overhead, and streams frolicked in joy. Then dancing sparkles of light began to run riot in hearts, and gaiety of life flowed, impudent and mischievous. In those days, Naftali Berger's heart also trembled with hidden gaiety, that very Berger who had been agitated for eight months straight in Mrs. Hashkis' yellow chamber, while his head leaned on his hand and his knees were crossed, one over the other, and a stream of sorrowful, powerful nostalgia flowed over him, and secret, demanding dreams began to suck on him, and he yearned for beautiful thoughts of innocent childhood, and the bold appetites of the exulting spring struck warm eyes that looked into the soul—and why indeed not with love? He dreamed of new and young life that could, in fact, satisfy the soul. For what—was it not enough? Or perhaps he was unworthy? People come and take up life and make it into renunciation after renunciation at the dawn of their spring—and for what? For even the truth of things was entirely different. And in those days, there were joyful and intimating dresses, and the sounds of longing throbbed and promised, and yearning souls trembled and peeked and listened in feverish distress to every rustle around—and days began to flow, yearning days of light, fervent, expectant with devouring fever…however, that was a dream—and it deluded people.

Right after Pesach, heavy, dull lead was again hanging like a basin, and it closed over people's heads from above and an ugly swamp stripped laughter away from them, dark and frozen below—and the days crawled heavy and dark, lower than low; and each was deafer than the next, and each was more polluted than the next, and they had no beginning, and they had no end, and they crouched together heavy and gray upon the soul, which was mute with anxiety, and they suppressed in the root every thought about spring and about a little light and about any kind of straightening up. And once again the roads were wide and gloomy and mournful, and the sky above them was low and gray and damp, and people were solitary, and they wandered shrunken and pale and anxious and suffering in secret and guessing something…and again Naftali sat in the yellow room and again the darkness oppressed the weary soul, and again the swamp shouted, and whips snapped, and the wagon drivers white with flour growled and panted and roared from their navels: "Na-na-na-na…na-a, volk tabi yesh…"

And once he sat silently at his window, as in former days, and his knees were always crossed, as was always his way, and his head was leaning on his hand, as from time to time, and his ears listened to the faint, even voice of his pupil, who babbled and recited his lesson to him on that day as on every other day. In one of the nearby rooms a thirsty infant cried bitterly, and in the kitchen, Mrs. Hashkis rained fire and brimstone down on the head of the cook, who was already crying, and she called her "bare-bottomed" [see Is. 20:4]. That morning in fact the sky started to clear and pure beams of light were freed from here and there, and they shined on the swamp, and dry patches began to brighten on the scattered roofs.

Something had certainly happened, so that Naftali turned his eyes slightly, without noticing, and he suddenly saw the sky, beyond the windowpanes, and it was freed, and it was high and deep, and he saw the tops of the orchard, which was beyond the tranquil roofs, and it was fuzzy, and it was green, and it had begun to blossom, and it was bathed in light. Then his eyes fastened on the distances of the sky, and his heart trembled and was warm, and he saw that it was flowing on and on to infinity, and there it hinted and winked and was lost to the yearning heart—and suddenly a rather strange thing happened. The chair beneath him was thrown backward with a great noise and fell, and a tormented plaint was noised and lost, and Naftali for some reason was standing in the center of the room with some bending of the head. The pale boy was alarmed at first and a shadow trembled on his white forehead, and he was silent. But immediately an irritated scolding shook him: "Re-cite!"

The boy, alarmed, quickly began his recitation again, and Naftali angrily spat and abruptly bent over, and, as he lowered his fists, for some reason, deep into his pockets, he immediately began to pace, as though trapped, from wall to wall, and from time to time he tripped over the children's green beds, which were scattered here, filling the room. And when streams of disgusted blood later flooded his face, and his temples became feeble, and weakness poured into his knees and chest, at the end of his strength, he approached the chair, which had meanwhile been righted, and lowered his body onto it with a sigh of weakness, "The dev-vil knows what's..."

Then the boy's frail voice flowed evenly, and there was silence and the sun was gloomy yellow, and a fly stubbornly buzzed and banged against the panes, and in the adjoining rooms Mrs. Hashkis clanged with her keys and scolded the nanny. And that silence was like the extension of a long, subdued plaint, which pressed his heart and closed it and told him of sadness, told him of fates that were lost in life, and dreams that withered in the bud, and life that was ended in error. Many, many had been the days of light and tranquility, and those days had been good and generous, and they were always dangling, like a proud matron, who had finally shown her grace, and nevertheless they pass and are lost, and there is no redemption. Gloom, gloom! There is youth in life and a person lives it only once in this world, and all his dreams are of it—and they wither with no joy and not a scrap of happiness, they wither even in the sparkling of the exultant spring, and they are always lost exactly thus, not so beautifully, without any basis or reason for it, as if it were not you, the person, who had already completely left childhood, who were their master, and not you, with a yesterday of twenty-two years behind you, who had fostered dreams for them, and not you—not you who had so many thoughts about them…

Zmmm…zmmm…

And when the veins of his temples twined and gleamed, and his jaws began to turn sickly purple, he crossed his knees with frozen calm and laid his head in his hands.

From that hour on, the days began to crawl long and yellow, and idleness was spread over everything. The outdoors crouched weak and barren, and the big sky had no desire at all, and Naftali sat at his window and only was anxious often lest the Viennese chair beneath him might be destroyed because of the burden of his weight. And in the heat of the day, the warm and fatty mist of the yellow room, full of many children's beds and imbued with the odor of various salves, completely oppressed his soul, and he would suddenly start feeling that his body was so polluted and truly full of scum—as if he and his body were of a piece and could not be separated from the mucky room, whose yellow windows were sealed all year long with strips of gazettes because of the frost, and that scummy greasiness ate at him for days and days and had already rotted him on all sides from the foundations to the roof beams. And even the breath of his nose became loathsome to him, and he would sit by his window without moving at all, and his face was boiled, withered, motionless, like a softened lump of meat, which has markings of a human form on it, and some clown had come and put gold glasses on it.

It always began at the same hour, when little Vera sat with her open book and handled a fly whose wings she had torn off, until the pale boy unwillingly recited that day's history chapter, that plague of a chapter, which always crawled lazily, like life without purpose, casting the soul into the barren, muddy pollution, just like it. The feeble voice of the weary boy flowed smoothly in that lazy silence, and it crawled with total indifference and related, as it were, strange things from such distant, such strange periods, and people fluttered, whose memory had long been extinguished, and wars, from which no survivor remained, and Naftali would half lie at the window and often hold his breath because of the filth and hear and not hear, and his boiled, and withered, motionless face was toward the barren street.

His eyes stared and were cold and crawled in a mute gaze from the dust of the wide path and slipped into the deep ditch to its left and climbed up the heap of yellow earth alongside it; and they clung to the old, low fence, and continued the whole length of the street, and they encountered the crooked, scrawled letters, which, apparently, one of the *shaygitzes*, who had certainly reached old age by now, had written with chalk, the swamp of his frozen soul would almost be shaken, and he would think, as it were, with a bit of revenge, that those rich men only know how to fill their important bellies in their dining rooms and to decorate their pasty bodies on the dusty promenade in the park—and in truth, they all lived like real pigs and they were always sunk up to their neck in mud and stink and coarseness. And a flaccid curtain of mist began to tremble in his oppressed heart and blur his mind and its mists, and at first it did not allow all that stupid commotion and annoying pollution to reach him, what was going on around him during all the days of his exile in towns and villages, in the country and outside of it.

They fluttered before him and were extinguished and came back again, and blurred shadows vanished again, and shattered people, and rooms, and rubbish, and wild shocks of hair, and the plumes of women's clothing, and parched voices, and scratchy laughter, and words, and running with no purpose, and in recent days, in the sickly days of the sun, in the bustling and depressed town, also anger, frequent anger, anger that eats the heart and soul. Afterward his head fell a bit, and his face froze completely, and Semyons, flooded-with-freedom, healthy, in high, polished boots would begin to be distinguishable in his mind, and lean Isaks in crushed collars and crooked ties, and Nastias with cropped hair, and hoarse Rachilkas with smoking cigarettes, and he abruptly began to accuse himself bitterly and think with irritated venom, that he was born in mud and he always lived in mud, and he would also die in mud, and the spirit of man is cursed. There are grasshopper people. Seemingly, if a man has a beautiful soul, it is not worth anything at all to him, that he should settle himself in a polluted swamp, like this one in

Yehudiliva, and even if they gave him a salary double the one they were giving him, and even if the thing were clear to him, that this sojourn was merely temporary—and all the more so…but here the darkness of his breast always emitted a kind of dull cough, appalling the soul, and his lips uttered a withered rebuke, "Vera…"

She released her fly and buried her face in her book.

And once he was sitting that way and caught his thoughts crawling and suddenly he remembered a certain Bendit, a healthy, yellow shoemaker, a "good bloke," whose way it was to stand and sway back and forth over a cup of pale tea and spread white butter on coarse bread with his calloused finger and answer threateningly to everyone who addressed him at that time, "Popka, I'm busy!"

At that time his eyes fastened on little Vera, who sat with her chin stretched toward her book and her arms crossed behind her, and she was trying to remove a button from her book just by blowing on it, and he intended to call her by her name, to stop her from doing that, and his lips uttered, "Popka…"

But his eyes immediately fluttered around, and he added, "Eh…Vera, is that how you do your lessons?"

And a few days afterward something happened. He was sitting alone in his room and waiting for the children, who were eating their meal at that time. There was silence, and flies buzzed, and in the dining room they banged with forks for a long time. Suddenly Mrs. Hashkis raised a frightful, alarming outcry, "Wh-at? What did you sa-ay? Popka? What's the meaning of that word, ah?"

After that the vapor was heavy, and the silence was yellow, and the stench emitted greasiness and Naftali's soul had a feeling as though a barber had smeared his face and his neck below it with hot lather. Later, when the stream of oozing tar, which scratched his back all that time, had stopped, he told him the day's history lesson, and, like every day, with a suppressed groan, he brought his chair close to the boy's and started to explain the following chapter to him with withering annoyance and weak reprimands, the plaguing chapter, which would crawl and oppress tomorrow exactly the way its fellow had crawled and oppressed today.

But when cups and spoons began to rattle in the house, and

keys began to bang against cupboards, and strange women came and chatted with "in general" and "of course," the servant woman began to run around in the corridor, and the children wore suppressed, mischievous joy, and Naftali himself sat at his window and saw the clean and idle dining room, and he saw a yellow patch of sun and a pure white tablecloth and fragments of tired light in the polished samovar and the transparent cups, and suddenly he clearly saw the beautiful mountains, bathed in tranquil light, and the river, flowing with streams of gold, and he wanted to be sitting alone in a boat, and he stood up and began to walk back and forth in the room.

The pale boy was busy with his lesson, and suddenly he performed a saucy dance and went back to his book, and Vera snored and hid her face in her hand, and the boy stuck his tongue out at her, and she began to laugh into her fist—and he did not notice, he paced, and he urged her with a fond reprimand and reminded them feverishly of words and sayings, which they frequently encountered. After the tea, chairs began to scrape the floor, and long dresses rustled in the corridor, and they looked for parasols while talking, and then Naftali stood and waited next to his window, and presently he saw the band, as it went out under red, white, and black canopies. And when he saw his Mrs. Hashkis among them, and she bore her corseted breast before her, and her black dress studded with rhinestones, and she lagged behind it, his heart immediately felt enlarged, and the excited band of ramblers in the square mingled and sang in his soul and soft syllables of song in the orchard, and dresses dragging in the crossroad, and the shouts of girls in the twilight dusk, and he began to look for his topcoat. The low fence before him was as though pushed into the earth, and it lost all of its importance, and the roofs were tranquil and sturdy, and behind them the gilded treetops of the orchard bloomed, and into the azure heights broke the blue steeple of the church, entirely hidden in the thick greenery of the orchard. Naftali raised his eyes a bit more, and he saw the pure, saturated dome of the sky with a lacy blue cloth below it, and a strip of pure gold twisting on the hem of the cloth, like lace on lace. The sun slipped toward immersion. Now a soaring bird darkened on the azure sea. There, in the distance, a white mass crawled, and its tail grew and grew: a railroad train. There was freedom under the sky and its expanses for an aspiring soul…

And when the children's mischief broke the boundary and suddenly halted his thoughts, he turned to them and saw two beautiful children, full of mischief, and he felt warm fondness for them, and he stopped their lesson and started talking with them, and mocking, and Vera, at last, climbed up and sat on his knees and asked if he had a mother and where were his sisters, and the boy, her brother, sat like an adult on the end of the table near him, and they chatted and laughed, and he told them, by the way, tales and stories, and they were enthusiastic, and their pure cheeks turned pink, and their black eyes were bright, and they asked and dreamt and drank in his words thirstily. When he told them Bible stories, Vera raised her glowing black eyes to him, and she asked feverishly, and the boy stopped her eagerly, "Silly." She was amazed. "If you only saw how he picked up the Egyptian—and craash!"

And when he left there, and the children accompanied him and ran after him mischievously and boisterously, and he saw the windows of the notary gleaming from the red sun, and the children were noisily raising dust, and the servant women ran, bearing hay in their aprons, his face glowed, and his stature was erect, and when he met acquaintances, he would answer their greetings loudly. But if someone wanted to talk with him at that time, he would answer feverishly, and excuse himself, "Sorry. I'm in a hurry now; but I'm sure we'll see each other again."

But when he got home, he wouldn't tarry there long. A gulp of coffee, some sort of translation, and a cursory perusal of the new *Ha-Shilo'ah*, and a cursory turning over of one of the Russian magazines—and the evening twilight began to murmur and to make demands in isolated corners, and from the distance the faint murmur of the bustling square stole in, and soft syllables of song floated and vanished in it, and great sorrow, with no explanation and no meaning stole in and dripped and filled the soul, rumbling and sucking the chest, and going on to boil the temples, and spreading and blurring the eyes, and gripping, pursuing, pursuing wordlessly and speechlessly outward…

—Whither?

The willow whispered behind the windows, and Naftali's hands were thrust in the pockets of his trousers, and his shoulders were raised and making his head protrude somewhat, and thus he paced, humming mournfully, sometimes groaning and sizzling in fury.

"What will become of him?—Lord of the Universe, what will become of him!"

Before he went outside, before he saw anyone, he already knew in advance whom he would see, and with whom he would talk, and what the other would tell him, and what he would say to the other. Even before leaving the door of his house, and even before his ear seized anything, he already knew quite clearly what his heart would say to him late at night, when he returned home and turned on the lamp and the walls would not even tremble, and he would fall with a groan on his bed and bury his face in the pillows, or that he would lie on the sofa with the last issue of *Emet* in his hand...

The night would not wait. The sky would become serious and gloomy and pure, and the many branches of the willow would whisper, and the darkness would increase, and the cat would watch from the corner, and the saturated dusk would rustle and rustle—Lord of the Universe! And now, young and healthy, you have nothing more to do but smash your head against the wall and bellow like a bull, or to bury your face in the pillow and allow an eternal sob to burst out and vainly bewail some eternal loss...

"The dev-vil knows what's the matter..."

2.

And in chilly twilight, the tranquil, wide post road lay, and the shutters of its pretty houses were white and serene, and above a huge, tranquil azure dome dreamed, in purest purity. However, at the end of the street, at the entrance to the park, under that very azure dome, ant-people bustled, and women in kerchiefs murmured, and noisy children laughed and raised dust. There was a blue wall there, on the left of the street, and its windows were wide open, and sodden *romansas* rolled out of them, and crumbling, hoarse songs, and the noise of gramophones accompanying them; and there was a white pharmacy to the right and the apprentice who worked there, that Jewish lad whose ears always stuck out, because he shaved his head, opened its windows to the street and began to scratch various musical phrases on his violin, with the noisy additions of his own.

And near those houses stood a cloud of dust and in it lads and servant girls frolicked, shouting, and tall Jews dressed in peaked caps came over and hit their boisterous children. And when Naftali saw the noisy bands from a distance, his heart was somewhat heavy, and his face guarded his soul and its secret property, and while he made his way among them, he listened to a wanton laugh from here and a plaintive cry from there, and he saw full, ardent faces, and he thought with some irritation about the coarseness that covered life, but he was puzzled about the reason for it; it is possible simply because that is its essence, and it is possible—precisely because its essence is completely different; but soon his breath grew heavy upon him, and the dust penetrated and tickled his throat and his nostrils, and he hurried and left the band and turned right to the square.

There once again was a long, high cloud of dust and pale gloom and a big stream of women's hats bobbling and white blouses fluttering and the flames of cigarettes reddening and fading, and the square bustled with a commotion and shouting and words. Naftali put one hand in his trouser pocket and lowered his head to his shoulder and made a way for himself and moved to the side and came, finally, to the yellow sand path, next to the church, and started to stroll alone there, frequently puffing into the handkerchief before his face. There he happened to meet a tall, straight lad, who was also strolling alone, and biting the end of his mustache and fingering his temples frequently, until his face twisted with repressed pain. This was David Ratner, Naftali's long-time friend, who had just returned, for some reason, from abroad, after living there for a long while. Naftali saw him, and his face took on a pale glow, and he approached him and greeted him with a withered shout of goodwill, "Ah!"

Then he joined him and asked, "*Nu*, where are you headed?"

They walked together in silence. The square bustled around

them, and enthusiastic boys shouted and the sound of coins rang, and
high school girls raced hand in hand and whispered to one another
and dapper men floated, standing straight, with pipes and cigarettes,
and hummed the walt, that came noisily from the park. They walked
in silence, and the dust penetrated their throats, hastily begging
people's pardon, though heard only by themselves, until Ratner could
no longer contain himself and he softly sighed, as though talking to
himself, while his hand pressed on his temples and his face twisted,
"Damn it! They're doing nothing but raise dust!"

And the other grunted, he, too, as if it were a slip of the tongue,
as though talking to himself, "Hmm, yes, plenty of dust."

And they walked on in silence.

In the first days, right after Ratner came back from overseas,
every time the two met, Naftali would surround him again and again
with great pleasure and various questions. Although two years ago he
had also lived in big cities overseas, along with this friend of his, every
single extra hour had been burdensome there, and even with the best
of his acquaintances from there, he always felt as though he were with
items only for decoration, as though with companions for a while
on a train—now, after about two years had passed since the day he
had returned from there, in his joy with Ratner, immediately upon
seeing him returned from "there," there was much of the saturated
joy, which bursts from the withered heart of a depressed, despairing
wanderer, when he suddenly meets an old acquaintance on a strange
and busy and oppressive street, someone from the past, from his
hometown, a witness to the days of his tranquility.

For a few solid days the boiling and stinking room at Mrs.
Hashkis's had been rather comfortable and even rather joyous, and
the beautiful children were so sweet and diligent and merry, and their
voices throbbed with such suffused delight, and even the long chapters
of barren history weren't so crawling and annoying, and sometimes
he imagined he even found interest in it. In those days he also said
to Mina, with such easy and simple affection, that she was pretty,
and afterward he took her hand, and when he strolled with Ratner
in evening, he talked to him a lot, and, with great pleasure. He even
remembered people and events that had no connection with him at

all, and, with a yearning soul, he would fall upon every trivial little thing and probe it and turn it over, and his words were enthusiastic, and his voice echoed a bit at the end, and at that time he would laugh childishly, and with sharp pleasure—and be wearied. Once, when they were walking together, Naftali spoke with enthusiasm and reminded his friend of a certain Pashka "Sparky," whose way it was to suck on a little cigarette and spit through her teeth, and he teased her a lot and tried to imitate her exactly, the way she would threaten with clenched fists and stamp with her feet and sing out of her hoarse throat:

"She would come into the world in all her power and glory…"

And suddenly empty weakness began to suck at his heart, and he raised his shoulders somewhat and spoke, "Eh, God is with them!"

And immediately his face tightened with bitter agitation, and he asked his silent friend with fluttering quickness, "Ah? What did you say?"

And he sighed. And the day ended. Comfortable darkness began to sway silently and cool the heavens and dim the lights and began to weave gloomy dreams. No, there is another truth in life…and only then did Naftali's soul speak and in his sorry style he broke the mutual silence and asked his friend, "Anyway, you've come back, too, David. *Nu*, what will be now?"

Then they went on without talking.

After the commotion in the square began to diminish and sodden humidity slowly lay down the cloud of dust, and the square was immersed in darkness, a single dress fluttered, and a laugh struck and died and a subdued whisper was silent, and Naftali placed his spectacles on his nose, and his eyes began to wander and look about him in suppressed gloom. On the smudged sidewalk near the closed stores, an unclear picture fluttered and moved away, and its footsteps clicked and stamped on the saturated ground. Naftali looked at it first and then spoke as though not speaking; however, when he was entirely in despair of seeing, he turned to his friend with a "hmm…"

"Look, David—isn't she one of us?"

At first the other answered curtly, "No!"

But afterward he also became a bit annoyed, "And if she's one of us—do you miss her a lot, lad?"

Then Naftali answered with a stifled "heh," accompanied by a squeezed out cough at the end, and if you wish—interpret it. Then he took off his pince-nez and began to wipe it well, and after replacing it, he began to look around him with great concentration, and sometimes Ratner would hiss out a somewhat crushed chuckle, "Hah. You're a fine lad, Tali. Apparently you're not completely dumb."

Naftali did not look at his face, nor did he turn his head to him; however, he clearly saw the judgmental laugh and its bubbling venom, and his heart suddenly froze, and it beat strongly in his chest. The tops of his jaws blushed in a sickly way. At first he raised cold and silent eyes to his friend, and then he stammered a little and began to finger his pince-nez.

"So-o?…Oho…and you're smart!"

Ratner chuckled; and when the other one didn't stop, presently he went over to a practical, decisive style, "Anyway, my lad! All of that foolishness, why does it come? You have desire for Mina—say it outright. In truth—what? What are those grimaces?"

And again they spat venom at one another, and again they walked in silence, and in silence they passed the church, and they turned into the wide street, that rose to the right, and they came to the house and attic, sequestered in lovely tranquility in the center of the green air, the house at the top of the street, across from the low fences of the gardens, that extended far off out of the town. There, on the simple bench next to the painted gate sat a single girl all alone, brunette, not tall, whose eyes were bright blue, and she smiled at them cordially, while they still saw her from a distance, and they started exchanging jocular, light, fluttering words with her. When they reached her, they were silent and sat down next to her. For a short time the three of them sat quietly. However, soon an empty, rolling sigh from the depths of the withered soul shook the oppressed silence, "Ha, hmmm…"

It was Naftali sighing. Afterward he placed both his hands on the knob of his walking stick, and he put his chin on top, and from that group a hesitant, yellow, weak, mournful hum began to come out, a fluttering chaos of various scraps of melody. The evening darkness continued to spread out and conquer the silent street with the blurred roofs of the town, dwelling on its slope, and blurred the broad fields that spread out there behind it, bringing out the distant forests, darkening far off at the end of the serious-mournful and pure sky. A grasshopper buzzed. In the distance the broad song of the field died away. Suddenly the bare cry of a woman burst out and whined from one of the nearby courtyards, "*Va-syotka, Va-syotka, Vas-vas-vas…*"

And immediately afterward a sow squealed portentously and then everything was mute again—and silence.

The girl suddenly started to yawn. She laughed at herself afterward with a bit of embarrassment about it: Ratner found occasion to spit venom at her by the way, and Naftali suddenly was aroused and snorted a silent laugh through his nose, with both weakness and venom, and without turning his head at all, he silently streamed broken pleas in the guise of playing the fool, "Mi-na!"

They laughed, and Mina answered, "On the contrary, Tali?"

Then he recovered the strength of his knees and hands, and meanwhile he spat and sputtered nervously, "What will become of him, Master of the Universe!"

And once again silence.

And when they walked back from there, the tin roofs were already frozen in the glow, and the shutters of the house latched and splinters glittered in the sand of the street. Repose filled the surroundings, and in the outskirts of the town a dog barked, and they walked in zigzags, and Ratner pounded with his stick from time to time, raising a small arc of floating dust, which immediately settled lazily, and Naftali also strolled with his hands folded behind him and his snout raised to the moon, which was over the forest, and to the brilliant beams of dew, that crawled and covered the beautiful expanses of the fields. For a long time they wended their way in silence. Finally a round and suffused hum began to crawl weakly and fight with the frozen silence and weaken and then pierce it again. It was Naftali pleading. Shortly a broad and suffused sigh lazily burst out and embraced the round, weak humming, and they joined together softly in the solid silence. Now their strength grew and the silence embraced clear and saturated words:

"Did they tell me the truth, as though/ it was the end of my swan's song ..."

And indeed Ratner had one reprehensible trait: strange venom often rustled within him. It seems, that people are walking, and the night is so fine...anyway, nonsense—let it be nonsense, if only, at least, the soul might rest a little, and suddenly, "Tell me, please, you fine young man—why are you alive, ah?"

And *hah-hah-hah* the night trembled, and if only, at least, the laughter had been appropriate. For in truth—what stroke of genius was in that joke?

And he still mocked, "What are you rustling about, boy? Are you a bit feverish? Ha-ha...eh! Vanity of vanities! The gods are still in the heavens, and death—they say, that it's beyond life, and I and you—fool, we still have leisure to smoke a cigarette when we want, take!"

And usually, most often, a joke like that ends in reconciled compromise, and sometimes after it they even come to have a friendly conversation, a fragmentary and shattered conversation, even, but easy and rather soft, a conversation that usually ended with Naftali lighting a non-habitual cigarette for himself and whispering with a whining and somewhat jocular voice, "But what's to come of it, David, eh?"

And the other decides, "Marry a woman, fool."

And Naftali complains, "Here you go again...in fact, never in my life did I hear you speak your heart's thoughts...I'm not complaining. Maybe that's the way it ought to be: but I can't, David...I'm losing everything...the devil knows, I'm nastily twisted and I don't know what...which...which...a cauldron of mud, the devil knows what!"

"Hah."

"*Nu!*"

And again they proceeded in silence.

3.

Once the two of them were sitting on a bench at Mina's, and they were joking with her in turn. At first Naftali also took part in the conversation, but he soon got up with a noisy groan, and with his head leaning somewhat to the side, and with his shoulder, he made his way and moved himself aside and disappeared through the gate, and soon his moaning song reached the ears of those who remained, crawling out of the open attic. Mina, who at that time had started telling Ratner the "story" that had happened during the winter at the Gymnasium and had stirred up the pedantic woman inspector against the senior girls, and she, Mina herself, had been in the throes of battle, suddenly stopped talking and her pure face took on a fond shadow, and she directed it directly at Ratner's face and called out sadly, "That man suffers a lot. Isn't that so, Ratner?"

And Ratner, who was looking at her face passionately all the time, suddenly also made a face like hers, and while stroking her beautiful hair with desire, he called out in her style, "That girl is rather beautiful and sweet. True, Mina?"

Naftali paced diagonally in the attic and lay on Mina's bed and sang in the darkness and groaned and went out to the railing and threw himself down on her bed again: and finally blazing heat burned his body, and his temples began to pound as though breaking apart, and when he went outside and sat on the bench, he found his friend, who was holding Mina's hand, and Mina was protesting and laughing and scolding him again, and he reassured her and teased and reassured again, that he saw no necessity in the matter, that she should take her hand out of his—simply, the thing was not at all good for her. True, he knew her and was aware that she was stiff-necked and a little stubborn—indeed, that was nice; but that her hand, so little and soft, should rest in his hand, which was nevertheless big and maybe also strong—let her say it, please: isn't it very lovely? What do you say about that, Tali! On the contrary. Here's Naftali, someone entirely on the sidelines, ha-ha, is it not true, Naftali? So let us depend on him. Good? Does she see? At first she refused the matter—because in general it was alien to her; now…*nu!* Already! But, devil of a fellow! How was he permitted to speak even to her—to her? Mina, and would that Tali speak, for example, even a single word?

Naftali sat with them and looked, as it were, in front of him, and his softened-frozen face was blurred in a hesitant smile, and he thought blurry and slippery thoughts, but burning and stinging, about eyes casting cutting sparks and about a special cordiality, that scratches the heart, one that only women are capable of, and about frivolity in relationships, that didn't fit his strength or his dreams at all, and about a certain principle, as it appeared, that if it was really so, then he had no heart for it at all, after regarding her he wasn't exactly—simple, he wasn't looking for that for himself, absolutely not that, and in that "not looking" now he was so weary, so weary and lacking strength, and he didn't need anything, anything…

"Ach, don't be foolish, David. Please, sit if you're sitting."

"I can't do otherwise, dear, there is one weakness in him, and it's called garrulity—and there will be his tomb. Don't you believe me? But how do you think, when you are by yourself? Aside from that, please ask. He's had many acquaintances, but perhaps only one will tell her, not like him and not like her; but you will only say so because in these days you have been wearing a black apron and your large, ardent eyes saw the way large, ardent eyes are supposed to see."

Indeed, he, too, was foolish in those days. Her full lips sucked his cheek, the very cheek, under which the teeth were swollen with piercing pain—and he was silent…

"Nothing, nothing." Naftali thought continually in piercing vexation, and suddenly he straightened his back and passed his hand over his face, and his lips uttered, against his will, "Mina!"

And his face immediately turned yellow and he started rubbing it continually with his hand, and he squeezed out, "What will become of him, Lord of the Universe!"

That time they sat for a long time with Mina. And afterward, when they made their way back from there, and they were silent and distant and dispersed from one another, the hour was already very late, and the moon stood over the top of the tranquil church, and the fence of whitewashed stones, which surrounded the pretty orchard next to it, was white and it shone more than during the day. The square lay silent and mute, and beneath one of the porches, which was near the closed stores, the street watchman yawned from time to time. From far away the blind windows of the pharmacy shone, and in the black shadow of the blue wall across from it, a kind of grayish whiteness fluttered and disappeared, and it was like someone in a woman's dress, and frequently the fire of a cigarette turned red, and softly a voice that had lost its form crawled and sawed the silence, *"Ti-ta, ti-ta, ti-ta-trai…"*

At first they made their way for a long while in silence and lazily, and not even the ordinary hum of the song was between them. Now an empty, dark groan shook the silence as if a residue of sickly phlegm was hanging at the end of it, and immediately it was absorbed, and everything returned to the way it was—the groaner was Naftali, walking alone and silently with his hands folded behind him and his face turned to the ground. A match went fiery with a scratch, turned red, and went out—it was Ratner, walking at a distance from him, lighting his cigarette, which frequently went out. Thus they came to the center of the square, where suddenly on the left the unbroken shadow of the row of low, closed stores ended, and a splendid street opened, imbued with the splendor of the moon, and the painted roofs guarded the pretty houses, and Naftali stood still. The leaves on the tall willows were pale and sparkling, and there, down the flat street, outside of the sleeping town, was a blurred chain of mountains, near the hospital, immersed and lost in the tranquil, pure light that recalled forgotten dreams. The heart trembled, and its distress trembled. There was an ambitious childhood and there were pure dreams—when did they vanish, and how were they lost? Immediately a sharp and boiling nectar began to ferment beneath his chest, and his eyes were covered by fog and suddenly a silent and bursting desire sparked within him, that he, too, might prostrate himself on peaks and dip into dreams in the fields and be lost in its reigning light, in its serene and festive light, of hers, apparently, he was lacking that sorrowful thing, that in us is called a heart.

"The devil knows what this is!" he squeezed out.

"What are you rustling about there, ah?" Ratner was a bit disturbed, as he came over to him then.

Naftali began to walk again and murmured softly, "Nothing at all. The night, I say, as if out of spite…"

And Ratner began to calm him down, first in his weary style, "A night like all other nights, boy; but…smart people know what to do on a night like this…"

Ratner's style, after a short pause in the middle of his speech, broke suddenly, as it were, and became different, without any prior expectation of it, he somewhat shifted Naftali's heart for some reason, and he started to mock, "And therefore they bolt their shutters well and snort with pleasure? Hah, hah."

The other began as though confirming his friend's words, and there was a kind of weary moderation in his words, "But what else? Or they're whispering with maidens in the gardens. There are also those who commit suicide. If a person isn't a complete fool, he finds something to be busy with. The honorable Kants, for example, are now finding categorical imperatives and the Schopenhauers—they're secluding themselves with awe."

But suddenly his walking stick slipped from his hand, and he was silent. After picking it up, he looked at his friend's face and called out in his usual style, "What? Why did you stare at me with calf's eyes? A person dwells in one town for six full months of the rainy season—and in the spring, afterward, he lacks even someone to stroll with him in a dark orchard after midnight. Ha! A man groans and whines like a woman in labor—will you stop looking at me?"

And with weary disgust he quickly finished the annoying conversation, "Fool, Mina is a grown-up girl—and you've come to play with her with children's dishes…"

He stopped, and Naftali walked over and began to talk to him in agitated sorrow. He said, "fool." But he wasn't the man. All of those things, and things like them, he sensed very well; but he wasn't the man—and nothing else. He had already thought a lot about that. For that an entirely other psyche was necessary. In truth…here he's saying, "Mina"…Perhaps, you're right. True, she doesn't need children's dishes; but he—what was he doing here?…Simply, that's true too. It's impossible to push away things like this with a straw; that is to say…a person is always a person, but…isn't all that—not that—even that Mina…He used to visit her often. *Nu*, it's possible that it was even good for him in her company—what's so surprising? But did he expect this? And is it the same thing?…Here, you see, too—what? The same muck all day long…

Near the church, from which they had already distanced themselves quite a way, a woman's dress suddenly began to make a noise, and a woman's hoarse laugh, and a man's shoes struck the pavement. Immediately a sharp and choked cry pierced the subdued silence, like that of a hen, when someone has grabbed it, and after it followed the broken syllable of a man's laugh, "Ha, ha."

And everything was lost again. Naftali did not return to his words, and Ratner woke up a little and lit a new cigarette, and meanwhile he muttered wearily, "Still, boy, it still isn't clear to me why you're alive."

Naftali spat with a hiss and again they walked, silently, and at a distance from one another.

And when Naftali got home later, he did not fall onto his bed with a groan, nor did he take the last issue of *Emet* in his hand. He scolded the stunned servant woman, without having intended to at all, for not opening the door for him promptly, and he said things to her, that weren't at all to his liking, and he immediately had annoying torments from that, and he opened the windows wide and lay on his back on the sofa, and he put his arms under his head, and he laid his feet on the edge, and he lay that way for a long time and fell asleep in his clothes. The walls of the room were heavy and mute, as though dead, and the big light that shined before him, burned his face and enflamed his weary brain, and it was clear to him, that all this heavy swamp, yellow and mute, had already existed once, even before it swept the barren plain of yesterday and the yellow wasteland of tomorrow; however, he needed no refuge. David also sat this time, pale and without strength, on the corner of the sofa, twisting the end of his mustache and chuckling in mockery; but Naftali saw in that mockery, too, that heavy and dry silence of the hereafter. And therefore he stood at first, even though his head was very heavy for him, and his tongue stuck to his palate, and he could not speak; but this time he managed to lower his eyes, and he started to look at the yellow lily-nail in the side of the sofa—and everything was clear to him, and he began to speak with subdued, thinned enthusiasm, "Let's say—hanging. *Nu*—shooting. But hunger? Hellish pains like that—with premeditation?"

Because this time he already knew well which way things were tending. It was something self-evident, that David quickly showed him quietly the stunned and frightened servant woman, running after Mrs. Hashkis—and her dress screamed; but he wouldn't deceive Naftali this time. True, the brain was burning and the soul was trembling and a loathsome genealogy like that was certainly not worthy of fame; but since everything was clear to him, everything was the same. All of that was; but on the third day, David relented from his dreadful decision—and he ate. True, not many days passed, and he stopped in by chance and again found him slipping a rope over a hook in the white ceiling, and then he no longer found words for him—then there were other days; but Mina, the grown-up girl, took him by his button and loathed the matter. Then she said to him herself, that there was no mystery or secret in it. Simply, something shameful—and nothing more. Long arms hanging and waving straight—back and forth, back and forth. Really, the thing was not worthwhile. But this thing, she said, depends on the feeling...and the watchman, who ran after the dress, stood before him as though seeing things and said, "Can she understand? Among us people—spittle! Among us the main thing is—the not necessarily in everything...how could it be, ha, ha!"

And he immediately began to twist his mustache proudly—as though he were sure, that David had not said those things to Naftali while they were sitting together on a riverbank in a village in Switzerland.

The next morning a mischievous sun struck his face with a full beam of burning light and his eyes were torn as though by tongs, the stink of the lamp, which was lit and whose fire was red in the black glass, filled the air of the room and the heat of the morning burned and a foul vapor boiled the bed and wet his dressed flesh; however, he was not about to get up, and his head hurt, and he gathered the rest of his strength to remember something, and his annoyance was great. Then a broken thought tripped in his shackled brain, and his temples pressed together as though in a heavy vise, and his brain filled with a blur and dry vapors, and for a short while, while the vapors rose, some weak echoes and annoying sounds vanished—it seemed, of what had just happened; but just then a scratching sawing began all over the wall of boards near him, and his teeth gnashed in torment. And just afterward the clock on the other side of the wall began to growl, ringing out the hour of eleven, something loathsome pounded his destroyed brain, and he remembered the crawling, polluted day, that was quickly beginning for him, and like someone suddenly seeing a snake at his feet, he leaped from his bed with a groan; but he immediately fell down backward as though struck by horror, and his legs were on the sofa, and his arms feverishly hugged his knees, and his chest squeezed out a tormented, sickly rustle, which was half a sob, "The devil knows what this is…"

And with one leap he returned to the middle of the room.

4.

All that day Naftali sat at the window in Mrs. Hashkis' dirty, oppressed room, and he felt all his destroyed, withering flesh as superfluous, as something annoying and irritating, whose existence was attached to him for some reason, and his mind was stupefied and could not grasp the essence of all the things. The street was barren, the fence dilapidated, and the field was weary and withered. A short peasant dressed in a long cotton dress bore her belly in front of her, and in one hand was a wicker basket, and a tray full of red seeds was in the other, and her feet were bare and pounded the dust. The silence of noon and heat. A woman's voice, "I don't understand. How a person assumes the right to talk about people, whose faces they haven't even seen. By our lives, that isn't even honest…"

And a man, who talks like someone with a hump on his back,

gets excited, and splinters pour out, "You think that way in vain. You think that way in vain. Whoever lives the life of the intellect…"

Here they are. Mina with her parasol and Moshe Hefitsh and his book. That very Hefitsh, who supplies Pisariev to the girl students at the gymnasium. They don't go to the Talmud Torah. The silence of noon and the barren street and the dilapidated fence…

And when Naftali came to his lonely and silent room, the evening had already fallen, and the sky was growing darker, and the windows began to pale, and the willow whispered mournfully, and the corners were so gloomy and mournful and softly demanding life and dreams and heart's desire…then he collapsed on the corner of the sofa, and his head fell on his chest, and his arms hugged his knees, and he sat silently and thought and dreamt and sighed. The room filled with darkness, and in the darkness the windows grew gray and the shadows on the floor and on the white stove paled, and he sat and shrank more from moment to moment and pushed into the corner, as though he intended to nullify himself in it and clear his place—the best of remedies: there is no Naftali here; and there is an end to everything…

Only later in the night, the sudden, impudent, ringing bark of a dog scared him, and he raised his head in confusion. Immediately another bark rolled through the silence from another corner; after it—yet another from a third angle, shaking the quiet, frozen night, causing a tremble in the sleeping street and dying away. When he went to the open window and stuck his burning head out, a fresh breeze hugged his forehead and came to his chest and opened his eyes, and the street was silent, and the darkness was saturated, and far, far away a running coach rattled up gravel. In the double darkness, between the white churches, on both sides of the street at the end, a number of dogs stood, black, and one of them had white spots, and they scurried with their tails and roamed about in place, barking angrily, and from the opposite end of the street others poured out barks to them. Naftali looked at them and raised his eyes and saw, behold, behind was the blurry mane of forest, at the end of the sky, the moon slowly rose, and it was as big as the sun and as red as blood. Then a smile spread across his face, and he sniffed, "Ahh, dogs! Ah?"

And immediately he suddenly straightened his back and stuck out his chest and spat, "*Tfu*, the devil!"

And as though a heavy burden had fallen from him, he turned away from the window and paced a little, erect, with his hand stroking the shirt on his chest. Afterward, he went out and sat on the bench near the gate. The freshness of the night penetrated his flesh, and the sodden darkness gladdened his soul, and he put his hands in the pockets of his trousers, and he lay one leg on his other knee and sniffed again in resentment, "*Tfu*, the devil!"

In the irrigated fields, behind the nearby river, a bird on foot began to screech moderately and confidently. The measured, considered screeches entered the silence and spread out in it and, together with it, penetrated Naftali's absorbent soul. Suddenly his ear discerned clear words in that screech:

—*Flee-ee! Flee-ee!*

And later, while he walked near the house, with slight haste, he kept raising his shoulders a little and rubbing his hands together feverishly, and beneath his chest a tranquil, firm light was kindled and began to burn, and it was firmly decreed within him to go to Odessa. It was too much for him, too much. This swamp of the provinces would grow even greater. For it was a laughing matter. A person loses his bearings and starts seeing abysses at his feet, and his soul withers in the end—and how, *nu*, how do we begin his story? A man lived under the dome of the sky, and he lived and lived—and nothing; and suddenly…what? What happened? What is the thing that he lost? What was changed with him from yesterday? And was it not a laughing matter—and nothing more, no. Away from here, away, away…eh! Ha, ha…eh—as Ratner says…

In the chorus of dogs, which had gathered not far from his bench, a fight broke out, and they started growling and getting angry and barking, and he abruptly leaned over and picked up a stick that was lying at his feet and threw it hard among them, while growling a suppressed and somewhat angry curse, "Get away, damn you!"

One of the dogs began to howl softly and limped away among the group, and the chorus parted. Naftali sat on the bench and spat and once again put his hands in his trouser pockets.

And when later he looked around him again, it was quiet and peaceful, and the dogs wandered about in a group again, and the moon rose up to the lower part of the sky, and it was even bigger, and its dim light was sown on the dusky street, and it brought out the shadows that the houses cast on the damp dust. In the dusky shadow between the churches, a dark figure, which was like a human figure, fluttered and vanished, and it immediately fluttered again, and its shadow began to grow and grow along the diagonal of the dark pavement. Finally, the figure of a tall, straight man left the darkness. It walked straight, and Naftali followed it with his eyes. Only after it had distanced itself from him, did he recognize Ratner in it. That finding was comforting for him, apparently. He hastily got up and began to rush after his friend, running cautiously and stepping on his tiptoes, and biting his lower lip. When he reached him, he fell upon him from behind and stirred his voice, "Grab the Jew!"

And afterward, they walked together, and Naftali spoke about Odessa and his decision to go there, and Ratner twisted his mustache and kept feeling his temples, and they reached the green bench, near the arched bridge that arched over the river that flowed through the center of the town, and they sat down. There was silence all around, and the river ran its waves in a gentle melody, and a silent light swung in the water. Ratner sat, leaning over, and his arms supported his head, and Naftali crossed one leg over the other, and his left hand lay on the back of the bench, and he looked at a pure bonfire that reddened in a distant meadow. Suddenly a slight tremor seized Ratner's shoulders, and later, raising his head, he turned to his friend with subdued haste, "*Mmm...nu*, young man...so you're going away, you said?"

"Ah? So it is. And soon, most likely."

Afterward, Ratner lit a cigarette and began taking long drags on it and looking forward. Naftali sighed and uncrossed his legs, and he, too, sat silently. Finally, Ratner began to busy himself with putting out the cigarette with the tip of his walking stick and spoke softly and moderately, "*Nu*...and what do you expect to do there?"

"Do?"

At first Naftali began to stammer as he spoke; but afterward his voice became full, and his style a bit more fluent, and he began to speak a lot, and his words were sad and plaintive. Do you understand? He was certain, that it was all the fault of the provinces. That is to say, completely—in everything. Was that surprising? For really was very much wanting? The matter was already evident, thank God. Here—a soft sofa, there, a chattering girl, there—a fine conversation of intellectuals—and everything was as if it had never been. Everything, he said…certainly. Had not much long ago lost its content, thank God—that means—a lot has shed its form…indeed, you don't deny it. On the contrary. But as for the real feeling, that a living person feels his real abilities in real life—surely that could have no relevance…do you understand? Because do you aspire to greatness? Everything, thank God, is already evident. But that vital suckling of the living soul that wishes to live, simply—do you understand? Truly like…like…like that frog croaking in the lake—do you understand? What did it have?

Sometimes you desire to grasp the sum of things—that means— to see, at least…and what good is it? Do you understand? Because what—what can you hold onto? For you begin, it seems, with what was so clear and so obvious—and you end…For everything is as if in order—everything. True. Frequent turmoil, burning stones, narrow rooms, many people, many words, annoyance, indeed, annoyance; but everything in order. Do you understand? A person has a grip on life—that is to say, simple. A basic, old grip. And suddenly…what happened suddenly? No one can say—but the essence of things was lost…Do you understand? Once he had a polluted psychological feeling. A long time ago, he thought, sometimes, for some reason, that he had a certain leaning for literary matters. He used to write, erase—the matter isn't important, anyway. Afterward he realized clearly, that he doesn't even have any spark of talent for the matter, hah-hah. *N-nu.* He felt sad—that is, he indeed had a polluted feeling…what he had afterward isn't at all important; but the main thing is—that he knew, at least…Do you understand? A person falls off the roof and becomes mute, deaf, an idiot—do you know? But now— now? Do you understand? For you don't even know when that began…you do know one thing, that he no longer remembers even the day when he breathed a breath at ease for the last time…

Ratner, who was sitting all that time and digging his walking stick into the earth at his feet, abruptly lifted his head and asked quietly, "Good. But what are you planning to do in Odessa?"

"To do?"

And Naftali spoke once again, and he spoke many subdued and boiling words, and bitter complaint seethed in them about the polluted and oppressive surroundings and the stupidity of idiocy, and he mentioned a strange and morbid attitude of people toward people and things—and in general…and afterward they sat for a long time in silence, and the moon was not high, and the surface of the river was dark and creased, and a fresh chill started to spread and raise gooseflesh, and over the irrigated fields before them white vapors began to crawl here and there. Finally, Ratner began to fuss with a cigarette for a long time, and he lit it and muttered something listlessly, and then he uttered a mute syllable from his nostrils, "Ha, a person always has demands, the surroundings—pollution—here—here. Marry a woman, boy."

Afterward he began to stretch in his seat and to get up. Naftali raised his eyes to him with mute hostility because of suppressed anger, and his chest immediately uttered a strange groan, half of which was a rustle, and his body swayed, not in the ordinary way—that is to say, he improved his sitting position and nothing more—and remained seated. In the distance a long row of trees extended across the large irrigated meadow, and behind the trees the orphaned bonfire died away, and white columns of smoke surrounded it and crawled and spread from it.

All around was silence, and in the area of the river some creature rustled and chirped pleas, and when he stood up from his seat after a short while, no one was with him anymore, and the street lay empty and dark and permeated with cold. First he put his hands in his pockets and grasped his walking stick under his armpit, and he walked delicately, and his head was down; afterward he took his stick in his hand and his steps lengthened, and he quietly growled: "And anyway, *nu…*"

And when a white strip widened at the edge of the sky, before his open window, he was already sitting at his table, and the wicker box was standing by him, and almost everything was organized, and the rest of his things were lying on the sofa and on the chairs, and his head rested on his hand, and his face looked out, and he said with a weary and sad-innocent laugh about Mina, who for some reason had pressed his hand with her little hand one, two, and three times that day, and her face was friendly and bright, "You see, I'm leaving…maybe you can tell me why?"

And when he got into bed, the morning had risen.

5.

One morning they found Ratner lying dead in his room, and when the day ended, Naftali walked alone and depressed on his way back from the burial ground. His face was pale and frozen in its distress, and his eyes sat deeply under his forehead. On his way, some of his acquaintances met him; and when they saw him, their faces became sorrowful and fearful, and the same question floated on their lips, which always was uttered in a surprised and uncertain tone, "*Nu*, what can you say now, ah?"

However, when they approached him and looked in his face, and for some reason no more spirit rose in them, and trembling and embarrassed, they, as it were, shrank into themselves, and their steps were as though they were unreal, and their faces were sunk into the earth; and when Naftali went by and drew away from them, their steps grew longer, without intending it, and they would breathe in with mournful relief—and God knows the mournful thoughts that wandered in their hearts for continued moments afterward.

This time, for some reason, Naftali's feet led him not to his own dwelling, but to his father's house, for his father also lived in that town. And when he arrived, oppressed and weary, he entered the not very large room and fell down on the sofa, with no strength. He buried his face in his arms, and the shining heels of his shoes protruded upward. He lay for a long time that way, and not even a weak groan burst from his chest. Twilight dimness began to wander in the room, and anxious silence reigned. Sometimes one of the members of the household would enter and immediately leave, walking on tiptoes, and his heart was full of hidden anxiety, and his face expressed a kind of recognition of guilt, which can no longer be repaired, "My arguments are blocked…"

When it got completely dark, and through the curtains, already dark, the sky paled and filtered strange dusk into the room, which was as if its soul, too, had wilted in anxiety, his father entered, a thin Jew, one of the petty merchants, who sometimes went to the rabbi's house, and he also read *Gazettes*, trying to see who was right. This time for some reason he entered with his somewhat gray, cropped head bare, and, while rolling a rustling cigarette, he stood in the center of the room and first sighed softly and called in a fallen, wondering voice, "*Nu*, Naftali…"

But he immediately stopped speaking for some reason, and as he neared the door, returning but not returning, he whispered with a long sigh, "*Uuach tu tu-tu-tu*, Lord of the universe, for that is all a man's fate; though…"

But he stopped in the middle; and from behind the door he whispered, "Serve some bread, Rivkah, he won't eat."

And later at night, when the moon was high, silence was in the streets, and Naftali walked alone and lazily, and his hollow cough, opening some dark and absolute abyss in the soul, would hesitate from time to time, and step, and be absorbed in the darkness, that absorbs everything. As he approached the bridge, near which he had sat the last time on that night with Ratner, it seemed to him, as though the thing had been long, long ago, and he stood at the railing and began to look down. The burbling of the flow crawled, and fragments of frozen light sparkled on the waves, and the hilly banks, reflected in the water, waved back and forth as though dreaming.

"Hah, a man always has demands…"

Naftali turned toward the banks, frozen in the light and silence, and presently he began to look at the water again, sparkling and black. A white lily raised its head and stopped and made the smooth flow of the water fade. His blurred reflection floated and suddenly lengthened and immediately shrank and once again broke up and straightened out, and it knew no rest. In the clear sky, which was under the hairy top of the reversed water-willow, a serene moon floated in splendor.

Then another reflection began to flutter and tremble in the water, and a woman's hat sent out lengthening and broadening tongues—as though a living spirit had come. Mina stood by his side. She had returned alone from the station, after accompanying her father. Naftali had only seen her in passing during the day. She had stood, he remembered, alone at the gate and was pale and feverishly fingered the tassel of her parasol, embroidered in blue, and then it had seemed to him for some reason, that someone had insulted her...

"Ah! Mina? What do you have to say about such impertinence, ah? He didn't even ask our opinion..."

The girl bit her lip and kept silence, pale.

"Or maybe he did ask? Why are you silent, then?"

Mina let her voice burst out and began, "I think, Naftali, that...that..."

But suddenly her voice changed and she finished, trembling, "Naftali, it's so heavy for me—and you...and you..."

She addressed him informally, intimately.

Then Naftali raised his eyes and saw, to his horror, two tear-drops hanging and trembling on her eyelashes, shining and full, and immediately his two hands grasped her hand and pressed it warmly, and he chattered with an innocent heart, with a full and mournful voice, "Forgive me, Mina...Mina..."

And when his ears heard her suppressed, trembling weeping, he hugged her soft hip with one hand, and with the other he brought his face to her mouth and kissed her soft and trembling lips. Then reflections quivered and floated on the water again, and her small hand lay submissive in his hands, and all around there was frozen silence in the light, and the burble-stream flowed lightly. Later the moon was in the river, and the water began to release mist, and Naftali accompanied Mina home, with occasional suppressed sighs, and Mina gripped his arm, and she walked silently next to him, and she sometimes pressed against his shoulder with sorrowful trembling. When they were standing in front of her house, Naftali looked at the open white door and the railing and afterward at her and again at the door and sighed, *"nu,"* and Mina pressed his hand and looked into his eyes for a moment and spoke familiarly to him. His face became somewhat dark, and he quickly chattered something to her, emphatically using a more formal way of addressing her. Then she banged the iron knocker, and its sound was absorbed in the darkness, and Naftali stood and looked at the white rectangle that was in the middle of that blue gate.

And the next day Naftali's hands were placed in the pockets of his trousers, and his black shirt was somewhat puffed out behind him, and he walked in a diagonal in the yellow room and groaned in suppressed manner and his teeth frequently bit his lips. The heat was burning, and the ointments steamed, and the children wilted, and he did not feel a thing. After he parted from his pupils and went outside and saw the windows gleaming from the sun and children raising dust and servant women carrying straw—for some reason he did not hurry as he walked but strolled slowly and often looked to the sides.

Then an old acquaintance dressed in a white topcoat met him. With one hand he was holding a stick, and an account book was thrust under his arm, and a bunch of keys hung from his finger. Each looked the other in the face, and then they tarried, and Naftali did not complain himself feverishly to him, and they stood together and conversed moderately, and their words rolled on, and Naftali began to tell him, that recently he had even decided to leave the town, but he still knew nothing clearly. The other listened to him and concurred with moderate nods of the head and told him that for his part, his wife also had a brother, who was about to receive a license to practice dentistry that year.

Translated by Jeffrey Green

In the Gardens

A leprous white spot blossomed out and quickly spread over the morning sun, causing the surrounding radiance to pale. The golden sparkle, glittering like the slow streams of water one used to romp in as a child, trembled in sudden fright and went out. In the open plain to the left, the lush vegetation had earlier been laughing in green contentment, its flowers nodding toward the newly risen sun in a blaze of yellow and red and white; but now, appalled by the sudden disappearance of its shinning gems, it let its laughter darken into gloom. A cool breeze blew. From one of the villages nearby a rooster crowed hoarsely and lengthily, and the young willows by the river began to stir and rustle.

The sudden chill made me shiver and I took final leave of my troubled sleep. Trembling, I put on the jacket, which had served as my pillow, and uneasily began to take in the cold, black waters lapping alongside me. I looked about for the green iron bridge to which I had drifted with the current and where I had heaved my boat to when I was overcome with fatigue; but the bridge must have been a good distance behind me, for it was completely out of sight. My boat rocked gently where it had become tangled among the dank reeds along the riverbank to my right, which was covered over with burgeoning truck gardens. I was accustomed to being deafened by the strident croaking of the frogs near the bridge, but the noise had stopped, it seemed, as soon as light had begun to appear on the eastern horizon. All around me I could hear the heavy breathing of the morning stillness in the fields, the hush that with the burning heat of the day begins to oppress the flesh and overpower the senses. Yellow lilies floated by noiselessly, and the wavelets whitened in mute fear of the dark current. Somewhere a bird emitted a single screech, and among the scarlet poppies beside the young potato plants a grasshopper chirped and fell silent.

The shady plants in which my boat was caught exuded the cold morning damp and the air was charged with the sharp smell of moist earth and pungent foliage. I took hold of the paddle, and the boat made for the center of the river. Slowly the water was beginning to regain its hue; here and there the dark surface was flecked with gold. At first my surroundings appeared a trifle strange. I had always loved the quiet, beautiful river of my birthplace, and had known it well; but a few years of travel often efface far more important memories, and among the recollections my Wanderjahre had blurred for me in my overwrought state was that of the beloved river which had fostered my childhood.

In the broad plain to my left, far off in the distance, a tall chimney stood out against the sky, sending up wreaths of black smoke; and beyond the truck gardens that stretched out to my right, far beyond the grove of gleaming white young birches atop the mountains bordering the gardens, a shimmering parapet shone silver in the air. I had forgotten all about that parapet, and how I used to see it in the old days jutting out above the huge manor-house belonging to the nobleman of the village, the one who owned all these trees and the gardens on the sloping banks to my right. It came back to me that Big Nose, the coarse, ruddy fellow who provided our community with fish, rented these lands from year to year. His crude cabin lay hidden a short distance away in one of the sloping gardens. I was shaken a little by the extent of my forgetfulness.

It was already eight in the morning, and my second day of

ceaseless wandering upon the river and through the fields. The whole
excursion was beginning to sicken me; all I wanted to do was rest,
and I let my hands move listlessly to paddle. But as I did so, I became
aware of the sound of two empty buckets creaking nearby. Turning
round, I perceived not far off a small, open stretch of sand I had failed
to notice before, where nets were spread out over upright poles, and a
cluster of boats, some small and some of medium size, were moored
to a stripped stake that projected from the river bank.

And now, in among the gardens, on a narrow, winding path
behind a line of curved, luminous birches, a vaguely familiar figure
came into view and intermittently emerged from and disappeared
behind the foliage as he moved toward me. He was carrying two
empty tin buckets and it was these I had heard creaking and clanking as they swung from a pole lying across his shoulders. By the time
he had made his cautious way through the white potato blossoms
alongside the river, I could make him out as a hulking, sallow Jew,
clad only in shiny knee-breeches, high boots and a spare grimy cap,
beneath which shone a hard, narrow, bulging forehead.

The man's face was unusual: it was tanned by the sun, filthy
with unwiped sweat, and slightly swollen from sleep; and each feature
had its distinctive peculiarity. The lips were especially striking; forming
a red, wet protuberance between his tawny mustache and beard.

Odd though it was, I remember clearly that when the man
reached the river and started to lower the pole carefully from his
shoulder, casting a straight, piercing glance in my direction, my first
sensation was of my blood beginning to stir and my senses beginning
to swim. This was all the more astonishing since, as I now realized, I
had met him time and again in the past without anything like this
ever having happened before. Perhaps my state of exhaustion was to
blame, but it somehow seemed that this was no man, a human being
for all his gross and strange appearance, but rather an incarnation of
the oppressive tremulous stillness of the field, who was now bearing
down on me, breathing heavily and overpoweringly, and wafting
to my nostrils the tainted effluvium that arose from the profusely
flowering scarlet poppies. Their stifling exhalation, though obviously
odorless, was laden with the faint, disturbing provocation of fulfilled

desire. My head whirled and I could see nothing before me except the moist, protruding blob of lips in the approaching face, lips that reddened brazenly in the brightening sun.

Not quite sure of himself, the man coughed harshly and said at last in a raucous voice, "Reb Ephraim, I think…No? Isn't it Reb Ephraim?"

Then he was certain: "Of course, it's Reb Ephraim. Well, well. Good morning to you. And what are you doing in our part of the world without a word of warning?"

When I failed to reply at once he continued, "Eh! What's the matter with you? Don't you remember me anymore? I can't believe it, I just can't." He spat with all the zest of a farmer on his day off, a swift casual expectoration followed by deep sighs of contentment.

But I had already placed him. I had recognized him and my surroundings, too, and I felt hopeful. With one stroke of the paddle I brought my boat up to him; then offering him a cigarette, I replied, "Ha! What a thing to say! That I wouldn't remember—that of all people I wouldn't remember you!"

His Jewish name, Big Nose, had always seemed perfectly marvelous to us; and now here he was, our Big Nose—our acquaintance of years back, the same red prodigy who without fail used to give us a snack of black bread and fresh cucumbers and a drink of cold milk, whenever we sailed forth in straggling groups for a boisterous hike along the river. He had always been a rather strange fellow. All his life he had lived on his farm, and every day he would bring to our central Jewish market the fresh fish he had caught and the vegetables he had raised in the truck gardens he held in tenure. After selling his produce he would repair to the synagogue for his devotions, booming away in his coarse farmer's voice and garbling every single word of the prayers. Then he would return home to tend his gardens, keeping himself aloof from the rest of the world. During the rainy season he would disappear entirely, showing up in the market only once a week, on Fridays. On *Simhat Torah*, however, he would stagger about the streets dressed in a top hat and an ill-fitting, rusty black frock coat, wheedling and whining in broken bear-like grunts, "*Oy*, for-for-for-forgive us…excuse us…par-par-par-pardon us…as I am a J-J-Jew."

Though quite well to do all his life, he had never been one to spend his money freely, even where his own pleasure was concerned. As far as I can recall, he had remained a widower; his first wife had died of a woman's disease, which he loved to describe to a chosen few among us. The sons that she had left behind her he packed off one by one to a yeshivah, the merits of which he had sworn by for years with a conviction as absolute as his faith in the existence of God. After a long period of silence the sons would send him a letter from Yaktrinoslav telling him that they were alive and well, and held such and such positions there, and that they were paid so many rubles and received such and such gifts per month, and that they hoped and were confident that, God willing, they would one day make good.

In addition to these sons he also had an only daughter who, however, was an imbecile. She resembled her father in her protruding facial features, except that hers were completely obtuse. Suli was the only one of the children who had remained at home with him; her close-cropped, scraggly black hair, invariably full of feathers, and her grimy inert hands always stood out sharply between the whitewashed stove and the whitewashed wall. Sometimes when we were sitting in that room on the long, high, narrow benches around that large crude table, he would go out to fix something for us, and then there would always be somebody or other in our group who thought it fun to have a word with her.

"Hey, Suli!" he would call.

She would lift a stupid bovine face toward the speaker and mutter in a toneless, masculine voice, "What do you want?"

The boy would then ask her a bawdy question, and while everyone guffawed, she would once again mutter a reply, the words tumbling out in a coarse rasping voice:

"Sons of bitches! Drop dead, you and all your families! Bastards, dirty bastards!"

At the sound of her voice, Big Nose would come in from the corridor where he had been busying himself. Suli would immediately fall silent and pull her head into her shoulders while her father removed the whip that always dangled at the doorpost, brandished it in front of her, and said fiercely, "So you've forgotten, have you?"

He would often spend a good deal of time talking to us, and even joke with us in an odd sort of way, but he always left me with the dreary impression that I had been speaking to a piece of flint. He was, in fact, a hard man—hard as his hobnailed boots, hard as his powerful gnarled hands and as his squat swarthy neck, which was crisscrossed with a network of stiff wrinkles like the dark, webbed foot of a gander.

Now I saw a friendly look come into his face and my hopes rose—though I did not let them run away with me, and with good reason, as it turned out. When I said I would like to come to his house and rest a bit, he made a long face, scratched his forehead, and fixed his eyes on the distant horizon ahead of him. He looked ludicrous at that moment, and I was sure that such chance visits as mine, with the tips that they brought him, always overcame his stubborn will. But what was the meaning of that fixed gaze? What could he be looking for on the distant horizon?

The sun, in the meantime, had begun to blaze down fiercely. Catching fire, the river flashed with a blinding glare and gave off sultry vapors. A sibilant hum started up in every corner of the gardens, where all was pervaded with a strange stirring. I was overpowered by the vast, potent, whispering hush of young plants germinating; my head began to burn and everything turned hazy. I took off my jacket again and in my nervousness at the suspense undid the buttons on my light shirt. Beneath it I could feel my flesh quivering.

"What's the matter? Why don't you say something, Reb David?"

He evidently had come to a decision and looked straight at me, searchingly.

"Well…all right, come along…sure, come along…I'll find you a glass of cold milk…but mind, nothing else."

He rapped out these last words with great sternness, yet in them I heard a softer note, as if he were pleading with me. Then, with a deep sigh, he at once stooped down and began hastily filling the buckets with water.

Suddenly, from out of the surrounding stillness, carrying over from the garden slope that was concealed from view, there floated toward us an eerie, rasping voice—rough apparently in the way that a man's would be, though its owner was attempting to mellow and sweeten it. The voice sounded repulsively petulant as it kissed each word it brought forth, "Suski…Muski…Hi! Hi!…Where are you?"

My companion shuddered and the blood rushed to his face. Before I could get a word out of my mouth, his broken growl rolled through the silence, casting a pall of terror over the sprouting gardens, "Shut the hell up!"

Then, placing the pole with the two buckets fastened to either end on his shoulder, he faced me and said with gloomy resolution, "No. I can't."

He turned to go. It seemed to me, at that moment, that the sun abruptly took on new strength and the reeking river began to mock me with deliberate malice. And good God in heaven, the incessant hum that filled the germinating gardens—what did that mean? I felt as if a foreign body had been stuck in my chest and throat all night long. Suddenly, I was sure I had lived my whole life up to that point for the sole and exclusive purpose of obtaining that cold glass of milk. If I did not get it, I would never be able to go on. Huskily, imploringly, I called after him, "Not even a glass of milk? Look, name your price, anything you want, only let me have it."

He stopped and faced toward me. Temptation was obviously beginning to overcome him. He vacillated aloud, "A glass of milk?… There's milk…Maybe…but…well, all right…But you'll have to wait for me here. I'll call you. Because, you see…"

When I came to the house at his call, I found it odd not to see the scraggly black head standing out between the stove and the wall; but the impression quickly slipped from my mind. Besides, I was not particularly anxious to talk to my host, who was serving me amid an oppressive silence. Nothing, I saw, had changed inside the house. The same whitewashed walls, spotted with filth; the same flyblown picture of the solitary general on the wall; and the same small windows with their yellow panes blackened by hordes of buzzing flies. The whip, however, which formerly dangled at the doorpost, was now hanging from a nail above the head of the broad bed in the corner. All was still; and the stillness was pervaded with a muggy aura all-redolent of the strange effluvium that the owner of the house had brought with him to the river's edge. The flies swarmed about relentlessly. A stillness suffused with an aura of this sort always arouses a feeling of utter heart-consuming loneliness, which bores its cruel purposeful way deep into the breast even of the man somehow reconciled to his surroundings, and battens on his blood without pity. I perceived clearly that here there could be no rest, whether I willed it or no.

When my host went to bring me the milk, I got up and went outdoors, but felt no easier there. The heavy stillness inside the house was only part of a mightier stillness, which seemed to reign over everything in the open air. Feeling as though my heart was gripped by a pair of tongs, I started to walk down the sandy path alongside the house. I looked at the yearning, languorous growth about me, my head heavy and burning, and my mind full of nothing if not reverence for Big Nose, the coarse, crude fellow who had the courage to live here alone, in utter solitude, and raise his potatoes and vegetables simply because they were potatoes and vegetables. The hectic, unceasing growth all about: the rustling stillness that eats ardent desire for light again and again without sating its ravenous lust—for him all these somehow did not exist, or if they did, they had been created just so that his potatoes and vegetables might flourish, and if the sun became too hot for him, he would wipe his meaty face with the sleeve of his coarse shirt and go back to what he was doing.

When he returned and found me strolling outside the house, he did not call me back, but went in, brought out a glass and silently filled it from the black pitcher in his hands; and as I emptied the glass he filled it again. When I had finished, all that remained was for me to depart as quickly as possible. Without saying a word, I pulled out and deliberately gave him a full half-ruble for his fee, and then made off toward my boat, leaving him scratching his forehead. I was already a good distance away when I heard him call out after me.

"Don't be too angry, Reb Ephraim, because…because, you see…But milk and all that you can get from me any time…"

Remaining in the vicinity, I presently tied my boat to a tree at the bottom of a steep bank—the one that was crested by the young birch grove which marked the boundary of Big Nose's gardens. Then, though I was exhausted by the effort and kept gasping from the heat, I dragged myself laboriously to the top of the hill. There I spied a cool retreat under one of the shady bushes growing along the edge, where the height dropped away to the sloping plain covered with truck gardens that separated the hill from the river flowing at its foot. I sank down amid the rustling twigs in the shady spot and inhaled deeply. The entire scene below lay spread out before me like a map—the brightly glowing, luxuriant green plain with its golden-brown birches, white potato blossoms and scarlet poppies; Big Nose's crude cabin, which from afar seemed scarcely higher than the ground it stood on; the narrow courtyard surrounding the cabin with its litter of broken wheels and wagons and its rags hung out to dry on poles; and at the very edge of the plain, bushes through which glistened from time to time the waters of the rivers below. All this lay outspread in silent yearning, steeped in generation and growth, sprouting, budding, flowering. But a rank invisible aura arose, stifling and oppressive...

I lay there a long time, unable to fall asleep, probably because I was so worn out. Mosquitoes swirled about me, whining in my ears. I lit one cigarette after another to ward them off and finally tried covering my face with my handkerchief; but this forced me to breathe in the stale air that I exhaled, making me feel worse still...

When at last my eyelids dropped and I was on the verge of dozing off, from the bottom of the mountain there came to my ears the sounds of a peculiar groan that held a hint of strange laughter. I heard it again, then a third time. At first I ignored it, but curiosity finally won out. Looking down below me, I saw in the tall grass at the foot of the hill the seated figure of a rather tall, full-bodied woman. All she was wearing was a homespun slip that left much of her body exposed, and the shadows cast by sun and leaf rippled and glided softly over her ample shoulders, which were bare like her soft, full upper arms. Her head was bent forward and she grasped her shoulder in her hand, offering it quietly and with obvious pleasure to the blazing sun. Occasionally she would change hands and hold out her other shoulder. Suddenly she raised her head and emitted the same groaning sound I had heard before. I recognized that black, scraggly head, and started back in trepidation.

"Good God—it's Suli!"

Tiny balls of hard, coarse laughter began rolling out of her chest like peas.

Then the strange voice I had heard that morning by the river began once again to kiss out words languorously, sweetly, "Suski... Muski...Hi-hi-hi..."

Her voice held a strange violence—an aggressive quality unique of its kind. I somehow felt that I was in very familiar surroundings where I had never been before, that I was looking at very commonplace things which, till that moment, I had never yet seen.

After a brief pause, during which the girl listened attentively, she resumed in a louder voice, "Suski...Muski..."

She concluded with a wild, interminable wail, "Hooo-oo-oo-oo..."

Soon I heard a vigorous rustling among the leaves near the girl and in the distance, I made out Big Nose's figure, recognizable by his husky build and slow, powerful walk. The whip I had seen in the house hanging in the corner at the head of the bed was dangling from his clenched fist; as he drew closer to the seated woman, I could see his harsh red face and the knotted muscles in his dirt-streaked forehead.

"What's going on here again?" he growled from the distance in a choked voice.

The girl at once fell silent and hid her head on her shoulder. He drew near, stood by her and began staring at her darkly—at her bare shoulders. At first I did not understand, but when I saw that squat, thick-skinned neck of his begin to swell and turn a fiery scarlet, I realized the significance of the way he was looking at her. My heart began to pound violently, and I gasped for breath. I recall that I remained lying as I was, stiff as a board, with my arms stretched out before me. As if to brace myself, I gripped a clump of grass in each hand and pressed the blades together with all my strength...

I did not begin to feel the pain caused by my fingernails digging into my hands until I saw Big Nose rise to his feet, flushed and panting like an animal, and fasten the clasps on his breeches. He spat noisily and growled, "You scum, I'll murder you. You're a whore, a whore!"

And with the last cry, the whip in his hands whistled through the air, snaking across Suli's bare shoulder where she lay. She writhed and sat upright, wailing in terror, and as he turned to leave, she took her hands from her welted shoulder and cried out quickly in her coarse, toneless masculine voice, "You son of a bitch! Bastard, dirty bastard!"

Translated by David Segal

Uproar

There by the long, plain, flour-dusty carts, which usually stood idly in the middle of the spacious empty square, beside the pot-bellied road which sprawled somewhat in the spring sun, with the scrawny little horses which seemed from afar to be frozen in rigid dreams, standing like a wall-painting, but for the occasional switch of their lazy tails at the troublesome flies about them, a multitude of loud voices suddenly erupted in ringing laughter, and the rather desolate square, eternally strewn with wisps of loose hay and sunk in flaccid sleep, suddenly shook feverishly and its immobile space resounded with bright waves of, "Oh ho ho ho!"

Along the low wires strung beside the broad road, from one pole with its white lamp to the next, perched a flock of staid sparrows, facing the brilliance; alarmed, the birds all took off at once, with a frightened rustle.

Whrrr...

They flew off and began noisily to bathe and swirl in the tranquil azure light under the vast and friendly sky. *Whrrr*—Come, let them be, those floury, busy creatures down below! Let them fuss in their rows of squat, dismal shops on this insignificant patch of ground. Let the Duke's abandoned castles and clipped orchards serve them for beauty and the bright steeple with its proud, foolish neck serve them for height. *Whrrr*—in truth, are all of these worth one deep breath of this pure wide azure, and the sublime dreams of its distant horizon?

Whrrr...

Down below there was clamor and the area was suddenly shaken and full of voices. Dumb Yoli, a yellow, snub-nosed carter whose speech was incoherent, was apparently one of those speakers, as he lolled in his cart and excitedly emitted a strange yellowish roar, with a pointed conclusion, "The blagues of Egybt take im! Eh? Ho ho ho bull 'im, bull 'im, the blind dog! Ho!"

And his comrades, the other carters, shouted from their carts with voices like hammers:

"Ho! That cock, let him go to hell!"

"Ho ho! He's just a blind dog! Eh?"

"Ho ho ho! Throw him out! Out of here, Chicken!"

"Cover it up, my boy!"

"It's the truth, as I'm a Jew, ho ho!"

And suddenly the original loud outburst broke again and drowned the voices.

"Ho ho ho ho!"

It being a partial Christian holiday, the doors of the shops were partially closed. Soon the shopkeepers came out or peered through the shutters. At the butcher's a little way off, the thumping of the cleaver was suddenly stilled. A window-pane rattled in the notary's office on the second floor, and the casement was opened wide; then the fat chambermaid of the Central Inn, a low, many-windowed hostelry, who regularly appeared with her skirt hitched up and her arms bared as she meticulously emptied her pail into the rising black swamp opposite the shabby hallway, stood and rested her idle, longing gaze on the gang around the distant carts. It was quiet and the square was still again, the morning sun being sleepy.

Nearby, in the apothecary's yard, the young redhead Prokhor, who served as a coachman, was grooming his master's horses and placidly chanting psalms in a strange, churchy voice. Over there, by the long carts, where that ringing, extraordinary clamor had been raised, the wretched horses stood as if lifeless, while the robust, floured men sprawled wordlessly in their carts. One of them, a stocky, broad-shouldered fellow in a floury apron, stood beside his horse, his whip tucked under his arm, tying on a nosebag full of hay. It was quiet, and in the blue space above them a single sparrow turned and then descended calmly and settled on the iron wires. Had it been an error? Or a delusion, a dream of the ears that ached with the agony of the frozen stillness? A cock began to crow beside the distant river.

But human hearts had been aroused and could not be quieted at once. A wave had broken over them, and even if it were a dream, they would have another in its place. An error, you say? Oh no—do you really want, my merciful Jews, to see human life as devoid of all interest, like a dusty breeze? What else can the more intelligent among you have to offer?

A dream...the dream of a suffocating soul stuck in squalid idleness and dreaming of salvation? These are the vapid thoughts of a professional idler. No. Those ears heard laughter—will you please tell me what that laughter signified? The gods are kind, and those voices were tremendous—what did they mean, eh? Now people began popping out of their holes, grasping at straws. Soon they began bringing out rickety benches. Empty crates were shaken and thumped, while the shopkeepers sat outside their shops, expectant. What were they waiting for?

See here—the gods are kind, but not as kind as good people. One of the carters, Kopei Bendit the Chicken, tall and robust, somewhat cross-eyed, with one hunched shoulder, suddenly stood up in his cart and pointed his whip at his stocky, broad-shouldered brother-in-law, Chaim Lemi the Orphan, the one who was tending his horse. This same Orphan was always running away from his stumpy, sickly wife, who resembled her tall robust brother in having a crooked shoulder and was even more cross-eyed. She used to go to the Rabbi and wail in a deep, incoherent voice, and get something in writing, then wipe her nose and travel to Starodob, where she would drag her husband from the circus and take him home. The Orphan had married her more than eight years before, moved partly by love, a lonesome orphan's love, instilled in him by the halfpenny stories he devoured in the traveling circus's filthy stable, where he had been employed in his youth, and partly because he had had enough of the circus. Kopei Bendit, the tall, robust, cross-eyed fellow, had slapped him affectionately on the shoulder and cried:

"Take my word for it, brother! After all, you're not a baby. You see that piebald and its cart? They're yours. Yes! Wait a minute! Pillows and featherbeds too. And that fat samovar, that's also hers—hey—spit, brother! We'll have a swig and be brothers—What more do we need? By my life, eh?"

Only when he took his place under the wedding canopy one clear, icy night, his hand tucked under his arm as the elders led in the bride, and the harps and flutes played, he saw his little woman weeping, a single drop trickling down till it reached the tip of her nose, where it winked at him like a star on the rim of those blue heavens. And when they began reciting the blessing for him to repeat; he stammered and stumbled at every word, the merciful Jews correcting him in unison; and he did not recover that night except when his tall brother-in-law came and sat beside him and gave him a hug, already fairly drunk, and chattered, nodding weakly, "Mmm...Mmm...and so forth...You understand? Brothers—and so on...Don't talk too much with that witch...Don't! After all, you're not a baby—that's what it comes to..."

Suddenly he got up, struck his chest with his fist, and bellowed mournfully, "Come to me! You understand? To me! I'll blunt her teeth I promise you, as I live! Mmm...Mmm...Let's have a drop, brother—and so forth!"

The Chicken was half out of his cart and apparently preaching, and floury caps began rising out of the other carts. Now and then someone laughed briefly, or a whip pierced the air like that of the Chicken, and voices began to rise. Ha! To hell with them.... Their wives must have been stingy with the beans today, or that crust of bread they're mourning about—aye! Carters, what do they know...

Then Reb Israel Leib Sweet, a prosperous shopkeeper who dealt in sweetmeats, rose and began strolling along his shop, the one under the notary's office, and slowly moved on, while his fingers clumsily rolled a cigarette. He wore his usual black coat and red neckerchief, with the worn cap on his head. Reaching the opposite corner of the road he stopped and carefully licked the edge of the cigarette paper. Reb Mordechai Ber Shchavil, another affluent shopkeeper who dealt in flour, observed him from the further row of shops across the street.

He was a broad-shouldered, well-dressed person, with a full beard and red nose, and a black mole, which sprouted hair. He too rose and left his shop with a loud triple groan, "Ah," he said. "Reb Israel Leib…Would you please, just a minute, Reb Israel Leib…I would like to say, if you would be so kind…this afternoon they will open the mill, and I would like to reclaim my carts—maybe he could lend one a small sum?—I will pay it back tomorrow—eh? Those carters, why are they so noisy today?" Someone in another corner saw them and began yawning and got up for a walk, while on the edge of the square, behind the steeple, a different scene began taking shape, and soon the old square resembled one of those scenes of the resurrection, such as children imagine in their dreams, with figures moving about, tall and short, bent and straight—moving slowly, individuals and groups, grunting and sighing and even talking.

Meanwhile that gang was also changing. The carts were empty and people, some floury and some not, crowded about them. The Chicken was there too, holding forth, but he was not alone. Many others talked in excited tones and ringing laughter, and the gang swelled. The Orphan was gloomy and ranting, "You animals! Savage Tartars!"

That was the language he remembered from the circus and the halfpenny stories he had read, and he always resorted to it, especially when he was angry.

"What did I say, what? I said you were all a pack of donkeys, all of you! Aye, as I am a Jew. What's your life worth? You're like dumb animals, savages, Asiatics, damn you! All you do is eat and drink and snore and…Shut up, Nosey! Human beings—you are human beings? Have you ever been to a show? Ever been to the *teatre*? You asses! Asiatics! Living with you! It's hell living with you. As I'm a Jew! How can anyone live with you? *Pfui!*"

"Hey, hey!" These words got up the nose of one of the gang

and the commotion grew louder. The bystanders began joining in, even those who had not come to watch. Kopei Bendit was silent, his flushed face stilled in dull wonder, while his companions whispered in his ears. Suddenly it seemed that something pierced his feeble brain and he pounced like an animal on his brother-in-law, and his voice rang out, "Whaa? That's what you want, you uncircumcised Antichrist? To go back to being a tramp? Starodob's calling you again?" He gritted his teeth: "Shut up, you dunce! Hey? Or I'll squash you right here, like…like a flea—*pfui*!"

The gang fell silent and crowded closer. They were exercising self-control. But the Orphan started again from the beginning, in the same dark tone, "You animal! You African Tartar! What do you want from me, eh? What…"

But he did not finish. At the end of the opposite lane stood Moishe Butcher, a redheaded Jew who was always laughing and whose white teeth always gleamed in the sun, together with his filthy apron. He suddenly jerked forward with a resounding cry, and in harsh tones, which sounded like the pounding of the smith's hammer cried, "Aha! Shut him up, Chicken! So the fine lad has started again? Shut him up, I say!"

The Orphan desisted. The blood rushed to his face, but he paled at once, turned his shoulder to his brother-in-law and began to defy him.

"And what if it is Starodob? So what, Starodob—What then? I'll run off to Starodob, if I want to! Hey! So what?"

Suddenly a heavy sigh burst from all the listeners and the men took a deep breath. Then the excited voices rose again and the uproar increased "Oh ho ho! What a plague! With a wife and children! The nerve! Oh ho ho ho…"

Dumb Yoli's dirty, burning face came forward and his angry bellow pierced the eardrums:

"The Antichrist! The horsh and cart, Topei! The horsh and cart, as I'm a Jew—let him go to hell! Hey!"

Moishe Butcher's hammer resounded from the sidelines:

"A con, is he?" followed by: "Flatten him, the crook, flatten him!"

The clamor grew and burst like a dam, "Crush him! You, Chicken! Stick it to him! Squash the unclean animal! Hit him! Oh ho ho!"

The heads began to move apart. Suddenly there was a crack of a broken board in one of the carts, and a short, broad-shouldered figure burst through the crowd, its shorn head uncovered and its shaven face pale and bleeding on one side, its apron drooping, and it began to leap and charge and scream wildly, flinging its whip about, shouting and bellowing, "You Tartars, the plague take you! Animals! Eat and drink and snore...Animals!"

The group fell silent for a moment, somewhat stunned. Dumb Yoli, who had marched in fury to the harnessed horse with the fodder-bag and taken the reins, left the whip to dangle over his shoulder as he stood with one foot on a wheel axle, remaining thus with his dirty face flushed and rigid. The Chicken, standing immobile, his big mouth wide open, breathed heavily like an overworked horse. The Butcher suddenly groaned from the depths of his belly, "Animals?! Hey? Finish him off!"

The gang shook. The heads came together again. The more respectable began to sidle away, while others, who were ready for a fight, fell into a commotion. The big Chicken closed his mouth and was the first to jerk forward with a strangled cry, waving a thick wooden board in the air and resembling, from a distance, one of those cheap prints showing Moses breaking the Tablets of the Law, while his hobnailed boots began stomping on the cobblestones. Moishe Butcher groaned and followed him, cleaver in hand, while the other carters swayed and moved on. The commotion swelled. First it was Yoli's roar that thundered:

"Hey, you bastard!"

But the roar was drowned in the great tumult of voices that filled and overflowed the boundaries of the square.

"Ho ho! Get him, Chicken! He wants Starodob, damn him to hell! The Antichrist! With a wife and children, plague take him! Get a move on, Chicken!"

Suddenly a runaway cart began jolting down the road with a deafening clanging of metal, with Dumb Yoli standing up in it, his strong legs wide apart, whipping the wretched horse which swung from side to side between the shafts. His roars were jolted wildly amid the tumult and he growled like a beast, "The horsh and cart, damn him to hell! The traitor! You rotter! You unclean shaushage! Damnation!" And more shrilly: "Leave your wive and children to berish? Well, you vilthy beasht!"

A sudden wind swept over the spacious square, which had always been rather desolate, strewn with loose wisps of hay and sunk in languid sleep. Columns of dust rose and moved like waves, and through them could be discerned the rushing Jews, dogs scrambling from the butcher's shop, barking frantically, and women shouting in the yards, while here and there windows slammed shut, and Yoli and his cart made a deafening racket, and the heavy door of the post office creaked and banged, until the raging storm conquered the square.

But once Yoli and his cart were gone and the pillars of dust slowly began to settle and dark knots of Jews formed, women clustered at the windows and a bunch of clerks gathered beside the post office and the notary's bald pate shone in his second-floor window, not a trace of the storm remained. Silence fell, and the barking dogs vanished, and there was no more shouting. Far from the heart of the deserted square, at the end of the street, there appeared a dark crowd of men, swaying strangely, having apparently forgotten what they were about and fallen silent, the broad-shouldered Orphan at their head, his whip under his arm, followed by the tall Chicken with the wooden plank in his rigid hands, and then the rest of the carters, leaning forward as they trotted at a steady, lumbering pace, only concerned, apparently, not to spoil the formation. It was a strange parade, and the onlookers, who had not witnessed the start of the row, watched it in amazement, searching for an explanation.

What was the meaning of the race run by these grown men, for their enjoyment, or perhaps not? What was its object? But even those who might have provided an explanation, in the secret smugness of the sober-minded, for which their arid hearts yearned, even they ignored the nudges and whispers of their companions who did not know the answer, ashamed to admit to them that they too had been carried away, beyond the usual limits. They preferred to remain

silent and gaze at the wordless, moving throng so as to avoid looking at their inquisitive companions. The square must have been too
spacious for the small gang to conquer, and the dusty low roofs of
the shops suddenly began to complain: What a dreary life it is, this
life of ours, oh good people…

From a distance the gang caught a glimpse of Prokhor's red
shirt beside the apothecary's squat, white, proud little shop. He was
standing, combed and bareheaded, on the slightly raised porch at
the entrance, and his usual psalms were suddenly recalled in the
true purpose of the race. Moishe Butcher shouted in a ringing voice:
"Prokhor, hey Prokhor!"

Prokhor shook like a hound at the hunter's whistle, and
abandoned his verses. He vaulted over the railing of the porch and
dropped down on the fugitive, who swerved like a cat and ran back
to the square, beside his pursuers, who were unable to follow him
because of Prokhor, who had misjudged his jump and to avoid falling
hopped up and down in the street, his body leaning forward and his
legs apart, kicking out. By the time he regained his balance he had
reached the steeple on the other side of the street, and blurting out
a curse he burst out laughing and resumed his tranquil recitation of
verses. The gang found itself facing the market again, and continued
its silent run in the same formation. Only when they reached Mordechai Ber Shchavil's shop, which was open at both ends and had
a door on the street where the Rabbi lived, the Orphan suddenly
stopped still. When he saw Mordechai Ber's sickly son sitting in the
doorway with his hands on his cane, close to his chest, he gasped and
growled, and for some reason shook his fist at him, "Spoiled offspring
of a rotten mother! Her atonement, are you? *Pfui*!" Having said this
he ran through the shop with the gang at his heels.

The square was visibly relieved. A filthy apprentice, holding
a shoetree in his black hand, shouted to one of the lower windows,
"To the Rabbi! As I'm a Jew—to the Rabbi, Mendel!"

Children broke into a run, and women laughed, and the Jews
chatted and whistled. Mordechai Ber the shopkeeper turned up near
the post office, to tell the gang of clerks all that had happened. His
companion, Israel Leib, was enlightening the notary, whose head

emerged from the second floor, with many Russian words and giggles. At the Central Inn the fat chambermaid was gleefully expounding to the guests who came out, and one traveler with a sleepy face and red blotches on his cheeks kept getting behind her to pinch her on her bare neck. She let out a shriek, which subsided softly, "Och, my trials…Mr Rosilkroit!"

In Shchavil's passage shop the sickly young man, excited and pale, lips trembling, groaned and voiced his complaint to the crowd, which was dwindling as people went by the opposite exit to the street, which echoed with the laughter of women and the pranks of the children, with and without shoes on. The Rabbi's house stood wide open, its windows packed with children and adults, thick as flies, as were the dining-room and corridor, while the black tail of the crowd straggled into the street.

Inside, everyone was talking at once, a noisy racket, in the midst of which a little cross-eyed woman stood beside the red curtain, holding two miserable, frightened girls by their hands. She was sobbing in a gruff masculine voice, blowing her nose and bellowing unintelligible phrases, while the Rabbi, who had come out of his private room with a great book in his hands and his spectacles on his nose, stood beside his great chair and listened with difficulty to the Chicken's roar, "Hey! All of a sudden, the devil knows what goes on in his dirty mind. A man goes to sleep at night, healthy and sound—and then she says, Rabbi, he's got fire in his belly!"

Chaim Lemi stood by the wall, pale and crushed, the trickle of blood on his cheek now dry and his head covered with a sort of crushed silk cap which had been found for him in the Rabbi's house. He was silent, his pale face looking as if he had just broken the bonds of a strange dream and was wondering where he was. The Rabbi, still standing with a hand in his half-opened book, was saying something, it seemed, and asking several questions, but did not hear anything. The Chicken was close by, wiping his dirty, low brow with his filthy sleeve. It seemed that he had finished speaking. But suddenly the Orphan's face flushed and he emerged from his corner, ploughed through the crowd to the Rabbi and shouted, "Rabbi! No…Rabbi! I ask you…what I want to ask you…For example, Rabbi…when I married the woman—doesn't it mean…Doesn't it mean that I'm the man? Me? I'm the man, aren't I?"

He stopped and glanced at the Rabbi's face. Seeing the Rabbi's face turned to him he banged his fist on the table.

"The hell with her! When I say beans, that's what it should be, beans! Isn't that so, Rabbi? Should be beans, say!"

Suddenly he fell silent and his face once again turned pale. The uproar began again. The Rabbi sat down and laughed, and his twitching shoulders revealed his growing anger. The woman continued to chatter unintelligibly, and the tall Chicken began to yell again. The crowd was aroused. Dumb Yoli's piercing scream resounded from the street as he approached, now on foot, scraping his hobnailed boots on the hard ground, and Chaim Lemi looked down and backed away to the wall in a daze. Suddenly the woman began howling again, and Chaim Lemi looked at her and saw her cross-eyed face, faded and wrinkled like an old boot, and from the swollen tip of her nose hung a trembling drop, and unable to restrain himself he charged at her, roaring, "Home, you witch! This minute!"

One of the frightened girls began to cry, while peals of laughter filled the place and the racket started again. The woman was alarmed and her face fell even more. She put up a hand to shield her lowered head, as Chaim Lemi suddenly spat: "*Pfui!*"

Rushing to the open door, he roared: "That's enough, you animals!"

The onlookers, shocked, moved out of his way. In the corridor some tried to block his way, but he grunted and someone fell down with a curse. Once in the street he stopped and shouted up at the windows, "You, witch! Hey, tell that witch of mine to go home now. Right now! I want something to eat!" He roared out in conclusion, "You wild animals! You savage Tartars! The hell with you and your dirty hearts…*pfui!*"

That afternoon, when the doors of the flour-mill opened and the carters drove up their noisy carts, including Shchavil's two carts which he had reclaimed, Chaim Lemi stood by, urging on his lazy horse and lighting his cigarette with the burning end of his brother-in-law's, who was also whipping his horse forward. And when the

Chicken saw the other's apron hanging loose, as it had that morning, he growled, "That witch, the plague take her! Is she too sick to sew it up so it won't hang down?"

He sucked on his cigarette and handed it back to his brother-in-law, spitting with excitement.

But Chaim Lemi seized his brother-in-law's thick paw and touching the end of his cigarette to the other cigarette, exclaimed as he inhaled: "To sew it?…And what about food?…Women—She made a Yom Kippur for me today!"

The Chicken recoiled as if bitten by a snake, and his neck swelled and reddened, "What?! That's the sort of trick she's up to?—The idiot. I'll teach her a lesson!"

He fixed his cross-eyed gaze on his brother-in-law, who had lit his cigarette and was puffing on it to get it going. He seized his shoulder affectionately and straightened it. Then he promised him, beating his fist on his heart, "You listen to me, brother—you'll see! Don't let anything stop you—just slap her down! One-two-three—slap her down! Hey hey, stop right there! Ah, that's the way!"

Translated by Yael Lotan

The Time Before

Ephrat, Uriel Ephrat, a rather tall and pale young man who, for some months now, had been constantly biting at his lower lip, received a telephone message one spring morning, a message for which he had been waiting so anxiously several days previously and then had ceased to wait for it because he thought about it and had discovered that, in truth, it didn't really matter to him. The message turned out to be, "Heh…eh!—"

Uriel, who was then sitting there, reluctant to return to his own room lest he lie down on the bed, suddenly forgot that it didn't matter to him. As though still thinking of something else, he jerked his head to the mouthpiece. "What? Who is it? Is that you, Pozer?"

It was Pozer, his friend, Chaim Pozer. This friend had promised him that he would let him know immediately if he succeeded in obtaining money for Uriel's journey.

The devil take him! What kind of an answer was that? The moron, what was he yelping there like a horse?

"Idiot, stop neighing at me like a crazy colt. Talk plainly."

His landlady, that woman of refined taste, in whose house he had a room, was at that moment planted in a rocking hair in the corner. She uttered a startled moan, as though her chair were about to break beneath her, and then began to complain, "*Phoo*, Yuriel. What's going on here?"

Already a trifle heated, he turned his face to her glumly. Look at her! Phoo, Yuriel! What was he doing to her? And what's more, the way she pronounced his name. He hated such comedy of manners. He had a good, simple Jewish name. Overcoming his distaste, he called out, as though to explain to her his resentment of the other, "A person shouldn't be such an idiot!"

Meanwhile the telephone yelped out again, "Heh…eh!"

Uriel bent over as though he had been struck. What nerve! Did that skinny bespectacled mushroom there think that he was playing around with a dirty brat who had made in his pants?

He thrust about furiously for a stronger epithet, but in his confusion, missed the mark and called back, "Idiot, do you hear me, you blockhead? Look, I'm packing my suitcase and coming to the port, and then…."

What would then be he couldn't quite say, but the fellow at the other end took alarm at the threat and gave him no opportunity to finish. The telephone buzzed back at him, "Alright. I'll also be there soon. The ship leaves at two o'clock. What? Sails at two."

The telephone fell silent. Uriel lit a cigarette and sat still. He felt slightly unwell from the sensation of his rejoicing heart. But he hesitated to pay too much attention to that. All those absurd symptoms, really absurd, that had been bothering him in the past few days had already afflicted his sorely overtired and much distressed soul. It was better for him not to start groping about there, if only that would help. There was something disgusting about it—such nonsense; except that there are things, apparently, that don't have any need to be understood. Ha ha…

Only a few days ago, Uriel had been at Dr. Shalshelet's office, the same doctor who had come from Paris recently; and he had yawned a lot, drunk coffee, smoked cigarettes, and just looked out the window into the street or at the bald pate of the one who sat opposite, in a bathrobe, open at the throat, bare feet enclosed in sandals and humming to himself whilst scanning the crowded lines of a notebook; except that this humming to which Uriel had already become accustomed, was at times even agreeable, and the coffee, into which the Doctor used to mix liquor, made him sleepy. Afterward, when he returned home, he lay on the bed for a long time, sucking at cigarettes, ruminating proper and improper thoughts and dozing apparently. And then he saw his old soft, black cap that he had worn with such pleasure a year ago when he had come back from the cities of the seacoast, and he went up to it and laughed mournfully, saying, "You see, cap? I didn't die."

These were ordinary aspects of the absurd symptoms. But, afterward, on the very same day when twilight was lingering in the room, and the samovar was boiling woefully and the tram car occasionally passed with a shriek outside, his heart became so hotly oppressive and his throat so full and warm, as he had not known it to happen for so long now, and were it not for his landlady, who came in just then and sat down next to him, sighing inaudibly, he would certainly have wept, much to his disgrace. But it eventually turned out that it was she who had come in who wept instead.

Afterward, the experience that began to trouble his weary soul while he was lying on the bed depressed him completely. Like a storm that sweeps up the haystack in the field and scatters the straw to the winds, it came and snatched up his anxious soul and sucked his strength and cast him down, forlorn and weary—so completely worn out and sorrowful. It started as a savage, inner cry, a hoarse cry that reverberated in him long afterward, "Let me speak as a child!"

Marvelous. And it seemed to him as though he uttered this cry aloud. There was a time he recalled when he used to wonder at the tenacity of certain childhood memories; what have they to do with a grown up person? But the question only drifted through his mind and quickly vanished. Because, first of all, Tzavar came, Mendel or Chaim Tzavar, that tall, dark, thin student who always had something "phenomenal" to disclose, which he would do while staring at his long fingernails and waxing mildly enthusiastic, this Tzavar, whom Uriel had not seen for over two years and could hardly recollect. His face had then been much darkened by a frown and his forehead furrowed, as always when he wanted to say something serious. At such moments

97

he would contemplate his long fingernails and bare his white teeth and he would begin, slowly raising his face and squeezing out the words, "We, human beings who have already grown...."

And at once Uriel felt the pinch in his heart, and again he submitted to everything. For what did it want, that grown creature in him? What was it—foolishness? And who were they—those who matured? And that cripple, seen of a morning, sitting by the fence next to their house of prayer, the one whose long white hair and beard and proudly wrinkled forehead reminded him of one of the disciples from the past, would approach him on his crutches and say softly, "What's the difference, my son? Is not the truth always one?"

And afterward the odd disciple would be silent for a while and conclude with a harsh sounding phrase and a fierce tap on the forehead, whose violence made his docility suspect. Then one morning Uriel saw him sitting there, apparently so still, holding onto his empty bowl and looking up serenely to heaven, "And if you should say—of course, it would be all the more blameworthy."

By then Uriel had already made up his mind, and he wanted to tell it to the soft black cap lying at his feet, mouth down; he would have liked to say, in clear, simple words, that he couldn't go on any more, that the situation, as it was, was terrible, and that he, the same Uriel Ephrat who, the cap would doubtless recall, had treated the cap respectfully, always putting it on carefully in front of a mirror, was in urgent need of a refuge. All this—really childish. Precisely that—childish. What was worse, he wanted to weep. Simply to stretch out, with his face to the ground, to chew at the green grass breaking into leaf, and strike the earth with his fists, and pound it, to really pound it with his toenails, like a wild sun-struck beast of the desert, and then—to weep, to bitterly lament his soul and his dreams. Because—vanity of vanities!—why shouldn't a man weep? Is it a matter of dignity? Or nice or not nice? Restraint has to burst, like a bubble, being the kind of stuff that merely adds flavor to the dreams of schoolgirls or the discipline of soldiers. Ach—philosophy! But the very next night he remained in Madam's room and returned to his own room only at about two o'clock, when all the windows were blue. And afterward, when, in his insomnia-laden rest, he remembered the postcard that he had received a few days ago from his father in Z., he thought, "Perhaps he's right. He wants me to come home; maybe I really ought to get a bit of a rest?"

And in the morning, as soon as he rose, he hurried to find Pozer, who had promised him whatever it was he had promised with such genuine gladness. Ha, ha, that would be marvelous, said Pozer. He used to always wonder why Uriel so completely forgot that congenial corner of theirs. Yes, it would be marvelous. Of course, that particular corner had its annoyances, too. Sara Leah Maria. But actually, she was so agreeable. He would soon be coming to live there himself. He went to live there every summer—as a lesson in childhood. Ha, ha…it'll be marvelous.

After that, Uriel's heart seemed to become quiet, except that he began to spend more time in his landlady's quarters, and her dark features, often rather melancholy, lit up from day to day. Yesterday, at noon, Uriel was just sitting there in her place, lapsing into long silences, smoking one cigarette after another, when he rose suddenly, went to his own room and reclined on the bed, his face buried in the pillow, and lay there like that for a long while. Afterward, when Dr. Shalshelet entered and began to talk, he surrendered to him the room, his body, his face, everything but his eyes, which he kept for himself. And later, when the doctor remembered and told him that Tzavar, Mendel Tzavar, the tall law student who played the violin, had written to him from Metsel Forest, near Z., that they were waiting for Uriel to come; Uriel admitted that there was some truth in it. He had indeed received a letter from his father, inviting him to come and rest a bit, except all this talk of rest was a lot of nonsense. Ha—as though he needed it. Really, did he need it? And even if he did, it was certain he wouldn't find it there. Then what? Just to see the folks? But that had lost all content. One occasionally remembered a dear face in a congenial moment, on a bright morning, on a serene blue night, as though—but that was nothing compared to what there was. Nothing. And what there was—no place is free of Him. The Lord of the Universe is everywhere, old chap. And when he noticed that the doctor's French beard was retreating somewhat and that he was about to reply, remorse suddenly pressed on him and he began to argue and then he lay back quickly and called out, "Ha, ha...And as to being cared for, my dear doctor, when it comes to nursing, we ought to take into consideration the qualifications of our friendly landlady, the good Irene Vasilovna. Isn't that so, dear Vasilovna?"

But afterward, when the doctor took his leave of them, he again began spending considerable time in Madam's room, and he would remember his own room with trepidation. This morning, all that nonsense returned. And that silly heart began to rejoice and even...no. The decision was final; he was going—and that was that. It was all just nerves, apparently, and had to be taken in hand at once.

Slowly the previous light feverishness recurred, and he rose up. Phoo, what a clumsy oaf he was! What was he groping for? Couldn't he see that it was splendid? Really wonderful? That it meant—it was all over and done with! His silly life! Hadn't he used to look forward to this very thing—and yet, now, suddenly, it was something else? Phoo!

He began to walk up and back in the room, his hands folded, his chest raised high, feeling light. Pozer had answered that he would be at the port; he said he had managed to get it. In other words, that silly rhymester had just obtained passage money for him and he was going, going away and an end to all this nonsense! Ha, ha. And it wasn't simply nerves? He was fed up with this agreeable room of his, and even with his landlady whose teeth gleamed between her pouting lips.

And indeed, could it possibly end otherwise—living with her and fermenting like old wine? In the morning—kisses and eggs and milk and doughnuts, and at night—kisses and eggs and milk and doughnuts...Good heavens. Even the great Shakespeare would not have been able to extricate himself of a morning from one of these milk doughnuts fried in butter that she used to offer him. And besides this—the town itself, Kiev. This loud, rushing, boisterous Kiev with its far too many inhabitants, perspiring in the heat, anxious and hurried, irritating and irritable; and those faces, moist and itchy, and the red cheeks, and even those hearty meals in the restaurants. No! Out! Out! To the fresh air of the Creator! To the open spaces and the feeling of liberation which he had lost sight of. The devil take it!

Two days and more of blossoming spring on-board ship, down the Dnieper that he liked so much, and then Homel—maybe a few days at Homel, with those clowns who, long ago, had been so amiable. One of them, the one who looked like the star of a successful operetta, on warm days wore practically nothing at all, going around in shorts and singing, laughing aloud, and writing verses; verses that seemed to have something in them of Rachel's smooth, clear, lovely neck—Rachel being his healthy, laughing sister, who was probably married by now. And the other one who drank, how he drank this second one of the lot, the one whose hair never grew on his face to his immense disgust, and always if you looked at his pale, sunburnt face with its pug nose, you expected to see also a bump on his back; but, disconcertingly, he was rather straight and good-looking. He would drink by himself for hours at a time, and he would not budge from the piano, or he would be telling jokes or writing caricatures of his acquaintances. As for the third, the one whose thick nostrils were always dilating, and his protruding, full lips seemed as though they were about to spread in a broad chuckle of pleasure, except that his glowing eyes concealed some ominous secret—this one would keep rolling on the sofa, his body thrust to one side and his legs propelled along the wall. And suddenly his chest would begin to heave with a long, noisy humming *ha-ah*, and he would scramble to his feet, the noises coming to a stop suddenly and he would finish off with a resounding oath in Russian. Amiable clowns—how could one forget their fresh openness and their lack of constraint? Ha, ha. And that mother of theirs—she, too. A tall, strong woman, the gums of her teeth always biting at her lips, and always inventing new epithets for her children and fighting with them and gesticulating, his heart full of the delight of battle. He would only stay there a few days, maybe two or three. And thence—to the enchanted valley! To the serenely waving foliage of his home town, to those quiet streets with the white houses hidden behind tall, blossoming trees, to the clean, straight rays of light in which white butterflies fluttered silently and silently chased other butterflies, just as white and silent as they, to the long, low fences along the broad roadway upon which starlings perched chirping and then swooped down upon the fleeing grasshopper. Ah…the devil. It would either be the end or the beginning—it made no difference. He needed nothing now; he desired nothing further any more.

Soon that throbbing in the temples, when walking becomes difficult and with every step one feels in one's chest an old, worn rubber boot instead of a heart. Uriel stopped pacing and glanced at his landlady who, all this time, had been sitting disconsolately in the rocking chair, as one offended though inoffensive, her small hands gripping the arm rests. He sat down aggressively in the corner of the sofa opposite her and hastened to light a cigarette. The devil take it! Soothing words—never at hand when you need them. Why is she sitting there like that, making a long face? He-had no liking for such ridiculous scenes. After all, what was he taking from her? Or had she thought that she would have someone who would lick up her eggs forever. Ha, she looked as though a lizard were in her throat. Was it his fault that her Foka Avilovitz, that short, thickset engineer with the pink, bald scalp was away from home for months at a time?

Afterward, however, she gave him breakfast, and Uriel sat and smiled in front of her and she also smiled sadly, accepting her fate. Soft-boiled eggs? Of course, of course. What? A glass of milk to finish off? *Ach*, that will be fine. But—doughnuts! Good Lord—doughnuts! Those imps! How buttery! A little red and burnt on the outside—as though dry and hard; but put one in your mouth, and it melts under the tongue. Upon my soul, they're marvelous! *Ach*, and from these he was taking his departure—leaving it all, and Irene Vasilovna...

In the afternoon, while Irene Vasilovna was singing and packing his things, Uriel stood nearby resting against the windowsill, looking out upon the street, his hand turning over and over the picture post-card he had just received in the mail. Outside the sun splashed over everything: a healthy, smiling spring sun, playing upon the passing carriages and glancing off the well dressed, hurrying pedestrians, the gallant officers and the large billboard signs. The tram cars clanged past, sending off blue sparks that disappeared into the clear, luminous air. The windows of the houses opposite were streaked with gold, and the light blue canopy of the sky blandly reflected the crimson blossoms behind the trimmed bushes in the gardens and the green flowers on the verandas. And there, behind the broad, glittering street,

in the sea of tranquil, illuminated space, far, far beyond the red university and even further, were the anxious, invisible, pure yearnings
of childhood, and the furtive dreams—dreams that existed once and
are no more, and dreams that will be and will vanish in their turn.
That young woman, whose dreams were certainly there as well, what
did she want of him? If only one could be like the column of light
smoke rising there far away in the open fields from some indiscern-
ible chimney, a slow-rising column, expanding and dissolving into
the vast expanse of azure sky.

Uriel snorted and lit another cigarette and again directed his
gaze on the postcard in his hand. A melancholy young woman looked
into a stream while standing by a tree, whose shadow was reflected
in the running waters. What is she saying to the reflection? The tree
was bare of leaves, and golden strands of light glided through it. Ah,
once there was happiness and happiness will not return. This siren
had written underneath:

"My dear friend, come to me in the early morning. Come and
listen. From the day it happened I am sad in the early morning."

Uriel took a clean postcard. How inevitably the things she said
aroused a flurry in one's soul. The devil. Her long, black braids of
hair, coming down to below her waist had also, it seemed, something
of that flurry. What did she want of him?

He sat down and wrote quickly:

"Lord of Mercy! But you are poetry, my lady of sorrows. By
the grace of God, you are my blessed one, my dearest, now and for
always. Bowing silently, Uriel."

When he gave the card to the servant to drop into the mailbox,
he thought, "What do I want of her?"

And afterward, when again he looked out, he began to laugh
to himself so bitterly that the pain of it lacerated his breast. Madam,
who was at that moment fussing in the next room, checked her song
and hastened to his side. His face was poised between laughter and
anger.

"What is it? What's the matter?"

"Look there…The wind is carrying it off. The doctor's, one of
the doctor's unfortunate notebooks…ha, ha, ha…"

The woman came to his side and looked out. On the veranda protruding from Dr. Shalshelet's apartment opposite, Ullita, the doctor's big servant girl was standing, her legs wide apart and her bare arms outstretched as though trying to catch a runaway chicken. On her coarse, heavy face was a frightened look of impotent futility. And, in the still air around the veranda two pages of closely written handwriting were floating. As they descended, the servant lunged against the railing of the veranda to catch them and Madam let out a wail, apprehensive lest she fall, and then burst out laughing and Uriel began to mimic the doctor's complaining whine, "Oh, *diable*! That servant again, that servant! A wild ox, no good for anything except to be cut into steaks for the drunks in the saloon! What a creature, God forgive me! You're a cow! *Tchort Vozmi!* A red cow, do you know what that is…oh, *diable*!"

Our landlady nearly burst with laughter at this and called out weakly, "Stop! Stop!"

Uriel desisted and began to talk in his usual voice. But the odd pain in his chest did not leave him.

"Ah, someone has come along and is picking them up. Look, there, do you see how she has pounced on him. Must have the blood of bandits in her, ha, ha…And the poor doctor probably doesn't know anything about it. '*La grande conception d'humanite*' is in such danger—ha, ha—and he knows nothing about it…He is no doubt sitting on his upholstered chair, dressed in his *pidjole*, sandals on his feet, bending over so that his bald pate is directly exposed to the sun, smiling, his clipped moustache and his French beard wagging and his hand busy, writing, writing, writing closely crowded lines—viewpoints, absurdities, general harmonies and modes of living and *la grande conception d'humanite*, and, in any case, there was no salvation in all this…Ha, ha. But look now. There he is in person, coming up the street. What luck for that wretched servant girl! Before dinner and already on the street? But now, she also sees him apparently. Upon my soul, look! His beard has begun to flap. Is he talking to us? Irene Vasilovna!"

Uriel opened the window and extended his head. "Ha, ha. Bonjour, Monsieur le docteur. Bonjour and also, adieu. What?"

"How come? Is it true?" the doctor remonstrated. Someone told him yesterday and he had argued with him that it wasn't so. Is it? He was going away? For sure?

He came across to the tiny garden in front of the house and thrust his nose into one of the roses.

Hmm! That's what comes from modern man's tendency to talk so much. Ha, ha. But is it possible that he wouldn't even drop in to see him? First of all, he also has something to do with that corner to which he was going. He had even promised to go there himself. In fact, he had already written to his brother that he was coming. Besides which, yesterday he had finished that article entirely. Ha...ha. That's no article, Mr Uriel; it's a precious tropical fruit from Corfu! She was quite correct, after all, Mademoiselle Talisha. Oh, *diable*! And he had argued with her about going. She said: he's going. And he had said: no. She—going. He—no. The result being that he has lost a bar of chocolate. Ha, ha. What was he looking so surprised at? Mademoiselle Talisha...she, the one he had met at the theater...she said she had heard it from Pozer...

"Mademoiselle Talisha? Ah, Mademoiselle Talisha—the one that..."

The one that? Ah, a real joker that fellow...Eh? Does he maybe have definite indications about how things are going with her? Ha, ha. But why doesn't he finish?

"What are you talking about, Doctor? What indications? But I just recollected that I didn't mean that at all."

The landlady, who was busy nearby and was listening to this exchange with the doctor, interrupted, asking him with a muffled laugh, "Is that the one you said had a dripping nose?"

"Ach! Ach! Ach! Oh, *diable*! That awful ox of a woman. Again! Again she's scattered the pages to the wind. That damned servant!"

And it seemed to Uriel that the angry, screeching tram car that passed by just then snatched up the doctor in its passage and swallowed him whole, leaving not a vestige of his presence, except perhaps the open gate to the garden and the blossoming rosebush, over which still hovered his parting words, "Ach! I beg your pardon. See you at the port...Mademoiselle Talisha is also leaving today...Ach!"

Afterward, Pozer came. Uriel was then already half-reclining on the sofa, knees crossed and one leg in mid-air. His landlady, who had finished singing, was sitting at the other end of the sofa, glum; and the luggage was all packed and set down against the glass door opening upon the veranda. Pozer's face was swollen and at the tip of one of his temples was a soft, red pimple, from the heat. A bundle of newspapers was in his hand. Ah, the bag already packed, eh? That's the way, old boy. He dropped into the chair opposite the sofa and at once took hold of the yellow shoe of his left foot and placed it on his right knee. Then his hand groped around his full lap rustling among the papers.

Hell! The huge, swollen nose was thrust aside; spectacles glinted and began to move from side to side, reading the picture postcard that he had extricated from his lap. Ha, ha.

"Original," he says, "and no virgin. See? That Mili—damn it." Ha, ha.

"*Ach!*"—she writes. "*Ach*, were it not for that nose, that big swollen nose, that my miserable soul finds so repulsive, as repulsive as those slimy worms that jerk in the mouth, Pozer, like when you gave me to eat them in the rainy days at Somadoni. He doesn't wet his nose a little, dear Pozer. In his nostrils isn't it a little cold, like something moistened?" Ha.

"But write, dear man. Write to this seemingly crazy Mili. My dear Horatio! Who can tell me what the day will bring forth?"

A flame, he says, and no virgin. And then, once again: "All those feelings of respect I have for Shalshelet, the dear Doctor Shalshelet, please pass them all on to him. With all it suggests…"

He has already seen her today. He was very pleased, and he took her address. *Ach*. To be sure. And here in the corner it says: "And where is Uriel?" Ha. He begins to restore the post-card to his lap, and his spectacles shift about searchingly.

"A witch," he says, "no virgin. Damn it! Got a cigarette, Uriel? Irene Vasilovna ought to know her—no? Ah, I'm sorry. A real character," he promises her. "Irene Vasilovna, what news does Foka Avilovitz write from his Asia? Huh? Where is he? In Tchinkent. Tchinkent. Ha." He remembers. "That's near Tzet Kizil-Kum. No?

Ha. Tchinkent. Khodzent, Tashkent—Asia! But Irene Vasilovna, she also has here a sample of a real Asiatic—does she know? A genuine citizen of Palestine, eh…"

He took a cigarette and put it into his mouth in his own fashion, with taut, outstretched hand, the thumb extending almost to his ear, and his lips protruding; and when he began to draw at the cigarette, one had the impression that he was pleasurably sucking his finger. Uriel suddenly remembered the caricature of him that one of his wit-loving friends had sent him some years ago, and he laughed aloud. Irene Vasilovna also burst out laughing, after she had cast a questioning glance in his direction. Pozer looked at them, somewhat perplexed, and then he, too, began to enjoy the situation. Ha. That letter, that's what amused them. *Nu.* She's some virgin. *Tcha!* He had already decided that he would visit her on his way home. Drop in to see her, no matter what. Afterward, maybe he would take her with him to Palestine. She had written him already, quite specifically, that she very much wanted to go. Ha. This year will really be gay there in that corner of the world.

And again his head leaned over and his hand began to rustle among the papers in his lap, and he began to extract letters and to quote precise dates and figures. Tsavar is there. Tsavar has been living there now, they write to him, for some time. In other words: there are groups and skirts also…ha…Yefim writes that at his place they are expecting guests. They told him that those in Homel were going this year to Metsel Forest, the Switzerland of Z. Ha…Dr. Shalshelet told him today that Mademoiselle Talisha would also be there. She had spoken of it to him as well. He, Dr. Shalshelet himself, would certainly be there: he had already arranged to leave together with him from Kiev. That would be as soon as he could make it. In about a month, or possibly less. *Ach*, if only he could also get rid of this damned calamity of his. She had already caused enough trouble, that heartbreaker! To hell with it! And you sit all day and scratch and scrape with a miserable pen, as though…to hell with it! And he groaned and his hands again gripped the yellow shoe on his knee. That's the way it is—my good friend. But it's already one, Uriel, we had better hurry a little. Ha?

2.

Three days later, early in the morning, before anyone else was to be seen about in the town, Uriel, after an absence of over three years, again walked the broad quiet streets of slumbering Homel. The streets, sprinkled with the dew of night, seemed gloomy and immersed in dreams that had once seemed so close and now were become so distant, and they reverberated dully with the strange thud of the footsteps he had brought with him from afar. The sky was immense and tranquil and lost in sublime contemplation, and the shutters were barred from within. Uriel breathed in the clear, calm air and his soul thirstily drank in the restfulness, and the joints of his arms and legs, together with his weary thoughts, stumbled pleasurably along. Intentionally or unintentionally, a certain barrier in the heart lifted and a certain childhood dawn was recalled, resplendent morning, after a glorious night in a boat. The still sleeping marketplace and the resounding yawn of the watchman. The spotted dogs crouching in front of the shut butcher shops and yesterday's heaps of hay, bright with the dew, telling of white aprons, twilight stillness, stolen joys—this dawn slumbering in the corners of the hometown.

How strange and distant, how fabulous that other dream had been to those participating with him in this quietness, how their eager, listening ears had absorbed it, beating about in despair and shouting defiance. And had it not been a dream, the dream of a restless and lost soul, that sad face, the pure, sad face that had become pale, apparently forever here, in one of the dilapidated corners of this old, worn yard, with its pitifully decrepit house. So very strange and distant had been that strange letter, with the barely legible, hastily written script, that letter still lying, it seems, in Uriel's trunk:

"Batyika we found the next day in the stable, her head and body thrust in the ground and her outspread feet pointing upward…"

Strange and distant, like the elusive echo of a forgotten myth. Uriel looked around him and he kept saying to himself, "My corner of the world…my obscure and worthless corner…"

But then the woolen sky brightened and reddened, and the

white clouds, like clustered thoughts, began to disperse, in despair, each one solitary and proud. At the same time, a bird fluttered by, chirped and disappeared. A clear light breeze came and carried off a remnant of a shadow and was gone; and after this something trembled in the broad expanse behind the distant railway station, where the vast plain stretched, and the sun began to come up in the east. Rays of light danced in the air, glancing off the golden dome of a mosque. Uriel looked at the green lumps of moss peeping up between the broken slabs of the sidewalk, laughing and crying at once, and he looked at the shrinking shadows of the worn fences, there where the many berries and the acrid-tasting leaves grew, of which he used to be wary, and he forgot his obscure corner and suddenly felt very tired and somewhat irritable. The devil take it, that sickly panting in his weary chest, that miserable dryness in the mouth…Ach, to rest a little—just a bit—to leap, as he once used to, into the soft, quiet bed in his mother's room, to curl up and hide his face in the pillows and blankets and to lie there relaxed in long, unbroken and all-forgetting slumber. Ha. Those things in the mouth—what did he need them for? What a fool he was making of himself, eh? Why did he rush to them? Did he have something for them? Or did he think he would find something in them for himself? Ah, it was a lamentable matter, nothing would come of it. Besides, he probably wouldn't be able to get to the train in the morning.

Meanwhile, shutters along the street began to open and doors creaked. In one of the courtyards a samovar was struck and at the same time, there came the gurgling hiss of its fire. In one of the houses with open windows, a child began to recite "blessings," making mistakes, and a father, or whoever it was, corrected him with a hoarse reprimand.

The day had arrived. Uriel lit a cigarette and glanced up at the sun whose golden purity gave promise of a long, yellow afternoon, and he suddenly remembered the ship on which she had arrived one morning. At first he remembered the barren bays of the Dnieper just beyond Kiev, those that, in daylight, made no impression on him. Then—the troublesome yellow sun that was so bright just as he approached the ship, and the band of peasants dressed in filthy blouses and eating stinking fish and cursing and knocking one another in horseplay and laughing loudly.

He remembered the second-class cabins full of noise and confusion to which he had descended; the bags and luggage blocking his way, big-bellied Jewesses sitting on piles of bedding, their breasts bared, the children clamoring and the mothers silencing them with quiet whispers. Two Jewish girls, one with short hair and the other in a blue skirt, were eating salami with relish in one of the corners, and conversing vehemently.

Jews, with either heads bare or heads covered, sat around drinking tea, talking, joking with the women and laughing. Two of them were playing cards, slapping them down in front of them fiercely and a third, who had taken off his jacket, began to pull at one of the two by the sleeve and cry out, as though to save the fellow's life, "Thief! Murderer! Ah. Ah! Let's see your money: ha, ha…that's how we play here!"

Uriel was recalled to himself by the pang that seared across his chest beneath his palm and stabbed at his temples, and he uttered a faint groan and took another cigarette and lit it with the butt-end of the one he had just finished. What utter nonsense. To rest! As though that confusing tumult, which in his childhood fancy had lodged there in that broad plain now cut by the Dnieper. As though, in truth, its net was not spread before him, before him too, even if there, in that lovely light behind the railway station, the trees of his homeland seemed to bow down to him and it seemed that also the soft, quiet bed in his mother's room was waiting for him. Simply enough, to snatch a little sleep would do no harm at all; but can anyone who wishes do so? Ha, ha. That Mademoiselle Talisha, to whom he had been gallant for these two days, she whom Dr. Shalshelet had brought to the port to be "entrusted to his care," she and her large guitar which she had put into a black bag—how he had laughed and enjoyed her frequent outcries as they sat at the prow on the forward deck while she fervently strummed one melody after another from the lovely songs of her country, and stopped every once in a while to call out in rapture, "Lawd! Can it be—that I'm not in Pawis?"

And now at last, the same street. It was entirely exposed to the sun, and people were hurrying up and back along it. Ha, ha. This was it, just as it used to be. Here was the sign, at a man's height, with the big shoe drawn on it that could be seen from one end of the street to the next. But—the devil! Could he have forgotten? Was the sign before the courtyard or after it? Ah, here it is. Those clowns—how quiet everything was. Uriel paused at the low gate, which was ajar already; the old lady had probably gone out, busy as ever. The yard was large and clean and the narrow pathway already swept, and the healthy green lawn alongside it lay fresh beneath the blue sky. There was the red wall at the other end of the yard with the orchard in blossom behind it. The windows were open, but the dark curtains were still drawn. Could they still be asleep? Ah. What's this? A new fence for the vegetable garden by the wall? That old lady and her patch…Ha, ha.

Just then Uriel heard a sudden noise behind him and the leaves in the garden rustled. Then came the sound of a muffled laugh. Could it be Rachel? Could Rachel still be staying with her mother? But here was the harsh, piercing voice of the old lady from the same direction.

"Ah, ah, big Dropa, ah, ha, you're caught? Wait!"

Then the same blue garden gate opened, amidst the sound of laughter and voices, and in charged a straight, lissome girl chewing at the cucumber in her hand, long black hair down her back, covering her shoulders and the sides of her pale, white face. Uriel stood still. Good Heavens! Could this be—Merka? The little girl—how she has grown! And how well shaped, the devil—a second version of that she-devil, Rachel. Ha, ha, she didn't ever seem to be dressed up. What did she have on instead of a blouse? Some sort of a big, blue shirt. Ha, ha, and this Sara Riza, the old lady, how she chased after her with a stick. But here she was, coming back.

The girl came running up to the brushwood fence by the orchard, and turned to the right to the path leading to the wall; and when the old lady also turned to the right, she swerved sharply, with a giggle, and darted back toward the gate. When she saw Uriel, she burst out with a shrill cry and flew, gleefully, into his outstretched arms. As she lay against his shoulder, her full chest rounded itself against him and her breath came in spurts, and her skin was warm.

III

The old woman, who was not aware of any of this, continued to brandish her stick, shouting in mock anger, "My girl, you'll not steal any vegetables from me! My overgrown schoolgirl!"

Then suddenly, she stopped in her tracks.

"Ha… What? Bulbiel? So grown up already! Does he think that it's Racheleh he has here? Or should I be afraid of him. Let go. Let her go!"

Uriel laughed and patted her with his hand:

"You're saying, Sara Riza, that I ought to be afraid?"

Merka, who continued munching at the cucumber, called out from where her face was pressed against Uriel's shoulder, "*Kish-kish-kish*, Saga Ceza! Ha, ha, ha. If you please, Madame…"

Meantime the old lady bellowed out: "What's going on here? A plague on my head. Are you her mother? Eh? Bulbiel!"

But the latter continued to placate her in jocular fashion:

"*Nu…nu!* Sara Riza. Is that the way to receive a guest like me? After all, we're not strangers, ha, ha. Say hello nicely and show me in and tell me what's new and how life is treating you. Isn't that what you ought to do, Merka?"

He fell silent for a moment and looked at the old woman who also gazed at him, and then he finished pensively, "You've grown a little older, dear Sara Riza, eh? It's not, not worthwhile, they say…"

The old woman grew indignant at this and was with difficulty appeased. Grown old? Of course she's an old lady, what did he think, age overtakes you quick enough if, day and night, you have to take care of such a chick as this one. The other chicks? Did he want to know what happened to them? Flown. All of them. Only this healthy woman is left, unfortunately. If only some fellow would come along, like the one who came to the dancer, and take her. If he would only make an appearance, at least, even if he were a heretic. Ah, those artist friends of hers have already got her used to anything, thank God. Yes, anything…What? Where were they? Ha, ha. Dear me. He was asking her? That actor of hers was wandering from country to country. He will probably keep rolling along, and one of these days he'll turn up bringing his impertinent "excuse me" as a present to mother. Didn't

he know her Shmer'le? And you? (turning to the girl) Troublemaker!!
If at least she'd only let me have some of the cucumbers. Give, here!
Nu, and that delicate moth of hers, that Shual'ke, the dear fellow
had been taken sick at the beginning of spring and had already been
to Warsaw and now he was growing bed bugs in that place of yours
over there—at Naot Deshe.

"Alone?"

The old woman was munching at the cucumber she had sal-
vaged from her daughter's hands. Alone? She had only yesterday come
from there, a tender-looking one, who had also been there with him.
And you—what are you standing here like a lump of dough? Can't you
see to it that Henya gets the samovar boiling? Prepare some tea! Get
on with it, girl! Tell them there to put the fish on the fire. That should
be a meal to stuff the fellow's mouth. *Nu*...And that afterthought of
hers, that dear child of her old age, had also got himself there.

"How? Heinke? Was he there too for health reasons?"

"No, not really, just counting the skirts passing. For health
reasons! That's all he needs—fever and cold fish. *Nu*, come along,
bird of passage. Let's go into the house, and you'll rest a bit. When
did you arrive? Come on."

The old woman turned around up the path, with Uriel behind
her. She sighed and talked as she shuffled ahead, "That's how it
is—Bulbiel—ah? So you've just come home—from what part of the
world? Ah? The same fine face...ha, ha! Slender, proud! Ask; how?
And ask; who? Oh our dear little friend...Ha, ha. The world of the
good God is too small for them. *Oy*, I'd show you. I'd talk to all of you
and give you a good smack, that's what, one, two, and...You'd learn!
You'd get soft and cuddly quick enough in my hands! But—you're
all so clever..."

"Ha, ha, upon my word, Sara Riza, you're as smart as they
come..."

"Smart? Oh no—you're the ones who are clever, as I say...you.
Oh silly Bulbiel, are you also thinking of joining those mad-happy
kids of mine? But come along, you unencumbered soul!"

And when she came to the staircase inside, she lifted her skirts with one hand and climbed the few stairs, shouting out, "And what about that scoundrel of ours!—Merka? Is he thinking of getting up today—or does he intend to postpone it till tomorrow?"

The scoundrel, as the old woman called him, turned out to be Hatzotzra, Zelig Hatzotzra from Uriel's hometown of Z., or as he used to be called by everyone, Yefim. A thin, good-hearted person, who liked only good people and tea with milk, he worked as a dentist all day in his room, which was also an office. The midwife Liza, his tall lady friend, she with the slightly bent head whom one met frequently at his place, used to prepare a samovar for him and sew his buttons, looking at him with a sad, pale countenance. This Yefim, Uriel recalled, used to receive visitors informally in his room, which he had fixed up especially for these rather frequent guests, and he would show off his sink, wiping his hands on a towel slung over his shoulder and make a sly face and complain of his weakness these days, and that there were two many patients and in a confidential whisper tell about "this Liza" and her pure protective impulses…Does anybody understand him? Very simply, a great, noble soul…And he would leave his sentences unfinished, until someone, biting a lip, would remind him, "But there are sick people waiting, Yefim."

When afterward Uriel stood at the sink, his chest and arms bare and his head under the open tap, the cold water running all over him, he suddenly thought of Tsavar, Yefim's friend in the old days. He remembered how in childhood the tall, thin stiff one used to measure the broad sidewalk slabs like a pole moving from its fixed place, and his companion, the smaller, thin, agile one, used to frisk about him, trying to catch his eye. Tsavar himself, when he used to tell about Yefim, used to relate long episodes, his dark face flushed with pleasure, and he would recollect the name of a certain Theodore, a Russian young man, and a certain Patrus, also a Russian youth, you know, and he would list the names of several girls and laugh a lot and conclude by saying, "A fool, who even has something phenomenal about him; but a good person. A good person."

Those clowns, ha, ha! Tsavar used to divide the people he knew into categories: *de jure*—serious people and people who weren't serious; *end de facto*—people he was afraid of and those he wasn't afraid of. With him there were never simply fools or clever people; either they were phenomenally foolish or phenomenally clever.

On the other hand, Yefim divided his own acquaintances into people who were good and those who weren't, while the clever ones were generally really bright, you know, and the fools were rather miniature fools. And when Yefim used to begin talking about Tsavar, he would also reminisce about Pitke and Pidke, wonderful fellows, and really good chaps, you know, and he would tell about the Jewish girls at the "Kostinkobitchi" and at the "Surage" in Warsaw and in Starodub.

From what one learned, this Tsavar, who was an excellent lawyer, was also an ardent violinist, and had once had, or still had, a Jewish schoolgirl admirer who listened to him with deference when he spoke about men and books and Roman law and who sympathized with him when he suffered with all of her innocent heart. And then too, he had another girl, whom he respected very much and to whom he used to write long letters, full of enthusiastic insights into the nature of coloratura in music and how he hoped one day to be among the more eminent contributors to the art and he was always waiting to hear from her. And this one too, it seemed, was very sympathetic when he had anything troubling him.

Yefim used to finish his description while still holding up the dentist's drill in front of a patient's open mouth, a mirror in his other hand.

"I am not saying anything, you know. The fellow is my friend… But really—that is, he is only a sort of 'Hlestakov,' a kind of imposter, not in miniature—no. But still, you know, with style."

When Uriel finished washing he felt as one resuscitated, and entered the spacious dining room, humming to himself. It was spotlessly clean and the walls were cheerful. From the boiling kettle a translucent cloud of steam rose, shining only where it struck the golden morning sunlight. Merka, who had already managed to put on a white blouse and a clean dress, was smiling and chatting while smearing butter on a slice of bread on her plate, and the old lady was also sitting there and sipping tea. Uriel seated himself and Merka handed him a glass of tea.

For a while he spoke to them both and made them laugh a little and enjoyed the morning light and the clear unruffled rhythm of his pulse, and his lightheadedness. But soon enough Yefim appeared bringing another atmosphere. His small, parched face was mournful and he did not even look at Uriel, his gaze going past him, and when he spoke, his voice quivered, as though unable to pitch itself, and his words were muffled and unclear and rather whining, complaining of a torment that was undeserved and a sort of revulsion against both God and man.

It was very much like those other times when he used to take to his bed, in a kind of oppressive grief, on account of something "between him and her" and would lie there all day, groaning lamentably with his hurt feelings. And at such times, one of his "Yenta" clients turned up, one of those matronly ladies wearing a big red brassiere under her huge petticoats. He would talk to her kindly and begin to unburden his heart to her. Uriel now sat and observed him and tried to make out what he was saying, and suddenly he remembered that tall midwife, with slightly bent head, who had remained in his house in Z.… He remembered her dumb fears of this dried out little man and his heart began to falter and hint at something. Sadness. A breath of light sadness floated through him and he drew at his cigarette and let his hand glide over the glass of cooling tea. But this did not last long. Yefim quickly came over and sat next to him, as in the old days, and looked at him candidly, pleased to see him and laughing. He talked about Sara Glazer, that insolent, saucy girl who, Uriel remembers, was considered to be his "eternal enemy," ha, ha! And about Tsavar, who was staying at Metsel Forest and whose pupils were in and around the town of Z., so that he had to spend most of his time on the train. Ha, ha. He had just met him yesterday; he had talked of Pidka, who it was too bad Uriel had not yet met, and of Pitka, who may be in Z. next month; he'll be coming for a rest, if only, if only…And altogether, if only his strong shoulders don't throw his whirling head to the dogs all at once, ha, ha.

Ah, that's a chap for you! A flame! And Uriel sat there gently, gazing down at the tea before him, and it seemed to him that it was a long, long time now that he was listening to this daily, irksome tirade, and soon he would stop the fellow's talk and, as every day, would get up without saying anything and go out to the quiet streets of his home town and meet up with brazen Sara, carrying her books, and he would exchange some flippant remarks with her and he would part from her and run into Chaim Tsavar, and listen to his monotonous raptures, look at the pictures of women that he would show him with pleasurable trepidation and secrecy, and he would then go home and flee from there too, to the fields or to the forest by the river, where he would wait for the night. At night he would lie there, and then he would get up and go back to the old, wet, dim-lit streets, and return perhaps to Yefim himself.

Then there would be much bustle about the samovar or concerning the need for a "third hand" in a game, or the gathering of a party for a boat trip…Afterward, when everything would be ready and they would be rushing each other and Liza the midwife would be fussing with the samovar and the glasses, which Yefim liked to take with him to the river in order to have tea and milk, he would suddenly go home again and lie down. The others would appear to be indignant at this, though secretly they would be pleased and they would all disperse, each to his bed. The next day they would talk about it and laugh and make jokes at each other's expense, Sara Glazer being particularly saucy, and then silent—without realizing it.

And when Uriel would afterward come to Yefim's house, he would be accosted at the door of the office by the dentist who would wave his drill at him and his parched face would light up as he said, "Uriel, you're a real snake. But now I haven't time for it…"

And now Uriel indeed put a stop to the fellow's flow of speech and rose all at once. But then he began to stretch and yawn. He, what was it he wanted to say? Aha…ah…he did not want any tea—definitely not. His head was much too heavy—he had better lie down and rest first. Could Merka please show him some place where he could lie down? *Ach*, how she resembled her sister, Rachel—the same clear, smooth neck and proud tilt of the head, like a panther, or the lioness body of a sphinx. What was he thinking? The devil take it!

That sweetness, as though, and…ha, ha, Merka. My tender bird of the vineyards, my green grasshopper. My daydream and my night thoughts. My girl—the little beloved one.

He suddenly found himself on one knee before her, and he took her rather firm, white hand in his and slowly bore it to his lips. The old woman squinted at them between loud sips at her tea, and Yefim's face, with its slightly open mouth, took on the look of one prepared to leap to the rescue. While the girl herself, who remained fixed where she was, her other hand sinking to the table clutching the bread she had just buttered, suddenly began to laugh, and her laughter sounded a trifle excessive. "Ha, ha, ha—Mama! Mama! look, here he is, the 'demon of the marshes,' the one you prayed for. Ha, ha, ha—isn't he, Mother! Isn't he the very same demon-lover, who comes to me? *Oy! Oy!* He's biting me—Mama—he's biting. Ha, ha, ha…"

Soon after the old woman rose. She mumbled something under her breath and adjusted the hairnet under her kerchief. She then reached out to the hanger by the door and took down her shawl with its black silken fringes and said: "*Nu*, enough, enough. He is probably tired. He ought to get some rest, instead of making a fool of himself or listening to all this prattle. I also have no time for all this whimsy of yours. I have to get to the bank before it's too late. *Nu.*" She was going. "Merka, make sure that Henya doesn't forget to fix the chicken. Are you paying attention? And if that tall, stooping merchant from Minsk should show up, let him wait for me here. Don't let him go. Is she listening? Ha? What? Is that rascal coming too? Let him hurry then. Where is he? *Nu?*"

Afterward, when Uriel remained alone with Merka, there occurred that rather odd incident which she would later like to describe to an incredulous audience of the good people of Z. Her audience would smile and then wait to hear the long-winded explanations of Tsavar who took pleasure in discussing matters of a phenomenal nature, introducing into his words the names of acquaintances and flavoring his speech with quotations from Roman Law and relating, in parenthesis, stories from the lives of the great musicians. And still later, when Dr. Shalshelet arrived in Z., Merka's audience also liked to hear his enthusiastically rendered explanation, with its warm regard for the extraordinary capacities of human beings, which the French call so-and-so, and of the total unconstraint in the soul, which, in types like Uriel, for instance, came to the fore of itself, so to speak, because of the lack of a certain great fundamental grasp of things. This fundamental feeling or grasp of things, *"la grande conception,"* as the French philosophers have called it, being common to personalities like, for example, the same Dr. Shalshelet of Vitebsk, who is seated here partaking of coffee and rolls, and *nu*, William Shakespeare of England, who once sat in a similar manner some hundreds of years ago and wrote the "third tablets" (yes, precisely that, the third tablets of the Law!), for a future humanity, and...a certain wild, God-stricken Indian who some thousands of years ago breathed his last beneath an obscure fence in the Hindustani Peninsula—this same philosophical grasp, common to all of those mentioned, is completely absent, and has perhaps never even been present, in those other types and is a basic deficiency, just as there are people born without hands, or feet, or who lack a sense of smell or are deformed in some way.

To be sure, it was a trifle odd; but Uriel would never have bothered much about it, not that day nor afterward. The room to which Merka directed him had once been the very place where the "gang" had liked to sit of an evening, at twilight or at night, very close to one another, bodies touching, laughing, singing, joking and also drinking, hiding the bottles from the old woman by thrusting them behind the sofa. Except that the wallpaper was different.

Along the wall by the door was the same old sofa, and Uriel found the shoe marks of the fellow who used to walk on the wall above it; and opposite on the right wall was the opening to the hall where the wallpaper and furniture had had a deteriorated appearance, even then, and where a piano gleamed in the corner. The same hall led to the old woman's bedroom, which opened again to the corridor. The curtains were drawn here too, as well as in the hall, and in the quiet dimness a few weak rays of light fell on the large chest of drawers. One sensed the air of a vanished glory, the smell of wilted mayflowers and decayed birds' nests. And when Uriel was left to himself in the gloomy interior that evoked so much of what had flowered and withered, he was overwhelmed by an immense melancholy, blind, heavy and beyond consolation. He felt a constriction in his throat, his nostrils became blocked, and at his temples the pulse quickened and began to obscure the already dim light. A moan rose from the depths of his being, "In vain, Uriel —it's no use, chum…"

And Uriel stamped heavily with his foot on the floor and then flung himself on the sofa, opened his shirt with a single, blurred movement and sat there breathing heavily. Ha! The devil take it—what's this nonsense now, eh?

"Phoo!"

And he groaned again and began to take off his shoes.

But soon, when his knees were drawn up on the sofa, and his stockinged feet were pointed at the chest of drawers opposite, he suddenly began to stare, with curious fascination, at the flowers embroidered in the blanket cover. He stared and stared and then bent over, bowing, his fists thrust into the sofa, his lips compressed, his head bending lower, lower, slowly, as though against his will; and when his forehead reached his knees and then touched the blanket, two long legs suddenly fluttered in the air, their white stockings far apart and turned over with a somersault, falling on the edge of the sofa, and Uriel remained lying there, his flushed face becoming pale again and staring at the ceiling, defiantly mirthful…But then to his consternation he noticed Merka standing there at the entrance to the hall, clutching at a pillow that she was bringing him from the bedroom, and laughing gleefully. He leapt up. When she saw his disheveled hair and the mirthful defiance on his face, his open shirt and the stockinged feet advancing on her, her laughter faded, the pillow dropped to the floor and with a screech she took flight through the door of the bedroom. Uriel stood there ludicrously and muttered, "What's going on here? It's no use…Let it be…But…What is it?"

With a groan he cried out in a voice that was not his, "Merka!"

But she was already gone from the bedroom. Uriel, for some reason, went in pursuit. In the corridor he saw her leap down all the steps to the courtyard and he ran and called out in his voice that had become strange to him, "But Merka! Are you crazy?"

She paid no attention, only her dress swished with haste as she ran; she stopped to look with alarm to the right and then to the left and then plunged through the little blue garden gate. Uriel chased after her, not knowing what had come over him. When he finally did come near her in the garden and stretched out his hand to seize her, she suddenly veered, like an eel, and evaded him, flying to the other side of the gate, by the orchard. She then bolted the gate and puffing and squalling, she entreated, him, without many words, her green eyes flashing, "Ugiel! Ugiel!"

Uriel stood on the other side of the low brushwood fence, breathing heavily, and then with a tired motion of his arm he muttered, rather irritably, "Silly girl!"

Upon which he laughed aloud and called out in a voice edged with annoyance, "Open up, dumbbell, and let me rest a bit at least. Ha, don't be such a silly kid, afraid of your own shadow. Or are you scared of me? Ha, ha."

By then, she too was giggling nervously, and she began to complain that he was so strange, one could take alarm. That she was all alone in the house, and he—ha, ha, ha…

Then she uttered another frightened squeal and sprang aside, "Mama…"

In a single quick leap over the fence, Uriel had flung himself to her side while she spoke. He grabbed her and embraced her, laughing into her emotion-filled white face and mimicking the old woman's vibrant voice, "Ah…Prope, my big, healthy girl…You're caught."

She looked at him with a rather queer stare, but at once her face lit up, though she was still breathing heavily, and while one elbow was held firmly in his hand, she raised her other hand to his lips which were seeking hers out, "Please, young man! Do you think I am Racheleh? Ha, ha…Or maybe you think that I was just a little girl then and don't remember anything, eh?"

Uriel smiled confusedly. "Ah, ah…" And suddenly: "Ah, she was a rare person. A real woman…Where is she now? Ah?"

And she laughed, "Where? You'll find her if you look hard. Come along. Do you want some berries? There are plenty of them on the bushes here…"

Soon after, Uriel found himself lying in the shade by the blackberry bushes in the orchard, his body somewhat tired and heavy, the vivacious Merka no longer looking up after every light kiss on his forehead to watch the silent butterflies hovering in the sun about the bush. She was already responding with a muffled giggle and patting him on the shoulder with indistinct sighs and nipping at his biceps with bare teeth and kissing him under his chin with a luscious fullness and then becoming suddenly still and weakly submissive.

And the sun shone down from the heavens directly upon the orchard and a brightness of molten gold flowed everywhere around them. Uriel lay quietly, his gaze fixed on the girl's soft shoulders, their pink whiteness barely discernible beneath the light blouse; whose shoulders seemed to want to give themselves to him voluptuously, but his face was like the face of one born blind, pale and remote and anxiously attentive, and his soul groped about for something that seemed to be very important, to which he had clung with such anguish and cruel certainty, and which he now dreaded he would lose forever. In vain all this going around in circles; the thing would stalk him always like a shadow and there was no escape—although suddenly did it not seem to stop of its own accord and leave him, or was it he, Uriel, who had disengaged himself from it with a bold shrug and it remained far, far from him, in those forgotten and God-forsaken places where he himself had once been.

Uriel lay there, looking up at the smiling blue sky which reminded him of the serene innocence of childhood, of a time beneath the green branches of the trees, with the insects humming on the grass, the silent butterflies, white and red, hovering about the berries and a grasshopper prowling about, and everything so new and remarkable and his soul expanding with the wonder of it.

There had been bustling cities afterward, it seems, and the people there too had been near and far at the same time and there had been events, agreeable and disagreeable, and the clamor had been irksome—where had it all gone? Had it indeed existed? But it surely must have been—so far away, so distant...

At this moment, however, when a bird twittered nearby and vanished and he began to obscurely recollect, as in a vague dream, some low brushwood fence over which he had leaped into a certain orchard, his soul became troubled slightly and he clutched for support, trembling and raising himself a little and he began to fondle her eagerly, she who was clasping him, and he immersed his face in that round, ardent breast with a desperate heedlessness as though to find there in that oblivion, once and for all, the ultimate refuge. And she, who at first chuckled with pleasure at the renewed sign of life in him, and even kissed him again under his chin with a sigh, now began to resist him with all her strength, flustered, her breath coming in gasps, and pushing him away, "Ugiel, Ugiel...That's not nice, Ugiel. Ah... It's not right...Ha, ha...*Oy, oy*...Wait, Ugiel..."

All at once she lay still, weak and submissive, but her face unresponsive and her lips very pale. Whereupon Ugiel raised his head and released her, and she emitted a weird-sounding moan, and wrenched herself free with a rustle of dress and leaves and was gone. Then the silence descended heavily, broken only by a humming on the ground, and Uriel lay there, like a ruin in the sun, the same green grasshopper prowling across his bloodless cheek and down his right ear.

3.

As the day withdrew, a dark, blue night descended, with a wan, crescent moon at the edge of the murky sky and a few pure, bright stars above. That tall young man standing at the other corner of the balcony at the end of the lurching train was looking out upon the night and singing; dressed in a student's long cloak, he was accompanying his broken recitation, which sounded like beans crackling in a frying pan, with appropriate gestures. When Uriel came out from the interior of the train upon the balcony, he did not notice him, and went directly to the window of the end door opposite, which looked out upon the broad curving fields of the land. These fields, lying in their blue darkness, did not seem to recognize him, nor he them; for as he remembered them, they had once been so ponderous, so close to God, breathing the same great sadness of His inscrutability; and now they were so frivolous, running and bounding like colts, not at all in accordance with their dignity, and losing themselves in the darkness as though this had never been, and in their stead came their companion fields, with the same silly, jogging dance past, so unbecoming to pot-bellied dignitaries.

Maybe they did recognize him; but did not sense it…There was only the distant clump of trees like a black stripe on the horizon, absorbed in some old pensiveness; but she too swept past, in a most indecent manner after the nimble dancers who had openly cut loose. Ha, that silly old woman, who could tell her "for shame?" Was it indeed worthwhile, all those forest flowers and shrubs and soon blackberries and even the red foliage of autumn—all these secrets of grown-up children that she has kept to herself now with such a sense of self-importance for hundreds of years—are they really worth it? That an old crone like her should, for their sakes, act so improperly, without the decorum of—let's say—a certain persuasiveness? And perhaps—God knows! Maybe she does have the answer and has no doubts whatsoever; and were it not that she was bound to her place and disheartened by the centuries of suffering—she perhaps would not have hesitated at all to throw herself indecorously into the jogging dance, together with those others.

Uriel let his head droop and he watched the wheels turning, swiftly, with such loud screeching and earsplitting rattle. Ha, ha. He was really very sorry that such penetrating and original thoughts should choose to pass through his mind just when he happened to be alone here. Fine thoughts were all right, however, only if communicated to another. Ha, ha. Though to be sure there is one of two possibilities. If the other person is a man—he begins to argue and gets excited and starts to present his own stupid version, and one may not be in a mood for that. But if it's a girl? Ah, a nice, Jewish girl, that's something else. Her face becomes tense, her feelings are touched; she listens with drooping attentiveness and occasionally casts at the one discoursing with her soft, warm glances, those marvelous glances which are always so agreeable, even to a thick-skinned person like himself, ha, ha.

And finally—finally a "coat of many colors" is embroidered for him as a souvenir, or else she knits him warm stockings for the winter—and Uriel had to spit out again, and the wind came and blew the spittle against the train.

Meanwhile that tall young man who was standing at the other

end of the balcony became more enthusiastic, and his vehement music-making became loud enough to be heard above the uproar of rattling iron, to the sound and jolting of which one had become accustomed. Uriel turned his head and recognized him at once, observing also how the young man used his hands and feet as well as his voice to beat out the rhythm. At first Uriel casually lit a cigarette and just looked at him; he then yawned and bethought himself with pleasure of the empty seat in the train which he had all to himself; but as soon as he glanced at the profile of the other, he became uneasy and tiptoed to the door of the train, opened it quietly and entered, biting his lips, a strained smile on his face and the words that Yefim had spoken this morning echoing in his ears:

"He, Tsavar, travels up and back every day in the train. Good Lord. Ha, ha."

Inside the railway car, columns of curing, reddish vapors were exuded by the dull lanterns and the roar of train wheels was interrupted now and again by a jarring clang of something loose overhead. A group of peasants had gathered together in the corner for companionship and had lit a thick candle and were making merry, passing around a bottle with shouts and guffaws.

Uriel went to his seat in the opposite corner, which was in semi-darkness and where, opposite from him sat a bald priest with thick shoulders who had been sitting there alone before this, peeling oranges with a kind of touching meticulousness, stroking his broad beard and wiping his shiny forehead and listening attentively with an occasional nod of assent to the confident words of a large, argumentative Jew, dressed in a black fur cap and smoking a fat cigar. Uriel approached them and waited for the Jew to remove his big foot stretched out on the opposite seat. The man tried to catch Uriel's eye so as to vouchsafe him a friendly smile, almost as though he knew him, but Uriel deliberately avoided his glance and looked away, spread his blanket and lay down with a shiver of pleasure. "Good God"—he said to himself—"That's all I need here is Tsavar."

Uriel then pulled up his collar and sank his face into it and lay swaying with the movement of the train and suddenly remembered that curious letter he had received more than a year ago from

Tsavar, when the latter had been in Odessa. Ha, ha. He had then chosen far better places than he had and had taught them to Betty, his friend's clever child, that pink and charming little girl who had barely begun to speak. And when afterward she wanted to impress him she would stand in the middle of the room and straighten her slightly bow-legged, full limbs and clasp her hands behind her back for some reason, and would recite in fluent, child-accented Russian, with a French pronunciation:

"And those waves, like the clarion calls of spirits…Where is she? Where is she? With the sound of the pounding of the heart of Prometheus, she beats the rhythm with her sharp back…"

And she would always end up by falling at his knees and calling out, "Confucius used to s-a-y! Ha, ha…"

The contents of this letter were made known to Uriel only later, when he came to Kiev, and Dr. Shalshelet had asked him, incidentally, one day, whether he had any idea about the wonderful musical composition, truly par excellence, that Tsavar had composed last year. Ha, ha—the next item was coming up. The day will certainly arrive and Uriel would be wearily sitting in some corner smoking one cigarette after another, and the other would be standing there before him, in one hand a violin and the other propelling a bow, and his dark face would flush and he would talk and talk and talk…

And suddenly Uriel trembled at the sound of the assured voice of the Jew opposite him:

"Ah…Excuse me, Monsieur Ephrat…May I trouble you for a match?"

And Monsieur Ephrat continued to lie there, holding his breath. *Ach.* This calamity, where did it come from? Uriel lay still, aware of every stir, like a dissembling cat trying to play a trick on its prey, and he sought to remember that fleshy face and that assured voice of the Jew opposite who had resumed talking to the priest and was in fact now looking at the one he was addressing, and Uriel's listening ear caught only a few phrases of this rush of speech, "By us in the Talmud…Ha, ha… In that I see Jesus, the Nazerine…Certainly…Ha, ha! But that is completely absurd, even if one were to discuss it…"

Uriel suddenly felt profoundly awake. It was the smell of his hometown. But why should he feel as though the fluent speaker was glancing at him out of the corner of his eye? Had he not given up the idea of entering him in conversation? Ha, ha. How sweet sleep was, my dear elder Shalshelet. Sweet sleep—and peace in the night!

Uriel now remembered who the Jew was, one of the chief tobacco traders of Z., known as Reb Heshel Shalshelet at the school of the Rabbi and in the houses of most of the important families of the community, and as Yossi Gregorovitch at the Merchants' club and at the homes of the doctor and chief of the Post Office, who used to converse with him on the wonders of the wonderful bathing places to which he used to invite them every month, even sending his horses and fine carriage to bring them there and to fetch them back since they were his guests.

This famous Mr. Shalshelet, the older brother of Dr. Shalshelet of Kiev, was the father of those "babies," as they were called in Z., three big, red-faced fellows, who were not to be separated from Uriel's memories of his hometown. They were always up to something, providing the good merchants and their wives with something to talk about, whether it was spreading forbidden literature, political or pornographic, or—getting the children of the pale citizens to prance about the streets crying, "Jew! Burning Jew!"

This Shalshelet he would probably not even have remembered but for a certain childhood incident, long ago. It was on the night after Yom Kippur, the Day of Atonement. That morning a golden autumn sun had warmed the city streets and Uriel had gone out for a walk. He had met many other Jewish boys in holiday clothes, some of them rushing to the synagogue, some looking furtively at one another, with a pining look of sanctity, "How will we sin today?"

Uriel also met others whom he knew. They asked him to join them, speaking in a kind of feverish passion. Come on. To Shalshelet's house. Come along. Enough of this silly caution. All together. In public. Why not? What? Beginning to object already? All that's trivial. They are well acquainted with his pretenses. In short—coming or not?

As every year, there was a "secret meal" for friends on this holy fast day, at Shalshelet's house, and not only the family participated with Mr. Shalshelet at the head, but also certain of Uriel's friends, who upon meeting him in the street would greet him with that smirk which seemed to say, "Ha, you and I share the same secret, that there is no God in heaven…"

And on the evening of that particular Yom Kippur day, Shalshelet had been at Uriel's home. Uriel's grandfather, one of the brilliant pupils of the great Rabbis of Lubovitch, a gray and bent old man, was then the Rabbi of Z. and had just come back from a day of prayer in the synagogue and prior to the recitation of the final benedictions, was walking up and down a little in the large hall that was dimly illuminated by the remnants of the special Yom Kippur candles which sent out more flickering shadows than light. He was walking to and fro in his long white *keitel*, prayer robe, his soft sandals weakly tapping the floor, clapping his hands every once in a while and his voice chanting in a warm, fast-weakened, but ardent bim-bam of praise to God. Uriel sat in an obscure corner of the hall, watching his grandfather tenderly and with much sadness. Suddenly this Shalshelet came in and sat next to him, at ease and smiling and with a look of one who has suffered many torments, motioned to the old man and said in a confiding manner, "What do you think? Real peace of soul can be found only among such as these! Peace of soul and health of body. Health! But that's completely absurd, even if one were to discuss it. They're people surrounded by certainty and inwardly certain…"

After which he sighed and covered his knee with his fur cap and lit a big cigar.

Uriel dozed for a long time. When he opened his eyes, the train was standing still. The priest was no longer sitting there opposite, and the Jew was also gone. The railway car was quiet and immersed in shadows. The peasants had fallen asleep and were snoring. In another dark corner, someone was relating something and his listener yawned. There was the smell of liquor and of peasants in their woolen vests. Uriel lifted his head and looked out the window. The platform was empty, a reddish glare rebounding from the white walls. The black letters of the sign opposite focused into his vision, twitching at his heart: Metsel Forest. So we've already arrived at Metsel Forest! But, the devil take it, why are they waiting here like this? Oh well, might as well enjoy the rest from that shaking and noise. May as well—here at Metsel Forest. Ah, if only one could go out here and buy another ticket and return, return to wherever the wind takes one...Ha, ha. Silentius, Horatio, my friend! Let us forget for a moment...

From the other end of the platform, lost in the great gloom of night, came the sound of the station keeper's footsteps crunching on gravel, and a call from the other end, where the locomotive puffed and hissed, "Is there any?"

And from the other side out of the gloom a solitary voice answered, "There is!"

And again the first voice called, "Har-la-pin-ko!"

After which came the sound of nailed boots running on the stone and a helping-voice rang out, "One, two, three!"

And Uriel lay back again in his seat. The silence returned for a while, and in the depths of the heart, he felt the same pinching pressure with its dire misgivings. But then came the conductor's whistle at last, and on the platform there were indistinct shuffling noises and a vibrant cry was heard, "Ah—Hurry! We're late!"

Then when she stepped onto the train and into the car, by the door next to Uriel's seat, she was still breathing heavily.

A well-modulated man's voice said: "So? Has Linka gone?"

And she answered quietly. "Heh, heh... gone..."

Uriel put his hand under his head and snorted to himself. Ha! Again that long-necked heron. The devil take it!

And the man's voice continued to speak, "A young woman with something phenomenal about her, I say. She insists—chocolates. So go and argue with her. Ha, ha. As a matter of fact, she is quite right. I did promise to buy her chocolate, if I get the letter. But here, we have a vacant seat. Ah. Pardon me, sir, is this seat taken? No? Ah. He's asleep, he is. Anyhow, it makes no difference. Let's sit here. Ah, we're moving!"

The engine rent the night with a vigorous hoot and the train began to lurch forward and then back and the iron rails clacked loudly. Tsavar sat in the corner, his elbow resting on the windowsill, his other hand on his knee. The girl extricated her white hands from under her cape and began to manipulate the clasp that fastened the shawl to her dark hair. At that moment, from outside was heard a burst of rowdy laughter and she put her head through the window and called out in a ringing voice, "Lina! Lina! Remember to come home early tomorrow morning! Alright?"

The train was already gliding along and from where it had stood came the hasty answer, "Alright, Sara!"

But that distant cry had fallen on Uriel's heart, and he raised himself a little and emitted an irrepressible moan and looked at the girl seated opposite him. Yes, it was Sarah. Sara Glazer. She was as beautiful as ever, and as proud as ever. Ha, Ha. Those hands and the same fussing with the clasp. But that other—could it be Lina? Her younger sister, Lina? Ha! That Linka, she has probably grown, if she is already on such terms with her sister Sarah, who is so much older. Uriel recalled that this very Sarah, suddenly so present before him, had once been his "arch enemy," and he remembered those passing suspicious and fleeting thoughts she used to arouse in him, and he became light-hearted. Ha, maybe they just had to be friends, the two of them? He lay back, began to stretch and called out slowly, "*Nu*, how is life, Miss Sarah, my dear Miss Sarah?"

Tsavar, whose head was slightly bent to the window straightened up, and with his elbow still resting in the sill and a hand on his knee, he opened his mouth. Sarah, who had recoiled with a start when he began to speak, uttered a cry and called out, "Ah! Uriel!"

It seemed to Uriel, even in the darkness, that her face had turned pale. But she immediately gave him her small, white hand, which she took out from under her cape and laughed good-humoredly, "Lina is crazy. She got into one of her moods and didn't want to come home with me today…Ha, ha. Will she be mad at herself!"

And Tsavar was by now seated by Uriel's side, tapping his fingers, excited and shrugging his shoulders.

"No! How come? This is indeed phenomenal," he says. That he shouldn't recognize Uriel? That he should look straight at his face and not recognize him?

Slowly Tsavar bared his white teeth and talked more composedly about Lina and the chocolate he had promised her, and he related in detail how and why he had decided to spend the night in Z., while Sarah sat there opposite them, not saying anything at all, half-resentful of and half cordial to Uriel, and Uriel half reclined there in his dim-lit corner, his lower lip protruding a little and his brow slightly wrinkled. Then he lit a cigarette and interrupted Tsavar with a remark in the fellow's own words and then he laughed and asked Sarah, "Yes, this is phenomenal, isn't it? Ha, ha. Really, Sarah, you...and Tsavar as well—you're sitting here and we're talking normally, as though it hadn't been more than three years since we've seen each other. Isn't that so? But good Lord...good Lord, Sarah...Ha! I seem to be sure that things have changed. My soul lives...I could swear...ha, ha. Isn't that so, Tsavar?"

Tsavar looked away and studied his fingernails, and Sarah, it seemed to Uriel, who had listened to his words with some nameless concern, became cold and silent and then she said, rather petulantly, "And I am sitting here in confusion. Is it possible that Uriel lost all his charm? That would be such a shame...But—no, of course not."

Uriel snatched the word from her mouth, "No? And are you so happy? Really, Sarah?"

She lapsed into silence again for a bit and then rose and said, "Ha. I have the feeling that I will also begin to believe that I am going back three years."

And as she straightened, she sighed to herself, "This awful sadness—good God."

After this she put her head out the window and withdrew it and shrugged her shoulders impatiently, as though unable to see an end or a meaning to her laborious life. Then all at once, she thrust out her chest and her sonorous voice began to resound within the rushing train:

"Life, what, Lina, Lina?..."

Tsavar was soon waving this big hand in the air and beating the rhythm with his foot and beaming with pleasure and humming along with her the last stanza of the song. But she stopped singing all of a sudden and sat down and asked him, in a thoroughly subdued manner, whether he thought of spending the night at their house or at Shalshelet's, where, she believed, he had a lesson in the morning.

A pale, white light flashed by the window and then the train pulled to the left, lurching and heaving, and the locomotive let out a long wail. Sarah leaped up and began to adjust her shawl. Tsavar rose and fixed his coat, complaining for some reason that the pharmacy shops would probably all be closed already. Uriel remained seated, smoking his cigarette: that light pressure in the heart, that had begun a while ago, now increasingly became heavy and oppressive…But here the platform came into view, full of people, and the porter came in to collect baggage. Sarah looked at Uriel and went out to the balcony. Tsavar began to carefully take down the violin and briefcase from the rack and Uriel, with a groan, rose up and folded his blanket.

4.

The light wagon, drawn by a single horse, which Uriel had hired, bounced and swayed through the quiet streets, grinding at the stones and sending sparks flying, incensing the dogs in the white-walled yards. And these dogs ran and barked and they jumped at the horse, toward his chin, obstructing his passage and then ran after the wagon for a while yapping loudly until they gradually desisted and returned to their places, growling into self-justification, "*R-r-r*…So what? Do you think we're good for nothing? You're the athlete, eh? *R-r-r*…"

The wounds of rage subsided and silence reigned. The wagon turned off the paved road and began to roll softly and soundlessly along a dirt road, soon standing at the green entrance arch, long since faded into the prevailing pallor of the street. Uriel sensed a certain relief in the fresh stillness, with the fragrances of night, which rose from the gardens in bloom. He descended leisurely from the wagon, took his bag and placed it on the steps before the house, which, with its five white shutters all closed, except for the one, in the center, seemed pleasant and placid to the eye.

This he had once called home. To all appearances, everything was as it used to be, somber and quiet under the mass of the roof.

The same stupid cat had sauntered along the top of the fences, her tail dragging behind her. The flower garden, with its scented breath, the drops of water falling from the green pipe leading from the tin roof into the empty barrel below. Ha. The devil! Has any of this even ceased to be theirs, even for a single day? And if so, what was missing? He felt the prick of a sharp, painful sadness, tipped with the poison of regret. A huge, frozen wave melted and rolled off him and another, almost forgotten, pressure squeezed his tired chest. "Ah, in vain, in the depths of my heart—truly, Uriel, in vain…"

Uriel sat down with a sigh next to his bag, and lit a cigarette. From a stable nearby came a single high-pitched neigh of a horse. Then the sound of crunching behind him, it would seem. In the courtyard of his home, a cow was reclining and breathing heavily and evenly. This was what people said: It was like a dream…How life was suddenly empty of content and so hard to grasp. Like a dream…Had all the bitterness and hardship been only a dream? Or was this only a dream? Ha! The whole thing was somewhat strange, and also slightly amusing. Really, you want it, and then you sit here, smoking and listening to the screech of the owl on the other side of the river, and everything becomes faint, as though it had never been. Everything yesterday was the same. Today. Tonight. This air, forever absorbing, and without rest, even from its living impressions. They hovered all about over the flowers in the garden and played with the shades still vivid of the past. Bat'ke, Bat'ke, the pale, sad-faced, wonderful girl, so cherished and so close to his heart. And so vulnerable! Here she was climbing and struggling by the garden wall—her outstretched soft arm reaching out to the beautiful lilac blossoms on the other side, stretching and unable to reach—to her great disappointment. How avidly she craved them! *Oy, oy*…look please, her soul lives, Uriel…Uriel! What would be lost by plucking them for her, eh? But what a wretch he was. Not only that—he even sat there and made fun of her. Was she not worth even this trifling effort? Not worth it? Really? And then she ceased reaching out and the still air absorbed her sorrow: Yes, she was worthy. Truly, Uriel. What a miserable creature she was!

And the next day she would come again. This dear girl with her beautiful sadness, she would come at dusk when the sun was declining in the red-tinted sky and the cries of prayers rose from the mosques. She would come silently, a white figure against the red sky, and silently she would glide along the walls of the house and leave a bunch of fresh roses at Uriel's open window, and he would not see her.

A bunch of fresh roses, she arranged in her own inimitable way with the addition of a few forget-me-nots and daisies. She would put them down gently and go in to see Linka, his sister, and soon after she would be sitting in his room looking out of the window. The treetops in the orchard would be luminous and gold. A golden radiance smiling on the windowpane. Patches of sky would turn red and yellow and gray.

The scene would make him catch his breath, and she would be pale and sad and yearning for the beyond, and the sun would be red and weeping and departing, going down. Suddenly the windows would be obscured in shadow and it would become cold. Darkness would fill and a silence would rise up. Where upon she would approach him, flitting across the room, and quietly, in a hushed whisper plead with him, "Take me to the mountains, Uriel—to the rising of the sun…ah?"

Uriel looked around him and again lit a cigarette and for some reason or other remembered, and reckoned that he would die like a dog. He would die like a dog, alone, thrown on the rubbish heap. Then the darkness broke and it seemed as though a great curtain descended on the stage of the theater hall in the orchard. The dogs began to bark in the streets and a ripple of applause spilled out staccato-like. After which the orchestra struck up a tune and Uriel rose and took up his bag. But before he came to the brown door, it was opened from within and the man who opened it did not even look at him who was coming and returning home, instead he slowly raised himself on the bars of the ladder in the narrow corridor, his one hand grasping a rung and his long jacket dangling with the bars. Uriel remained standing in the doorway. He looked at the tallish figure of the man, his rather broad shoulders which hung down erratically on both sides. And in his weary heart, a warm sense of innocent tranquility surged mightily forward, that deep, quiet affection lost forever, which had nourished his frail, anxious soul in the bygone days of his childhood, when he would be gathered into the warm, secure lap and embrace the broad chest shyly. That chest that began at the top of the always open-necked shirt and ended in the long white strings of the ritual fringes that hung down from the sides of the waist. Uriel did not move, calling out in a suddenly grown tender voice, "Father!"

The other came to the entrance and stood there, turning his face to Uriel, a face framed by the side-curls and a rather thin beard, and peered in his direction with that concentrated gaze that used to cast such confusion on many of Uriel's friends when they visited him. Uriel smiled back at him weakly, and again said softly, "Father!"

Making his face out at last, his father called out, "Ah—*Nu*, Good, good. What a surprise! And I just said—that it was our Sufa coming. *Nu, nu*—come in and be welcome."

In the large dining room into which Uriel finally entered, it was quiet and dim because of the closed shutter, and in one of the corners, the cat was dozing. Uriel put down his bag and took off his coat and stood at the door. Old and oppressively familiar, the same big severe room still held its red table which also looked severe. Above was the rather low, white ceiling, red-stained by father's lamp, which stood out from the bookcase with the many large books lying around, one of them open. Along the two opposite walls, in the gloom that gathered, there were two red curtains and a huge clothes chest, which yellowed in its place to the left of the door. Father entered first and spoke in a whisper, gesturing to the closed white door at his right, "But be careful. Careful. Mother is sleeping."

He then sat down with some deliberation in the warm, upholstered chair. In front of him were strewn many papers, some of them yellowed with time, all of then filled with closely-crowded hard writing in the form of an arch, and Uriel recognized the "writings" which for days and nights in his childhood, he sometimes used to take of father's dictation, the "mystery writings" as he had then added, full of professed hints and secrets and addressed to the faithful. They were full of revelation and concealment, trial and error, and the strange play of letters and numbers, which, whenever he used to ask their meaning, his father would smile with pleasure, and explain that when he grew up he would understand better. Next to these pages, tossed there in a casual, friendly way, were father's spectacles. Father sat there and looked at the pages, in preparation for speech. Uriel gazed at him in the lamplight, and an odd shiver ran though him. New wrinkles had appeared in the high forehead and at the corners of the eyes, and others seemed to have deepened at the slightly broad nose; all of them full of a cold rigidity that was not blithely open to any human being. And that pallor: the skin went gray beneath the side-curls and the tangled beard…ah, how many thoughts had it not stirred in him. It would seem, now, as though indeed, nothing had changed. Uriel looked dully at the faded curtains and thought:

"But what did you expect?"

And with an intense pressure in his heart, he took a chair and said, as he sat down, "After all, it's close to two, father, and you…"

But he caught himself and grew silent. Ha, I'll get a rebuke soon enough—and a deserved one at that…

"Hm! Hm!" His father, fussing with the papers, one hand reaching for his spectacles, raised his face to him with that impatience of the absent-minded, his side-curls swinging a little, and Uriel's ears heard the short exclamation, "Talk man, *nu!*"

Uriel silently procured for him his spectacles, and his father put them on his nose and then, distractedly, put out his hands to Uriel, "*Nu*…Which means, that…will…you probably brought cigarettes…"

But by the time Uriel offered him his cigarette case and opened it, he had already withdrawn, and his left hand was holding the spectacles at his temple, and he was examining a written page, murmuring to himself as he read. Uriel took a cigarette and thrust it into his father's right hand. Upon which the old man turned his head then and cried out with, "Ah? *Nu*, good, good."

He then stopped his reading and carefully lit his cigarette with the lamp he took from the bookcase and smoked with deliberate puffs that made his forehead wrinkle.

"*S-s-s*…*Nu!* So that's it. *S-s-s*…that's it: You've come—so you're a guest. You're a guest…*S-s-s*…"

After which he said nothing for a while, giving Uriel a penetrating glance, and then after inhaling quickly at the cigarette, he extinguished it and again muttered, "Which means that…*S-s-s*…*Nu*! I am glad you've come. I am, truly, yes, very glad…"

His left hand then moved to the spectacles at his temple and he concluded, in a low voice, without lifting his eyes again from the page, "*Nu*…get the dust off…You can…what? Look around—you'll probably find something to eat…*Nu?*"

And his father immediately returned to his studies and to his quiet murmuring to himself as he read. Uriel rose and looked about him, in a dull despair. The corners opposite were empty and somewhat forbidding, and the walls looked back at him with a strange and cold look. The dreary spectacle that was to the east of the house also held out no promise of joy. At first Uriel diffidently went up to one of the windows and stood there and began to draw a queer diagram on the window pane, but then he uttered a groan and went into the dark dining room. There the samovar and the old utensils were gleaming in the corner, and the tall chairs were empty and stiff along the wall and the red armchair to the left of the door was occupied by a purring cat. Uriel went up to it, as though reminded of something unpleasant, and thrust the cat away with an irate shove. The animal rolled softly to the floor, stretching, its fur swishing dryly.

And Uriel sat down and leaned back in the big armchair, fuming, "*Ach*! You…Ah?"

Shortly after, Uriel was kissing his mother who was lying in her bed, her small face, with the film of sleep on it, beaming with a happiness that caused him consternation. In a while he held her warm head in his hand and looked at her intently, inquiringly, and then, as though solving the riddle of this face, with its cruel lines and wispy, white hair, he trembled and drew down his own face to hers and said with heavy-hearted benevolence, "And you here—getting older, eh?"

Her small, restless hands roamed over his face and collar and down his shoulders, and she chatted and laughed with that feverish happiness of hers.

"Oh, leave off! As though that's something to worry about. So long as I am left in peace and father is alright...*Ach*, Uriel, my child! I didn't dare hope you would come...I didn't let myself hope...that you would listen to your old father and mother, and...Ah, children, children! But here, I've forgotten that my children don't like such talk...*Nu, nu*. I won't talk about it any more...So long as you're here...You've come, you're here, *ach*! Oh why such silly woman's talk. You must be hungry, and probably tired...Right away, I'll get everything ready...when did you leave Kiev? You came from Kiev, didn't you? Oh, this silly chatter of mine."

Uriel suddenly felt helpless; this happy old woman, squirming with joy in her bed...it is all an illusion, my dear. He was no more than a shadow; all this was alien and strange, even though he had returned to the source of innocence and peace. What would happen if he were to address this old woman in clear words, saying, "Mother—you think I'm Uriel? Ha, ha! Uriel is gone, already lost, ha. He went away, left this house, you remember and...May God keep him...May God watch over him...I—I am someone else, old woman, and I want to sleep."

Instead he sat at the edge of the bed and soothed her and tried to persuade her that all was well and that she should think of something else. In vain. She hastily donned some clothes and kept on, garrulous and laughing with pleasure. Ha, ha, what was he talking about? What did he mean? She herself had not dared to hope, nor even...but then, you see. Oh, that crazy servant girl disappeared today of all days...Oh well...Ah!

But you know, her heart really felt something yesterday. They were sitting together, she and father, may he live, at their evening meal and the cat suddenly begins to lick herself all over, ha, ha. She doesn't care even if he does laugh at her. Still—she did say to that old lady, who drops in occasionally, she said to her: "You know, Grandma, we'll have a visitor tonight," and the other woman sat there, knitting, and she answered: "Probably Linka, it will be Linka, you think, Madam?" Ha, ha. That's what she said, and she, it would seem, agreed, and said nothing. To be sure, Linka, may she live...But her heart told her otherwise...Still, she was afraid to say anything...Also on account of Father, may he live…No doubt he had seen him already? He did see you? Ah, of course! This father of yours, she eats her heart out on account of him, may he live. He stays up so late every night, and hardly rests even by day. And she was afraid to say anything to him. *Ach*…She didn't dare utter a word to him. He would remonstrate her with his:

"Talk, *nu*! No, then…Get along with you, go, go…"

Ha, ha…His mother left the room, and he was left sitting in the dining room, a glass of hot tea and some food before him and a samovar boiling in the serving table by the door and a sleepy servant girl with red hands shuffling about. Then his mother came back and sat down opposite him and told him all the news, smiling and urging him to taste something else, which she was sure he would enjoy. And Father came in and walked up and down, one hand in his belt and the other stroking his thin beard and muttering to himself. Every once in a while he would approach the two at the table, and he would take his hand from his beard and put it to his mouth and his look would narrow and heedless to what mother was saying, he would ask, distantly, "Ah—eh?"

Before she had a chance to answer him, he turned back to his pacing and to his muttering, which had now become more gentle, "Ahh!"

Uriel remained seated, sipping occasionally from his glass, and languidly taking up a book from the pile on the table, opening and closing it again with only a casual glance at the contents. Mother spoke of the cow and of the milk, and Uriel's head grew heavy and confused, with a whirl of thoughts. True, true. This was indeed Father here. The father, with the secret of God in him, in whom Uriel the child had found shelter, and warm repose. This was he—Father. But what was a father anyway? What did the word mean? Father, and this was Mother. A shriveled-up woman, chattering away and laughing discordantly, was this mother? How odd! Had not that Irene Vasilovna and that Mili and so many other women asked him with a certain commiseration whether he had a mother? Was she the one they meant? Ha. And these moldy books, dusty and spoiled by lying here untouched, were the very books he had used to read, day after day for so long. Was it possible—that at one time these dead printed letters had spoken to his heart, so eager for life? To this very day there were bursting hearts, for life, for whom books were being printed with these queer, dead letters. He himself sometimes opened one of these books and his ears would blush, what was the name of this book, for instance, covered with the dust of already decomposed generations? Let's see. *Words of Peace: A Collection of Sayings. Golden Wisdom. The Voice of God on the Waters,* etc. Really, to be sure, to be sure…and next was written: *Parerga* and *Paralipomena* by Arthur Schopenhauer. Ah, all very fine, to be sure.

"And you know. You probably remember that father, may he live, never drinks any milk at all except with his tea, and even that only in the morning. As for me, may I continue to be so, praise God, I don't need milk."

All very fine then. Therefore, what was so strange? Was it perhaps that he had used to read so many of these books and suddenly stopped. Why had he stopped? Wasn't it all the same to him, though? Still why? He had had a reason, no doubt: but it was long forgotten. Be explicit. That reason had once been very important to him, very important indeed. Had he lost it so completely that its loss was of no importance to him? But then, what was important? Ha! An insipid question. But what was important? How shabby the words were. What was important? Ha! Corpses of meaning, fit for the books, affected wisdom. What was important? This was it—the rancid smell of dirty camels on the decadent orient, the stinking vestiges of the feeling of death, tainted by the decay rising from the ancient white tombs, which seemed to sprout in the heat like our own mushrooms after the rain…What was important?

Uriel stared dazedly about him and stood up on unsteady feet. What was the matter with him? A strange urge made him approach his father, who was walking serenely up and down, and to ask, in a pleading, passionate tone, "Father! It's true isn't it, there's a God in heaven. Ah? Simply—a God, who is great and good…or maybe even not so good…it's true, isn't it?"

Then he let out a savage moan, and his face went pale and he sat down quickly, biting his lip. And immediately after that he interrupted his mother with a kind of magnificent light-heartedness, "And what about Beril Lazer Galosher, Mother? What has become of him, eh? The old fellow is probably still alive and still singing the praises of his white goat who gives him a turn every year—ha, ha! *Ach*, I remember him clearly…No, Mother, how? No. What did he used to say to you?—'Ah! what do you say—Ma'am you're a clever one, what do you say to this? Do I have troubles. Ah! Yesterday two kids were born to my goat, both of them white, ah, yes. But my stupid old woman, the plague on her, my wife, whose housekeeping is…God have mercy on us, she, *forgets*, what do you make of that, now! She forgot and didn't notice which of the two kids was the first-born! There's a woman for you!' Ha, ha. I remember…And then how Father struggled with this, this 'problem,' eh? For two whole days, I think. Ha, ha. You remember what a tumult there was in the house for these two days?"

Mother, who was listening and laughing contentedly, screwed up her face and cried out with gratification, "Three days! That's what it was. Three whole days!"

"Three? Really, ha, ha!"

And she looked at him with that same gratification and said, "Yes, three whole days! You said there was a tumult in the house; ah, it was mad, like hell itself. You remember, there were three of them in the house then. The melancholy fellow who Father, may he live, was taking care of, and Moshe Rish of Tibetha, may he also live long, and the three of them were…ah? What was the name of that third one? I think it was…"

Father meanwhile had slowly approached them, and he interrupted her with a long "Ahhh?"

Mother then turned to him and began to ask impetuously, "Maybe you remember who was…"

But he was already somewhere else, answering with a reflective "Ahhh!"

And he went back to his pacing. Soon after, he came up to them again and asked Uriel for a cigarette, which he carefully lit with the lamp and then almost immediately put it out, mumbling weakly, "Na! My head is getting heavy. If you don't mind, I'll be going…you just stay as you are…"

And he departed to his room.

After this, Uriel persuaded his mother also to go and lie down. She then took him to his own room, which he had passed on to his sister Linka, and left him. Before that she lit for him the beautiful old lamp, with the soft luster illuminating the colored carpet and the pictures on the wall and the small chest covered by an embroidered cloth, to the left of the door.

When his mother closed the door behind her, the large mandolin hanging on the wall over the sofa resounded with a faint musical hum, and Uriel stood there, relishing the neat orderliness around him and it seemed to him as though here, in this room, the ceiling was higher than the rest of the house, and he suddenly felt a warm affection for his sister Linka, whose presence was so poignantly suggested. When he sat down on the immaculate white bed, and he sniffed voluptuously at the flimsy fragrance, that vague and ambiguous scent of the rooms of women, his face took on a certain glow, and as he slowly undressed, his thoughts were jubilant—a jubilation that always ended in a kind of oppressive shame.

This Linka—she must be quite a young woman by now…

But then the faint composure that had begun in his soul suddenly evaporated when he looked at the writing table and on it a still unopened letter. The address reminded him of something deeply familiar. He took the letter and opened it with some haste, his lips moving with impatience, "*Ach*—this Mili…"

The letter was written to him. Only a few words. Pozer, the inimitable David Pozer had written to her today that he, Uriel, was leaving Kiev for home. "Uriel, my dear Uriel! I want two days, no more than two days," she asked to spend with him in one of the large towns, whenever he so desired. That he should answer at once. If he does not answer her immediately or if, God forbid, he answers in the negative—then he would soon find her an unwelcome visitor at his home. "Dear man! Answer right away and let it be yes!" And here was her address also. *Ach*, Uriel.

Uriel put down the letter on the chair next to him with the tired shrug that used to irritate her so.

"What a crazy notion has got into her…"

And then he lay down in the bed and stared at the luster of the lamp, smoking one cigarette after another.

5.

Mili turned up one morning, tiptoeing over the mud that was already drying up after the troublesome rains that had started shortly after Uriel's return home. There had been many days of such loud splashing rain, beating against the windowpanes and squelching his high spirits, as with cold iron claws the heart is squeezed and dreams are made to shrivel up. It so happened that during many of these gray, gloomy days, Uriel had spent his time away from home, while on this particular day he played guest, being somewhat tired and feeling a pain in his chest. His tendency to wander was an old habit.

On the very morning after his return home, he had risen early and gone out. At first he prowled about the broad, open space behind the house, where fattened pigs used to lie grunting and flocks of geese used to waddle past; but by noon he found himself alone in the steep, green hills close to the hospital, which was quite far from home, and by the late afternoon, when he was about to return, he noticed a quiet running stream reflecting the light of the setting sun. It was the same murmuring stream that curled through the woods, trees bending over it and the wild bushes growing in profusion on its banks. He began to follow its rushing descent, leaping over rocks, clambering around cliffs, and being carried down the slope until suddenly he came upon Korni Ivanovitch, the heavy-set, amiable male nurse from the hospital, who once used to give him books to read, and he found him sitting alone by a bush, rolling a cigarette, one end of his fishing rod wedged into the ground and the other flung over the water. Korni smiled broadly when he saw him, and Uriel went and stood next to him, looking across at the green fields of grain, and they spoke together quietly. Uriel remembered the thick wood of pine trees at the bottom of the hill by the tranquil little village of Semtzi. It was in these woods that, alone and in the company of Antip, the robust son of Korni Ivanovitch, he had once spent many a pleasant day, Antip being a loud fellow who knew how to spit and who smelled of pork and hay and was in every way "different." Uriel, on a sudden impulse, took the man's little boat and paddled out to the middle of the stream and upon looking up he realized that Korni, the male nurse, was telling him something, "At Semtzi. In the second hut as you reach the village. Yes."

Uriel hastened to agree, "Aha! Aha!"

He paused in wonder and asked, "Ah, Semtzi? Is that so? Ah, Semtzi, Uncle Korni. Who?"

And the other, though busy with the fishing rod, the float of which was bouncing on the water, answered calmly, "Antip, I said Antip is at Semtzi. Yes. As you enter the village—the second hut. Directly opposite. Ah, that fellow lives well, yes—now, God be with him!"

Uriel moved along, and the banks, clearly reflected in the water below, slipped past him, the steep hills and the bent trees and the fields of grain, yellow and gold in the sunset, and other hills appeared, and he heard voices and saw the white kerchiefs of women at work. And finally the bridge came into view poised in mid-air, and the shining fields of clover, and a single bird flew up with a beating of wings and disappeared. The last rays of the sun were followed by a cool wind and the gathering of shadows and it was very quiet. A hush. Then he heard the sound of people talking as though in sleep and others singing, and the song seemed to come from far, far away. At the edge of the wheat field on the left, a bird began to chirp and from the field on the other side, an answering call came:

—*Tsrah, Tsrah, Tsrah!*

The boat continued to glide beneath the hanging trees and over the trees—silent images in the stream. He was startled by a huge lily that protruded from the water like a dead skull floating and held immobile by reeds or rock.

Soon after there was the barking of dogs and Uriel turned his head and a cry burst forth from his throat and his heart began to pinch and the pain, the pain expanded. Merciful God—Merciful God in heaven! He hadn't expected this—*ach*, this he hadn't bargained for at all. What a fool he was, not to have given it a thought! The devil!

Everything flows in one direction, everything! This that had once been a splendid forest of trees, overlooking the broad fields of wheat, these proud and soft woodlands were now a sickly-looking stretch of earth covered with weeds and the stumps of trees, like grave mounds.

Uriel released his grip on the oars and put his hands on his knees, his head hanging. It was very still, except for a monotonous cricket call and the mocking hurt of his strangely saddened heart. He recollected the thick woods, tall trees darkening the hillside, their vigorous splendor now vanished and gone, the bloom-filled corners and the curving paths, with flowers and dry thistles along it. How white with snow it was in early winter, the air so clear and black branches laden with ice quivering in the stillness. In March the god Pan used to gambol through the woods and fill the night with wild cries, the echoes of which could be discerned by day in the rising mist there by the birch trees.

The snow still lay white and pure then, only beginning to melt, and one's foot sank deep into it, and the paths became blacker and more branches appeared and the forest cries increased and the ice in the stream cracked and roared, and the line of birches, standing like sentinels, wept in the slanting rays of the sun. Ha! And in this March sieve, two human figures, black against the whiteness of snow, would flit among the trees, one a short stout fellow, his belly shaking often with laughter and a little gold chain with a cross under his open coat and jacket; the other taller and slender, his coat well-buttoned and his face rather pale, with a small blond beard and a fur cap, like those worn by gentlemen, and his hand holding a notebook and sometimes writing in it as they walked. They would converse and laugh and exchange cigarettes and estimate the height of a giant pine, rising to lofty heights and oblivious to the two tiny man-creatures on the ground. And then they would get to the horse and carriage waiting for them at the path and one would invite the other to share his bread. After which they would engage in solving the great affairs of the world and the small affairs of business and play a game of cards and part from one another, with a calm, simple word or two:

"Adieu!"

"Au revoir, monsieur!"

"The carriage!"

Ach…Pan, Pan! My overgrown god Pan! Don't you see we're both of us lost? Finished and done with! You'll never again gambol in a March woodland, nor fill the white nights with wild cries, and the poor walker in the woods who liked to tramp through the snow and let his face be brushed by the soft branches, will never again tremble at the soul-stirring echo of the triumphant god-cry…No—two young men, one short and stout and fond of laughter and the other tall and pale and given to writing in a notebook, exchanging cigarettes and sharing their bread! Ha!

Meanwhile the boat continued to glide like a dream on the light current and rounded the hill. A frightened wild goose screeched and rose up in the air with a loud beating of wings. The screech was shrill and woke a dog into barking noisiness. Uriel lifted his head and directed the boat to the bank and alighted and took himself to the second hut at the outskirts of the village. The small windows in this hut showed a dim light, and Uriel knocked and entered and found Antip, his friend, sitting and playing with a little boy with a laughing mouth and oddly luminous head, and there was a healthy young woman at her housework.

They did not let him go back that night, and in the morning those troublesome rains started and Natasha came, Antip's pink-faced gay sister, and Uriel remained with them for eight days. And at night, at night when the rain splashed heavily on the empty road and the opaque window panes were bright with running tears and the flies gathered in the black branches on the walls, Uriel extinguished the ancient lamp which they had dug up for him and he lay there in the darkness, and abandoned himself to fancying what it would be like to marry Natasha and live in a hut like this, he playing with a laughing, luminous child and she caring for the house.

But then he always felt for his own pillow and blanket. By the eighth day he no longer had such thoughts, and he slept soundly. At dawn, with a bright sun peeping through the clouds, Antip prepared to go to Metsel Forest to bring back a cow, and Uriel accompanied him. To Natasha's complaints he answered that he would not return with her brother, and when he came home, the rains started again, and besides, he found the brothers all there, even the one whom the mother called the actor, so he went home at this time from his prolonged wanderings abroad, and stayed with them for a while.

He found them to be as amiable as ever. The one, for instance, with a pug nose, who never used to budge from the piano, was now writing poetry, his poems revealing a style of his own and no longer making one think of his sister's delicate neck. As for the one who always used to write poetry in the past, this Actor, who was just returned from journeys abroad, was now beating the keyboard day and night, and not, as the other had been inclined to do, turning around to tell a good joke. The third, the one whose feet used to walk on the wall, only yesterday accompanied Uriel home, carrying a full jar of something he wanted to have analyzed at the director's office in Z. In the railway carriage, Uriel crouched in a corner, next to the window, stroking his mustache and smoking, and this young man sat opposite, his hands on the windowsill, looking out into the darkness, lit by the reddish smoke from the locomotive, and he recited the last lines of the poem that his brother had recently composed, these poems soon becoming the common property of all the brothers. These words seemed to say everything:

"Be still! There's a voice if it comes lightly,
And the heart already began…"

At home, Uriel found Mili's postcard written in haste to Linka:

Oh, excellent Linka!

I came and didn't find anyone and was concerned. I was worried lest—oh, I just couldn't let myself think of such a possibility—lest you have already gone on your own to Metsel Forest. Please, dear Linka, be so good as to postpone it till tomorrow and we'll go together.

Mili…

Mili was fairly certain that he was there, at Metsel Forest. Sara had told her, having heard it from a certain village girl she met. *Hmm*—No. The thing has to be settled at once. This mountain they were making out of nothing—those silly kids. Ha. And Lina, the schoolgirl!

In addition, Uriel found a sealed letter, addressed to him, out of which he could make nothing, turning it over and over in his hand and only after some hard thinking was he able to understand what it was all about, and then he flung it from him angrily. It was that tall, slightly angular midwife, who for years used to patch Yefim's clothes—she now wrote to Uriel, her only true friend, in the following vein:

> *My only true friend, Uriel!*
>
> *Life has lost all content; but cultured people do not ask so many ordinary questions. Life has lost meaning—it's nothing but an empty, superfluous thing to which we're still attached, recognized only by the writing on the blackboard at the head of the bed in the special room in the hospital. Do you remember? That hospital at the foothills, where in the warm nights are heard the passing freight trains and the river flowing and the sky overhead is vast, and I was foolish—ach, I was so childish and silly then. No. It's all gone, and my heart is now bleeding. But even if they have all betrayed me, you won't forget me. You will come to save mine! Ach, it is all very funny really! I, a midwife who, all my life believed in people, have ceased to see the point of it all, and they, good people who have never paid any attention to me, and, I am sure, haven't ever pronounced my name, they come up to me now with such respect and make me promise that I will try to live. Ach, I am weak from laughing, really!*

The handwriting of this letter was shaky, the letters large and uneven, and underneath the blotched signature, in even more agitated scrawl, full of exclamation marks, was written:

"Come!!! Come!!! Come and save me!!!"

The form of the letter so perturbed him that he picked it up again. The devil! She didn't seem to be pretending. That angular midwife…and a smile stole into the corner of his mouth and he recalled Korni Ivanovitch, when he knew him as a male nurse in the hospital. But suddenly he felt dizzy, his head and cheeks flushed and his temples throbbing, everything became obscure and sliding swiftly into a yawning abyss, and his hand clutched the bedpost, and he dropped onto the chair nearby.

Before Uriel returned to awareness in his chair, noting that he was sitting securely on it, Mili was there, sitting opposite him, smiling and chatting. She had beckoned first and then had opened the door herself and seeing him, her face had become pale and she bit her lip.

"*Ach*—"

Now she was already seated quietly unpinning her headdress, a slip of paper dangling from her right hand, swinging against her face; and she spoke. She hadn't expected…She had thought that Lina…she wasn't, after all…anyhow, she was a precious child…She herself had so eagerly waited for him—it had given her no rest.

Gradually she unfastened the shawl, the end of which fell out of her hand at her feet. Uriel watched the white-gloved hands pull off the gloves one from another and the shawl, raised from the floor, being folded carefully and placed on the bed next to him. Then he raised his eyes to her, looking at her for a long while as though seeing her for the first time and remained strangely silent, so that she rose nervously and said:

"*Ach*—how hot I am!"

And she began to move about the room like a graceful deer, taking down the mandolin and strumming a single confused chord on it; and then she laughed, sounding unlike herself and continued to mumble nervously. *Phoo*! If there was anything she detested—ha, ha—if there was anything, she maintained, it was this particular musical instrument. This instrument—and needless to add, also all these women close to Signor Uriel, altogether…Ha, ha! It was no joke. There was a certain Sara—what was her name? Clazer, she thought, no? Good heavens! Why Mili's own sister, who was getting a little on in years, and not very good-looking, this sister of Mili's never hated her, like she hates her… "Ha, ha. Oh, I beg your pardon. But it's time, Signor Uriel. I detest this 'Zraza,' if Signor knows her, and the English pudding and that big fellow, oh dear. *Nu*, ha, ha. Whenever you meet him, like now: What will you have, my friend? Take a look in my mouth and count my healthy teeth. This mouth is so splendid in that disagreeable area around." *Ach*—Mili? Perhaps—Mili? No. Really—Mili? "Ha, ha. It's all very phenomenal. The very thought that I would eventually sing his latest songs. Ha, ha, now there!"

In the mirror on the wall opposite Uriel, there suddenly appeared the black, shining braid dangling below her waist to her soft hips; and in the air floated the slip of paper that had been dangling from her hand when she entered, which now fell on the corner of the sofa.

Ha, ha…That one had already managed to thrust some notes of his music on her…

Soon after she turned an expressionless, stony face on Uriel, one hand clutching the other, which held the folded gloves. Then, looking at him directly, she approached him and said hoarsely:

"See, here we're enjoying ourselves, Signor?"

On encountering Uriel's vapid smile, her hand groped about blindly and struck the chair at her left and she sat down. "Alright, ha, ha! That's what I say: Alright, Signor! Good Lord, we ought to be expert at enjoying ourselves—what's the good of it, really?"

And her lips trembled and froze, and a red spot appeared on her cheeks, which quickly became pale again.

"We're quite expert, my poor Signor…" And in cold, straightforward tones, she added:

"But it doesn't matter to me at all—really. I just wanted to ask—why didn't you answer me anything, eh?" And she remained standing before him, leaning lightly against the chair, which she had placed before her, and waited for an answer.

Uriel's face contracted with a spasm, and he moaned weakly; but immediately thereafter he lifted his head and laughed politely at her, his eyes flashing, and he said:

"Perhaps…Miss, will you permit me to lie down on the sofa there? I am really very tired today…a little ill, my dear."

"Uriel!"

She turned pale and stamped her foot and held herself very upright as Uriel weakly raised himself from his place. Her hand did not relinquish its hold on the back of the chair, and she watched him dazedly. Why didn't he stop this posing, which was to her so odd, so unlike him. Why doesn't he stop, she wondered, and then asked him outright.

Uriel stretched out on the sofa, one knee over another, his brow cold and furrowed. He watched her, himself looking rather sickly and full of silent entreaty: What do you want from me, child that hasn't grown? Don't you see what sort of a person you're talking to? He continued to stare at her, coldly and helplessly, whatever it was he wanted he say to her becoming stuck in his throat: *Ach*, how glad I would be, Mili, dear Mili, if you would only let me rest a while, rest like a log in bed. Nothing more—Mili—that's all I want. But his lips only mumbled:

"Please, don't be angry, Miss. *Ach*, don't get angry…*Nu*, suppose you did ask, so…"

And suddenly he touched her face and realized how wearisome the whole affair was. The devil! What did a fool like he want to tell her—and what did he have to tell her? The only way out of this senseless farce was to put an end to it at once—and here he was continuing to exchange pleasantries with her. Ha—was it his fault? He became peeved and searched for words that would not come and then he cried out:

"I am surprised at you! Is it really so important to you, whatever it is you're asking me? There was something else that you wanted to know. Well then, the answer has already been given, more than once."

She stood there, astonished at him and muttered, "More than once?"

Uriel was now more irked than ever at himself. He had babbled again, and she was all ears.

His eyes flashed again, and he returned to his former tone, and he was at first rather taken aback by its slightly mocking quality: "If only our immature girl would say what she wants of me. Ha, ha! Specifically—I don't want to marry at all, *nu*! This was clear, I'd hoped, no? Please be quiet for a moment, and then talk. What? Can you doubt my reasoning? It was so distinct. Well then, say what you want. Who could make me—really? As for that friendship, and our being close—well, my own soul wasn't close even to me. Ha, ha, and further…it should be pointed out, I wasn't making fun of anyone. Moreover, just to marry a woman because it is comfortable that way, as people do? Don't you see?…There was comfort and there was comfort; as far as you were concerned, everything was resolved by a woman—everything except the rest and comfort that I wanted. Except for that kind of rest. But what then? To marry—just to have a woman…Ha, ha! You realized—it was a problem, as certain of my friends would say—for a very long time to come. And meanwhile, but meanwhile, there was society, my dear girl—that very thing which people like us, and others too no doubt, like to belittle. And with justification. Nevertheless…it was tolerant of me just the same. Very understanding…Ha, ha!"

Uriel felt tired all at once and fell silent, and she remained standing before him, pale, and biting her lip. She watched him slowly light a cigarette and lean his head back on the soft upholstered sides, and then as she took her veil and began to pin it to her hair and to fasten the clasp, she asked coldly: "Have you finished?" And then, impetuously:

"And don't let our Signor dream anything like what he has been saying. He is quite alright and merely inclines to fantasize, it were best not even to dream that it's so. Ha, ha! It has all been rather trying for me, and I simply would like for us to spend some time together…"

Uriel interrupted her with a cry of weary disgust: "*Ach*…No!"

"No?" And her own response defeated her—frustrated her completely.

It had come out of her in a way that deprived her of all comfort, even before she finished uttering it. The word hovered lifeless in the stillness that followed, broken only by the buzzing of a fly. And she, from whose throat had come that despairing cry, stood stiffly by the window, her face to the dull yellow roadway, and on the abandoned chair in the middle of the room, she lay her head scarf with a long pin attached. Uriel groaned with hopeless weariness and continued to lie where he was, staring at her long, shining braid that hung down behind her and rested on her luscious hip, immobilized now at the window. It was quiet and still, with a yellow sort of rest, and everything was fine and he was not responsible—he couldn't be held responsible for that buzzing fly, and the rooster and the braid of hair that lay so full of possibilities against a hip. All this was living, it was all called life; yet he was tired, tired, tired. No, he wasn't responsible for anything at all. And suddenly his head began to turn with weakness and a wan smile appeared and vanished at the corners of his mouth. Ha, ha. Congratulations to the excellent director and his wagging beard. Laissez-faire, my dear, laissez-faire...*Ach*, Uriel, Uriel!

On that very night in Kiev, the slightly strange night following the morning when he first met her at some friend's house, on that night when these same hips froze into immobile voluptuousness in the gloom of the silent room, had he then been responsible for what happened? *Ach*, of course not. Those were matters about which the cleverest of men were utter fools. The entire house had then been immersed in the still darkness of midnight, and one's ear caught the faintest sound such as a rustle in the kitchen or in one of the other apparently empty rooms, or the steady, monotonous click of a pendulum, and a mechanical cuckoo bird calling out at intervals the sum of these clicks. Her hips were still and unmoving then at that moment, and her braids hung down caressingly over them, and suddenly she turned to him with a pale, expressionless face, and her long, delicate fingers began to move nimbly, like the legs of a spider, over her black blouse and her dress, clasps and buttons swiftly became unfastened, and Uriel sat there, his face unable to compose itself, while she herself yawned broadly as she approached the bed, tranquil and unconcerned about her open dress; and when she started to take off her blouse, she asked in the same offhanded manner, without ever looking at him:

"If you wish, you can turn out the lamp; if you can't sleep with a light on."

Uriel shook himself free of his riveted immobility and stammered in confusion, "Eh, no. But, after all...As you wish...I...I'll go out to the next room."

But she was already in her dressing gown, which clung to her, revealing as well as concealing the soft contours of her body, and she lifted the blanket and turned her expressionless face to him and said in that same unconcerned voice:

"Don't bother. As far as I am concerned, you can sleep on the sofa."

And when she was already lying in her bed, she yawned again broadly.

Uriel did not go to the next room, instead he stretched out on the sofa and lay there, unreasonably angry—How silly!

All at once he laughed aloud.

Ah, he would like to see what would happen if, for instance, some great Tolstoy or other were in his place…Ha, ha, ha!

And the next morning, when he accompanied her to the tram-car station, the very sidewalk seemed to reveal a frozen grin and the gray walls were wet, and she walked at his side with all the people and the noisy traffic around them and she expressed her concern for her girlfriend who probably had not slept that night for worry about her—all on account of this silly whim of hers. No. Of course, it was true that she—well, it was dangerous for her to have anything to do with people who hadn't really grown up. The girlfriend was right, in her own way, she was right. How sorry she was to have caused her to worry about her…And he was really good-looking, the young man, without exaggeration…And why didn't he make her go home last night, eh? Why? *Ach*, good heavens, good heavens! What a baby she was! Ah, simply a baby, an unweaned infant, that's what…

However, as she stood with one foot on the step of the clanging, impatient tram, one hand held out, clasping his hand in farewell, she had giggled and confided:

"Goodbye, goodbye…ha, ha…my heart, this heart of mine…"
And he had told her right away that he was a poet. *Nu*. To be sure, you wouldn't find a mustache like that among ordinary folk. Ha, ha. Or even that smile at the corner of his mouth…Let him be so good as to tell her, please: "You are at least a little more clever than a poet, eh? Ha, ha…"

Uriel had then bowed, for some reason or other, and had kissed her hand; and then as the tram began to move, he felt a troubled gladness, but at that moment she leaped down from the step to his side.

The tram departed with a harsh, grinding clamor. Ha, ha. The same silly situation! She really didn't have to take the tram—she preferred to walk! Good Lord! It's all starting again: she wishes to walk and would he mind accompanying her? He will escort her, won't he? Eh?

Yet, at the corner of the next street, she stopped and made a face.

Ach, she was tired of him. Would he please go home and leave her alone? She had worn herself out. But he shouldn't worry—here was a carriage; it would take her to wherever she wanted to go.

And she had vanished into one of the wet and shining carriages and was gone.

Uriel hardly noticed that she was moving away from the window and that her hand was outstretched, groping sightlessly for something, which when found, turned out to be her veil, and that, as she began to manipulate the clasp, standing there by the bed, she peered intently at the large picture of the "sacred forest" on the wall. He lit himself a cigarette with the butt of the one he had just finished and looked at her and looked again and suddenly it seemed to him that she was only standing there with the white kerchief in her hand and on her face—and in his mind something flickered against his will and he nervously stroked his mustache, and a certain grimness stole into his countenance. At which he grew angry with himself. By all the demons in hell! What are all these symptoms to him? So what—let her cry, this baby, or let her dance or do whatever she feels like. It didn't make any difference to him. He wasn't responsible—he was just tired, tired, tired.. And that's that!

At first he held his breath and deliberately refrained from saying anything: he felt nothing. He was just sitting at the edge of the sofa, just as he was accustomed to sit—that was all. But as he became aware of her strange stillness, the way she held herself in check, a rushing whirl flashed across his temples and his heart danced and fell back, and his lips coldly accented the words, "I'm afraid you're crying there, Mili—eh? You're…"

With a shudder, he rose to his feet. *Ach*—the devil take it!

The sharp, uncontrolled wail that was wrung from her repressed weeping interrupted his words, and then she remained still, as she had been before, except that her face was now enclosed in her clasped hands, so that Uriel's extended hand found no response and came to rest on her quivering shoulder, and it was his voice that fumblingly took up the burden of consolation... "*Nu...nu*, Mili...I wouldn't have expected this of you, really...I didn't expect...Mili...After all..."

He was unable to find the right words, and his voice sounded to him inane and irritating. Suddenly he groaned, realizing his helplessness. "After all, it's you who have made the situation, Mili..."

He observed how she bit her lips with her small, white teeth and then removed his hands to reveal a smiling, glad face. At first he hesitated and a voice within called out: You're an idiot, Uriel—*ach*, what a stupid fool; have you never noticed a mean billy goat thrusting with his horns at his shadow for following him? And his face turned pale. But he immediately directed his attentions to the girl, bending down and kissing her throat and hair. She trembled; a light cry escaped her and in one springy movement was on the edge of the bed. From that vantage point, she threw herself on his neck, entwining his body, her lips feverishly devouring his face.

Uriel stood there, stupid and unresponsive. The hand that encircled her waist still held a cigarette and his face seemed to be making an effort of some kind to express the proper things and his lips pleaded: "*Nu*, enough...enough, Mili..."

But she felt nothing; she remained leaning against him, the opening of her blouse now altogether opened and her body warm and trembling with pleasure at his touch. Her braid had become loosened and an abundance of black hair swept down her back and tickled his hand and his face, while her own face, held slightly back, seethed with ferment and blind passion, and she kept murmuring feebly:

"Mama! Mama!"

This prayerful murmur made him suddenly anxious and sent a twinge of regret through his being. Aha! Do you remember at all, Uriel, what divine purity is like? *Ach*, don't you remember anything, Uriel, of the pure dreams and yearnings of a distant childhood? And he froze from within, and his face fell. *Ach*, Mili——it's all in vain, this prayer of yours. Your mother is far away, dear child, and you love a stranger, a man who is all ice and deception inside, a strange man and a stranger to men and a man far removed from God…

But then he couldn't help noticing her bare throat and the shadow between her full white breasts and a wild thrill seized him. His lower lip held tight between his teeth and his forehead wrinkling deeply, he took her in both his arms and carried her from the bed to the sofa where he deposited her carefully, disengaging his head from her clasping hands. And then, when he moved away from her and the chest by the door, his face was again very pale and his lower lip was trembling slightly, and he absently took up a little sculptured figure that he happened upon. But he quickly put it aside and emitted a hoarse moaning cry and passed his hand over his forehead, and then glancing at the wall calendar, he turned over the leaf and read: "How to prepare pancakes from eggs and other ingredients."

He read aloud and then turned to her to see that she had remained as he had left her, expressionless and unseeing, her throat wide open. At first he thought that she was looking at him, but then he went up to her and bent down to her face. She did not react. He tried to talk to her and even took her warm hand in his—but it was passive. Nervously he straightened and returned to the chest and then to the bed and to the other corner and finally left the room altogether to sink into an armchair in the large hall. It was quiet here, with a familiar quietness, and it was clean and fresh, the white tablecloth gleaming and the gold embroidered curtain in the corner reminding him of a hotel lounge. Uriel endeavored to pull himself together. No, no. This that he felt was no longer some Mili, or a splendid idea of a free spirit or some stupid laissez-faire or anything of that sort. No, it was peace, that's what it was, my friend. The only real peace there was, the peace of soul. However, useless to talk about it. Say nothing.

Uriel then rose, not without a groan, and lit a cigarette. Returning to his room, he found it empty, the door open, splotches of sunlight all about the room, the air of which seemed to exude a vague fragrance as of Mili's soft hair.

That evening, when the young man who had visited Uriel yesterday returned, bringing some small packets with him, he found Uriel still in bed, the shutters barred, his clothes flung on the chair. The other rooms were immersed in twilight stillness, and the dim outline of the figure in the bed was every once in a while illuminated by the reddish glare of a cigarette. The young man threw the packages down on one end of the sofa and tossed his hat on the other end and let himself sink down between them. He said nothing, and the twilight silence returned, broken only by the sound of a cow being milked in the yard outside. The young man breathed heavily and Uriel tried to make out his features with the moving nostrils. Wearying of this, he turned his face to the wall and asked, in a rather hoarse voice:

"Will you spend the night here?"

The other kept quiet. Outside a cricket chirped endlessly. In the courtyard, the cow stamped with a heavy hoof and the scatterbrained girl who was milking cried out complaining:

"Stoya."

And again the milk spurted and spurted. And the young man breathed heavily, and the sofa creaked beneath him. It would appear the fellow couldn't make himself comfortable. Ha, ha. Got him there below the ribs. Ah. But then he too fell silent, and even his breathing was no longer heard.

Just as Uriel was about to fall asleep, the young man rose hurriedly and began to fuss with something in the corner, and to mumble a long chain of old, familiar oaths, and then, as though to himself, that fierce Russian expression, which was always accompanied by a vehement spitting, and Uriel, who had almost forgotten his friend, asked dazedly:

"What's the matter?"

The other had meanwhile found his hat in the gloom, and he gathered up his packages and made for the door.

"What's the matter?" he asked again irritably.

After a short silence, the young man, who already had his hand upon the doorknob, turned his head only a little to Uriel and in a voice tinged with emotion, so unlike him, he said:

"There's a form of strength, I say…What do I mean? That…We are ruled by the whip, ha! That for thirty years a person should give up his body and mind and everything else—whatever it is you call them—the 'little' things and the 'big' things, the 'nice' and the 'not-so-nice,' the 'good' and the 'less good' and so on, ha! I mean: that a person should get excited and then disappointed and full of hope again. And what with despair, joy and weeping? The devil! Even if one only climbs the walls out of idleness and for thirty years gets himself scolded—so that...for what? So that a single pan of water to wash the feet, to the eternal shame of the mother, should come one fine morning and pronounce his doom? *Ach—nu*! It's as though I were reading from a book, no? Come along, will you accompany me to the station?"

Uriel laughed harshly and yawned, "Why did you finish, eh? I was only just beginning to fall asleep!" He yawned again, and the other closed the door behind him.

That same morning, feeling rather composed, Uriel began to reflect:

Our lives—he reckoned—are what they are. How right was the doctor from Vitebsk with all his icy cleverness and fiery phrases. A righteous man indeed, and goodly too were the daughters of Israel, those who matured and those who failed to mature. There is so much beauty in life, in poetry and everywhere one turns; and it is worth a man's while to be alive and, what is more, to anticipate his dismal end, and even if only for all this, it is worthwhile. Our lives!

So he reflected in apparent tranquility, covering his head with the blanket, a book falling from his hand to the floor and thrusting out the sounds of the world:

Ah! One Homer, for example, can make tens of thousands of us to feel the Divine presence. Thousands upon thousands! Ha, ha. We, of Israel, are compassionate—speaking, that is, of those who have black coffee and rolls of a morning and engage in their private affairs, affairs of business, and affairs of the spirit while buttering their rolls, and speaking of people, of books, of seduced servant girls and of ladies who shower us with attentions, and of art...Ha, ha. We, compassionate Israel, should really forgive him that sort of eloquence, the flavor of which comes to our spoiled senses, perhaps, from the mad thoughts he had the honor to reveal to us. And these—we ought to remember—are matters dependent on the root of the soul. That's what he says—the root of the soul—no more. And indeed, there is, if you please, such an expression: root of the soul. No matter. Well—some lord or other once told us that even Homer himself had been known, at times, to be fond of sleep. Homer, whereas he, Uriel himself, was not even one of those who were *not* upright in the tower of pigs.... *Ach*, no. To his disgrace—no. Now, here he had tried to express what had come to his mind on reading that book, which had fallen to the floor, tried to think aloud, calmly, as befits the subject:

"She appeared and departed in the soft darkness, pink-horned—she, Iacus. He too rose up—this Iomeus, the upright one in the tower of pigs..."

This very true and splendid book, which he had a while ago picked up at random, by stretching out a hand—and which, if we care to delve into it—was a result of the intense wish for *something else* than what was present, this book, true and splendid as it was had slipped from his grasp as the darkness came, and was the subject of his reflections there under the blanket. Soon thereafter he pulled these covers away from his head, realizing that he was breathing like a fish on the dry, hot shore. His cheeks flushed... Oh, begging your pardon, had he not over-seasoned his dish with a redundancy? Very possible, indeed. Nevertheless, if you please, Israel does forgive, you know. No more eloquent phrases then. He will try to see himself with the eyes of someone who would, let us say, undertake to write the story of a certain young man—, let's see!

He sits in the corner, his tea becoming cold. His mustache is grown and he has a flair for philosophical poetry. . Write that, if you please, just like that. And begin so: It was morning in the streets. And the street was full of the morning light and the gentle shadows, and spring was in bloom, the same spring that blossomed year after year, even in the days of the great Homer, whom the gods loved and the daughters of the gods adored, sitting at his feet, and which continued to bloom ever afterward, in the days of the lamb of God, who sought to pacify the gods and to impress the daughters of God, and which continued on, blossoming every year through all the other ages, replete with both god and man.

This is due to his flair for philosophy, as you can tell. But it's only to his credit.... Let's proceed. Thrushes chatted in the garden and chased the spring worm. The air was full of muffled sounds. The dining-room door was always open to the yard and nearby the orchard was in bloom. The semi-darkness in the room, caused by the closed shutters, was also full of thrilling sounds and smells, and only suggesting the presence of the light round about, were golden rays that stole through the black shutters—and these, please write, began to weave the same pattern of daily life, in themselves sightless, they nevertheless groped their way to the old heart and spoke, like seers of the Divine light and mercy. *Ach*, this Divine light and the mercy of God! If you please, write that too, but then: This passage of the seers, or the prophets, it's rather short isn't it? And quite devoid of deep meaning. Altogether, the routine form of expression is so commonplace, it's disgusting. And yet, once it was like the countenance of holy men, impressing itself upon the heart, like the great wind on a melancholy, golden day brings tidings of coming autumn:

"Isn't that enough, Uriel, end it...Oh you're such an idiot, if you can even dream that anything will ever stop..."

Will you please, write further... If you don't mind, write: And this gray weave was started. Like a living thing, it was there one inarticulate day, yesterday or the day before yesterday, or a year ago, one inarticulate day, depressed by the weight of generations. And it reminded one of another day like it, whether before or after, that used to draw him into the nettles by the roadside. And both of these were mixed up with still another day, which either was or was not, a weary, yellow day in which a feeble, sickly boy ran from someone who was pursuing him, crying bitterly, clutching a piece of bread in his hand, and his heart hurting terribly. The gray weave began. And again the barriers were down and in his chest he felt the same, once frightening sensation, now familiar, even if uncomfortable, of a movement in the body, a walker in the blood vessels, like a tramp seeking shelter. Quite astonishing, perhaps. It may be indeed, astonishing in a way. Still if you don't mind. Please write, as follows: And the end of the matter was that soon after everything was alright. In the head, which had begun to disintegrate, but didn't, something superfluous danced about, something instead of a brain. Breathing caused occasional discomfort, and a pain in the chest, dull as a disagreeable dream, became increasingly oppressive...

Uriel had launched upon these reflections when his mind had seemed to be composed; but now it was as if a great stone rolled over his being and his heart was blocked and breath became difficult. And when he realized that he had put his head under the blanket again, his first impulse was to put it aside, but then, in a spirit of revengeful spite, he overcame this stupid impulse, which seemed childish, or petty bourgeoisie—but suddenly his strength failed him, his thoughts ceased, and he felt as though his soul had grown old and full of sin. It seemed to him as though this soul of his was choking in the falsehood round about and was grounded in mystery and struggling, like a slaughtered pigeon, in the dark net of dying. *Ach*, sin, a single, infamous sin had lived with him all these years, day after day, year after year, and this vicious sin was of the very breath that man drew...Ha, ha. The devil! No—this was already more than rhetoric, Uriel.

Truly, a little too much, ha, ha. What are you laughing at? No...What are you so...

And he suddenly became aware of his head and his chest, cold with moisture, and his heart, that caged lion, squirming with imprisoned discomfort, and the rushing sound at his temples grew louder, overwhelming all else. When he felt a little better, he found himself sitting on the edge of the bed, his cheeks flushed and breathing heavily, his bare feet entangled with the sheet which had slipped to the floor, shuffling about in search of his shoes. What happened? Eh? Ha, ha. No—what could happen to an idiot like himself, *ach*? Nevertheless—it was funny. He was moralizing, was he? Bewailing the fate of the soul—ha, ha? A sort of moral struggle on his part, eh? The great struggle for God and His Word that a certain wandering young man, a rather agreeable and slightly melancholy young man, had once fought against the multitude, who, though not very friendly, had laughed and hurried and jostled each other through the streets of one of the big cities. Ha, ha.

A pale end lonely young man and the voice of God crying out from his heart—to the crowd of blind, rushing people who fulfill their obligations to the great Divine by setting Him up in a birdcage or in a picture-frame on a bookcase, ha, ha. In spite of which, they were healthy, these cattle: full-blooded, enjoying their sins and overcoming life, these blind wretches, squatting in a swamp, ignorant of the word of God and not wishing to know it. Ha, ha. Or maybe this multitude belonged.

Perhaps, however, for him it was the same multitude whose camps now covered the scorching surface of the desert, those upon whose heart His word had fallen like a hammer and whose hair had been grasped by His mighty hand dragging them into this wilderness; and there they have followed Him, their heads bowed and their quiet songs borne aloft on the wind, life-giving, making the dry sand and the stone give forth green grass and flowers and fruit-bearing trees…Ha, ha. Uriel! It's the same, Uriel, the same God-figure with nothing much to do—Uriel!

Ach—nu! Better get up, eh? That's what he ought to do—what has got into him anyway, dwelling on all that nonsense about the soul and suffering? *Phoo*, get rid of it! That's what it was—asceticism…spiritual anguish.

Uriel then lit a cigarette, assuming a calm bearing, suited, as far as he could gather, to someone in a situation like his. The house was completely wrapped in a restful stillness and the clicking pendulum of a clock only augmented the quiet. From the adjoining dining room also the slow hiss of the samovar called to him, and a log on the fire in the kitchen crackled. What a fool he was—wasn't he home, eh! Wasn't it peaceful here? Ha, ha. And he stretched out full-length on the bed, his hands under his head.

Shortly after, new sounds of activity and bustling were heard, and Uriel guessed that his sister Sara had come in. Ah, it was she, hopping restlessly like a bird, from one room to another, lightly, softly, with almost soundless tread, leaving a snatch of song behind and a shred of laughter, and Uriel, listening to her, felt that a morning breeze had entered:

"How idiotic! Always closing doors and windows, as though thieves were waiting just for this opportunity! Did you ever see such a thing? All shut!"

And the grating noise of a bolt pushed back and then the sound of a light tap on the windowpane, and a call: "Sara!"

And again the soft tread and the swish of skirts, and silence. He clearly distinguished the fire's blaze and crackle and the thin hum of the boiling water in the samovar.

Uriel did not stir. That voice that had just come and gone and merged into the silence was a strong, clear woman's voice, reminding him very much of the same voice when it still belonged to a girl, the same owner and yet so different, and it was also the same voice he had heard on the platform at Metsel Forest, when he was sitting in the train. And then he was suddenly glad to hear this voice and he rose and began to dress; but he thought better of it, yearning instead to see the railway tracks curving into the distance on the landscape behind the house, and he returned to his bed. No. These encounters—too much. Was there anything more difficult for someone like himself than such encounters? And especially when it was a slightly suspect girl, one who was in many ways a baby, to be treated with reservation, yes…

Lying there, Uriel hardly noticed the shutters of his windows opening slowly, without a sound. He would not have been made aware of it at all but for the flooding of the room with golden sunlight making the curtains smile, and the muffled voices from the garden coming through, clear and gay. Whereupon he rose, closed the curtains and uncertainly sucked at the stub of the cigarette in his hand. At first it was Sara's full-throated laughter that he heard, followed by Linka's melodious, light-hearted chatter:

"Ha, ha. No! How happy I am! Really happy. And don't make fun of me. Don't you see, you silly goose, that…just the thought…that Uriel…Oh, you are a goose! Ha, ha. Forgive me, Sara; but I really am so happy…"

And again the laughter rang out from the other's breast, merging with the chirp of a bird nearby. He took another cigarette and listened to his sister who continued to speak in a more serious tone:

"You see, my dear Sara...you may laugh if you like...This running about and searching of mind...And in fact...You see? I—I believe in Uriel, Sarah. You may doubt it...But I say, there are all sorts of people...Well...A silly person like myself has so much, so much, Sara, to talk about and ask about...You know how it is...Girls like us need...And I am so lonely here. Just lonely...No. You don't believe me? *Ach*, my dear Sara, there are times when a person feels that the sky is tumbling around him. *Absolutement!* Ha, ha."

The chatter gave no indication of hastening to its end, so that Uriel grew impatient and called out in the name of the devil that he would hear no more. But since these cackling geese continued to converse and giggle beneath his window, their voices interspersed with the twitter of birds, Uriel took to singing to himself:

"A tall, pale youth..." Ha! How was he? How did he sound? Not bad. The devil, how those two just kept on chattering. What had he to do though, with the subject of their childish conversation? Ha, ha...he was home. Home at last! Arrived yesterday, from a great distance—and today he had got up, and it was morning and he was singing. Lying back on his bed, to which he had returned, he let his voice ring free and idle, tripping merrily over the tune:

"A tall, pale youth rose from the city,
Rose and tra-la-la-la...rose and tra-la-la..."

Ha! Pretty good, eh. But then there it was again, that sickly melancholy, the sadness of the pure and noble soul which desired, or which should wish only for...or so it would seem...for faith and a great aspiration. For faith and utter devotion to faith and sanctity and the purity of faith—ha, ha. More specifically—behold, a youth. Sing praises! Ha, ha. Here I am, all of me, just as I am, and you—you had better prepare a salve for a fresh blow from me—*Phoo*!

"But no. He is really a nice boy, Sarah...He's had such a hard time of it..."

The devil take it—ha, ha.

Rose and tra-la-la—la...rose and tra-la-la.

Rose and rolled his sleeves, with a wail full of guilt and grief...

Full of guilt and grief...ha, ha. That same voice that called

out after the departing train when Sara Chazen had charged her to
come home tomorrow…Ha, ha. If that fellow, in a cap—if said to
himself, doesn't sit there with the girl through the night, a night in
which all the dogs are barking and all the cats are caterwauling, and
if he doesn't sit still without looking idiotically at her ivory forehead,
so cool and fresh, as far as Uriel could remember, and if he doesn't
think of the anguish of spirit: *Ach*, that ivory forehead cool and
fresh—merciful God! Ha, ha. *Phoo*, what was he thinking, what rot?
Will all this nonsense never stop?

> Rose and rolled his sleeves with a mighty wail
> Full of the guilt and grief of the earth—
> Their Creator, this will be her reward…
> I am sorry for the poet, sorry—
> Sorry and tra-la-la-la…Sorry, tra-la-la.
> And he will cook whatever beans he's got…

Then, when the straight, white-skinned girl was at his side,
taking care of him, her long golden braid swinging down her back,
and a bright smile like the daybreak lighting up her expressive face,
Uriel lay passive, trying to smile back at her. But when she adjusted
herself on the bed and bent down to him putting both her hands
on his chest and he saw from her vivid face that emotion was beginning to gather there, something in him stirred and his pale forehead
became troubled. Before she could utter a word, he moaned, and
she hastened to remove her hand from his chest and her face took
on an anxious questioning look. He extricated his own hand from
under the blanket, which he had drawn up to his shoulders when
she had come in, and caressed her cheeks and golden hair; and then,
throwing his gaze at the embroidered bedspread that hung nearby,
he asked her, absent-mindedly:

"Have you already had tea, Linka?"

She looked at him, a little surprised and tossed her head, as
though molested by a fly and answered, in all innocence:

"There's tea. If you want to get up, but…" She fell silent and
stared at him and repeated: "There is tea…"

And suddenly: "Ha, ha. You see, Uriel—I've got so much of the little things…"

Upon noticing his bleak expression her own words froze and she again gave him a long bewildered stare. She then leaned toward him and asked in a caressing voice that sounded like a continuation of her astonished silence:

"No. You want to make me angry, Uriel?"

Uriel felt ashamed of himself. But then he looked at her directly and thought: If she weren't his sister, honestly, she would also be asking him, with great commiseration, if he had a mother. Wouldn't she? And his eyes hardened as he said, carelessly:

"No—not so, Linka." He had caught himself in time. Her face became calm again and unsuspecting, and she proceeded in her former tone:

"I was sure of it. You see, Uriel? I have been waiting too long a time for you to come home…"

Uriel began to laugh aloud, and he couldn't help bursting out: "*Ach*! You! Innocent lamb of God!" And then, extricating himself from her, he said: "Let me get a cigarette."

His heart was pounding somewhat excessively. What silly thing are you up to now? Better not. Don't you see, Uriel, that you ought to keep quiet? Just don't say anything at all. But after he lit the cigarette his temples were throbbing:

"Ha. I am amazed at you, Linka. What's all this beating about the bush? If you have something to say—say it. If not—I'll ask and you'll answer…That would be better? Tell me: that Koli character, does he have a mother? Ha, ha."

The girl drew herself up in her seated position, her face showing real bewilderment now and her hands nervously stroking the blanket: "Koli? What are you talking about?"

Uriel's laugh grated: "Or Simple Simon. The one you left in Metsel Forest. What? He isn't so simple?"

Her pallor turned to deep red and she stood up with a stern rebuff: "Shut up…Shut up, I said…*Ach.*"

And she bent down to brush her skirts and continued, as though speaking to herself:

"These beastly manners of theirs…"

Afterward she took herself to the corner of the room, between chest and door, her hands busying themselves with the braiding of her hair and complaining awkwardly, still as though to herself: "And I was always so sure that in Uriel I would find a real brother. Someone with whom it would be worthwhile talking, frankly and honestly…"

But Uriel was by now thoroughly incensed and couldn't restrain himself. He cast at her the old, bitter complaint of men against their nearest and dearest: *"Nu*…Stop it…Don't be such a baby…I can't bear hearing such rot…honesty, shmonesty…"

He then drew up the blanket again and covered his shoulders and said conclusively: "Talk to me like you would to anyone else—or leave me alone!"

This was both stupid and unnecessary. Ha. So stupid, and completely unnecessary. How could even his punch-drunk head ever get around to it? Yes, it was in every way foolish and superfluous, because…the devil! Because no one could be blamed for someone else's upset stomach. Or…or, let be, that was the essence of his life…So—no one was to blame…

A short while after, Uriel stood at the window, tying the knot of his tie, his hands lingering on his neck and his face dangling in mid-air, and he kept asking himself over and over again: "What do I want of her—upon my life, what do I want from that child?"

Only when his eyes met a clear blue patch of sky, suddenly showing between the layers of white, woolen clouds, did he feel any release from his oppressive thoughts:

"That is eternity, big and blue…"

And he reverted to adjusting the knot of his tie: How awful he was…*Ach*!

6.

The afternoon was warm and peaceful; insects swarmed across the dry leaves in the garden and a sewing machine hummed in a neighbor's house accompanied by a very audible tailor's song. It was too hot in any of the rooms or in the garden, so that Uriel sought a cool spot in his father's room, his father having gone out. The leaves of the wild bean plant climbed up to the open window, and the books along the walls round about seemed to exude a dusty coolness...He lay on the old sofa, covered with worn green stuff, and his hands were playing with a yellow stick with a large round head, and he couldn't remember how it had fallen into his hands. And another Uriel who had once used to sit on the other sofa, also covered with some green material and just as worn, the one opposite him, his shaggy head with something vaguely, irritatingly arrogant about it, and his knees crossed as he was accustomed to sit when feeling at ease, and his shoulders, leaning against the pillows, slightly sloping, in a certain telling way.

He felt impelled to confess everything at once: Fool, why all these antics? Why? After all, everything is plain and clear...And then as that peculiar, confident smile flickered across his pale face and got stuck on the corners of the closed lips becoming something mocking, as though to say: catch me, if you can, Uriel's dumb suppressed complaints against the shaggy head became hard as granite and unbearable. And the more he looked at the lines of that apparently tranquil face the more was he convinced that it was the smile that contained the restless prison, that did not let him draw a single, proper breath, it was that smile that made itself out to be a knowing, clever smile, and which seemed to be rebelling deliberately against a certain truth, a truth that everyone considered essential, but which also concealed itself mockingly from its seekers. Ha...how much filth—oh mercy, how much filth of soul was stored in that shaggy arrogant head, with the hair soon to fall out, as though—and how amazing it was that a man could live and breathe without choking under all that filth.

As for that calm smile at the corners of the lips...Oh, the devil—no! He couldn't stand it anymore. It was utterly wearisome...Ha, ha. Does the honored sir get it? He repeats: he is tired of that filthy smile that consumed his heart until there was nothing left...Stop it! He said that the young man sitting there on the sofa should stop smiling like that—or...or he will get up and split his shaggy head with this walking stick. Ha. You think he couldn't do it? Eh? The devil, he thinks, the young fellow can hear well enough, and he'd better not treat these serious matters so lightly. Ha. It was no joke, my dear sir. He meant it; he would have at that detestable skull with this yellow stick here! Ha!

Uriel was suddenly aware of the spittle in his mouth and on his chin that seemed to be jerking about of itself, and he cursed and grabbed the stick with tightly clenched fists, which became white with red splotches like the claws of a goose, but the other, who was seated on the opposite sofa, didn't seem to pay any attention. He just lolled there, smoking pensively, the gray columns of smoke emerging from his mouth curling around his shaggy head. And suddenly, his eyes glistening with mockery, he said, with melancholy deliberation: "It's a foregone conclusion, my dear friend…"

And were it not for a sudden general weakness that made drops of perspiration appear on Uriel's forehead and made his chest sink in, the fellow would not have gotten away with such insolence. What brazen insolence! This was not even the impudent vulgarity of an ox, which could not be considered blameworthy or unhealthy; it was more like the arrogant insolence of someone getting rid of an over-attentive girl. But, God—he was so helpless—impotent and helpless!

Uriel suddenly felt his cheeks burning, cold sweat on his brows, and he was losing his breath. No—this was ridiculous, really. What did he care about the repugnant ideas of some fellow who was going bald? Really, what should it matter to him, let him go right on with his smart prattle, he didn't care. Just keep on if it makes you feel good.

He himself would just sit there, calm and detached, looking at the leaves of the climbing bean at the window, and they were indeed worth looking at, so magnificently cool and green. And you can be sure, my dear sir…what was it he wanted to say? Ha—yes…My dear sir, you know, he had never had such an odd sensation in his hands, as though they were utterly alien to him. Alien, as though belonging to someone else.

Very odd—ha, ha. And he would like to add, it's just as well he felt no particular need for these hands. Ha, ha. The things cultured men will think of…ha, ha. Culture…If you please…What was he saying? Ah, that he should not be misled; he was not at all feverish. Not at all. On the contrary, let us hear something gay, something to laugh at. If you have something funny to say, that is, ha, ha! What?

It's a forgone conclusion. In other words—since we are so set on living, which is a central principle—and the fated portion, I say, of those like ourselves—the women who have already granted favors...*Ach*, please. The face of an innocent lamb—why? My dear friend, you can be clever when you want to—so I'll be brief.

He lit a match and brought it to his cigarette; but on impulse he held it out at arm's length and watched the tiny red flame: "Please note—Already granted—which means, very simply that they bestowed, gave...Granted—take that skull and smash it against the wall. Ha!"

And Uriel again brought the match to his cigarette feeling as ill at ease as before. What was the matter? The other fellow was still conversing with him as though indeed eager to hear what he had to say. But, good Lord! God!

Then the fellow played some trick, disappearing and appearing again and finally sitting there with that calm, penetrating look. And Uriel grinned back at him and said:

"An example? Ha, ha. You really are pretending you don't know, aren't you? Well. Let's see. I'm *not* speaking even of that Irene Vasilovna, for instance...You remember? She cried, oh so bitterly, when I left her. Really, a warm roll, that one. You do remember, don't you? Or have you also begun to scorn the tears of women? Ha, ha. No...is that so? But think again, old fellow. This deprecation of tears, even if we do assume it to be grounded on some higher truth, this same truth is itself the object of an even greater scorn—isn't that so? How did you put it? There's a truth you can forgive in certain high-placed English lords and certain German or Russian officers, but which you cannot forgive in ordinary men like Hillik or Billik. Ha, ha. It's all the same, though. Whether they're lords and officers and you're only a callow youth from the Jewish Ghetto, even if they're men of genius, the salt of the earth, and the others are common ruffians, Hillik or Billik. What I mean is—this philosophy altogether—seems to be a good hook to catch fish like us, my friend. Ha, ha.

May we not conclude from this…you and I that is—who can tell what the future holds? What? No? Have you really stopped? I am sorry, old friend. You see—after all, it is entirely different if a person is a child or a "creator" or just a dreamer of dreams. If, at least, he were a common person, vulgar, simple—some sort of Hillik or Billik as you called him. Ha, ha. You remember? Yesterday there was a woman's comb left in this room, forgotten, and in the yellow afternoon stillness there lingered the pathetic fragrance of soft hair. At first, you recall, I was apparently very calm and sure of myself, and the girl, also not without justification, was sure of herself, just as that poor comb, for instance, was certain of being found and set to right. And what is more—you would think, a fervent hand would be found to stroke that soft hair as though seeking there the "essence" that was missing in this stupid life…Really, it was quite a jest, when you think of it. But you astonished me in one thing, my dear friend—I keep trying to understand but don't seem to be able to grasp it: Why then did you wander around that day, idling at all those other places just to avoid being in this room? Just not to be alone in this room? Ha, ha. Very odd. Why should a person pick himself up and run away and find no rest for a whole day just to avoid the rather pleasant smell of soft hair? Ha, ha.

It may be that Uriel only imagined it, but it certainly seemed to him that he was listening to this tirade through its troubling and irritating end: "I am quite sober, as you can see from the quivering corners of my mouth…"

These words were uttered in a whisper, the face ashen pale from weakness and weariness, and the shoulders leaning back on the cushions. Poor fellow, he looked feeble indeed. Soon, however, he was talking again:

"Possibly I was prone to take detours, but I never saw any danger in it. These detours, you see, are perhaps good for a man. One may sometimes find things that are not always available, even to someone as smart as I am. Ha, ha. Forgive me, this is really a bad joke, but I'd like to finish. I'd like to finish what I began.

"This is it—Irene Vasilovna, I said—she is not a Jewess, if you please. She is healthy, well proportioned, with a firm neck, although by the afternoon she is already suffering from the heat, and she is married, married to a man who…ha, ha. This Irene Vasilovna with the big teeth…Should I perhaps talk otherwise about her? Are they so sacred a topic? Well, I say…"

And suddenly, vehemently, he continued: "Ha, ha, ha! You're a beast, my dear friend—simply an animal, like a donkey. Ha, ha. A donkey, ears dangling and flapping…and I'm telling you, when you get rid of me, you'll be well rid of a nuisance. Women who have bestowed favors…ha, ha. I am really enjoying this. A person leaves me in possession of a great new truth and he just thinks about it, then goes out, has a good time and—bless the lord! Ha, ha, it's all gone, give blessings for what we have received!"

He began to laugh, and his laughter was like a slippery eel that is severed in two, each part slithering on in the throes of death; and Uriel was somewhat alarmed at the change in the other's usual calm, proud face. This face was now restless and nervous, furtive glances were cast in all directions, and it seemed to Uriel that the head seemed to shrink down upon the shoulders and the voice became anxious and fearful. The devil! Of course, there wasn't much air and the leaves at the window were not stirred at all by any breeze; still—oh, how pleased Uriel would have been at the obvious discomfiture of that wretch, if it were not for their conversation—*Ach*, he felt that his words would continue to be as disagreeable and insolent as ever, if they went on. He would not get out of this easily.

And the other was not whispering: "Hee, hee. Do you remember that tall, slightly bent midwife? You see? And when she got all blocked up—What, what did you say? She was no longer able to speak sweetly, eh? Ha, ha. Or do you indeed believe, Uriel, that she too will get better and go off to study somewhere at a nursing school. Oh, that gawky midwife! *Ach*, Uriel, Uriel!"

And Uriel was getting seriously troubled by all this. Why doesn't he shut up: "Keep still, you! Shut up!"

But the fellow was bent on having his own way, and he was even rather pleased about it so that Uriel had no choice but to listen, emitting a last despairing groan.

"Of course. That vast stretch of eternity you glimpsed isn't even blue; in fact, it may well be rather empty. Not to be denied—it may well be. But it certainly is not—terrible. Truly, it isn't. Or perhaps you also need a verification of that particular delusion. Eh? Do you want it written out, signed and sealed, for instance, that it was worthwhile for a certain son of a carpenter in Nazareth to go up and down the hills of Judea and Galilee—that, for instance, this or that food is absolutely kosher? What are all these foolish calculations, Uriel? A man's ship is wrecked at sea. It's all over and done with!"

Uriel felt his will flounder and his teeth began to grind, audibly. He listened to them: "Ahhh!"

He breathed in deeply, and his clenched fists made an effort to lift the stick, and he rose up like a feather. No. He was free! Were his hands free? Ho, ho! This young man would receive his just deserts!

And the terrible, savage cry that had been struggling in his soul and had got stuck in his throat, now suddenly burst out, and the stick was lowered with a fierce slash of hate, which was not easy on the hand, directly on that wretched skull. On this very wretched head, despicable and growing bald! But—merciful God. What impotence! Impotence! This wretched, despicable skull, which was his, and hard as stone, only broke his stick. How hateful! The head was still there, with that leering smile on the lips, mocking him, defying him…But no…no. He was free at last! His hands were…

Uriel suddenly was stricken with anxiety. Something flashed through his mind: "The devil take it!"

He stood there, his head buried in his shoulders and wiping his face with a handkerchief and looking at everything as though for the first time—the leaves at the window, the books along the walls. And then he felt his other hand, the still-clenched fist, releasing the end of the broken stick. The other end of the stick lay near the empty armchair on the floor. How strange, he thought, the end of a broken stick…

He lowered himself onto the creaking sofa again, for once more his temples were throbbing and his lips were trembling, and he was struggling for breath. Had he dozed off? No, how could he have fallen asleep. He was just lying there, weakly, like a newborn babe, and his mind was a blank. No, he had not been asleep. Certainly not! His chest had become heavy and something seemed to have got stuck in his throat...

Later, when his mother entered and came up to him, Uriel greeted her with the look he would give to anyone who came up to him on his deathbed, if, that is, he did die in front of people; and he let his eye rest vacantly on her face which was moving agitatedly. She was speaking. Ah, what was she talking about? About Lina, it seemed, and another girl, her friend. He listened to her final words: "And she hasn't come back..."

"Hasn't come back?"

She was obviously very worried and her limbs were twitching nervously, as she said: "*Ach*...All that going down to the river for a swim...A person has to have something to boast about...*Ach*, I got so frightened when I first heard what had happened. She's such a child really. Goes out of here, happy and healthy...It was with the girlfriend, who came to call Linka, and they went down together laughing and skipping...And suddenly...my blood froze. May such things happen only to our enemies. *Ach*. What was the name of the other girl—Mili, I think...No? How I begged them not to go...Girls, I said, please don't go..."

Uriel couldn't grasp at first what she was saying.

When he finally did, he asked: "Have they pulled her out? Is she alive?"

Her fidgeting hands found a momentary rest on her apron strings.

"A neighbor said—Malka, the tailor's wife said that...she came back...but I don't understand why Linka hasn't come home...I don't understand...I'd like to..."

Uriel smiled to himself and moaned through his nose and remained frozen in his place. It was all a mistake...They were taken ill perhaps. An upset stomach from one too many sips of a thousand-and-one nights. And that particular daughter of Israel was, in his eyes, a little suspect...ha, ha...But he had better not sin with his lips...She is just a trifle suspect...And she, for instance, he says—this particular girl will probably turn up tomorrow to receive her reward...Of course, of course...Ha, ha. When we love!

And he said to his mother: "She will probably be coming soon…In a little while she'll be here…" And against his will, he added: "And may her companion be well, ha, ha…"

He caught himself and was silent; but the old woman's head was nodding as she said: "He laughs…how can you? How do you know what's happened? Were you there? Or maybe…"

Uriel fumbled for an answer: No, he wasn't laughing…That is to say…It was said…Someone used to say that it would be alright… that a certain yellow Jew told him everything will be alright…

And again Uriel looked at her with the look he would give before his death, and he rose up and staggered to his own room. There the windows were open and on the leaves in the garden, sun-beetles sat and that broken music box that kept pulling and pulling so far, remonstrating pitifully out of weakness, seemed in this concentrated yellow stillness to be making its way with great difficulty and wasting its last ounce of strength in some futile effort, and getting lost, alone and aimlessly, in some vast, yellow swamp in which it was finally swallowed up completely.

Translated by Yehuda Hanegbi

Beside

For David Frischmann on his jubilee

Over the broad fields, breathing in the subdued silence of the night and its saturated dusk, a bird suddenly sawed in a hoarse, angry grating that filled the distance. The old man Archip, with his son Prokof that Ephraim had joined this night to fish by the bonfires, suddenly sighed, removing his extinguished pipe from his mouth to spit foamingly to his side.

"Look, he's fallen asleep here—that nice looking youth? Eh?"

He started to stir. When he got up, he looked around once and hesitated, apparently, and looked twice and sighed again, but already completely convinced, he started buttoning the buttonholes of his sheepskin coat that had seen far better days.

"Asleep of course! That would stand to reason, wouldn't it, that he's fallen asleep, eh?"

He gathered his many tools, which were all lying in a big heap not far from the place he himself had been lying, bowed, and pinned them beneath his armpit, while he took up the remaining collection in his other hand, and with that hand started to fumble and push and was lost in the thicket of dusky fleeced shrubs next to the riverbank.

There, among the many meanders of the river, between the jagged range of the dark mountains that looked like teeth, the fish were surely already asleep. It stands to reason that they would be asleep in those places. And that fellow—why isn't he showing up? There's nothing for it, but to go over there and see what's holding him up, after all. Eh? Only...only that Master won't be the only one to worry about the devils, eh? But there isn't much room in that rowboat. Hey, that outlaw! When he'll vacate it—he says—he'll leave it, then he'll come back here and take us. Eh? Of course—in the name of God! Hop!

The small rowboat, which had been hidden in the dark reeds and thickets which bend down to the water and are reflected crowded on the riverbank, shuddered and sprang forth from its darkness, being completely filled with a heap of moveable belongings, and Archip himself among them, bobbed and slid slowly down the stream. The rowboat moved toward the back of that green and overgrown bridge which looks as if it is suspended in the air and held there by a miracle, when you are thrown here, under one of those shrubs, and see it from afar. Ephraim remained there, pressed under one of the shrubs on the lower riverbank, looking at the scattered floats of the fishing rods, which stayed stuck in the earth where he was, floating and flashing on the smooth water and shuddering with the gentle flow.

Opposite, there was a long range of mountains next to the lone hospital with its spacious yard and its scattered buildings; there were slopes descending from the top of the mountain, surrounded by one long low fence and situated on the second bank of the river, arranged like an open chart, and behind those mountains the moon emerged floating, already blue and pure. And the small clumps of trees, which were scattered opposite those mountains, seemed to move, as if, with one heave of their shoulders, they were throwing off the heavy darkness which before had made them null and void; and that darkness fell away from them as a cape slips away from a man's shoulders, and remains thrown off, completely covered and shrunken, like the foot of the trees, whose summits stood out, rising out of the pure, bright mist, which had began to crawl ponderously and evaporate here and there, emphasizing each and every branch. They were single and clear like those dream-like treetops you can sometimes find in the paintings of great artists. They were radiant, but with the kind of frozen radiance that springs forth and turns the whole area around it into dreaming marble, a remembrance of other radiances and other moons. And his heart was distressed. Distressed because it was already clear that the heyday of youth was gone completely and the heart's flowers had faded at the height of their bloom, never to bloom again! And as for the trees and their dreaming tops, those that had once spoken to the yearning soul had nothing more to say—nothing at all.

Completely finished, my brothers of compassion! Tongs like ice pointed to the heart and a bridle sent out to arrest. During the night watch, the winds of judgment come out and chatter, like that same black box: since all His ways are justice…And that's justice, compassionate Israel? There, in the many meandering niches that are among the mountains opposite, those that grow wild with entangled shrubs and old trees bent over, there is running and confusion and laughter once in a while. Small gangs of youths, some dark and short and some pale and a little taller, and groups of girls, white-faced and melancholy and ruddy-complexioned and slightly less melancholy—all go there. There, they compete in running races and mischief, climbing the stairs and catching their breath with the effort, they play "touch and go" and "cat and catch." They may freeze quite suddenly in melancholy reflections. This enthusiasm of silence, the same enthusiasm that does not roar, but secretly yearns and gradually spreads over the soul, that does not emerge from them until one tall youth, a youth whitish and curly, suddenly takes up his mandolin, fluttering, and with shuddering hands plucks at its melancholy strings—what is this if not the very same instrument that this tall, curly-haired youth, quiet and remote, carried from the remote parts of Poltava only days before to the streets of Chicago and New York, busy and insolent, and the expanses of Baltimore. And then, deaf and yellow, he was spewed out in the crevices of this wild mountain…

By this frozen, numb radiance, a radiance white, blue and washed, which whispers and whispers to the dumb soul hinting of another moon and another radiance; a man feels and senses with his whole being, senses everything that has happened in his thirty

years of continual wandering, senses that even a little less than this
has gone by and there is no way of repairing…and the future…ah,
what will or will not be, this also is enough to scorch the mind of a
man, even if it were made of iron, and to turn it into an empty and
hollow container, from which some mists of filthy steam evaporate.
Its emptiness is more overweight than any weight—by the light of
that radiance a man doesn't see too much danger, even if he were to
enter the edge of the grove of "philosophy," and even if that man has a
foothold, so that he would worry a little about his soul in his proximity
to that forbidden grove. Who, after all, if not him and those like
him? Does he really worry about his body? And Ephraim pondered,
pondered as he drew back, pondered, and yet one should worry that
he did not recognize at first about what he pondered. More or less
as if: those youths…no matter. Those young men—why I, too, am
a man of Israel. They will bear fruit when they grow to a good old
age or a not so good old age. But those sad and beautiful souls…ah,
would I were a partner of God Almighty…

Those sad and beautiful souls—those pale daughters of Israel.
But what, really, were to be the fates of those, if Ephraim Margalit
was really a partner of God Almighty? Of course the intentions of
that same man were desirable. However, precisely because of that,
apparently, he didn't bring his ponderings to a conclusion. *Oy*, this
lovely magic which one of those days would become the silent radiance
of that same blue moon—was lost. Exactly—lost. Even one
desirable intention is no longer possible for a man, so that he could
bring it to a conclusion, and even if that same intention is no more
than thought alone. One heartbeat is enough for him, one projection
of any sort on the path that a man decides and explains to his
soul in that same frozen calm that locks his jaw, clenched with the
force of a decision.

It's the fur hat, dear sweet Rabbi, the fur hat that had been lost,
as it were, by the man who had once been a fool. His teeth began
to chatter again…Ha!

And meanwhile, the night's strength is beautiful. There was
brightness, and the treetops flashed indistinctly and creatures whis-

pered in the grass. In the distant grove the nightingale began with
his flute striking out clearly and with him a Cuckoo sorrowfully
prophesied. A footsoldier, living in the fields, sawed from time to
time angrily and his friend answered him from his remote dominion.
The square below was buzzing. Choruses of croaks rang out. In the
grasses, small creatures jumped and whistled and rasped and called
one to another. One small being, the kind of creature that gives
advice, was hidden in the bright grass below, and would celebrate
its victory, apparently, and conversing with someone in an Ashkenazi
pronunciation flushed and hasty.

Ha, vain and empty, will you take a dried fig? Will you take
it? Will you? Will you?

And her answer was always beside her and it too was flushed
and hasty, but with some rebellious intention, that lays poison:

I'll take! I will take!

And Ephraim, who had thrown himself down beside the fishing rods, stooped into the water, his face facing down into it, and
the tip of his feet reaching toward the sky and moving one after the
other in the air, was both listening and not listening to all that same
bustle. He snorted into his mustache, grown slightly annoyed, the
call he remembered.

But his feet remained in that place, and he lowered his face
and abandoned it to the tickling of the wet grass underneath. One
long, wild, wheat stalk pushed through and came to his lips, and he
caught it and began chewing it all together. Those lovely melancholy
souls…that is to say mumblings of the blurred tones of the soul…Ha!
One like them, one resembling those, wandering among those crevices: a soul, also beautiful, and sometimes slightly melancholy too, had
said to him in the many days before, whitened with the hard-boiling
suffering of a rebellious soul:

"Ah, merciful God! That Ephraim! I'm fed up with him! I
already want something else—Almighty God, I already want something else…"

And that woman, if she had been a little more experienced,
would surely have noticed straight away how the face of that youth

had suddenly saddened somehow, and how his high forehead had swelled and reddened as if a dark void had opened up before his feet: Alas, it had now been said…here!

Yet she was at present quite flooded with the aversion boiling in her soul, and that full mustache of his had a chance in the meantime to make something like a motion, and he stuttered in a bit and tried to correct this in his usual style, by dint of a blazing flash that cleft the burning pupils:

"Hm…hm…could it be that the woman means *someone* else? Ha, ha…"

One of the company laughed merrily. Another, it seemed, was laughing too: Vera, the elder sister. But the woman fearfully shut her two ears and began to protest, her feet rapping:

"Ah…Ah…"

When she felt the power of speech leaving her, she fled to her room and closed the door from within. Even so, afterward, when the household had dispersed each to his own corner and he remained reclining alone in that armchair which the tall flowers in the corner and their large sepals darkened, blowing forth the smoke of his cigarette, he had that very girl sitting on his knees and pulling at his mustache here and there, and suddenly her lips fluttered quivering upon his high forehead, and she stammered a bit at first and laughed at him:

"But you are filthy, my fine Ephraim, in the name of God!"

That very night, lying in bed and tossing sleeplessly, Ephraim resumed that thought of his which he had already cultivated concerning thirty years of life which were in the case of a person such as he, if the truth be told, something beyond all limits of decency—the devil take it. What a keen thought: it would actually be worth one's while to live thirty times thirty for the sake of such, except that in a way all of them have a whiff of simple scum to them, even after taking into consideration that privilege with which they favor a person's spirit.

That morning he had plucked a yellow lovely lily in the swamp—he had thrown it away in aversion. Much later his hands were yellow and strange to him. And when he was convinced, at last, that this would be a night of continuous restlessness, he promptly put his clothes on and went out, wandering about the empty streets of the town, and he found himself standing behind the big bridge across the broad avenue by the railway station whose many feeble lamps were lost in the distance on either side of its corpulent roadway, and he saw a thin light in that splendid house which stood alone with its three white windows and its airy curtains darkening and dangling, and he went up to the foyer whose projecting extremity was roofed with green metal sheets, and he knocked; Dina, who had come, it seemed, from her bed, let him in, a light shawl wound hastily about her bare, shrinking shoulders and her teeth chattering a little and her breath a bit loud, and, bringing him to her rooms, she was dismal and silent. It was as if she had been waiting for him, certain that he would come, and now that he had come she was grateful to him.

"Ha, ha, yearning…this too is yearning, my distinguished fellow. The holy yearning of that very beaver hat of beloved memory, ha, ha…be still—like a fish, be still…hmm!"

In one of the treetops of that neighborhood which had frozen in brilliance, a dormant bird apparently shuddered suddenly, and in the broad pastures which began beyond the distant ditch at the edge of the commons, near the horizon, some horse-driver's horn began wailing, wailing some ancient, naive melody, a brief melody that would break up and return and be repeated; Ephraim quivered somewhat as if the piercing cold had gripped him suddenly, and his shoulders began drawing him off to the stream before him, and he began quite intently observing the water below.

On the top of the mountain in the distance, a single deserted bonfire burned and flickered, having been kindled by the members of that gang before they scattered and went off to the clefts in the slope, and its reflection reddened and skipped along the water bottom, beneath the great huddled shadow of the mountain, which swayed there dreaming. Beside it swung, growing and diminishing in turn, a single lonely figure, about whose fluttering reflection could be discerned only that it was a person. Ephraim raised his head and looked at the top of the mountain in the distance. There actually was a figure caring for the deserted bonfire: rather tall, a woman whose shadow was great and black and dancing alongside. She stood at first somewhat bent from her waist down as if moving warily away from the place of the blaze, while one of her hands together with a leg dangling somewhat in space were removing the skirt of her dress from the embers, it seemed, and her right hand extended for some reason toward the hissing bonfire; but she soon straightened up completely and remained standing upon the mountain ridge where it stopped short and descended in an inclining erectness straight to the stream on the slope.

She remained standing with a cigarette hissing now and then in her mouth and one of her hands stretched out behind her and gripping, out of sheer habit it seemed, the lower part of her dress, and she looked away and observed the stream at her ease, its laughing fragments below, and she drank in the blurred brilliancies in the distance. The tumult of subdued voices below had moved off, it seemed, to one of the far clefts, since the ears caught it quite unclearly. There, far away and gay, rang the voice of a woman which finally stopped. Someone began a song, which could not be recognized, coming closer together with its echoes, and another was calling and cheering, in a run, it seemed, and his voice echoed and went mute at once:

"Zina! Oooh!"

Again nothing could be heard, and the fields' stillness rustled, and an eagle owl perched beyond the distant graveyard, the low huddle of whose trees blackened the dark horizon on the left, whining on and on.

Meanwhile a miracle occurred and one of the floats, which were floating and flashing in the water's quiet smoothness, began dipping down again, and Ephraim sensed this and grasped that rod and removed it. The water splashed about in a hush and was silenced once more. Opposite the moon, some writhing object flashed, its scales sparkling coldly, and Ephraim felt in his hands something shuddering smooth and cold that had a spark of life in it, and his heart was bewildered. A shivering to which he was unused suddenly gripped him, and his heart roared within him out of some latent fear. A splashing sound reached his ears again, a flash dove into the quiet water, and he saw to his astonishment that he had cast his catch into the stream once more.

At the same time he was suddenly confounded by the mighty laughter of a woman, a sound of laughter which was somehow not strange to his ears, mocking fiercely away and tumbling and descending from the mountain peak in the distance, and his heart was seared with the venom of that obliterating woman's revenge seeping through him, and his temples began to blaze. It was as if he had been discovered stealing a chicken, and his head and legs began tucking inward little by little, and thus he stayed properly bundled up beneath the damp bush so that its black shadow darkened him.

But he suddenly grunted with wrath and raised his head to the mountain ridge. Standing there was the same figure he had seen at first, except its face was turned toward the slope of the mountain where the clefts were, and its head and neck were stretched forward a bit, reaching in some odd gesture, the gesture of a lurking beast with its kill already in hand, and her hand was supporting, it seemed, her inclining breast, and her laughter went rolling and deriding in the purifying expanse. Suddenly she bowed and her neck stuck out a bit further. Ephraim was at once at peace and puzzled in his mind:

"Could it be she's still alive? Ha, ha, ha…"

This very question had a rather odd ring to it, the same ring which is not perceived except by the ears of the privileged to whom, of course, it would be capable of revealing the tip of some new horizon, and had never anticipated. To that somewhat twisted definition of the word: woman. Thus, for example, a woman might speak in the ears of her favorite, who had been her heart's desire on a day past; thus she might speak in the ears of her proper lord to whom she had been wed by the law of Moses and Israel.

"Could it be she's still alive? Ha, ha, ha…"

And Ephraim fancied some shortish youth at the bottom of the mountain, a blondish youth perhaps, with narrow shoulders and glasses on his nose and maybe with his mustache trimmed a bit as well, and he was carrying her coat and her parasol and her great beaver hat and he was climbing and falling and climbing again and falling once more, coming at last to the top of the mountain all wrapped up in himself like some locust one has taken up in his hand, breathing heavily with his empty hand waving and with a white handkerchief cleaning his knees that had been covered with dust, and his face grown red and wet, carrying all to her with a dedicated "hey-hey," not without its satisfaction. Even so he forgot this at once. Ephraim forgot this imaginary fellow of his just as he had first forgotten his own inner quivering. Something was writhing in his heart, writhing softly and slowly so that he was not aware of it, and suddenly it was as if all were lost, and slanting genial patches of light, patches of new pure gold, were sporting and dancing in the big signs and the flashing windows of gleeful Krishtchatik Avenue in Kiev and in the great square beside the National Center. Snows were thawing and places were blackening and melting and laughing under the sun, and beside the stand on the corner a gang of students, all sons of good citizens were scurrying and laughing, and the trolley cars were rushing and scurrying and bearing fresh tidings from one side of the host to the other and bellowing out of some repressed joy, and people were scurrying and striding upright, and the faces of the women they met were as if ripened just this minute so that they would laugh hotly, and there, on the near horizon upon the slope where a light hissing mist soared and melted in the face of the laughing sun, the broad Dnieper lay puffed up and groaning, while buttoned people strolled along its shore and waited for something, and unbuttoned people were taking care of their many caches and overturned rowboats and fuming tar, talking loudly and laughing and bellowing a song; and an axe was clanging there and a saw roared and beside the scattered tents beyond the broad river farmers fluttered, their short hair uncovered and their tunics red as they sighed, boards over windows that had been sealed and now opened.

It was three years ago. Three years ago the heart was a bit more foolish; and when a man's heart is a bit too foolish, why he discovers another relish even in the raw cucumbers he eats. This is common knowledge. And for this very reason Ephraim enjoyed a more upright stature at the time. With those three women all residing on the same street which he loved at night, the Street of the Beatification of the Virgin, laughter was quick and that evocative inner light which could not control its natural urge and pierced the laughter with its mute swishing beams, it was twice as quick; and when one of the three went out with him to the dim hall, to escort him, yet another other would hurry to peep after her slyly, and the third would suddenly recall something and pursue him till he was caught, so as to ask him in mischief at once bewildered and gleeful, "Ah…what was it I wanted to tell you? I wanted…ha, ha, ha!…"

And he would leave the place, with a cigarette stuck idly in his mouth, his hands set in the pockets of his mucky coat and his blazing face transfused with that flush fertile flux which attentive ears always discover in gardens and orchards before the matured grape blossom has opened. Beside a great flashing shop window in which a wheel moved leisurely displaying sapphires which sparkled and twinkled in the light of day and the palish incandescent lamps left on there night and day, he suddenly saw the difference between the gang of people standing there looking and Zina Adler, she who that very morning had been sitting beside him in silence and whom he had found later at the three-women place sitting in silence, later rising to occupy herself beside the cabinet in the library and for a bit beside the mirror and its implements, until he suddenly took notice of her not being in the room, no one having seen her departing. This was a rather but not overly tall woman whose face was oval and always palish and whose pupils were always dilated and always alight with large luminous membranes whose whiteness was a bit dark and utterly radiant, so that when she looked at someone, he would somehow believe himself an old friend of hers, and then he would regard her closely and discover that one might have his doubts about this. When Ephraim first saw her at the house of one of his acquaintances on one of those strange autumn days, he greeted her and amicably inquired, "So what do we find? How then can our brothers in Israel be living in…Popova Hora, for example?"

First she looked at him, and her face made no motion; then she responded in that very same manner of his, "Unfortunately I can tell you not a thing of Popova Hora; if, sir, you are at all interested in the brothers of Surazh and their sisters—I am at your disposal…"

Suddenly she began laughing out loud, and her laughter was, so it seemed to him then, too pure and too robust, and she went on: "It appears, sir, that you have been imprecise in your wording.

You should have asked: how can Jews be living in the province of Chernigov…ha, ha!"

Incidentally noting the aspect of her portrait as reflected in the large mirror opposite her, she looked at him once more straight in the face and grinned. Meanwhile night had descended and she went out with him to the theater. Since it was a bit late once the theater was over, she did not wish to return home and knock, so they went on strolling through the streets that had largely been emptied, to the top of Vladimir's Mound, the plain sprawling at their feet with its black river bedecked with the necklaces of many lamps, and she said much to him and did much laughing, not leaving him until day broke and the shops began to open.

Not many days had passed before she found an apartment together with Tsili, a tiny bustling woman of the dark daughters of Bobruysk, who at first wept a lot at night, crying out loud, and during the day wandered about the streets and went back home and wrote long letters and burned them and went on writing others in their place; and in time, after having dropped over once or twice together with her new companion to Ephraim's apartment, she began telling her at night with a somewhat odd laugh about how Ephraim would kiss her, when she occasionally dropped in on him all alone, and how he would lift her and carry her and stroll with her about the room, like some mother carrying and quieting her baby. And her companion did not weep; but during the day she took to wandering about the streets.

Meeting Ephraim she would tell him about that woman, her tiny roommate, telling him what a wonderful soul she was and how she, it seemed, suffered many agonies and how she was beginning to love her…Every day she felt all the more that she was beginning to love her. Moreover she was concerned: that this love would be no simple thing for her…no simple thing…here she was speaking obscurely because…because there are some things better not said. There are some things that…in brief, there are. She was laughing a lot as she spoke. Only then did Ephraim begin to sense that her laughter was not entirely as robust as he had believed at first.

And in the twilight of that expiring holy Sabbath when he met

her suddenly on one of the distant streets of the town, it was with
her light short coat unbuttoned and her hands bunched up in her
narrow pockets, while snow fell large and wet in flake after flake with
its gray net spread on the broad filthy street, darkening the emission
of the light which was dim enough as it was, while the lamps, which
the watchman was then hurriedly lighting with his torch, were reddish, their light quivering and wet. Legs were churning in the black
roaring filth, and the turmoil in the street, a turmoil of drunken men
and women and coachmen throwing up slush with their wheels, was
bothersome, resembling some pressing alarm in a nocturnal dream in
the twilight of that holy Sabbath when he met her there and walked
on with her and she held him and told him much and told him
incidentally about some dolorous uncle of hers on her mother's side
of the family who had always been silent, never letting out a sound
and who was discovered last year in the dusky attic busy with a rope
which he had drawn through a hook he had found there.

Then the sound of her laughter was quite strange and his heart
began to hesitate and he had to stop with her at one of the stuffy
restaurants in that part of the city, if only to obtain for her a single sip
of water. The big room was full of the turmoil of drunks and the smell
of cheap tobacco and the scream of one unseemly woman sprawling
in the muck with her face bleeding, whereas she laughed wearily and
assured him repeatedly that she was very thirsty and did feel quite well
in such company; the liquor served them was indeed quite filthy—but
she did feel that her mood here was very nice; because in essence she
loved—she loved just such places as this…just such…and the proof
of it…she could prove what she said…no. What had she wanted to
say? Ah, she wanted to tell him this. She could prove what she said,
for when she was a junior in high school…

Since that stroll Ephraim met her no more, except once or twice
at the theater; and even then he was somehow incapable of more than
merely saying a few fluttering words to her. On that particular morning she had come to him again but was soon sitting silently, which
made him a bit uneasy: a person comes and sits there from the first
with the intention of silence. At noon when he met her again at the
three-women place she was sitting there too in silence, which made

Beside

him too a bit gloomy at first, but before long that impression was put
out of his mind by the great lively laughter ringing about. For this
reason, when he saw her on his return from that place beside the shop
window, he being on the opposite sidewalk, he told himself to keep on
walking; but she was standing turning aside at times, turning with a
visible fervor and regarding the faces of the passers-by here and there
like a person waiting for someone, and when she had recognized him
at last, on the opposite sidewalk, she turned suddenly with that very
same fervor and began making her way through the racing trolley
cars and scurrying carriages and emerged intact, heading straight for
him. He stood there beginning to look at her. Her face was palish
and a little feverish and the great whites of her eyes were full of that
radiance; and when she raised them to him and looked at him, it
seemed to him that he was once more her old friend, greeting her
warmly, "So you have been wandering all day, Zina?"

When he took her hand, it was rather large and soft and cozy,
lying appeased and nicely clasped in his. He liked it. "Spring, ha, ha.
Why this is the meaning of spring?"

When he saw that her reticent face had suddenly given bloom
to some blush of sudden frankness then suddenly paling again at
once, he did not stop speaking: "Ha, ha. Our pleasant Polisya has
begun cooing in private; even bulky Pantili, that night watchman
in the remote hometown, would always drop him a brief hint, after
a big ringing yawn through all the daydreaming streets: it's a touch
of spring, *panitsh-cheto ei hovorit*—what is there to say)! Could it
be that there is something that must be done? But she was at the
Dnepr? No? Ah, this he had never anticipated. Not without cause,
not without cause would she go to the Dnieper—honestly! He was
sure that if she had seen that black potbelly swelling with a waking
groan and if she had listened to the sounds of the distant axes ringing
in the rustling, bustling space alongside, and if there, at the tip of the
distant and somewhat blurred horizon, might have appeared to her
a white fuzzy column of mist, the remembrance of a bellowing train
lifted and lost there in the covert distance—no, he was sure that she
would not stay here even a single day longer.

He was sure that she would at once take up her cane and bag

and with a great blazing gladness of the heart would return to that far-off reviving province of hers, to those broad potbellied fields groaning with the ponderous enjoyment of some great animal and softening and opening up in an agony of invisible love beneath their many snows which had begun to thaw, opening and soaking up the fertile masculine marrow, while at night they soared up and up with the purr of that same ponderous animal whose covetous pleasure had been fulfilled.

Ah, what are they and what can one make of them, these days of spring here—pardon me, what are they and what can one make of them here, in this noisy town all of which are walls and copper and iron and carriages and signs and nets of electric lines and stifling heat and unceasing tumult? Go and search here, in this desert of inert stones, for the wild groans of the wondrous rising day and night in the coppices of the homeland, those awakenings and swellings and blackenings day by day; or grasp the cutting uplifting honk of wild geese returning from afar, that which pierces the blurred space rustling with new and untold things.

By all means, go out in the morning and find here compasses of spread wings that revolved here at night in the soft softening snows and make your guess with the merry gladness of the heart: hurrah, it's the wild roosters returned, the wild roosters have already returned; I saw their circles—upon my word! Circles I saw in the snows of the fields! Ha, ha. Pardon me, go and search here for the puddles of gold that rush and sing in the shining streets, and for the chicks calling and stumbling with inexperience in the scoured yards, and the freezing cows warming themselves by the walls, and the smell of warm manure seizing the breath to whet it; search here for even one dumb Christopher or Listochavor as he is undoubtedly called there by the rustic maids wearing their big *shubot* and hobnailed boots, that village dunce whose head is already bare since he lost his cap, and whose linen pants are rolled up on his calves and whose bare red feet are already filthy looking for some wet puddle so as to stand in it pleasurably, he being gleeful as some colt cavorting toward all comers and cursing the noisy babes that tease him, and begging a "cigaroot" from every *panitsh* he met, and proclaiming in a flow of gladness and a pealing voice, "Ho, ho, good people! Spring will cooome; spring will cooome!...Ha, ha. Why is she laughing? But honestly—without cause! He...he would not have spoken thus in the ears of...some woman from Bobruysk, for example...he meant...Bobruysk, she could see...why Bobruysk had rather more to do with the...with the *Moralishis Gesetz*, say, than with the *Sterne om Himmel*, ha, ha...unlike Popova Hora, that is: muffled. Surazh..."

And here suddenly Zina began laughing in a great voice and her laughter rang out pure and strong, though in some ways, a little too dim.

"You're laughing? Ha, ha. No. You are not laughing. Ha, ha, ha. You were drinking in these words thirstily. Ha, ha. You drank them in thirstily. You listened to the words and your heart was hovering there, your heart cut loose and burst out to hover there—in the white fond fields of the homeland, where the wild geese scream and the chicks call and the *Patruks* and *Rishkas* are getting their plows ready and swabbing and cleaning their rifles and Father is signing promissory notes and growling into his graying mustache: what will it all come to—and what will all of it come to...ha, ha, ha...only when you began laughing before, you didn't begin laughing only, ha, ha, ha...you didn't begin laughing, only I did say: a woman from Bobruysk...ha, ha, ha...and here you were merely wondering—here you were wondering, ha, ha: that kiss, for example...the same kiss that a person...let us suppose even a person such as I give to some...woman from Bobruysk, ha, ha...could it be...could it be that it does not enter the realm of the...what did I call it? The realm of the *Sterne om Himmel*? Ha, ha, ha..."

Ephraim stopped suddenly. This laugh of hers, which had begun inclining more and more toward some slightly odd corners, sobered up his seething exhilaration, and his polished heart began to beam and grope in the darkness. Like a storm suddenly in his brain arose the talk of that very woman who had talked with him one day concerning that dolorous uncle of hers on her mother's side of the family, and at once he mocked himself and what he had absorbed of pathological theory and for some reason he recalled a story, a story that had been whispered in his childhood in his teacher's house, concerning a village woman, a healthy hearty woman of good family, who had been found one day roaming about by the crossroads beyond the village in her birthday suit, smiling merrily and winking at every man she met…Yet while he was simultaneously considering the uncle and that woman with his mind repressing the rustling disapproval of his that had suddenly bobbed up, Zina suddenly hopped back and a small broken roar burst from her breast, "*Oy!*"

He quivered and grasped her hand, but she embraced him laughingly and they walked on and she went on speaking: "Ha, ha…I thought you intended to eat me up alive—the way you looked at me. Is it a wonder that I was frightened? What? Could it be that I had no grounds for concern? Ha, ha…but I assure you it was not worthwhile. Honestly! Ha, ha, all in all I deserve, so I believe, a different, finer end. No? Ha, ha…if…if it really was my chattering that caused it, why I ask your forgiveness—I again ask your forgiveness. But in general—you should not pay too much attention to my talk. It's a habit with me. Don't you see—a little weakness? It happens, for example, that I might suddenly begin chattering about a deer that bloomed…that is—it happens that even my chattering by itself doesn't suffice…and this is worth remembering. No. Pardon me, worth remembering. It seems to me that I already told you this—or not? Apparently it was due to the family in my case…did you see—my father's old mother, for example…very elderly…deaf and always winding her ornamented wimple in veils and red tassels…when she is in a severe temper, why…why she never speaks a word, but looks up at the ceiling and begins singing to her own nose…ha, ha, she looks full of righteousness at the ceiling and sings in a raving bellow some ancient waltz…ha, ha, ha! No. I think I didn't say any such thing to you…could it be I did, Ephraim? As far as I can remember, I only wondered a bit…ha, ha…wondered a little, nothing more…and really, I am sorry, ha, ha, ha…I am very sorry I chanced upon that *Sterne om Himmel*, since…ha, ha—since a fine fellow like him puts such limitations upon his definition, ha, ha, ha…"

Ephraim listened on and on to her fragmented words, his mind wondering but clarifying nothing by her devious chatter; and finding no other solution, he resumed his former manner—actually with a little difficulty at first: "But...but did I say anything, Zina?"

She suddenly fired sparks at him as if this very start of his was what she had hoped for, and her face blazed, and she burst into that laughter again: "Call me Tsili, ha, ha...is it not all the same? Ha, ha, ha..." Her breath began to cut short and come back boiling: "Ah, how much interest there is in this, great God of her fathers! Ha, ha, ha, I remember that when I was a student attending some class, I had a friend..."

Only then did Ephraim begin surmising something, and he began to draw words from her mouth and even to laugh out loud. He somehow did not draw her away from her fancy but began telling and asking her about that woman, her roommate, and she told and laughed and withdrew no more from him, spending the whole night with him at his house talking a lot and laughing a lot and occasionally going over to pour herself a glass of water from the bottle and sipping a bit, drops spilling down from her mouth, and resuming her talk. When it was morning she did not want to return home alone; since they went together they did not find her friend at home, she too not having passed the night there, once more she was laughing and somehow regretful in her heart, assuring him that she would drop in on him that day together with her, and Ephraim left her not returning home that whole day. On the morrow, as he lay in bed, a postcard was brought to him and he read,

> *The Kiev Terminal...*
>
> *"I laughed the day before yesterday, when we walked together on Krishtchatik Avenue. I should have laughed more, Ephraim...and here I am laughing today too. Ah, those wild geese already screaming over that blurred space in the homeland, that dunce Listochavor (in our town—Karpocha Bosoi), with, as you have assured, his pants already rolled up, neighing away in his sonorous voice, like some colt let out of its stall! No. I can't go on. Let Father sign his promissory notes and let him growl into his mustache as*

he wishes—there is one basic feeling in my heart, perhaps
a somewhat odd feeling, as if something important and
irrevocable will be lost to me if I stay here longer. So good-
bye, Ephraim. Only—one firm request: might you not be
led one day out to that corner of ours? Please do not forget
me then. I have a mother there, my friend, whose peer you
won't find on weekdays, and she can make pancakes—par
excellence, *as we live!*   Zina

This was more than three years ago. Before long he, too, left
Kiev never to return and never to meet that woman again. When in
the last days of that summer he was at a resort near Odessa, he was
told by a black fellow dressed in a black bolero and white frock with a
sash about his waist that Zina was in bed ill; in the late autumn days
that followed, one night he met Tsili as she was busy with packages
and big paper boxes in one of the terminals at the northern junc-
tion, and she told him that Zina had come back to live in Kiev, and
that she was very very pale, and that she went around in a bob—she
had bobbed her black tresses, she had been terribly sick. She was a
hothead—that woman. Wasn't that the truth? A hothead!

She looked at him a bit as if in doubt about something and
suddenly lowered her head as if she intended to drink from the glass
before her, and concluded in the humbled voice of repressed sorrow:
"A hot head, and a silly heart..."

She looked at him again slyly. What did she mean? Once more
there was nothing to be heard. From that day on he heard nothing
of Zina and her doings. It seemed to him that from then on he did
not even remember her. Save perhaps on a sleepless night or two. So
it happens, for example, that a man in his wanderings will suddenly
remember a soft whitish beautiful sprig of birch he had encountered
and not noticed by the distant bare wayside, spread out under the
silent light of noon, where the hand of God had transported him in
the dawn of his childhood—he will remember and then again forget
it at once. Zina...once there was a Zina. Ha! Full of years the sun
leaks and emerges in the east reddening like blood and falling into the
great sea and every day people stir and people meet and people depart

and dreams are woven and dreams are borne off in the wind. And Zina—who is it who will remember Zina? Was she not a worn-vague legend he remembered suddenly from the dawn of his childhood? In lands and states he had never traveled, in generations and ages his fathers' fathers could never remember, there was once a woman…Why did he remember her all at once? Why did he remember her? That bear! That bear! In the cold snowy season that bear drew itself into its den and snuggled up tight and took its big paw in its mouth and sucked and sucked. It was the cold snowy season and the dark woods were already agape and the hives of honey were nothing, it seemed, but a failing dream—now it drew itself well inside and took its big paw right in its mouth and sucked and sucked…

In the lakes and big swamps nearby a bird was complaining over and over in a hopeless voice, and from the clefts behind the mountains came the humming song of a moaning mandolin, a hushed dismal song, humming and coming nearer, and Ephraim lay his head upon his separated palms which clasped and supported him, and his face was turned to the patch of water frozen brilliantly and flowing slowly, and his lips went on releasing their whisper: "In lands and states none had ever traveled, in generations and ages my fathers' fathers could never remember, there was once a woman…"

It was a wonder. What was this with his heart all of a sudden—what was it with this heart of his that began pinching away hotly under the frozen brilliancies of the moon, as in ancient years? That bonfire burning at first on the mountain peak was now merely a girl smoking, her gray smoke soaring as a bit of gloom settled about her. At the top of the mountain there was no longer anyone; but in the narrow cleft twisting through the black darkness between the far mountains and tilting and descending to the stream at their base, voices hummed and spoke. The voices were subdued but ever nearer. Soon Ephraim's ear had caught the confident and somewhat queasy voice of a woman, and then a second voice kept low by the hesitant heart of a man, a voice which Ephraim knew dwelt frequently upon his name. The man was wrestling and the darkness of the soul encompassed him. This, it seemed, was the meaning of the intentional moderation seething in that voice. When the speakers had reached the bottom, it seemed, of the narrow path, that very same voice quivered with an uncertain question, so it seemed, and Ephraim clearly heard the voice of…no. Surely his ears were playing tricks on him. No. Could it really be the voice of Zina? Of that same Zina? She called out to the other one, and it was as if her words went on infiltrating lowly: "David, I said…"

Her voice was cold as iron, and the other one grunted and was still; in the dusk of the nearby bushes a bird tumbled, having seen a black dream, and again that frozen secretly moaning silence returned, the dismal horn of the horseman in the distance began weeping hopelessly and subsiding and whining and returning and whining alone and faintly in those expansive mute fields—ah, what was this with Ephraim's heart, what was it all of a sudden with this foolish heart that once more began pinching and went on pinching hotly under those mute brilliancies as in ancient years flown away?

Just as in ancient years, when he was a boy and his blazing heart drank up dreams calling valiantly for redemption to the ends of the far regions and for lifted wings and a pounding heart with the breath teeming and stifled in the breast. The heart was secretly weeping and wailing and pinching without pause, and the drawn lips—they managed to release some slight foolish verse:

"In lands and states I have never traveled, in generations and ages my fathers' fathers could never remember, there was once a woman…there was once a woman…"

There in a hidden dim corner in the secret places of the mind, the same mind whose blood as it were had begun to flow engulfing it, there a mosquito was biting away spreading filth full of cringing venom: "Hi, hi…how old do the dogs grow? Hi, hi, hi…dunce, dunce—Ephraim is a dunce…"

But now fluttering in the exit of that narrow cleft and emerging was that very same image he had seen at first, standing at the top of the mountain in the distance. She emerged with a sort of fluttering caution, her hand holding the folds of her dress behind her, her feet hesitantly groping and making their way over the dry bulges she found scattered here and there in the moist area beside the stream. She was wearing a grayish dress and her tresses, set in a black bun upon her head, were uncovered, and the dress had a square *décolletage* not too low with a smooth proud neck a bit sad in its silence peeping and whitening from within, dark against the brilliancies of night. Behind her, emerging a bit apart and making his own way, was that shortish youth. He was dressed in black, not formal, with glasses sparkling at the moon on his nose, and he carried a large bundle of women's dresses, and his black cane hung bumping against that bundle at his feet. Now the woman was already approaching the empty rowboat perched on the bank of the stream and waiting, with its oars slantingly crossed, and she leaped into it. The sides of the rowboat beat suddenly upon the smooth water and went on beating as one oar knocked upon the other loudly—one oar knocked upon the other loudly in the great stillness of the night...was it in a dream his heart had heard this once upon a time? Ephraim, Ephraim, was it in a dream at night you saw this once upon a distant time vanished now, and was it you, were you the one that in a single leap boarded the lonely boats waiting on the banks of quiet streams while the waters gave voice to a low sound and one oar called to the other in the stillness of night?

"Hi, hi...how old do the dogs grow? Hi, hi, hi...dunce, dunce—Ephraim is a dunce..."

Now the woman was sitting in the stern, and she quietly took the rudder while the youth sat opposite her and the boat moved off and began steering its drooping bow to the right. Now it swerved its drooping bow steering it straight ahead and now it was sailing in a hush, slipping on in a hush with its spread wings flashing and dripping mute sapphires and dipping back in again, and the smooth stream left behind was churning gripped in tremors in which drops began to chase and dance until soon it resumed its frozen tranquility, and the boat drew further and further away ever smaller and lost—now it was steering its bow to the right again and now the oars were groaning in their locks, groaning softly and growing mute, and now it was fluttering again beside the mountains with their slopes and now it was lost, entirely lost, against the protruding teeth of the ridge and it was nothing at all, leaving behind it a sleeping stream immersed silently in frozen light, as it had been at first; and only the easy merry current of that divine brook, roaring without pause beneath one of the nearer mountains as its water flowed into the stream beside him, it alone was flowing and merrily chattering a beautiful somewhat sad legend it had brought with it from its unseen notches, chattering about a lonely winged rowboat that had passed by not long ago and vanished, chattering about a proud uncovered still woman sitting in the stern of that boat with her uncovered hands gripping the rudder and her dress grayish with a square *décolletage* not too low and a smooth proud neck a bit sad in its silence peeping and paling from within dark and silent against the dusky brilliancies of night...

Not far from there clinked the lonely dolorous bell of some horse bound and left by itself for the night, and that bird in the swamp was dozing and complaining and the many sounds of night moaned together, so that it would suddenly seem that there was nothing but the voice of a dog barking without pause in its ringing voice in some distant settlement...and it was only much later, when the moon had already begun inclining toward the lower sky to the fore, and in the stream small tatters of mist had begun rising up to wander dispersed, that the clear hum was suddenly penetrated by a low voice calling, like a whisper in Ephraim's ears, the speaker having wrung it into a low whisper from a distance: "*Panitsh!* Ah, *panitsh*, did you fall asleep?"

Ephraim rose in a hurry. "Is that you, Archip?"

The latter resumed his wrung whisper with a sort of confident tranquility: "Hey, *panitsh*, will you come with me?"

From the contortions of the stream between the mountains darkening on the left, a little fishing boat darted stealthily forth, a rather small torch reddening and leaping in its bow.

The new woman who had come over that morning to Vera's place came in with her purse in her hand and an odd smile, that somewhat wild smile that gleefully and frankly says: "There is my darling, another limit entirely"—was casting its light behind its airy facade, and Vera suddenly took on a new light meeting her with a sharp cry of gleeful joy and kisses full of affection, and little Ruchama was captivated by her from the moment she got a look at her. It suddenly seemed to that little woman that someone had come to her, one whose words were carefully considered, and greeted her saying: "You're right, Ruchama, you're right—now look and see if it isn't..." and it wasn't much, whereas that woman was already settled there easily reclining in the depths of the plush rocking chair in the corner where Ephraim always liked to hide, and she was sniffing from time to time the marble-white belladonna floating in a glass of water nearby, her nostrils stirring at the distant noble scent, and she was grinning from her nook with warm friendliness and speaking cleverly and laughing at abrupt intervals and taking one cigarette after the other from her large purse from which she would not be separated and turning from time to time to address Ruchama too, as if she were addressing a friend who was like her in every way; and that little one was already chatting with her as one would chat with an old bosom friend, and her heart made merry within her and her pure face was clothed in light.

Why it was wonderful—ah, it was a wonder how she could...sit there and how she could talk and how she could look directly at whomever she was talking about...no, ha, ha...now she was casually removing the ashes from the cigarette in her hand to the little ashtray that Ruchama had originally placed for Ephraim upon the stand in the corner to her rear, behind the tall ficus plant with its shady leaves: great God of mercy, how she extended her hand and reached down...ha, ha, reaching with a pampered ease representing some cryptic expressive meditation, reaching slowly and silently as fragile somewhat proud shadows stirred and moved upon her pure brow; now she was extending it and withdrawing it again and suddenly raising it again to her oval face and grinning that odd grin and again resuming her flow of words...no—this was a woman! This now—was a woman! Ha, ha...too bad Ephraim was not here—really too bad! If that filthy one could only see how lovely one of us can be, and how she could be a darling and how...and how...no. That Ephraim—he is really an odd creature...perhaps he has born her a grudge since that day? Could he really have a grudge against her? No. Let him come—he shall be paid in kind...inferior being as he is! For more than a whole Sabbath a person is neither seen nor to be found—as if he had sunk in the mighty waters...perhaps today too he would not come? Almighty God…no. Just let him show a trace of such a nerve…

But suddenly she quivered. Loathing her life as one whose shame was exposed before all. That woman in the armchair who had been so attractive to her that she already treasured her and stored her utterances in the secret places of her soul, suddenly she had begun laughing loudly with her face turned toward hers, and her laughter was quite full and excited with a certain placid somewhat brutal confidence, based upon some cryptic property of the mature spirit flooded with its own maturity, and Ruchama suddenly felt as if the other had snatched her up in her hand, and a small roar burst from her breast, and her blazing face grew somewhat bewildered searching for solutions in that whitish visage of her elder sister who, to her astonishment, was also looking and wondering a little.

When Ruchama turned back and looked at the face of the woman laughing, the latter was already looking straight at her grinning there in such close warm friendliness, that of a heart which hides absolutely nothing, and she too began grinning brightly at the other and her heart that had been hesitant began resuming more and more of its tranquility. That woman looked with her frank smile at Vera's attentive face too, which with all its wonderment was by now ready to concede, and she called with the hushed full ease of humming meditation: "It's lovely here at your place…God, how lovely it is! And you, it seems to me, were always objecting and complaining whenever you had to return home…Honestly, Vera, without cause…honestly! And that piano there—why, is it you who plays it?"

Then rising toward Ruchama, "And you too, surely…no?"

But the latter grinned at her, a bit bashful on account of the sudden pure frankness in her heart: "At times…if you can call it playing…" She lowered her head.

That woman who in the meantime was already standing beside the piano and had opened it, suddenly let one of her hands lie there on the white keys and turned her head and upper body to the little one, a gesture of inner puzzlement: "But…why you speak, dear, as if…"

However the elder sister, Vera, who in the meantime had also risen from her corner in the nearby chesterfield and was standing fixing her hair which she had loosened before the big mirror among the flowers, suddenly cut her short with a thin venom that bubbled and beat out waves from her breast: "We, you understand—we are otherwise...is it such a trifle to you—with us? Ha, ha...she studied on and on—for two straight years and more she studied; then one fine morning she reconsidered and suddenly began to dance, so inspired was she by the melodies of one Dina Barbash—ah, you wouldn't know her: a doctor, coming from a well-to-do family, who has lately completed her studies at Petersburg, slept here at our place and she plays well, and she stopped..."

She turned from the mirror to face her companion, her hands left dangling busy with her hairpins and her head bent forward a bit: "You shall laugh...but from then on she hasn't even come near the piano—she hasn't even come near...ha, ha..."

She had already begun turning again to the mirror so as to finish her task, but at once she turned back suddenly enthused: "No...how she could play! You can ask Tsavar—how she would play for Tsavar and even with Tsavar accompanying her...you can ask..."

That little one's face suddenly paled and she nibbled her lips and fixed her curls dangling to the front, and she began rising from her place and sat back down again. When the guest subsequently began urging her to play something, anything at all; well, for her...ah, no...could it be that she did not understand a deep feeling such as this? Why she understood it perfectly; nevertheless she entreated her: well, let her give in for her sake...only for her sake...then the other leaped up as if bitten by a snake, her face flushed and she began waving her hands in the utter distraction of seething despair and she begged the other: "No! No! Ah, no! Well...well, pardon me, don't let her ask her—ah, here she was begging her: let her not entreat her...she...she didn't want to turn her down...she...she couldn't—ah, almighty God!"

Suddenly the others began laughing out loud and she too began a somewhat bewildered laugh and sat back down. But when immediately afterward Vera went up and sat at the piano and began playing the piece she found opened before her, the guest looked from her place at that little one and caught her with her pupils burning as she shot her sister a single spark, a somewhat odd spark blazing and yellowish that darted from some dark hiding place, as a black panther darting from its den, and vanished at once. She caught it and walked silently up to the foot of the curtains over the little window behind those many tall flowers with the broad sprays, and sat there on the sill taking one of her knees in her hands and beginning to observe the straightened treetops that bloomed and were flitting down that quiet splendid street, and she slipped along the great pure vault of sky overturned like a great tub, so as to close up the white tranquil homes with their lovely gardens and her gaze was left dangling and stuck to that blurred distant horizon beckoning behind those green fields and numerous orchards stretched out behind the streets to be lost in the distance. She sat on and on—suddenly gripped by a light trembling she turned to look about her, looking as one who has suddenly come from afar, and she rose and darted out of her hiding place and went up to the angered Ruchama, who when she saw her approaching lifted her appeased face to her, and she sat beside her with a kindly somewhat dismal grin and patted her hand and head: "Why are you agitated, Ruchamka?"

The latter looked at her as one looks at the face of a friend after having divulged to him the absolute confession of the heart and then laughed at his own folly, and she honestly cried: "Ah, that was nothing but nonsense…honestly nonsense, nothing more…"

Meanwhile Vera went on and grew a bit enthusiastic in her playing. The sounds she produced had less style now resonantly moaning and the surrounding area began filling up with that musical moan sprinkling and captivating the hankering heart and suddenly making it as easygoing as common, not outstanding, music could; the guest, suddenly caught up in her soul which the music was captivating all the more, placed her arm on the back of Ruchama's chair and bending over a bit toward it, she whispered: "Lovely…how lovely…why she's playing 'Scenes in the Forest,' it seems? Lovely…Ruchama my friend, I love them!"

The latter raised her face to her again blazing with the soul's belief, "It is truly a song of wonders? Song of wonders! Yet…of what account is she?"

Her hand gestured at the piano and she went on in complaint, "Could it be that this is music?!…"

And all at once enthusiastically again, "And you, apparently, love music very much—truly?"

Then the other patted her head again and began laughing at her once more with the same great friendliness. There was in this then something of the rustling of an afflicted wind, knocking at closed doors to seek its own expression.

"Ha, ha…what I can say wholeheartedly that I love, why it's…toffee and sweets, my friend…bonbons par excellence, as you like…well, and owing to that majestic respect which a person of culture is required to bear for the heritage of his ancient ancestors, perhaps even—*tsimmes*, that red *tsimmes* they make on Sabbath eves out of all kinds of tubers…ha, ha, perhaps—whatever you love, Ruchamka…true, I have a little weakness for my mother as well—I have a mother, a good friend, who is an excellent woman…she has great hopes for me!…honestly, an excellent woman…ha, ha, when you come to our place—you shall come to our place, pardon me, I do not want further talk…when you come to our place, you shall eat the cheeses that she prepares, and you too shall admit to me…you see, Father—one I no longer love overmuch…in general—fathers, it seems, are rather a nation in themselves…how do you feel—are they not? Ha, ha…but music…ha, ha, I am no longer speaking of that which is neither bonbons nor offers any great hopes for its daughters—even from Father it is possible, at least, to steal a cigarette when he is not home. Ha, ha…no. That is perhaps a joke which is none too keen; but, honestly—I am not mocking, Ruchamka…"

But meanwhile she had begun straightening the cigarette which she had already extracted from her purse, and she was rolling and fixing it, putting it in her mouth and was about to ignite it while little Ruchama's face kept on grinning in somewhat of a blur, lifted toward that woman speaking strangely as it were and not strangely, and she was ashamed a bit and wondering a bit, inwardly retaining what had passed the other's lips. When the latter had lit that cigarette at last, Ruchama saw, to her astonishment, that her oval face had paled somewhat and she was nibbling on at her closed lips while upon her pale forehead those same light shadows she had seen at first were moving. But suddenly the other looked at her in recollection, it seemed, and returned again to her talk and previous manner: "So then?"

Yet immediately she was again still, looking straight into the face of that little one sitting by her, and she was as if looking beyond her; but immediately she began grinning at her affectionately and resumed her talk: "So then? There are things...namely, take, for example, those very 'Scenes'...I myself am much of an expert even in matters of music; why should I lie? But those...why here we have, for example, Vera...that one...ha, ha, *entre nous*, my friend—could it be possible to say even of her that she is not among those who excel? In general—why she can play...many daughters of Israel can play...but when she plays those—listen, listen now...ha, ha...no! I picture in my imagination: a person whom God has endowed with a fruitful soul, and God has returned to endow him so again—that fruitful soul has its own expressions as well...there are in the contemplative brain, in the writing hand, in the drawing brush—many heavenly emissaries...no!

"How would that very woman, Ruchamka, that woman whom you see sitting here, why I say how she would labor on in an excess of pleasure, laboring and never ceasing, once her soul had absorbed those sounds moaning here resonantly in that moan that captivates the heart like a secure dream of childhood, and opens it, as a pure wind of God hovering over the high mountains...ah, perhaps your lips will flutter, Ruchamka: a luxurious *atelier* in Italy, praise and glory, the palaces of counts, the wealth of Croesus...ha! Like a bee, my friend, like that laboring bee whose labor alone is its reward. Like a common bee, laboring to give of its honey and lost...lost..."

She suddenly felt that one of her hands, which had at first been lying idly upon her knee, was placed, in a little feverish one of that girl's who was sitting by her, squeezing it with a heartfelt warmth while her soul moaned on. Meanwhile even Vera had managed to finish her piece and she rose beside the piano. The guest took with her empty hand that little one's, returning her squeeze warmly and strongly and beginning to laugh out loud: "Ha, ha...once upon a time there was one who always assured me that by day I was different and different I was by night. Ha, ha, he used to say that when he remembered me, he never remembered me except as I was by night. But that is not the essence of what I am saying; the essence of it is merely this: that I on my part used to agree with him, at times. *Ça bien compris*—in the secret places of the soul, ha, ha...why you are the one, you, little vamp, who have caused this, ha, ha..."

She tapped that girl on the face once or twice with that grayish glove she had taken from the approaching Vera's hand, and she threw the glove upon the couch that was there nearby, and again she resumed her flow of chatter and warm laughter. Again Ruchama was sitting thirstily drinking in her considered words with her soul gleeful and her face alive in the achievement of the soul's splendor.

And when the guest had taken Vera with her and in leaving had squeezed that little one's hand with a heartfelt warmth and again cast light upon her soul with that odd smile, which emitted rays of a certain splendor from beneath its facade, that somewhat wild smile which battered down walls saying: "There is, gentlemen, another limit entirely," and had departed by way as of that warm laughter in a flow of chatter, and the other had remained alone in that subdued parlor stillness which suddenly prevailed all about, she was at first fixed in a stance as if by nails, and she looked straight at that white door, restrained by taciturn politeness which closed behind those two, and her face was extended, attentively frozen, her soul shut tight. It seemed as if she were the one standing, keeping her solutions from that taciturn door. Nevertheless in the end, with the coming of that steady and broken ticking that had been caught at first in the stillness and was suddenly distinguished from that stillness, driving into her mute soul, she began emerging from her frozen state, and her former face came slowly back to her, turning toward the inner rooms, and her lips went on moving to no object, as if of one trying to utter a sound out of his strenuous sleep—suddenly she returned again and looked at the door, her lips easily extricating, as if reading what was written there in a clear exact accent: "Zina Adler..."

So it had been with her as well on one of those not too distant days, when the German instructress at her academy clarified for her class the laws of *plus quam perfectum*, and for many days she could not grasp them. One morning, as she was already dressed with her books under her arm and her mouth finishing off the expiring doughnut in her hand while repeating in an abrupt roar that day's academy lesson, even then she had stood before the door with her face extended and attentively frozen even then—and suddenly she had begun emerging from her frozen state and her former face had slowly come back to her, and at last her lips had gently released, as if she were reading clearly syllable by syllable what was written in front of her on the door: "*Plus quam perfectum*...."

Suddenly she discovered that she was exceedingly hot and her nostrils, moving, began breathing with difficulty, and when she sensed that the lobes of her ears as well were seething, her heart began bouncing from her breast right up to her throat so that it seemed to her that there was not enough room for her in the house. At first the girl understood nothing of what was about her, falling in her distress upon that empty armchair in the corner while her heart roared for Ephraim, who was not there, but suddenly seeing the piano which had remained open before her she jumped up and sat upon the chair beside it, her hands directed toward the whitening keys.

In her soul, lifted and vanishing in a moaning storm, were the scattered chords of sundry melodies with one groaning phrase staying a little longer until she beat upon the keys once and again in the enormous aspiration of her soul—and sighed in utter despair, dropping to the little window nearby and putting her head out to see the broad empty street, in whose distance she managed to recognize the open parasol flashing at the sun and belonging to Zina, and the tassel of her airy wrap that waved and wound behind her.

They were fluttering, and together with Vera, all dressed in white, were lost by the far corner of the street, and she remained frozen looking straight in the face of that ruddy student bedecked in white who had sprouted suddenly on the sidewalk before her, hastening greatly on his way while raising his beaver hat to her in a sort of wrath born of utter dedication, as one saying bitterly: "Ah, let it go to the devil, this beaver hat!" She did not return his greeting, except inadvertently and when he was already far away. Only when she had returned it and her odd voice had penetrated her ear was she too awakened by a dread in her soul, and she began again dashing about the house, her shoulders quivering at times, until she came across a light cape in the wrong place and threw it over her shoulders, taking out a large airy shawl in which to veil her head and face together, and going to stand by the outer door she began for some reason to draw quite carefully over her hand a single white glove she had discovered bound up forlorn in the shawl. But soon her neck stretched suddenly forward as she recognized Ephraim by his walk, recognizing him but unable to turn away before he had rung and come into the hall, so that she was pale and troubled and like a quivering bird began to search about to get her a place, finding refuge in one of the corners, till regret suddenly entered her heart and she squeezed herself into another corner, sitting hidden by the side of a couch that stood there, while she did not leave off drawing her glove over her hand with that same feverish care she had taken from the first.

Soon azure snakes began racing and winding and spreading over the large spots of sun making merry in that room, in whose space they went on drawing various strange figures in the style of those embroidered curtains which descended to darken the windows, and of those flowers in the vases beside them, which were tall with broad leaves and ample shade. Ephraim was sitting in his place in that armchair hidden in the corner, his head lying behind the shady leaves of that great ficus plant, and Ruchama was sitting at the side of the open piano opposite him, the tips of her little feet peeping from beneath her dress at the tall chair beside her, her own black cape over her body. Her shawl was folded over her head and her hands, propped upon her knees, were playing with its many tassels as she chattered in his ears about what she had already and what she had never in her life chattered, speaking of people she knew and of those she did not, telling about cities she had never seen and about the life in those cities of whom all were wont to talk, while washing their hands in piety, and her enthusiasm grew as was her custom and was not at all, so that she began suddenly mocking some of those acute shuddering tragedies, those of the beautiful soul, as it were, which "uncommon" people would hang in advance upon their grown-up noses—for a decoration, ha, ha…the spiritual transformation of those noble orders and jingling medals with which retired military men adorn their chests in conspicuous display; more than once she recalled "those daughters of Israel" who had "fled" to centers of knowledge, there learning to laugh with that easy flitting arbitrariness born of excessive wit, and to smoke cigarettes with an air of saying: "Such a trifle—could it be worth caring for much, eh?" And to speak in a roundabout way of music and literature and subjects of beauty in general—finally concluding with a sentiment of restrained innocence: "'With my master's permission, ha, ha; but really I cannot bear them!'"

Suddenly she began to laugh, laughing as was not always her custom, there being in her laughter something new and rather odd—the very same that is to be heard in the untaught crow imitating roosters who have not yet learned to crow properly; Ephraim's heart began wondering and moaning heavily, the tip of his mustache moved a little, and once he had absorbed a full swallow of the cigarette in his hand he discharged graying spirals in a single windy sigh stifled but long, and reflected, "No…this is no longer a girl; no—this is no…"

Then suddenly, "And one fine morning I shall get up early—with a bald spot sprouted upon my head! Now this one has—sprouted!"

Then it seemed to him that his collar was rather too narrow. At first he stretched his neck forward, as one whose collar is really too narrow; but once he had sensed that his scalp was suddenly wet, he rose confusedly to leave. When he opened the outside door his head was somewhat bunched up between his elevated shoulders, as that of one whose back is extended to receive a blow.

Upon returning, he met that whitish kinky fellow whom the dismal banks of the Psel had nursed and the yellow prairies of America had cast off, lights were laughing with one another and the many gold tops of the mosques were sparkling in the square from whose green lawns beams were streaming while the yellow paths of sand grinned, stretched out between the lawns like those towels stretched out to dry beside the pools, and that fellow was standing gripping Ephraim's lapel and speaking much to him in his fashion, which was a bit odd seeing as it was always seasoned with words and even many entire sentences of English, speaking, it seemed, with the great enthusiasm of the soul as his face was lighted by some subdued confession of the heart.

Ephraim thought this puzzling even if only a little; but he stood facing the other looking straight at his whitish face upon which a ruddy redness was playing, looking while it seemed as if he looked and saw an open space, his regard, which had frozen, penetrating and perceiving and wandering among the clipped broad treetops in the orchard behind him, then lifted to slip onward to that pure horizon of the end of all great, truly great, lying there in its entirety, tranquilly embracing mountains and weaving its secret thoughts...yet suddenly he caught himself feeling his hand that patted away at that fellow's shoulder, and sensing his lips moving about, voicing involuntarily in that same jumbled fashion of the other: "Fine, fine...very well, sir..."

Simultaneously his ear caught an uncertain question, which that fellow was mumbling, asking most politely: "But...excuse sir. I wished to ask—perhaps...maybe it is possible for you—at once?"

He noticed that one of the other's hands was holding a large wrapped scroll of paper, and at first he began laughing at him again with that same roundabout friendliness, as he too chattered, "At once? You mean...at once?"

But suddenly his face quivered in recognition, beginning to let go of that light mask of appropriate reflections, which had darkened it at first, and he cried decisively, "No. I can't at once. I...I can't today!"

Squinting with a worried suspicion at the large scroll of paper, he put out his hand to him. The latter took it; but he kept it a bit not releasing it: "But we are going together, it seems. Sir—thither?"

Ephraim looked aside in an embarrassment of small anger and encountered the large sign of a coffee shop sparkling at the other end of the square, a little way off. In the large shop window, upon the heights of the white decorated sugar tower there on display, was written in large black letters: Today—ice cream.

"I…it's very hot…I should like to stop first at that coffee shop…"

The other was suddenly enthusiastic, "Ah, that is an idea…but, upon my soul, that is—*nice*, as our brothers, the sons of Israel, say once they have begun feeling their oats there taking in a nice dish of cool ice cream in such heat—that will be *very nice*…hello! I shall stop there too."

As they walked, Ephraim began suddenly to laugh and speak, "It is possible that this is a bit puzzling. Indeed, it is possible. Yet in general—why this is folly. Ha, ha, I open my mouth to wonder? But, honestly, it is not worthwhile…Not at all worthwhile. Ha, ha, could it be…why I say: could it be that I ever anticipated, for example, that one might look at that whitish face of yours and regard that stance of yours, erect, European in every sense of the word, and suddenly recall…ha, ha, suddenly recall no less than…Africans, than two Negroes—simply, Africans, ha, ha? Two Negroes—and another, third, Negro?

"Ha, ha…as previously mentioned, this is nothing but sheer folly; but when I was shriveled up, seeing not a single lovely hour of sun together with myriads of people such as I, so it appeared, in that charred metropolis by the sea, I would daily regard in the terrible torrid filth of the afternoon two clipped Africans, standing facing one another in the large shop window on a street corner bustling with people and beasts and steam, standing in primitive attire while the great heap of ground coffee which they were sifting, it seemed, interposed between them, and from time to time they bared white teeth clamped in suffering so that their black jaws were silvery pro- truding with some black luster—apparently due to the cruel heat, and maybe due to the oppressed longings of a warm heart moaning for its tranquil hut in the distant homeland, if not for those elegant haughty women passing there on the nearby sidewalk, even farther off than that homeland…ha, ha, and I remember the morning my ship left for the sea with me standing on the deck observing all the smoke of that European Sodom and its blurred chimneys, a black Negro came up and stood beside me, he too returning on that very ship to his yellow sands in distant Africa. His clothes were black and pressed and his face was black and pressed with only his collar and teeth and cuffs milky white and a gold chain hanging on his chest and field glasses in a case at his waist which were new—new and flashing. Ah? No. If I am not in error, he was busy as well with something resembling a guidebook, ha, ha, so it seems to me, he had a guidebook as well. He stood beside me remarking frequently:

"'Delightful? Delightful! It's delightful!'

"Suddenly he laughed at me with his white teeth—took the pipe out of the drooping corner of his mouth and laughed at me with his white teeth. 'Goodbye, *hee, hee*...goodbye, sweetheart!'

"And he sighed with the subdued belief of the soul: 'Twenty years!'

"Ha, ha. I on my part glanced at his black hands sparkling with much and some false gold, and I thought: *twenty years*...how many heaps of ground coffee has this one finished sifting there in that period of twenty years and how much have those black jaws flashed in the heat of day with that same luster...twenty years! Ha, ha, I too stayed there half a year...and you sir, how long? Two years? But...what was I referring to in this? Ah, ha, ha...as previously mentioned, this is nothing but folly; but...always, whenever I see you, I somehow remember those...by the way, those very Africans had enticed me beforehand, as well, to something else, and I...in brief, my friend. I shall be pardoned, and it is no lie if I say that...ha, ha, why I confess to him that I made nothing out of what he said to me previously. So much for it. Now I forgive him his weakness for that *nice* and *perhaps* and so forth, and he is therefore obliged to forgive me my own little weakness for...things about an open mouth and a deer that bloomed...ha, ha!"

The other was laughing at him confusedly with one of his eyebrows lifted a little: the essence of it all—what is the essence? But once Ephraim was done, that ruddy redness began playing again upon his whitish face and he began, in a slight embarrassment which he tried to suppress anew. "So much for it—*it's right*! *It's all right*! If in peace—you too have come in peace! Yet all in all—what do you want from me? I would like you to read this story of mine and tell me…that is to say, tell me—I have already published several stories in the *Forverts*, even one big one; but those are not important at all. So, at least, I think. It was a beginning. In other words, not that they were not important; but…*yes*. And secondly, those had been written in Russian first and had been translated into Yiddish. Not so this one—it was written in Yiddish from the start. That is to say, since I have been told about you, sir, that you are…"

However in the meanwhile they had come up to the glass door of the coffee shop, and he opened it letting Ephraim enter first, and once he too had entered after him he resumed his talk no more, because Mrs. Viltsiva, who was sitting hidden in the secret place under that flashing horn in the corner, was screaming there not at all in jest, and also because he suddenly saw sitting in the special room open opposite the door Vera Reshel, that soft whitish one whose initials, V.R., were inscribed at the head of many short poems that he kept in a bulky notebook in his box, and that new woman he had first seen not long ago, when he had gone one day with a certain large gang for a trip in the mountains, and afterward had seen her once more at night in a dream, she being with that new fellow with the glasses, the very one with whom she had fled then in the boat, unseen by anyone—he with his black cane and his white straw hat hanging on the top of that cane, and his grin, somewhat odd, that grin of his, certain as it were, of something that was really not certain at all.

As they sat they were fanning at times with handkerchiefs while their mouths blew upon the little spoons in their hands, which were full of cool ice cream, and the tip of that Vera's wrap, drawn a bit aloft, fell from time to time so that she would fix it once more with her right pinkie in a languid small anger, and that whitish fellow, seeing this, was completely dismissed by her. Ephraim, who had shut his ears the minute he had entered and was laughing at Vera and marveling at how could she sit there in utter tranquility without crowing, at least, like a rooster in that medley, looked as he spoke at the visitor and saw that her face was somehow cold, as if deliberately so, and hesitated and put out his hand to her and to that fellow beside her as well. Sitting down, he took part from time to time in that conversation of Vera's in which that whitish fellow was engaged with her, while he reflected upon the woman sitting at his side who had managed to mature to such a considerable degree and had suddenly become quite distant, so it appeared, and he wondered a little while his heart moaned a little for that face which had once been so close to him and had moved away such a distance, and he quieted his soul from time to time in some hidden shame of the soul by means of that clever implication, "Basically...well—why it's quite clear...this is quite clear, ha, ha..."

He ordered a dish of ice cream with a certain spiritual grandness, which suddenly began celebrating in his heart. But his very own voice, a somewhat pompous voice that resembled, so it seemed to him, the voice of a rakish rooster proudly surveying the barnyard audience of his women, it was that very voice which spread sharp venom in him at once so that he was suddenly struck by his soul already being troubled, as it appeared, too much by the clarification of that matter. One way or the other now s feared, was already troubled too much. Really she was overdoing it a little. That sonorous moan which suddenly began to stir and quake in his chest...no. He would have said that even in this there was some...preparation—some preparation for "war," as it were, was there not? My master Ephraim! Ha, ha...the honored elder—my master Ephraim. Why are you sitting and looking and surveying that woman intentionally—pardon me, what is the meaning of that foolish regard, eh? Ah, if that woman were only a bit more clever...and maybe—maybe she was really just as clever? No. It's not nice...ha, ha, but what is this fear, my honored one? And why then isn't it nice? He was right, apparently, he who said...what was it he said? *Il a des choses que ces font, etc.* Right, ha, ha. And maybe this was no proof. No. Really this was no proof.

It was always a firm principle: better that they think me cruel than a fool. Is it not the truth, my master Ephraim? Yet—do you see? Such are her just deserts, not to be clever. Now that lady has reconsidered and has begun peering at us, as one who has been hired for this...or perhaps—perhaps these were things at which the more clever people put their foot down? Ah, how far you have gone, honored Ephraim! Now he was already being accosted by those nocturnal thoughts which old scholars in a womanless state are always afflicted by…so much for it! Pardon me, fond lady. We—we are surely among those who understand! Indeed we had seen that very face before it reconsidered and began peering at us so…we had seen it only a sixtieth of a minute ago, before it put on this hard mask…yet…hmm…at any rate—it is a bit puzzling. No. It is puzzling a bit, my master, the honored Ephraim—not in accordance with the nature of any of us, who would suddenly rejoice like an eager colt that has not yet reached maturity…I say, it is not fit—really, not fit. So then? Hmm…you see—there is something in this, which is perhaps worth caring about a bit. It is something else.

For example, those women…ha, ha, women those…those lovely animals, indispensable domestic animals, raised in humanity's eating place, fattened from the beginning of time and soft of flesh, limp as those nurtured cats from the Siberian lands when they sprawl in the sun at noon dreamily licking their flesh at their pleasure, and savage and perverse as those very cats when this limp pampered flesh suddenly begins seething with the fundamental blood of the wild which long generations of civilization have not bested, and it goes out for its prey ravenously…really, this is something which is perhaps worth caring about a little. Ha. There is a fellow, wandering idly by day under the blessed vault of sky of the Holy One blessed be He, and remembering one of those animals—ha, ha, unfortunately he remembers one of those animals too much, whose fashion it for some reason had been to nibble constantly at strands of cotton.

It was that sort of time of life for her. It seems she had had a toothache then and had neglected to see a dentist. Ha, ha. And whenever she would come up in haste to that little cabinet hanging on the wall and open it to take something, as had ever been her fashion, she would not find it, remembering incidentally to seize that large wad of cotton and stick it in her mouth just as it was and with her white teeth slice a generous portion from it, as the man slices with his teeth a portion of raw meat, and that portion began steadily vanishing there—quite incidentally and casually while she was entirely occupied with another task: when she threw the wad back into the cabinet, closing it, and when she drifted away incessantly turning to the right and searching to the left and beneath the couch and behind the mirror on the wall and when she gave an order to the maidservant in the other room—then that fellow's heart began bouncing right up to his throat, and rather than words of any human tongue he began bellowing within his chest, like some animal that had been startled out of rest...*a propos*: that animal of whom I have been speaking, lady, was of very early age, an utter infant that had not even been fully weaned yet, and her figure was marvelously shaped and her dress clasped her flesh in the mornings and afternoons with a certain grandness, breathing with the ease of natural forces, and her shoulder was smooth and somewhat full and quiet, quiet—with a little effervescence moving in it...and when her rosy lips which apparently had never ceased nicely absorbing her mother's milk would be wiped dry with some keen sharply stirring pain possibly born of that very fellow whenever they met by chance or not in a distant quiet room, he would completely forget that a bitter day was coming when he would be stretched out at that one's feet wallowing in his flowing blood while she would not even turn her face to him and not even a laugh would sound within her; for pampered from the beginning of time and naturally eager for her portion of cotton which she would then slice with her clamped white teeth, as the wild man slices with his teeth a portion of raw meat, she would drift away from him passing on quietly and a bit languidly without even suspecting that she was in need of any evidence in her defense...*yes, nota bene milady*: her man, that pale somewhat weary doctor whose beard and pupils were always black and flashing would always pat her on her warm fragrant head and call her most lovingly with the peace of belief: my innocent lamb! My innocent lamb!

So what do we have? So what do we have—nothing. And you might say we find, just a bit of a bit, that in all those many capers we too have achieved a certain perception...and a small little turn to the side, lady: those who understand will understand anyway that these capers, of which we have been speaking, are nothing to us but a cliché, as they say. Capers are what we in such cases are used to calling matters of plain consciousness. Not so in this, my lady. For in this there is room only for that organic effervescence which we find in all organic bodies and which we are used to calling, in their case as well, consciousness. In brief—this is nothing, as previously mentioned, but a small turn to the side. Know therefore: a certain perception is now ours…ha, ha, why her, for example. Now this is a way to sit, the devil take it! Do you see? First of all—why we are cold. Cold we are, like that ice upon the rivers, and we sense nothing of the existence of anyone about us. So then? Perhaps someone or other will come and say to us clearly and concisely: excuse me, why this is Ephraim Margelit sitting here—Ephraim…well…the same Ephraim Margelit? But that name seems so strange to us…Ephraim? Ephraim Margelit? But—honestly, I remember nothing.

Absolutely—nothing. Ephraim Margelit? I—of course it matters not a whit; but I am—Zina; I am Zina Adler from Surazh, Chernigov and maybe from Kiev and maybe from Odessa—and even that matter is of no great importance. And I have many acquaintances—and maybe not just acquaintances; but I am capable of guarding my property alone in that very Kiev and that very Odessa and wherever you wish, even in exalted Switzerland. And what shall I say? It is quite possible that I did once meet a fellow named Ephraim Margelit…Ephraim Margelit? But—no. Absolutely. I remember nothing. Nothing…ha, ha, the devil take it! Such subtle grappling on the part of some…primordial effervescent being—why this is really quite amazing. Yet…yet I fear, my darling, that you serve, if not as an indispensable domestic animal, at least as a sort of ladle rejected by the great cook of that exalted mankind, may its glory be praised, and such subtle philosophies on the part of a ladle which has no longer any function at all, why this, it seems, is much more amazing…the devil take it! About what you said before, would it be worth caring, my important fellow? Those women—women those, as you said, or the fact that one Zina Adler has forgotten or has pretended to have forgotten your most lofty honor?

Suddenly he sensed that his little spoon which he had extended to the plate of ice cream before him, had returned to his mouth empty. Vera too sensed this, since she had turned to him just then in her talk, and she began laughing out loud so that the others too noticed this and grinned at her politely, while Ephraim began wondering and covering up his embarrassment: "Puzzling, puzzling, it is a bit puzzling, assuredly…"

Then all began laughing out loud, and at first it seemed as if their hearts had suddenly drawn a bit nearer, afterward returning again to their former chatter. When Ephraim observed his surroundings, that Zina was sitting grandly smoking a cigarette ("she smokes cigarettes?" thought Ephraim incidentally and tried to remember something. "This is something new for that one!"), and listening at her ease to the words of that fellow with the glasses, who was sitting whispering most earnestly into her ear so that she laughed from time to time, looking with great distant innocence at those about her, and with that very same innocence "including" Ephraim "too." Vera turned from time to time to Ephraim, apparently with some incidental question of merry laughter, as it were, and he answered her, it seemed, correctly—did he not? ("She smokes cigarettes—this very woman." So Ephraim reflected and thought again. Suddenly he recalled the words of that little one who had spoken to him previously of "those daughters of Israel who had fled to centers of knowledge there learning to smoke cigarettes." "Aha!" he thought. "That little one! Or perhaps—perhaps even in this it was merely that primordial being speaking from her mouth, ha, ha? But *pfui!*"). The whitish fellow with that ruddy redness playing on his face was speaking and again speaking the praises of some *liberté* in its broader sense—simply: in its individual sense, *personal* in their language, and in our own—*national* as well. He told of some "literary circles" in America and of how those in them would speak ill of a certain Colon and Semicolon (these apparently being names of writers)—perhaps they remembered that great story: *The Victims of Love?* Very likely not. Since they read no Yiddish. That very Double Apostrophe was the one who wrote it. Naturally it was to be understood that nothing modern or universal was to be found there except to a very limited degree; but they should read that story, a real, as they say, *Span, thrilling*, as had been said: *A very thrilling novel…yes.* That was the basic standard of criticism employed by a certain *éditeur* who was one of New York's finest. Incidentally, that very same *éditeur*, for example, had told him…

Ephraim suddenly felt that this place was very nice. Ha, ha, yet what had he believed? So people lived—and you go learn from them. So people came into a place and so the ruddy redness found its place breaking out on the cheek and so they lauded everything "dear" to their hearts—life would come anyway and all would be quite well. All would be "dandy." Those whose ruddiness broke out because of a whitish girl, and those who found enjoyment in steady earnestness; those who sought and found themselves some *éditeur* in New York, and those for whom it was just nice—they had in common a bowing of their heads to receive the great grace of God, ha, ha.

Of course at times a bothersome thought would come to disrupt the train a little. A person—not a god; and it happened that due to an untimely drop, too much a man's flesh would reach the point of contradiction; however things of too much thought always have their limits, set by the ancients: so very "great" were those who blazed our trails...well, a man's flesh—certainly. So people lived and so it was nice. Ha, thanks were due to that whitish kinky fellow—really and truly, thanks were due to that whitish kinky fellow. For where would he ever have been had he not met up with that whitish kinky fellow...Ha, ha, the field, the field...Ephraim suddenly lost the thread of his thought and that buzz of flowing chatter beside him had seemingly been removed.

The field...he suddenly rose, as if his place had cast him off, and strolling about the room once or twice he bumped up against his chair and sat down again. If it were silent there, the woodlark would ring out aloft. It is proper that a man think out his thoughts beside those green still humps, with the distant woodlark ringing out aloft. All about there was a great stillness as that of dusky temples, and the distant vault of sky shielded thoughtfully overhead and the broad earth below was contently flat and one's thought gushed, fresh and plentiful, having a certain sharpness to it and a foaming effervescence and a sweet powerful fecundity—that which is to be found in the finest of vintage wines, as one sips them with that deliberate enjoyment and concentration of the soul pampered by sip after little sip, filling and penetrating with that same fresh keenness to every individual drop of the blood, just as with those fresh thoughts full

of effervescent emotion which the soul absorbed beside those still
humps, absorbing every single thought individually in receptive pleasure—and with them their powerful fecundity and their stimulating
keenness and their plentiful effervescence…if it were silent there, the
distant woodlark would ring out aloft. Yet surely there was a stirring
and a whistling and the blazing heat of noon there…a stirring and
a whistling and the blazing heat of noon…ha, ha, great is the power
of the field, blessed by the Lord!

It is proper to wander alone in the fragrant intoxicating grain
and to clip the dandelion heads on the borders with one blow of a
stick and to throw little stones at the birds hopping and lost in the
sea of kernels laughing and frozen at last, and to observe glittering
creeping things whose vast populace swarmed and scurried over the
carcass white as lime that bared its teeth lying upon the plain at
the foot of the green mountain. From there one went on into the
adjacent coppice hiding at the base of the tallest hump as his lips
whistled whatever melody came to his mouth until he suddenly began
screaming, screaming like a wild ass in the wilderness, one of his
settled thoughts coming forth and beginning to bother him. Happy
is he who has tried going down to the nooks of the coppice, winding
and warm in their attentive dusk, and has taken his clothes off as the
snake takes off its hardened tube, and has climbed to sit at the tip of
a high tickling branch of one of the higher trees, warming his back in
the scorching sun and abandoning his thirsty stirring flesh, so that it
might go on absorbing those piercing sharp beams, absorbing them
with the sort of frozen dullness born of crude bodily enjoyment, as
a mare will freeze suddenly at noon in the field.

It happened that one would be sitting on that branch embracing the fragrant cypress trunk attentively awaiting every blazing stab
and freeing himself of the feeling and the ghost of the feeling of all
else—suddenly he felt he wanted to weep. Not to complain or to
pander to anyone—to weep, to scream like a bull. There was a ball
as hard and strong as rock lying in the breast year by year and life
was not easy and breath was so heavy…oh, of whom were you afraid?
Why were you not as shamefaced as a loud baby, lips suddenly wid-
ening as you called from your ill moaning heart: *oy*? The voice came

out wildly as if rag after snipped rag were hanging from it all as it echoed throughout the coppice finding no place for itself and you lifted your head to the sun and began whistling with your lips what one would whistle: *pfui pfui pfui*, in other words: I am not abashed and not ashamed, for has something happened to me? Even so you soon descended from the heights of that branch. Descended…ha, who could gain entrance to the secrets of that lonely closed house in the heart of that coppice, the memento of a tranquil country lodge now destroyed? That desolate house with its ruined halls encompassed by nettles and thistles all around, and its opaque impervious windows through only one of whose partitions it was possible for those who knew to penetrate to the interior? The second story of that house was worth inspecting from time to time. Ephraim's feet had banged about there often, the shuddering floorboards beneath him sighing and groaning as he strolled and sniffed, his nostrils moving at the smell of some archaic vacuity rotting away, the smell of the strange thoughts it nourished. He would pick away with his stick at the padding of straw and stubble heaped there in a corner to serve, it seemed, as a bed some night past—for whom?

He reflected upon the extinguished cigarette butts tossed about here and there, and the cheap toffee wrappers fouled with garbage, and he would read and read again the winding fleecy sketches in which he was already well versed, those which had been inscribed and carved on the yellow windowsills. Verka—be snuffed, oh flame! So it had been written there in one place. And below—in big letters and with wondrous errors and numerous exclamation points was a brief concurrence: "Let her be snuffed!!!" And there was another inscription nicely chiseled by pocketknife, a cryptic inscription apparently mute yet full of sound, in which the heart's reflections might find quite pungent nourishment: "June 12, 1908. My Darling!" Ah, who was she and what was she, whose quivering heart his heart had divined? Whose pocketknife had served her as a chisel? Had she wept then or laughed then? Had he been standing then on her right kissing her softly on the barrenness of her neck or was there only his distant image fluttering opposite her? And what had happened to her in the end—what had happened in the end to that one whose soul, it seemed, had remained here as an orphan distressed in this desolate ruin?

Yet it happened that he was suddenly seized with utter weariness, and he would sit down in the heart of that rotting ruin and take...*pfui*-no! A person goes out by himself to the field where loneliness peeps at him from every corner, and the sharp pain in fragmentary portions is thrice as great, so that he is brought to his knees, actually brought to his knees beneath the load's weight...ha, thanks were due to that whitish kinky fellow, the one to whom some *éditeur* in New York had told whatever he told—thanks were due to him and would that he tell again...oh, I am for peace—why I am for peace, merciful people, if only...ah, do not send me away by myself, for myself knows devastation...and here—how lovely...ha, ha, how lovely it is here...

"Would you like a glass of beer, my friends? They have cold beer here and it is very nice...honestly!"

He jingled the bell beside him and removed his hat and lit himself a cigarette with a hearty grandness. What?—beside him a tall full-grown maid was standing grinning at him. Ah—truly, he had ordered beer, cold beer. As long as there would not be much of a delay; will there be much of a delay? Vera, she would drink a glass of beer—would she not? And the visitor? Surely she too would not refuse? Well, and the "buddies," ha, ha! With my respects? Nice! Very nice!

Yet in the meantime that fellow with the glasses had risen, and he went out to the buffet for some reason. When Ephraim turned to Vera with a question, half of which was a fluttering implication, and asked who he was, and she found herself slightly embarrassed her cheeks suddenly blooming and she lifted her face to her companion as in despair, he saw that now the other one's tranquil face was celebrating its victory with a hidden smile: Congratulations, my important friend. More than once—would it have been better if he had not asked that question in front of her? But then Ephraim suddenly put his hands down before him and began looking straight at her with a sort of odd tranquility, his face laughing openly at her: "So much for it...please tell me then, how are you feeling, Zina, ah?"

Yet before he had been able to finish the statement that other one too, who had been bothered a little from the start, was already regarding him differently, the whites of her eyes growing, as it were, and growing as she began crouching and slanting toward Vera: "Mister...Galit, I believe..."

Suddenly she turned back straight at him: "Ephraim Margalit—is it not?"

And Ephraim began laughing out loud: "Ha, ha, if I am not mistaken..."

She put out her hand to him and was as one wonder-struck, and suddenly she began grinning a somewhat strange grin: "Why... you yourself are in doubt as it seems?"

Again that quite actual and quite soft hand was lying in his own, as it had been more than once in former days, and it was, as it had seemed to him at first, actually nestled in it just as appeased and nicely embraced; yet she did not let it tarry there long and that blurred feeling began again, its blur giving rise to a moaning suction in the breast.

"And I...did not recognize you. Absolutely—did not recognize you."

"Ha, ha. Because I have been changed."

Ephraim had already considered the matter and found that he was somewhat sorry about that good comfortable hand he had lost once again, and he tried to put on a smile. But she dallied with her words while on her forehead those light shadows of hers were moving at their ease as she apparently pondered: "Because you have been changed? Possibly...very possibly...yet more likely—because...that is, because I did not anticipate meeting you here..."

He was already laughing at her tranquilly and did not cease looking at her face: "But my heart is whispering to me, Zina, that it was neither due to one nor the other...ha, ha...ah, my heart is whispering something else entirely, ha, ha..."

She was a bit embarrassed and began, as had ever been her way, laughing loudly, "But due to what?"

"Ha, ha...but...but due to your meeting me in the daytime, Zina...in the daytime and not at night, ha, ha..."

She was at first astounded, as it were, a little; yet her laugh remained frozen upon her face, as if in hiding, "That is to say?"

Suddenly she recalled old memories: "Ah, and here I had completely forgotten, you, sir, are *incorrigible*, ha, ha, ha..."

Yet suddenly that laugh of hers broke off, breaking off at once, and her face was seemingly wondering and asking: Could I have been laughing—could it be possibly that I have been laughing? She immediately turned aside and began chattering out of that frozen strange tranquility she had had at first, chattering with Vera and her kinky companion and greeting with the fondness of open friendship that fellow with the glasses as he entered bringing many little bags of stuffed paper.

However, the sages have said: Once a woman has laughed, wait, for she will laugh once more. That little bunch did not come apart all that day and all the following night. In the twilight of dawn, as the distant east grew pale and pink while they returned together from sailing in a boat on the river and sat down for tea *en masse* in Ephraim's room, that Zina was already sitting beside him doing much laughing and much chattering, having already chattered to him of a certain aunt of hers on her mother's side or on her father's side who would suddenly rise in the middle of the night and grasp that man of hers lying beside her, a famous merchant in those parts with whom she had already married off sons and daughters—she would grasp him by his shoulders and begin shaking him with all her might and clinging to him with a fearful question born of despair: "But who are you? I do not understand—who are you? Now tell me—who are you? Ha, ha, ha..."

Then she had already resumed her talk of her mother, so very good, and those wonderful cheeses she prepared which were good and possibly better than she, and of her father who for some reason had begun trimming his graying mustache and whose way it was of late to ask every single one of her acquaintances in particular: "Fine, fine. Everything is fine. But perhaps you will tell me, my friend: where does she think she will be in the end? Pardon me—in the end where does she think she will be? Ha, ha..."

Finally she lit a cigarette and leaned over to Ephraim, one of her arms stretched to embrace the back of his chair, and asked him with a hint of laughter at that fellow with the glasses who was sitting at the other end rapt in literary conversation with the kinky fellow who was already a bit hoarse: "Please be so kind as to tell me...how is it—could it be...you no longer inquire...as to the meaning of—this? Ha, ha..."

Ephraim looked at her and after a brief silence leisurely remarked, as if in doubt: "I no longer...have need of this, it seems... does it not?"

He surveyed her again and laughed decisively, "Ha, ha. It seems I no longer have need of this, Zina..."

She on her part began laughing loudly and moved her chair away without a word, going to sit beside that fellow opposite her who began laughing to greet her with a sort of feeble obsequiousness and mopping his flashing forehead with a white handkerchief, and she leaned over to him a bit and began reminiscing with him, with the heartiness peculiar to great friendships.

Those were the days when little Ruchama began to her great pleasure to stay with Dina Barbash—she began staying there frequently with that very receptive pleasure of some special lust. Her lovely home, always closed in, which emerged from the rural street like a wedge in the face of the spotted broad fields on the bank of the bridged stream which separated it from the rest of the community, was to the moaning soul of that little one a symbol of the tranquility of easy beauty; noon by noon, when the great stillness following despair would prevail over the mute area, and she would for some reason begin sensing in that weltering soul of hers that it was not by dint of the heat alone that this effervescent filth had been cast upon her, her ear would then suddenly catch from within the blurred dream the healthy lucid tones of the sledge hammers spurting out of the bowed blacksmiths' huts standing to the rear of that distant bridge, and her soul would begin to take nourishment from that lonely house and its fenced orchard emerging tail-like in that strange corner, and would thirst and hanker for that tranquil somewhat cryptic existence in which this house always breathed as did the lonely creature within it.

Ruchama loved to drop in particularly when that other one was not at home and old Teodorovna would let her in and lead her with open fondness to the "chambers," while she herself would leave, withdrawing to her place of rest in the apartment within the enclosed yard. Then she would stroll at her pleasure through those tranquil somewhat proud rooms whose scent was always easy and somewhat distant and would always penetrate to the fundamental soul with some never clear dreams of hinting beauty, dreams which had been dreamt by others in the distance, dreamt in a blur or not on a distant tranquil day when all about had been padded with fresh grass flashing spent dashes of gold…was it not you who dreamed them? Ah! She would go rummaging through the many pages of music scattered and buried together beneath the cover upon that flashing piano which in that woman's home was always open, and from time to time she would stick her head with a certain cryptic caution, which she herself did not understand, in-between the heavy red curtains that fell descending toward that piano and served as an entrance to that spacious room while affording light to that polished little chamber always immersed in a cryptic half-darkness and bearing within it some mute secret, a secret stirring in every dim corner which always frightened Ruchama a little, driving her out of there just as it drew her in.

What was it she found there? With an enjoyment imbued with stirring venom that hurled some dismal bile into the soul, she would grip and leaf through that bulky album, the one she would always find in the basket hidden in one of the many-shadowed corners and covered with an airy little cloth, and she would peer and simply eat up, as if fevered, with only a look, every single line of those many and various countenances which peered out at her there, peering in the manner of people coming suddenly from a distance, peering in the manner in which new creatures of the most improved sort would if they were to stumble and come suddenly down to us from some other spheres. Dreams of childhood—those forgetful dreams and their foolish ways. Ha, ha. Was this not the cry of wanton voluptuousness of which that Vera has been so fond since the day she returned from those clever cities of hers? And that Ephraim—he too took up her manner: a dismal baby dreaming dreams! Yet she wondered on. Why then just dreams of childhood—may you be so kind? Was this not a great world and wide? In every single generation, so she believed, there were people quite correct and decent, there were people of the exact same form and feature of those woven and living in the dreams of every "dismal baby," if she were innocent of spirit and did dream.

They dwelt wherever they dwelt and wove secretly with no fanfare that simple permanent truth lying at the base of life and searched for in vain along all the noisy ways, and that great absolute beauty which filled and encompassed their entire existence and from which the entire existence about them was nourished as well. There were—and the pure heart divined them everywhere...everywhere...hmm...her quivering heart demurred: which heart was pure and which was not?

Hmm...certainly not the twisted heart of a filthy baby like her...and a pure heart all in all—how could it be defined?...Ah, let this heart of hers be twisted—let it be twisted; however here it was that feeling she was discussing, that moldering feeling that never left one alone. Now we here always dismiss this saying: a matter of innocent childhood, a matter of innocent childhood—and going with our spirits steady and our hearts tranquil into our bedrooms and the vanities of our toilette completely forgetting that not all hearts are equal. Of course not all hearts are equal. Are there not other hearts—there are more honest hearts and therefore it happened that even some light album, for example, which one had taken up by chance, would outweigh all those astute bucklers with which we armor ourselves in our daily lives out of the treasure- house of that clever exalted lady...a light thing of no obvious importance—and here the truth surfaced...here it was incisive...dreams of childhood!

A sudden weakness descended sticking its nails into her soul. The weakness of that certainty that conquers the spirit: the clipping of the wings. The vain spasms. Go then to be dung in the fields and do not be over wise! Then she would also see Dina, this familiar Dina extending her hand in a promise, and now she too was strange just as all those many countenances that had become strange to her, those whose living creating pulse she had divined from afar, strange to her because she was distant and because she was taller than she, could not catch up with her—in vain...never would she catch up with her—never...then she leaped suddenly from her place and her soft shoulders quivered and her throat began burning away as she dashed about in every corner, as a bird caught in a trap, until at last she faltered and fell into the dim corner of the sofa bunched up in silence, her strength wasted. She justified Dina...yet, little by little her distaste began again. She took spirit once more and her breath began emerging noisily and she was already strolling again rubbing her palms from time to time: again she considered that Dina of hers, that easy Dina laughing goodheartedly whose stillness bubbled with such warmth promising so much...why she was a child. If the truth be told—why she was but a little child, a feeble fledgling whose feathers had not yet sprouted, and that stirring life was for her and before her and now she would come and conquer and that hand of hers would create, that hand of hers, mighty and outstretched—oh, that outstretched hand of hers...so very outstretched!...

"Ah, Dina, this good Dina, why was she delayed?"

When she would hear, at last, that sound ringing brokenly, that sure somewhat spent ring and the patter of that Teodorovna's sandals in the hall, her heart would begin dancing gladly within her and she would dart out of her corner with her soulful faith upon her face and go up a bit ashamedly to that good tranquil Dina entering with a good slightly dismal smile that was in need of nothing and embracing her new little friend with a sort of open warmth of the soul, patting her on the head and shoulder and seating her in the soft corner of the sofa by the wall where she too would sit beside her, out of that warm slightly dismal tranquility of her soul, till the other opened her heart to her beginning to talk away...of what? God's brook is the soul of a beautiful person. She would talk excitedly telling of things and of stammered things...the more she told the more that little one would forget that in those streets and in the very houses she had left behind her, she had left a certain other existence and other people and other thoughts as well, and it was just such an existence and such people and thoughts of that sort that had to a considerable degree some connection with her own soul as well. She would not be aware of the airy curtains over the windows as they grew grayer and grayer, nor of the grayish shadows in the corners and beneath the furnishings as they came darting on out groping and searching one shadow for the other, nor of the fervent whir of the cicadas in the street as it drove through the open windows piercing the stirring silence of the place, that silence of twilight moving on in and moaning.

She would be aware of the black darkness when it had already descended entirely, so that the face of her good companion was wrapped in it blurred and lost, and from time to time her ear would catch the frenzy of a distant song that overcame her not overcoming the distance, and then there would be a cryptic keen melancholy, that of some awe incomprehensible to her, and it would begin pressing more and more upon her heart with a sharp searing pain, and her chest would expand as her breath was subdued drawing back and cut off, and it might happen then that her head would suddenly fall upon the tranquil warm bosom of the other whose grip was secure, she who was so good and so close to the heart, and her shoulders would begin dancing and her teeth would snatch and clamp nicely upon that light kerchief on the other's shoulders, hissing out from time to time to that stirring darkness with a suppressed stifled grunt—the grunt of a wild man without a tongue…and the other would speak nothing to her. She did not comfort her and did not coax her and did not make a sound: she would pat her feverish shoulder and pat her seething head whose black scattered curls discharged sparks in the dusk, and that warm tranquil hand would quiver away…

There was a form she found in that album, a large form whose features were rather outstanding impelling other dreams, and before it she would always stay a bit longer. This was a front view of Ephraim's face of long ago—in it were the remnants of excited voices expressing the dreams of his heart of distant days, louder days full, it seemed, of great emotion. It had then been a courageous open face with a trace of a mustache just beginning feathery-soft and the cheeks were somewhat full, as of one whose maturity was in bloom, and a pair of great open "lights" looked out confidently beneath the strong forehead, looking at distances, and the rebellious forelock was arched, and that mockery which could not be grasped, hiding in the corners of the flush lips, was full of light and confidence and just a little-dismal…remnants of excited voices expressing the dreams of a heart of distant days, louder days full, it seemed, of great emotion.

Dreams were hovering and ponderings whispering and distant stifled strings were moaning away—suddenly you raised your head as if astonished and darted out of that hidden corner, darting heavy of spirit with a nibbling wonderment in the heart: "Hah! This foolish excited heart—why did it begin weeping and for whom was it weeping there with such hot piercing pain?"

On one of those nights she suddenly remembered in the hush of the night that form before which her heart was always open, and she buried her face in her pillow with her blanket covering her head and did much weeping once more out of that odd wondering of the heart. The next day she went at noon and was quite occupied with that bulky album closing it and opening it again, and finally with quivering hands removed that picture from its frame and read on its opposite side this epistle, inscribed there in small somewhat erased letters scattered about in disorder: "On the yellow sand beside the sea of Rome. A dismal venom-filled filament is drawn from the distances driving through the great waste. Ah, it was divined in my soul: today I shall fall bleeding—in that great waste my heart shall bleed. Dear Dina! This is what I found today in my bag—an ember saved by a miracle from my great destruction. Take it and let it be for us a souvenir of what was—or was not. For it does happen that I too dream, Dina. Do you remember?

"Rainy nights and wet mists and a gray citadel and blurred lights in the puddles and rushed people stricken with filthy colds, and you and I were warm, you and I put on merriment and laughter all day long—warm and full of pure gladness was the radiant fire we kindled in our hearts. Ah, Dina! Might it flame up again one of these days?

"Those many loud nightingales that encompassed me days ago in that exalted Lanciano, itself already grown distant from me, were mere chatterers—and I had not even prayed for that. Incidentally, God is with them and their chirping—tomorrow I am taking flight entirely from this tanned Rome which has brought me nothing new, except perhaps that those nightingales are nice not only for dreams of love in the light of the blue moon. The innkeeper's wife told me that here their meat is used to make very nice pies which always arouse in the Russian generals, even those who are not stricken with gout, that special softhearted humor that yellows the faces absorbed in eating, and as the bald head moves from side to side without a word, the depths of the melting heart emit bitter loud sighs, being a memory of those distant fond days of a childhood that has passed and gone.

"And for proof, that Donna Chaya Leah stuffed me too that day with such a pie…what do you suppose, Dina—is it not that which is chattering even today from my mouth? Ah, it was already divined in my soul: today I shall fall bleeding, a dismal venom-filled filament is drawn to me from the distances driving through the great waste—and in that great waste my heart shall bleed. Dina, Dina, weep, if you wish; yet do not weep overmuch…"

To the side of that epistle she found these words inscribed, by now written in ink and in clearer letters. It seemed they had been written after his return home from the "yellow sands": "Detestable! Detestable! Yet you will forgive my error, Dina. It is this tanned Rome, it seems, which has put even these words into the mouth of one of Judah's pale exiles—and I want this picture to remain in safekeeping…and I shall seal it with a kiss, which only by its distance can be atoned for…

"And I shall seal it with a kiss…"

That little one's heart began pounding in her throat and her breath cut short. When she caught herself before long strolling fearlessly through the rooms with the picture in her hand, a sudden quivering entered her heart and she hurriedly began returning it to the place from which it had been taken. Yet then and only then did she suddenly feel that folded piece of paper lying beside it whitening at the edge of the carpet, recalling that it had been hidden at first beneath the picture and had fallen from the album as she removed the picture from it, and had remained at first lying in her lap until she rose and had not been aware of it, apparently, so that it had dropped upon the floor. This piece of paper was yellow with age, emitting a little smell of dust, and some forms not at all clear were inscribed within it on the smooth side. When she tried to unroll it, its joined folds parted with a light rustle. Ruchama, without thinking too much unrolled it and began reading from it, but she read with great difficulty because the letters were written in a woman's hand, it seemed, twisting and scurrying and scattered. Inscribed there was something whose form suggested a poem, and beneath it and to its sides many heads of horses had been drawn and heads of sheep and even the head of a woman whose curls were scattered and arms went straight down as she hung by her neck from some hook, it seemed, that was dangling in space. Ruchama mustered up all her strength to fit one word to the other, and finally that poem was produced which she later preserved in memory many days. It was written thus:

> *If it be that he return from wandering and come to my*
>   *land,*
> *I shall be tranquil.*
> *And if he visit my mother's home and I look upon his*
>   *face—*
> *I shall look again upon his face,*
> *I shall be tranquil.*
> *And if he look at me—*
> *Even if he should look at me and at the secret places of*
>   *my soul,*
> *as he did look,*
> *With his distant mercy and the great soulful melancholy*
>   *of a man—*
> *As a hero putting on his uniform*
> *I shall put on my dark tranquility.*
> *And if he extend his hand to me in peace—*
> *I shall receive his hand in peace:*
> *Quiet of mind I shall receive his great hand,*
> *His hot hand, embracing and rejecting confidently,*
> *And there shall be no memory of that foolish tremor in*
>   *my own palm—*
> *I shall be tranquil…*
> *Yet if my luck allow that he visit my dwelling even to lie*
>   *for a night*
> *Under one roof with me—in my mother's home,*

*Then I shall rise in the hush of night and grope softly on
    the tiptoes of my bare feet
And find his bed in the dark—
I will find his bed in the dark!
And he being stretched out before me,
gripped in the void of sleep,
His limbs quivering with the gladness of overpowering
    repose,
He will neither notice nor sense nor will his soul dream
    of my nearness,
I shall bow and kiss him on his chest—
Softly I shall remove the edge of the blanket and kiss him
    on his chest…
And that kiss will be the kiss of the murderer killing:
I shall guzzle his blood with that kiss!
And that blood will be mine, to quiet my thirst,
And it will be my medicine,
to quiet the desire of a lonesome sick soul,
    Wailing,
Like a she-wolf in her hole,
in agony for love
Embracing still stones,
A quivering soul burning in its flame for a kiss of love
And never kissing—
From the day it darted forth to thirst and be sick in the
    sunlight
Till it grew old.…*

Here drawn below was that woman with her scattered curls
hanging by her neck from that hook in space and an address was also
inscribed, of someone named Girasim. That little one unhurriedly
folded up the paper and stuck it back in place beneath the picture
and unhurriedly stood beside the mirror fixing the locks of her hair
and tranquilly and unhurriedly went out to the hall and returned
home. Yet when Teodorovna overtook her and asked her the cause
of her leaving without having seeing *Mademoiselle*, she did not listen

to her words nor did she reply…and when she came back home, she wandered about the many rooms with her memory as if in a dream, so that when she was spoken to she would peer into the face of the one addressing her as if peering from ultimate distances, and when she thought of taking up a lamp she would come and take a cup and a towel and a garment and an inkwell, anything but the lamp. So it was the next day and so the next day and the next on and on. Father, a shortish Jew whose beard and head of hair were clipped and graying here and there and who was always speaking of soffits and barge boards and certain odd fractional numbers and of business, spitting enthusiastically as he spoke, this father began sighing at night upon his wife's bosom, she already lying in bed and he taking off his clothes busy with little notebooks and papers, until he would complain: "I see it already…very likely the chapters will start again soon from 'In the beginning…' I see it already…courses again and Kiev again and papers again and dances and weddings—I see it already…I am already, thank God, versed in the subject!"

And he would fall upon the bed huddling well beneath the blanket and sighing concluding briefly: "So…so much for it!"

That Vera on her part began looking somewhat anew at Ephraim and when speaking to him she would not look at his face, and when looking at his face her look would go aslant and the pink radiant lobes of her ears would redden. Yet before long Ephraim asked her in slight wonderment: "This is a somewhat puzzling matter, Vera. Why you have been speaking to me of late…ha, ha, so, I remember, my fondly remembered mother would speak to Padka the carpenter, a great thief famed in our neighborhood when one of her hens had vanished at night from the chicken coop in the yard…"

She looked at him at first with a sort of shining gratitude and began laughing frankly: "Really, Ephraim, honestly, there is some truth in this. But…"

Yet suddenly her face reddened and her speech broke off.

Ephraim began laughing again: "But? You wish to say: But my hen did vanish? Do you not? Ha, ha…"

The tip of his mustache moved slightly and he began picking

with his stick at the ground below: "You see…it is a dismal matter, Vera. Without a doubt, there is melancholy in it. But…"

Suddenly he raised his face to her: "Ha, ha, why I too stopped after 'but,' Vera…"

That very night, when it seemed to him suddenly that his pillow was blazing beneath his head and he had jumped up, his seared tongue hanging out, to fling open the window at his side facing the outdoors, he suddenly began gnashing his teeth and his chest gave the bellow of a bear as he mimicked those very words of his wringing them out with a sort of stirring venom: "There is melancholy in it, Vera! There is melancholy in it, Vera! The grandiose complaint of a sentimental family of mature Dutch roosters…beast!"

Yet he simultaneously noticed the white stove opposite him. The shutters in the room had not been closed so that it was much whiter than by day, since the full moon was now at a point directly facing the windows and an enlarged shadow, darting suddenly from the dusk of the corner and stretching out slantingly on the floor, climbed up suddenly to blacken the whiteness of that stove and slipped away at once lost in the dim opposite corner, while Ephraim sat by himself at first growling in a whisper, as one who had found the proper definition of some term, "Twinges of conscience…hah, ha, why these are twinges of conscience, with all respects to your most high honor. Fine!"

He had even begun suspecting with the tranquility appropriate to the matter, that all might have merely been due to that drop; too much he had taken before bedtime out of what that gentleman had provided for him, as was his fashion. Flesh and blood of course are never other than flesh and blood—all the more so when the days were no longer the days of childhood and there were grounds for thinking that the "sundry curiosities of psychology" had already been stricken with gout…what then had he eaten before going to bed? Yet then he suddenly recalled that shadow vanishing and scurrying, and he stuck his head outside. That spacious street was asleep and somewhat moist owing to the chilly dampness of the night, its nearer side immersed in gloomy dusk and its other bigger side flat and padded with cool nocturnal light and somewhat absorbed in thought, while in the tops of its massive trees the many laminae were as clear and singly prominent as the impressions upon the plate of a negative, whereas their opposite sides were as silvery as fish scales in those brilliancies. In the blackening dusk beside the single decorated hall protruding from that large house painted vermilion across the way there was, ducking and moving beside the walls, the figure of a woman, veiled, it seemed, in a rather long cape with a white kerchief tucked about her head. Ephraim looked and suddenly his heart began growing warmer, moaning with the great faith of the soul and stifled, yearning, calling from its depths for his Dina, that hushed Dina, dedicated to him heart and soul, wandering alone at night beside his frozen windows with her ear quivering with every swish of breeze, waiting with a tremor in her limbs and withdrawing as her dreaming soul caught some rustle out of its latent dream, and returning again to drift by herself once the stillness had returned as before, and hiding rubbing up beside the walls where the dusk was penetrating her bursting soul, at last to the interior finding itself a wondrous route to his distant one at ease, so that, alarmed, he put out his head, as if moonstruck, to her—and keeping silent afterward. Silent she was in her melancholy, never opening her mouth.

When she saw him once in a blue moon telling him nothing while he might toss in his sleep and go wandering through the empty streets at night and seeing light in her rooms drop in on her so as to see the face of a living person and listen to the voice of a living person—and she would dedicate her humming soul to him and her seething body as well, dedicating them with that silence of great faith and that melancholy of a woman's utter dedication...

"Dina...Dina!"

Had he called? He had. But his voice was stifled and his lips quivered. Had she heard?

"Di..."

Yet what had happened to her—that one over there? In spite of her broad cape and that dusk encompassing her, it was quite evident that her limbs were stretching out suddenly, as if settled in a cooling bath. They stretched out—then she squeezed up against the wall beside her as if intending to squeeze through it, and froze entirely. She reconsidered—and that white kerchief on her head began moving slowly with no noticeable hand touching it, and now it was gone. It had apparently been bunched up beneath that black cape. Suddenly she shrank entirely and was swept away all at once fleeing with the rustle of her dress beating waves in the stillness, lost. Ephraim, who had been regarding her with a frozen look as his temples began freezing with pain, went back and fell suddenly upon his bed which had already grown a bit cooler, and he grunted,

"Ruchama…why that was Ruchama…great God of mercy!"

Hence he sat again forgetfully embracing his knees and casting a vague look before him as he suddenly recalled, mockingly, "No, Ephraim, passionately! Passionately!"

And loudly with arms outspread in exaggerated despair he flamed, "Ruchama! Aha, great God of mercy, why that was Ruchama!"

Yet once he had gone back and fallen immediately afterward upon the pillow, he remained lying like a log, drifting into the Land of Nod. It was just before rising that he suddenly saw before him one of those psychological curiosities, his mustache curled and his arms long with a tall top hat slipping forward upon his brow, wearing a full dress coat with prominent tails with his neck tall and his legs covered with feathers, as befitted the offspring of a family of roosters coming from Holland. This person came up to him magnificently and exclaimed most politely, "I am honored, my lady Mrs. Fault. I—my name is: Psychological Curiosity. Is it not true that the great repose suits us both? It is true. It is a melancholy affair, my honored lady; but-cock-a-doodle-doo…"

That crow, of the cock in the yard, woke him up.

That very day, as he went out before noon and meeting that Ruchama on the street walked on with her speaking to her and continuously regarding her face, she at first withheld her words due to some hazy anger, and when she did speak to him it was to contradict something, until suddenly her face blushed with some strange new fire that had taken hold of it and she began chattering and laughing brokenly in a great voice, regarding him a little audaciously and beginning to assure him repeatedly that all those foolish capers which she had sensed him making that day were to no avail—absolutely to no avail, ha, ha, and as for her why she was sure and so would continue to be that some strange dream had frightened him that night. It was his face which had told her, with the words his mouth had not found that day, ha, ha. A most nonsensical dream, a foolish dream by no means worth the while of a blue blood such as he, ha, ha. What was that dream, Ephraim—eh? He did not want to tell her? He did not want to—absolutely? Absolutely? So much for it—she was powerless; but sorry, ha, ha. Ah, how sorry she was! For she…why her very soul had blazed with curiosity—why it had always been her great desire to be privy to people's dreams, precisely those dreams people call nonsensical—no, precisely to those nonsensical dreams grownups have, ha, ha—that is, those whose mustaches are already grown and …and whose heads are already balding—no? Ha, ha. It seemed to her that he was quite concerned about this—are you not concerned about this, Ephraim? Ah?

Her voice fell a bit and that final "Ah?" emerged a bit devoid of content. Immediately following it she silenced, imagining that entirely different thoughts had come suddenly to toss her further, bearing her soul inward so that she suddenly forgot of what she had been speaking, not remembering if she had been speaking—suddenly her whole being quivered, quivering as if due to some inner chill that had come to shake her limbs and be gone What had that little one suddenly seen in the recesses of her soul? When Ephraim had sensed this, looking at her in slight wonderment, she grinned at him feebly, grinning in a hush out of some confessional weakness of the heart, and once more from her face that slight somewhat dismal pallor peeped, born of the faith of the innocent soul silently bearing its irretrievable fortune…

On a day of trickling sun Ephraim was lying in that ancient spacious armchair next to the table with his legs thrust forth at rest on the chair close alongside beneath the hanging mirror which extended in reverse from the wall. Before him he had spread that large scroll he had seen one day in the hands of that whitish kinky fellow. It was scattered before him in page after big page, inscribed and tightly filled with many lines and dots, while he held one of them in his hand, finishing with a slightly wondering attentiveness his reading of that story. In it were somewhat dismal matters nibbling at the heart.

Sprawling heavily was that black mute darkness of obscure nights of autumn. In the empty street the dryly-bare trees beat their branches roaring dryly, and the windowpanes that blackly flashed were painting in distant darkness the light of the dismal lamp in the room; at times they would quiver in the might of the arbitrary wind and ring out in fragments. There was no one to have sensed when it could have been possible—but some bug in the roof had already gotten itself expelled from its place, miserably finding rest no more, while a stranger, a black threatening stranger came and sat in some concealed coop beside the chimney on the roof, possibly within that very chimney, wailing from time to time wildly—its heart was full of disasters as it gnawed with its rotten teeth the knees upon its long shriveled legs and wailed from time to time wildly. On account of this the grieved heart would grieve all the more suddenly, finding itself open wide to receive various venomous thoughts out of a desperate melancholy while the teeth were pressed from time to time to the point of gnashing. As a beast of the field—so it was told further on—as a beast of the field gathers itself in at the start of the rainy season to its narrow dark den and begins to take nourishment by sucking its paws with its very mouth, so did the most lonesome of people and all those whom God had not gifted gather themselves into their mute beds and begin sucking their souls from within—gathering their heads and feet in beneath the feverish hushed blanket and beginning to take nourishment by sucking their throttled souls from within. Popping up, not wishing to be obscured, would be spacious soft rooms, comfortable rooms possessed of sufficient light and sufficient warmth and sufficient chatter flowing tranquilly; recalled and not expelled would be pale quivering children, children seemingly after the heart who were warm in the great nights of autumn and well with their quivering hearts so certain beside grownup father and his broad chest and beard generating all about him that wonderful certain warmth born in the tranquil soul of those privy to the secrets of a great god.

"Father...Father...God is in heaven and you are so good...you are so very good...Father!"

Yet in truth that father was no longer alive, and even if he had been—he would have been so distant and strange there being no warmth at all beside him, while the existence of God in heaven, as well, was already quite open to doubt, and even if it had not been open to doubt this would only have been because it was already all the same to one whether that hoary ancient was actually there in that gray far-off distance or not—and that David or Chaim in the story, a man whose field had been utterly swept away with no further remedy possible, lay in bed entirely gathered in beneath that feverish mute blanket, as in the fearful alarm of a nocturnal dream, and his crushed soul, that which had already begun divining its dark end, was silent and still as a mute fish whose river had cast it up on dry ground.

Yet that Chava of his, that eternal Chava as hard as rock who was always available and always good and always stuffed full of great fertile love and stirring soulful faith, she sat at his head smoothing his black curls a bit wet with heat and dreaming for him that lovely dream of pies in the sky: "It will be easier for those to come to live out their lives here—the life of this earth...it will be much easier...now a generation will be born, David—and every spare pale shadow of these bitter days will find its remedy...I am sure of it. Every spare pale shadow...ah, I see it and not far, I behold it, David, and not generations away—so I want to live my life as well...God! One day in the soft twilight grasshoppers will moan in the streets. Healthy children will laugh at a distance, and the distant rose of Sharon will give forth fragrance and unto her dreaming grandchild the ancient dame will whisper the words of a wondrous legend, that wondrous antique legend relating the song of those holy and sublime who came one day to water with the blood of their great hearts that inheritance of the happy generations, fertilizing with their fat and flesh that lovely vineyard of the Lord...God!"

And she added, after a little pause secretly complaining in despair, she added, "And we here...we here shall rest, David—we here shall rest...rest..."

Such was the conclusion of that story and such were its final words; yet beneath all that was written a small black inscription which at first Ephraim had apparently not perceived, neither what it was nor why, and in which was written with exceeding care in large precise letters: "s.p. KALMAR."

As Ephraim came upon this inscription, that slight wonderment of the heart which had been overpowering in the course of his reading was already beginning to melt and drift away, replaced by a stirring venom possessing something of the same provocation that accompanied a sudden disillusionment, so that he laughed harshly through his nostrils—and every time he raised his face in jesting enjoyment to that sun in its trickling, all of it scrambled like an egg upon the window before him, he thrust his head back, still abandoning his being to those flustered rays celebrating their holiday of gold and intoxicated with bursting blooming love.

And they, the moment they sensed this, encompassed him like bees, and they drove into him sticking to his flesh and freezing in his blood as those flies of death that stick to a person's flesh and freeze in his blood as if dead, freezing on account of their eager sucking, oblivious of all, and his face stilled and was very pale, as that of one blind from his birth. So he sat a long while, sitting and not making even a single move, and in such a half-awake state of mind that fragmentary thought which he had begun at first went on annoying him, never wholly frozen:

"Conquest, this is that same conquest...ha, ha...why this man, who only yesterday was quite ordinary, a wretch whose fate looked after him over his shoulder, comes today all at once to put his bit in the mouth of that mute eternity great in its honor, ha, ha—now he comes, as we have found, and takes his saddle and puts it none too artfully upon the back of that blind awful mare which is borne up to conquer the spirit of all flesh consuming it since the first generations...conquest—that is what they say: conquest...there is a foothold! And that fellow who suddenly signed so carefully s.p. KALMAR not for nothing has he signed so carefully s.p. KALMAR, ha, ha...conquest—this is a conquest...there is a foothold."

When Zina came in and saw him lying busy with the many writings before him, she stood at first as if somewhat in doubt; yet he suddenly sensed her and the scent of her perfume upon his breath and rose to greet her, laughing as he gestured toward those scattered pages.

"Conquest…I wanted to say…why that has always been my word, Zina. People lack the sense of divination—this is a sense they lack entirely, and that is their misfortune. Especially our daughters of Israel, ha, ha…a fellow has been going around here for days and months, a whitish kinky fellow, to all appearances, taking his pleasure, so it seems, in the light of the faces of our women, gnawing at our ears, so it seems, with nonsense and plain superfluities, and now—do you see? Evidently we could not take his true measure…"

She, having lowered the curtain on account of the radiance which even so was somewhat spent by then, and having bent over a bit casually toward those indicated pages, began straightening up with some languor and luxuriousness, and having moved back she exclaimed, while removing her glove, cutting him short, "Ah…you mean…that little pale one?"

"Little pale one?"

The *raison* of it all had already failed somehow in Ephraim's breast, even before he managed to finish his words and perhaps even from the moment of its origin; yet that manner of the other, which was somewhat unusual, and that characteristic tone in which she had said the phrase "Little pale one," filled up his dry spaces.

He lifted his face to her and smiled, and she unhurriedly sat down and lit a cigarette, then speaking: "Here you said previously: Our daughters of Israel. Perhaps you were right; however as for me it is all the same…ha, ha, as for me—now I have already reached a clear decision on the matter; a daughter of Israel these days is obliged first of all to marry—afterward it will be possible for her to concern herself with authors and ordinary idlers…that is a truth which I no longer question."

The speaker's face was as usual—somewhat, even too much; yet those words of hers lacked her usual fleshy frolicsome laugh, and Ephraim's heart began in alarm divining something in that talk of hers, that which had been one day in her very silence in the days when she had come and been silent beside him, once he had met with her in Kiev. He "girded his loins" and began laughing, sitting before her. "Huh? Ha, ha. Yet you did see…my field of vision was already much wider in this regard than yours. I, as I spoke, had only been speaking in a spirit of innocence, without a shadow of a jest, you see, and…and I had only been speaking…well, about that characteristic tendency I have always found in such matters. Because…now you do see, good friend…let us say, for example, thus…people are headed for utter extinction. People are headed for that great muddy extinction, my good friend, which admits of no reality but its own, and those, the purer among them, secretly divine in their hearts their great misfortune. Yet, you see, with us and within us there are things which, though in essence are nothing at all to that muddy monster, are nevertheless revealed to us as not entirely common—not such, for example, as all who so desire come and take. And we, the thirsty ones, even for a minute's reprieve, want to regard those things as an indivisible part of that horrifying existence, and in them we divine a certain refuge groping for a foothold—and because of this we see how people are always hurrying, clinging in bunches, as those bees expiring as the bitter season of snow draws near with its slumber, to everyone they suspect of having succeeded, sticking in their nails to gain a foothold upon that awful eternity always roaring for its prey…"

When he looked incidentally at the face of the other, seeing once more that somewhat hard luster give way in the big whites of her eyes, he sensed that he had better not stop and there was even a sort of provocative venom beginning to stir in him, yet at once he was inwardly stunned by it and resumed his talk: "No. And I had previously mentioned the daughters of Israel merely because…because you see…we, the men, we have, generally, a different tendency…when we see that our power is naught, why we…well, we advance all at once to the end of the matter, if we can manage it; or when power is meager and utterly empty—do you see? Why we seize upon the most cynical explanation of the matter, ha, ha—why we take all that mute souring despair and cast it together with the blazing head and the slender shadow of its final thought, upon…upon the dark reveling bosom of woman…with whom it is—otherwise. It is you, do you see, who have clambering hands, and the abyss is so terrible and the soul quivers so, and there are so many scorched stalks of straw for salvation, ha, ha, and you…but what do you want to say, Zina—you do want to tell me something. Do you not?"

This question, asked so suddenly, burst from his lips before it had taken shape properly in his own mind; yet he suddenly sensed that his heart was growing empty and such chatterings could no longer get the better of her, while that whetted anger which he had previously stifled within him sprouted and burst forth of its own accord in the form of that sudden question.

The other was indeed a bit astounded at first and even tried to rise from her place with a soulful quivering "I?"

However at once she sat back down with that same tranquility she had had at first, and she spoke at first in the same style as before with her face again too usual and her words again lacking at first that usual flashy frolicsome laugh of hers, "How sorry I am that you broke off suddenly, no—tell me what you saw in me to make you break off suddenly, eh? And I—why such matters are always so close to my heart…they sway my heart so…*et voilà*, there are nights when I cannot sleep. Ah, how did you say it? That great muddy extinction, ha, ha!" she suddenly began laughing harshly and loudly.

"And the abyss is so terrible and there are so many scorched stalks of straw for salvation, ha, ha, ha…well? And then—how was it then? However…would you kindly excuse me, for…for here is what I wanted to tell you, in utter frankness: now I want to split just once and get rid of all that burnt porridge of philosophy you took the trouble to spit out for me here. Do you have any objection? Ha, ha…now—I, for example, as far as I can remember, have never in my life been afraid except of one thing, if I may speak honestly and truly, and this thing, insofar as I had any conception of its nature, is quite different from, as in your golden tongue, 'that great muddy extinction,' ha, ha.

"It might happen, let us say, that one day I might meet a man, hmmm…I meet a man and I…and it is, shall we say, nice for me to be close to that man. Say of this what you will: say—close to his soul. Or say—close to his flesh, or say—just close, as 'close as the horns of the altar,' as you used to say in those days—I am not being exact nor does this trouble me at all. Well, that man…that man— whether because he is too proud, as would usually be thought by *les enfants innocents*, or because it is precisely his capacity for pride that is deficient, as would usually be thought by me, or, let us say, that the cause of the matter is otherwise, and that man is not as close to me as I might wish—this is the single solitary thing which always has the power to cause me the most awful suffering, that which, if you have any conception of it, any philosophy can no more serve than…than a fresh bundle of twigs that people bring so as to add to the consuming fire, if you would most kindly allow even me to employ the language of our generation's poets, ha, ha…however…ah, God be with you—our generation's heroes, as it were!"

She rose and began for some reason to pull her long glove on her hand. Suddenly she turned her head sideways to him and hooking up the glove, she began laughing a bit oddly: "Ha, ha. You asked me before what I wanted to tell you, but what can I say to…to fellows balding, as it seems, such as you? Ha, ha…perhaps only this: rather than sitting there and preaching of some extinction and other such inanities—would it not be more proper for you to go and learn a bit…about simple pride from…from a goat, begging your pardon? A bit of common pride! Goatish, if you would allow my saying so, ha, ha…"

Once she was silent, she threw down her coat, which had been hanging over her arm at first, and went over to the mirror and began fixing the fastenings of her locks which she spread apart all at once…suddenly she gave a little luxurious yawn and hissed some none too clear sound to herself and began laughing aloud at her reflection in the mirror turning only her face to Ephraim as her hands dangled busy with her scattered fragrant locks, and she asked, "Might you tell me this, at least, Ephraim, ha, ha. Would I be able to hope that one day I will find someone who will find his way to my flustered heart, eh?"

She laughed aloud again and withdrew to interests of her own.

At first, when she had only begun to speak and be angry, Ephraim was sitting with his face lifted to her following her with his eyes and thirsting for the meaning of it all. Yet not much later, once he had sensed that hidden fire which at times flicked out from beneath that hard chilly luster guarding the other's pupils, his face suddenly assumed an inspired look, and the veins in his high fore- head swelled a little as his pupils ignited with a rushing fire while his limbs began to stir with that sharp effervescent seething that shakes a man's voice when he opens his mouth to speak and imbues the moaning breast with a heavy spirit when he sits and is silent—when every more or less definite thought drifts out and away, replaced by a rise of light easy hazes of wool as the head revolves intoxicated by the respiring nearness of some dark reveling abyss, indicating and promising something else, so that the heavy soul is soon quivering with that enjoyment of the willful repose it finds in the sharpness of the feeling it has let go.

As the other let her hands dangle to her locks, standing as she was before the mirror, he saw that she was again wearing that gray full dress with the rather small *décolletage*, and he saw the smoothness of her neck whitening from within with a dark whiteness and a sort of inner expression, and he sensed the living warmth stored in that soft close waist of hers, that agitated somewhat strange warmth which had in it something of the gray cat's, that which apparently served as an entrance to an entirely different existence, and he was already stifling some wild scream within him and was already beginning to rise from his chair to her. He began rising due to that attraction which is neither definite nor strong, as one moonstruck before the moon has seized him; yet suddenly that feeling failed in his heart—suddenly he felt that all that great agony of the stirring flesh was too heavy and bulging for his own breast, for what was its power, that spent empty vacant breast that had begun shriveling with an irritating physical pain due to that wilting emptiness within it, and he dropped back and fell, like the beam of an olive press, his head falling to the rear as his face, which suddenly paled, began struggling with a weak little laugh of mockery, as it were, that concealed sealed mockery if you wish—it was the simple crude mockery one displays toward his companions;

yet—are you fastidious? Then it had something as well of a mockery turned inwards…let it be turned inwards…so he listened even to that final question she asked and to her loud laugh at the end of it. These did startle him a little as he reclined. He thought: "Aha!"

And he began to probe, "And if this were the truth? If this is the truth—I am sorry, ha, ha…now that gnawing at the heart has begun, ha, ha…"

And he chattered in the meantime, looking at her, "What? You asked if you could hope? That is, that…the one with the glasses is not so awful? Evidently he too is not…goat-like? Ha, ha…"

The other's hands froze in her locks as she looked at him, surveying him with her face full of some stirring expression. Suddenly she grinned and asked, "Hand over your heart, Ephraim. Didn't you wish to say something else?"

A little set back, he surveyed her and resumed speaking, "Something else? Possibly…what else would I have wanted to say? Ah, true…about that of which I was speaking previously: the goat…I wanted—yet this is more of that burnt porridge, ha, ha…I had wanted to say that whatever I had said was merely *a priori*, to use the language of those burnt philosophers. Ha, ha, *a posteriori* most certainly the crowning achievement of all there is and the ideal summit of all creation ought to be and so truly is—that goat; yet…yet…even if I were sorry—that is to say…"

But he suddenly broke off. Zina too, already standing beside his chair leaning over a bit and looking straight at his face, paying no attention to his words, suddenly quivered and with a stir of bursting anger turned away to the street. From the windows which were open behind the curtains, their ears took in a commotion of somewhat agitated voices, since these were not uncommon voices and unusually agitated, there was in their commotion, which had grown up suddenly, something that cast an unusual quivering upon that limp hush to which the ears were accustomed in that ever quiet street.

As Ephraim raised the tip of the lowered curtain he saw, first of all, the yellowish scrawny dog that was always dozing at its pleasure beside the far portico as it raised its chin growling and gnashing its teeth, and then he saw a Jew dressed in a black greatcoat, a well-to-do

merchant of the neighborhood whom Ephraim knew, the father of
two well-pressed undergraduate boys and a student girl infatuated,
with "Sonatas" and "Overtures," now with his chain out of place and
his cap dropping upon his shoulder and his spare grayish forelock
already in a tangle so that he stood as if lost, in one hand holding a
green singular and special envelope which he had apparently bought
as he had started out, while his other hand was hanging down so
that it was obvious that some sudden concern had suddenly arisen
to stop him from executing a certain very important enterprise. He
looked and looked dully about him as a lamb not yet seized by frenzy
and suddenly spit with a stir of inspiration and went back, bending
forward head and shoulders with his green purchase borne before
him most carefully and intently while his other hand began to be
concerned once more with recognizing the total importance of the
matter, cutting its route through the air.

Ephraim began laughing out loud suddenly; however he was
unable to explain that laugh of his to Zina, who had turned and was
looking at him wonderingly, and those voices which had billowed up
in the hush were already so close that it was already possible merely
to discern that all in all they were merely two in number, yet excited
to much too great a degree. Because of this, their boisterous echoes
were moaning and banging about in the quiet street, as if this were
a big agitated gang approaching. They already observed that one of
them was just laughing and breathing with that boisterous pleasure
of utter satisfaction in the soul while the other was speaking with
this weighty seriousness of an enthusiasm which had in it something
of a confident provocation as well, "Well, no. *Voilà*, perhaps it is
indeed a paradox. I say…a paradoxical jest is fine perhaps. However
this thought of mine, *elle est serieuse*. I say…thus, for example, we
are permitted to perceive that which was ever a maxim of Turgenev's:
'The inventive capacity.' I say…have you never taken proper notice
of this? For it was fundamentally…I say…"

Ephraim at once recognized the voices of that whitish kinky
fellow, he who was laughing and breathing with pleasure, and of the
one with the glasses discoursing, and he sat back down.

"Knowledge…knowledge…," he heard Zina's voice whispering

behind him. "Ah, what knowledge and what wisdom—great God of my fathers!"

All at once she was discovered laughing out loud—when he turned to her she was discovered busy again with her locks which she had not fixed, but with a certain obvious rashness, and her stirring physique was a bit bent over twisting like a wireworm, with her hands still dangling busy with her growing braid, as she laughed out loud: "Ha, ha, ha. Why, you remember?" She took the pins she held between her lips and began sticking them into the curls which were already arranged, "'Teo teo, teo teo, teo tinkas, ha, toto toto, toto toto, toto tinkas—so great Mount Olympus took its dive,' ha, ha, ha. My master will kindly receive these tidings. Here are those 'nightingales'—for you and your honor's sake they have come!"

Suddenly, as if she had assumed a new potency, she began gushing in a great boisterous voice: "Ha, ha, ha, ha…"

She stopped no more except when those two entered still in that boisterous conversation which did not cease, and even when they had entered she did not stop, meeting them beside the door and turning first to Ephraim, who at first was looking and trying to guess, "What does she want?"—and then at them, "Now we shall see…we shall see at once then…ha, ha, ha…we here were sitting in discussion. Ha, ha, ha…my master here finds me…he finds me somewhat extraordinary…ha, ha, ha…he assures me that my temperature rises too high at night, ha, ha, ha…"

Suddenly she grasped that whitish one by his lapel. Her laugh was gone and she turned to him with her face lifted full of faith, "No. Did you see? When I was startled suddenly by your awful voices from the street, he grasped suddenly at the pulse of my hand and called so confidently: 'Ah, why it already has something of the night in it!' I wonder…ha, ha!"

Suddenly, just as she had left off at first, she began laughing again. That whitish fellow was lightly tapping the cigarette he had taken out upon the cover of its box in his hand and his look penetrated straight to the other's face as he laughed at her, as it were, with a confident understanding, an understanding possibly in connection with this matter and with another as well, if there were such, and uttered, "Well, why this is a matter of reality…this is a matter which has existence in reality…this is…"

The one with the glasses reddened along his jaws, and as he stripped himself of his spectacles and began to polish them with his white handkerchief, he looked at her with that thirsty look calling out from the nooks of the soul—and it seemed as if even that red squashed spot that had been sanctioned by his glasses to settle upon his nose was calling wordlessly with an oozing pain, "Mercy! Mercy! I am so crushed by all this…" And he too made an effort to laugh.

Meanwhile Ephraim had come out of his wonderment and divination with a mere shrug of his shoulders, and he rose to greet the newcomers, extending his hand to them. When the other reminded him with the ring of her laughter which did not stop that he had all the same not clarified for her, at least, who had been the cause of this—for surely someone had?—suddenly he began to laugh a bit harshly, "Ha, ha…then was it another of those clarifications that you needed? Choosing two out of a gang whose members are but three—this, it seemed, was such a simple easy matter…especially when a person finds in his own soul some relationship to the matter…"

Then the other's laugh quivered a little; yet at once this was corrected as she began fixing suddenly, for that fellow, casually as it were but with something of a care that dallied too much, that tie about his neck, incidentally asking Ephraim briefly and without a laugh, "That is, as for him the matter is entirely clear?"

They sat down and Ephraim sat as well, and while sitting he gave her a somewhat spent look, murmuring, "If I have my own free will in the matter?"

He turned at once to the one with the glasses with a light laugh of fondness, "This unusual call which you have paid me, is there some meaning to it, or is it just a call?"

That whitish one who had forgetfully not left off tapping with the tip of his cigarette, which had already become filthy and mushy due to this, upon its box, had been looking about him at times and now was turning to his companion with the glasses and to Zina with a puzzled face as he asked himself feebly, "Is it possible that they have not been here? It is somewhat puzzling…"

They meant palish Vera and little Ruchama her sister. And as for that, there was something in it. The one with the glasses, out of whose entire life history was known to his new acquaintances only this that his name was Peli, whereas Zina called him David, and that in those good not distant days he had been the resident scholar of the "clique" having apparently even gained fame as such, had read that whitish fellow's story and it had made him most enthusiastic, since in it he had found the more complicated dilemmas of Jewish life at present exposed through a singular prism—that *ewig neis lied* sung here to the accompaniment of an entirely new melody. For, in essence, why it was he, that fellow with the glasses, who believed that precisely such works were the cornerstones of the foundation of every literature if its will be to live—they are the firm strata which these days of darkness have secretly created for us, to serve us in the course of time as the material of those lofty palaces to be built in magnificence by our history, the will of which is to renew our days and which has already begun to renew our days, and our proof of it has been revealed in Strindberg but take the great geniuses which humanity has created for us and take the apothecary's common maidservant—the matters were many and complicated and could have served as food for thought and reflection and the destruction of philosophies and their repair as well, while that whitish fellow's lips had of late been mostly set tight, and with his stifled breath and his kinky curls one might sit across from him and read upon his good whitish face, "Merciful Israel, has my sin indeed been so great before God and mankind?"

However things of that sort are always suppressed in the depths of a man's heart. At the most he does not make much of them in public. And as for that, his face had been bright of late with a consuming reddishness always blooming upon his cheeks and his chest rose frequently as his laughter rang out with its boisterous echo and his mouth spoke on—it happened that he would employ certain words and phrases with which he was not familiar, stressed with a certain prerogative. That fellow with the glasses, who, as had been made public of late, was he of the signature David Zinhes, the famous *Trumpet* of the city V. being published with his most frequent par-

ticipation had already sat down to write a complete scroll concerning
that story, the name he had given it being: "The Outburst of Social
Forces and Question of the Future," and the motto he had written at
its head proclaiming: *Dea Omnibus Dubitandum.* This scroll would
be sent tomorrow or the day after to the *èditeur* of the *Trumpet,* so
as to be set and ready for printing by the time of the publication
of the story—which, incidentally, had already been set up and was
soon to be released in a special issue of that very *Trumpet*—and in
the meantime he wanted to read it aloud to the members of the fond
company he had found in this remote spot. If the truth be told, he
merely wanted to read it aloud to Zina by herself, but it was she
who had already submitted that the reading be public. To this end
they had agreed to drop in on Ephraim that noon. From there, all
would go out to the river and the reading would take place right in
the boat or in the adjacent coppice beyond the mountains. Vera, who
had begun finding of late things always to be asked of or addressed
to that "little pale one," was supposed to come early to Ephraim's, so
as to reveal the matter of their decision to him before their arrival.
Hence the matter was somewhat puzzling. Here they had already had
the time to see the one they had wanted to and had arrived as well
whereas she was not to be seen.

"It is somewhat puzzling…a bit puzzling…"

In the meantime some fellows began arriving whom even Zina
had apparently not expected, as could be learned from those shadows
which began moving over her face. Among the comers were some
whom Ephraim did not know except at a distance and some whom
he had never known at all, yet they apparently did belong to that
gang in which the "author" and the "reader" were included. Skinny
fellows arrived, wearing narrow caps and stretching out their hands
to Ephraim with a sort of great inner power, and other fellows who
fulfilled their obligation with a mere nod, standing their rapping
sticks in the corners. Here and there cigarettes were lit. In the room
the tapping of moving feet began. Chairs were scratched, there was
a rise of phlegm and freshness, and mouths spoke subdued words
and when they forgot their words were not subdued.

Ephraim was sitting in his place and there was something in the way he sat that suggested a stranger, while he unintentionally extended his hand to offer himself the smoking box and its implements which were close by, and he began rolling himself cigarettes.

The "author," sitting on the opposite chair to his left, beneath that mirror which extended in reverse from the wall, turned at the question of another fellow who wore the cap of a university student, he being the student of law, Talalai, who had come up and addressed him directly as he had entered, engaging him in some enthused conversation. The "lecturer" was sitting and discoursing at the hub of another small gang assembled beside him in one of the corners. Zina remained sitting in the opposite chair, to Ephraim's right, a kind of opposite number to that whitish one who had turned aside distantly in busy conversation, and she leaned over and looked into Ephraim's face as she laughed and whispered to him: "'Kill or hearken to my words,' ha, ha. No. This—is my fault, as I understand it; but even I am not at fault, Ephraim. This is not what I anticipated. I did not anticipate an 'audience.' Ah, those 'Trumpeters'—they could never get along without a 'tail!' When I said: a boat—I thought: who would be with us in the boat? I said: there would be…ha, ha…did I think about it at all? Ephraim, why I said—I said just this, 'I shall enjoy his grace,' ha, ha… 'I shall be warmed by his light'…why…why I love him…why, for three straight years and more I have hankered for his shadow, like…some filthy silly little girl…I tossed and tossed in my sleep, and all repose was long since foreign to me. And if finally this time, in this biting bitter time, Ephraim, I have risen again to be transported from great distances like some storm—it has been only to him…why he…Ephraim, why he is unique, singular and special out of all I have seen and met in my many days of wandering…ha, ha…now he is looking at me…yet why does he look at me thus, ha, ha…I am a weak ineffectual woman and the filthy capacity for pity is, to my distress, so great in my heart that I cannot—honestly, I cannot look at such a frightened face without my heart looking within me—ah, will you not look at me thus, Ephraim, ha, ha…"

The cigarette and its implements froze in Ephraim's hands as he looked straight at her face. It was again as usual and somewhat too much, yet from its quiet whiteness a sort of special pallor was peeping which was not too usual in her, coming to rest upon the lower part of her white proud forehead, its lower parts beside her nose, and that gloomy shadow had settled, as that of the wrinkling rivers, upon her widened pupils as well, they burning stormily, roaring and calling him from the nooks of her soul that bled in silence—and he suddenly began laughing. He paled suddenly and began laughing loudly—and it was that short harsh laugh which a person does not finish unless his chest begins to ache and ache, as if he had fallen from the roof and it had been crushed within him.

The other quivered a little as she too began laughing out loud, and she hurried to conclude in somewhat stirring haste while rising from her place, leaning over to him: "Yet…yet it can be remedied…ha, ha, let him not be discouraged…it can be remedied…I…ha, ha, ha…"

Yet Ephraim was already spent as he sat, his chest aching and aching as if he had fallen from the roof and it had been crushed within him. He was already spent as he sat, thinking for some reason of that reluctant despair seething in the heart and boring an opening as it seethed: "Life is lost, poetry has grown ancient, being trivial and foolish—even its great suffering has grown ancient, being trivial and foolish; but life—life is lost…over! Dreams born of no wisdom and legs racing after absurdities and foolish weeping and teeth gnashing like a child's and nights without sleep in ridiculous loneliness and a whistle of lips with a goat-like keenness in the soul and flustered singing out of the stupefied mind and foolish trivial marvelous nights without sleep but not lonely—all of these many trivial foolish meager distant follies will never, without a doubt, be the essence of elevated life, the cream of existence, they being so distant…life is lost!"

Suddenly with some black soulful quivering, "Is that it?"

Only after both his hands had grasped the arms of the chair in which he was sitting and he had sensed that the palms of his hands were quite pained, did he manage to suppress that odd writhing tremor which arose to shake his flesh, owing to that black sense of compulsory death that had sprouted and grown suddenly throughout his being until it was more than just a sense, plainly stifling his breath, and he stilled that seething roar that bobbed up suddenly from dark secret places to beat upon his aching chest—which began aching all the more. Then he raised his face so that it encountered that of Talalai, who was already sitting where Zina had been and smoking a cigarette. Since he was already sitting with his black brilliant forelock exposed, his face seemed to Ephraim as pure and seemingly white and soft as the face of a pure child blooming and growing from day to day, and the slight shadows moving over it and darkening it a bit every time he put the cigarette in his mouth and sucked upon it at length, with some apparently stumbling reflection, they on their part added to it a certain expression of superior understanding and fresh thought—and Ephraim's heart was suddenly hot and foolish and as one who, having stumbled, extends his hand feverishly while falling and tries to hold on to empty space, looking for any sort of hold there, so his entire crushed being was suddenly drawn to the other and he rapped him upon the shoulder intentionally so as to touch him, feeling his healthy warmth, and laughing at him, "Ah, ha! So what is new, Talalai—Master Talalai?"

When the man saw that as he sat he was quite attentively surveying Zina, who was then standing not far away and talking to that fellow with the glasses with a certain excess of feeling, he laughed at him with a slight shadow of that vulgar playfulness, "That apparently is somewhat of a perverse matter—is it not? Ha, ha..."

The other looked at him. His face was full of the impressions of fresh observation and was really rather intelligent and even prepared—good grief, you have indeed wandered far, pure holiness of childhood with its fertile dew in the heart—it was even prepared for the colossal outburst of lucid soulful faith. He looked—and suddenly began laughing, and his laugh was lucid and healthy and full of merry strength, "Ah? No, ha, ha, ha. But..."

He bowed to him by way of approach and placed his two hands folded before him. It was evident that his mind was "fixing" some matter of thought.

"But did you see, good sir? I...that is—at times, I am merely a jurist. Why this is a matter of reality—with us. A person is no longer a person with us, but rather, do you see—let us say, a concealed sealed bill of indictment in need of defense and therefore requiring study and extensive investigation, ha, ha, ha. This is a matter, do you see, in which one can be rather interested, except that apparently not all are privileged—or that it requires a special familiarity. God knows! Thus, you see, now I, too, for example, have never been privileged—that is...I should like my good sir to understand me exactly...I have not been privileged..."

"To get as far as the very body of that defense, ha, ha?"

"Ha, ha, ha...upon my soul, good sir!"

"Ha, ha...and here too?"

The other was moved to a somewhat stifled whisper, "Here too...let him consider the matter! Furthermore—it does actually happen that thorns and snares attack a man's soul due to his actions—of his concealed wrath. Let my good sir ponder the matter. Here you sit and pick and probe thinking your thoughts and making your suppositions and discoveries—and suddenly you see and actually quiver: instead of that defense you had put at the base of the matter, it is that very bill of indictment which is stretched before us open and revealed, and as swollen and burdened as...as those fears right out of some legend! Thus, do you see, here too. Ha, ha, ha, the only place I found fit and fair enough for the unraveling of that Gordian knot was...why my good sir has no need of explanation...he indicated that fellow with the glasses. Ha, ha, ha! But you see, good sir? Lately it has been evident that such a one can serve me merely as a *corpus delicti*, as we say. Ha, ha, ha...as a *corpus delicti*, an important supplement to that complicated bill of indictment marked with the name of...Zina, it appears? Ha, ha, ha..."

He thrust his shoulders back a bit and with that healthy laugh of pleasure folded the palms of his hands together in space and bowed, hiding them between his knees—and in this crouch bunched up inward, he breathed out to Ephraim a whisper full of great implication, "But that is quite a woman, apparently! Ha, ha, ha..."

Ephraim laughed at him with that light somewhat chilly laugh of politeness and fell back upon the side of his armchair. When he turned to his left he saw that the "others" had already managed to arrive. The "author" had apparently already been put at rest and the former place of that Talalai had been taken by Vera who was sitting beside him talking and listening and laughing and observing as she wondered at the stirring "audience" round about. The lustrous whiteness of her cheeks had suddenly given bloom to blushing fresh roses.

Little Ruchama's airy shawl was hanging from her shoulder and she tucked it under her left arm, going up to Zina and speaking to her with a face that was for some reason rebellious. Before long one could distinguish in the midst of that buzzing stir round about the solitary voice of the lecturer, who was suddenly discovered standing beside Ephraim. He wheedled, "How they can explain…she talked and talked, and I simply did not understand what she was saying, *chem chem chem*…here we had a boat trip and a reading and everything *tout à coup*, and therefore I told them to call the 'companions'…"

Zina was already laughing and patting little Ruchama under the chin. Before long the lecturer was discovered sitting beside a little table, which had been moved. All at once the buzzing ceased. The assembled company began quickly and intently taking their places. Those who had found a place sat down. And those who had not succeeded remained standing in place. In one of the corners a stick fell rapping and was silenced. There were some who upon reconsideration readied their throats with mashed phlegm, and a subdued silence fell.

"'The Outburst of Social Forces and the Question of the Future.' Concerning a story by a new author. *Dea Omnibus Dubitandum*. Descartes. *Kachem!*" His was a voice a bit subdued and secretly yearning, and it was already apparent that it would not at all resemble that to which Ephraim had been accustomed in the case of that fellow. When Ephraim turned to face him, as if with a new intention, he encountered Zina, as she sat not far away, facing him and laughing at him, "Aha?…yet you too, apparently, are a baby…"

"We have found in Carlyle, who wrote in his book—…"

However there was then a knock on the door, which opened, and still standing in the doorway, a bit puzzled, was a new guest who had not been expected. She remained standing, with her hands placed in the pockets of her gray broad coat which descended to her peeping sandals, while her head had been hastily enwrapped apparently in a white shawl whose tips were dangling behind her shoulders, and her tranquil noble face was a bit puzzled as if she were searching about her. The lecturer suddenly broke off and all turned to her. She began chattering, "Please excuse me, gentlemen; but…"

However suddenly little Ruchama jumped up and called with fervent affection, "Dina!"

And she fell upon her. Sensing this Ephraim rose to greet her and that Vera darted with a little laugh of friendship out of her corner beside the "author." Zina did not turn her face away from the newcomer but moving to the side she leaned a bit toward her neighbor and asked him something in a whisper.

The newcomer said hello and smiled, "Why, you are having a kind of—*lecture*. Are you not?"

The sisters encircled her in the meantime with affectionate laughter; however she caught herself at once and began rushing. She turned to those seated and questioned Zina, who on her part had been surveying her and listening to the whisper of that fellow, her neighbor.

"Begging your pardon, gentlemen…I—at once…"

And to Ephraim with some stifled passion that had begun bursting and sprouting from the noble tranquility of her face, "Ephraim, pardon me—two or three words…is it possible—why it is possible?"

She broke off laughing again with affectionate friendship at Vera and Ruchama but already from a distance, and not waiting for Ephraim she turned toward the door. The other went out with her; yet beside the door he turned to the lecturer and blurted, "Please…he is free not to wait…he should kindly not wait!"

Once he had come after her into the other room to which she had brought him, this being his bedroom, that shawl of hers had already dropped from her head and her black fragrant curls were somewhat loosened and hence seemingly more numerous and fragrant than ever, and she turned to him placing the warm stirring palms of her hands on his shoulders. They were quivering a little while her face changed and was suddenly pale and blushing and suddenly open and stirring and aspiring streaming to him while her soul stirred whispering its fragmented words, "Excuse me, Ephraim; but...I can no more...ah, I can no more, my only Ephraim!"

Her seething head fell upon his shoulder.

Ephraim was somewhat astounded having been long since unaccustomed to seeing her so, and he took her by her seething quivering waist, "But, Dina..."

However she hurriedly placed her little hand that suppressed stirring agonies to his lips.

"Ah, do not speak, do not speak...all is clear to me—all that you could say, and I demand nothing; but..."

She raised her head from his shoulder and inhaled, her knees feeble and her face quite spent, and she dropped to the chair beside the bed at its head and caught her loud breath in her throat. "But my strength has left me, Ephraim—and I would make haste to find me a shelter...a foolish shelter, you will say; but I could no more...that black terror which descended and struck me suddenly...ah, if you would look into my heart, Ephraim..."

A big immaculate drop was quivering and sparkling upon the paleness of her cheek and she took his two hands and began kissing him intermittently in silence. As she looked at him from time to time from beneath her forehead that pondered a refined pain, her brown pupils widened, settling in fluid pools and full of that warm radiance gilded with the dismal blazing happiness dedicated to a gloomy fate.

Ephraim was sitting beside her on the edge of the bed next to her, and he suddenly found his head heavy and suddenly entirely unnecessary, while his heart shuddered with a rather odd feeling that had taken shape in him in the form of this misplaced desire of the heart: for some reason, were it only possible, he wanted someone to come so that in the other's presence his own soul would feel a tap apart from her, as one taps upon an earthen bowl when buying it in the market. It was plain to him that it would then provide the ears with that sealed sound fragmented from the moment of its origin, as that covered samovar once its water had boiled.

Thus it suddenly appeared full and filled and thus it appeared sealed and concealed. With what? Yet in matters such as these it was proper for a person to probe the least. Especially one to whom the matters were essentially not very new while the wings of that lung in his chest demanded in spite of all air to breathe; nevertheless if someone were to come and tap him brokenly upon his soul, that one too would understand perhaps—she too, struggling with the distress of her soul as a fly trapped in a transparent flask and battering its head and breast against the wall of hard glass. He sat and looked at the black numerous locks of the other which had already broken out and scattered entirely, spreading the fragrant stirring warmth of inner agony and flashing at those spent sunbeams that had already divined, apparently, their time for rapid departure and hence were dismal and silent, kissing whatever they met with long warm kisses clinging in stifled agony. Suddenly he was just thinking, thinking as one does out of idleness and as he had already thought more than once, with a certain passing form of sudden deep perception: "This, apparently, is the essence of that love of which they speak…"

And he recalled other distant sunbeams spent as well. In the still of that dismal noon a rooster sounded a distant crow of despair from the yards of the neighborhood, grown up with crowded treetops beside the river nestled in the plain of the homeland, and that crow went on complaining, as the sound of a wailing ram's horn and ended where began the open abyss of oblivion, from which its hook fished up certain memories neither clear nor distant, for some reason seeming very important and very dismal and very close to the wondering heart. The wisps of scattered hay and the remains of trampled fodder grown green and golden dispersed throughout the vacated yard were utterly without the purpose of their being, that purpose which not long ago had been so definite and so merry and so obvious and unconcerned by any denial or misgiving.

Their last hope lost—removed from joy, just as their being had been removed from its remedy—they told, telling with a mute wringing pain, dismal stories to the heart which secretly writhed emitting fresh blood, as the open neck of that hot bird just slaughtered, and listened. Those were dismal stories complaining about some fragrant village wagons decorated in vermilion which had been standing here not long ago with their spotted poles, and about some healthy pressed

smooth horses which had been munching their provender here with
great zest and would snort at night from time to time stamping their
cleated shoes, and about some in-laws of the village who had taken
his sister and black clothes that had at times emerged with large faces
quite yellowed to take care of something in one of the corners of the
yard and return with their hands chancing upon something to be
fixed beneath the flaps of their great coat, then turning on their way
to those horses and fixing the bags of provender hanging from their
snouts and attending with great affection to their most smooth and
flashing places as they hummed beneath their mustaches the tunes
which would raise a din within the house.

Those matters had seemed so dismal then—and there was one
story which seemed the most dismal of all. There was one story, which
seemed the most dismal of all, a story about a fresh ruddy merry
woman whom those large in-laws had brought and taken back with
them, a woman whose name was Tili who had been not very much
older than always having taken such great pleasure in stealing stealthily up to squeeze her long shielding warm locks secretly and he had
loved so to look at her blooming face shooting off fresh sparks and to
see her laughing at him with that great warm fervid friendship—there
was such a dismal story about this playing dancing woman who in
the commotion of a morning's departure would be most bothered
by something and also somewhat provoked, so that when she had
found him, after urgent racing, in mother's dusky room, her face
would be so odd as she snatched him up in her arms and kissed him
with a seething kiss upon his forehead and kissed him once more
on his lips so that her wet fragrant kerchief was lost beside him, he
hurrying to store it away with a gladness that quivered in his heart
while she flew out like a fleeing thief.

Stories and stories. Because those were no longer here and the
yard was empty and the rooster's crow quivering from a distance was
so despairing and the big well-swept rooms of the house held their
doors wide open with a hush sprawling in them while the *Talmud*
in the great hall remained open at the severe *Pi Parasha* tractate
and a somewhat angry father was waiting beside for him to enter,
and because Tili, that ever-fresh, ever-ruddy, ever-merry woman

would sit in the morning bunched up in that corner of Father's and Mother's hitched wagon, a bit pale with her lips swollen as she grew angry whenever addressed or asked something—because of all these together, the desolation of the heart was very great, drawn very tight while that warm flow that had been flowing in the chest beneath his hand since morning streamed in one place only, piercing on as if, stuck there and lowered in with cruel composure, was the finest of drills. Only when that flow finally rose all at once pinching him suddenly at the base of his nose did his mouth suddenly open as he battered his head against that tottering fence about the garden that blossomed in vain in the corner of that yard, and he began to cry with a great oppressive pain in his chest, his weeping arriving at a certain provoked revengeful pleasure, which grew in him greater and greater and only ceased when he chattered once or twice in an unlovely voice—a voice not his that had suddenly broadened, as that of the grown bull: "Tili…Tili…"

When he ceased, he looked at the desolate emptiness about him and growled with that provocation which had been part of the pleasure of his former weeping, "Like a wild bull…clumsy!"

Once he had grown and would at times recall this, he would even then think, for some reason, with a sense of that light-winged form of sudden deep perception, "Why this, apparently, is the essence of that love of which they speak…"

However, always in such cases that form, more or less distinct, would fade beside him flying off at once in air, while his soul would remain in him as if deceived and not out of any great cleverness, and a certain slightly odd phrase which had long ago been a saying of his gloomy father's and which had remained stamped on his own memory as well would then begin complaining and complaining soulfully with some effervescent venom: "This is established doctrine, my son—an established doctrine which we have studied: 'Keep your scabby head out of the clouds of wisdom!'"

But now two lips came seething and lush and suddenly beginning with that sucking attachment of the craving soul to guzzle the palms of his hands and to remind him of the lovely captivity in which those were held. He looked down at the black reluctant head, which had previously fallen to his knees and frozen beside his heavy hands with that sucking kiss which was mute on account of the groan bursting in the soul, and his own concealed soul moved. This seething head was mute and flashing dismally dedicated in silent despair to its fate and there was in this some piercing melancholy driving in to secret places—this melancholy—suddenly incorporating the agonies of people as it bore its own flesh in its teeth. This suddenly recalled a bereaved mother.

She weltered in her mute agony, and the palms of her pale hands stirred full of a feverish soulful roar as she caressed and kissed the body of her only son lying before her heavy and cold. She was remembered—and vanished at once. Remaining was that silent melancholy and the soul suddenly grew heavier as did the shoulders until it seemed so difficult and not worth living further. Then the shoulders were thrust back and that unnecessary head fell of itself to the tapestry on the wall, falling as one who having suddenly despaired of his strength hurries to fall at will, before his heavy burden over-comes him and causes him to fall against his will. Thus…ah, to be really lying thus—to be lying like the beam of an olive press, frozen to all thought and sealed and concealed to all feeling and dull and too obtuse to take in any impression at all…to be lying dead!

However he was immediately angered by something and again drew himself up straight all at once, "Lying dead…lying dead…tell me—for which woman is he playing the fop, this poetaster!"

When he looked then, seeing beside his knees that head again, seething in its agony and never moving, the matter already seemed to him somewhat puzzling. It was suddenly as if he had by no means grasped the essence of it. What was it—what was this here? A woman was suddenly wallowing and squirming beside him—for what? Now her head seethed with an odd silence—what was it and for what was that feverish stirring bursting out and roaring to him from this frozen silence? Distress—this was the distress and agony of the soul? Distress…agony of the soul…it was strange—so strange…

Suddenly—with some feverish provocation, "But what does she intend to extract from him? What is she doing here probing and pecking with her deadly lips? And why had she suddenly seized his hands—ah, why had she suddenly seized his hands? The devil take it! And you sit here—sit down, begging your pardon, like some ridiculous dodo bird, and let your long face survey the ceiling—survey it because that one has found her pleasure in seizing those foolish hands! No—what does she want of him? What is she groping for in her artless soul? What is this probing? What is this pecking? What does she mean to extract from him? Let go—ah, she should let go!" He already meant to withdraw his hands, which were moving out of her palms; yet suddenly he gave a little quiver and stifled his anger, his look fastened with some good intention upon that warm head freezing in agony as he began going on back to his soul:

"But, why she is Dina…this is Dina…Dina…"

However no echo was found in it. Instead the other finally left off his hand, slightly lifting her impassioned face to him. It was suddenly found to be oval and seemed somewhat full recalling the face of an innocent girl with no longer any resemblance at all to that face she would show in public, and she bared white teeth drawn to him with the thirsty aspiration of the soul, laughing at him out of some seething quite dismal confession: "No! You, Ephraim, are my mortal wound forever—forever you will subjugate my foolish life…ah, where shall I find my shelter—where shall I find me a shelter, Ephraim?"

She fell upon his lap and her shoulders began quivering; yet that odd provocation which had begun bubbling in Ephraim's heart had not yet come to a boil when the other suddenly rose, getting up and beginning to fix her locks coyly before him, with that weak somewhat moist laugh:

"Ah, what is the matter with me—perhaps you will tell me, Ephraim, what is the matter with me today?"

Once she was standing dressed before that swaying mirror carefully attending to her *toilette* with her white shawl wrapped again about her head, already greatly resembling the one the public saw, she spoke in fragments and with a shadow of slight coyness bearing something of a struggling soulful shame, saying that he should excuse her, that it was only proper that he excuse this foolish weakness of hers, that when she had gone out previously she had not even suspected that she would go to him, that such an odd mood as hers today she had long since ceased remembering—and suddenly she turned to him from the mirror, already fit and ready to go, and laughed at him just as she had previously laughed at Vera and Ruchama as she put out her hand to him in farewell: "Why...death in its fundamental essence is so foreign to me...Ephraim! Why I am so healthy..."

This had such a dismal ring so subdued dropping upon the surrounding hush without giving rise even to a quiver and renewing, it appeared, nothing; however, once it had penetrated and fallen to the dusky abyss of the soul...some feverish concern suddenly arose there while the chest and temples began moaning and a sudden aspiring urgency grew in the soul to look—to look and see again that dismal open face repressing and not repressing its stirring grief and laughing, just as it had previously laughed at Vera and Ruchama.

The soul blazed thirstily and when he raised his head again the other was not beside him. There was no one round about as that dismal ring expired and a scent of distant oils wandered somewhat mixed with the smell of the *eau de Cologne* on his table, that which the other had rubbed upon her face before going, and the effervescent stir in space moaned—and moaned an ancient tale. This too was vanity—for what were the words you found to tell her? He turned to the window setting his arms and chest upon its sill.

On one of the panes a mad fly was buzzing and beating, wanting to get out and he struck the frame opening it wide. The street was silent and on the far opposite sidewalk he saw someone who, his belly protruding, suddenly revealed his flashing bald spot as he bowed most politely, and at once she was revealed on the sidewalk beside this window of his which she had left just now, and she nodded to the other with that little polite laugh of hers while drawing back one of the tips of that white shawl, and beneath the arched portico of that house his lady, an educated woman from Cherikov, who had married without the consent of her well-to-do parents, was sitting apparently upon the green bench beside the door chatting with her neighbor from the house across the way who was very likely sitting on the other side of that door, and in her broad manly voice there was something of her bulky fattened dog's voice which had already grown a bit hoarse, in recognizing the great obligation of his heart and his faithfulness to her and his pride in her.

"And I say: *skakoi, eto stati, skazhiti pozhalsta*? I don't want to—and that's it! I do not want to and it is all over!"

Ephraim suddenly found himself reflecting with some odd tranquility, as one will reflect out of idleness upon matters of circumstance, reflecting for some reason upon that very chatterer as a woman blooming like a palm tree in the yards of that remote Chernikov of hers—joining the circle of the educated and fearfully listening to their lofty words until *livres étrangers* began falling from her bosom and she began "warring" by day with her parents "struck by blindness" while at night she would put her blazing head out of the open window in her room to drink in the tranquility of the sleeping street and bear up her soul to the distant stars in the dusky sky and to Leiv Borisovich her teacher and guide who spoke rich Russian and denied the existence of God…hmm…it was of course possible—certainly it was possible that this "lovely dismal spirit" was a bit too fleshy; maybe then this was just a little bit too much for that "lovely dismal spirit"—so much for it! Nonsense!

Maybe this was a most difficult condition only as concerned the pocked lustful mail—flowers of those days; however in the soul—the soul! It was within the soul that love blossomed and that love had burst the bonds. Then it would happen that that dreaming distant star in the sky would be dearer and more near the heart than all that bulky well-founded philosophy of life whose spread net was being woven as it had been from the earliest generations by clever uncles and merciful aunts and just plain, wise intelligent experienced Jews, while another life—a new beautiful lofty life was divined by flourishing dreams.

Perhaps you will say: Man was simply bound to life—bound to life in its most fundamental sense? There was no freedom here? Oh, of what account was it—this wonderful life, which gave an honest man the pleasant ability to stuff his flesh and bring it to that point of soft warm fictile fattiness, of what account was it then when frenzy gripped the heart of Leiovichka so that he left off writing her for a

whole half year? Would she not then have thrown herself into the
river were it not for the letter carrier who had met her right beside the
bridge and handed that letter to her? *Tout de suite*, once Leiovichka
had begun writing again, that life came back as well and was filled,
that wonderful life which gave a spiritually honest man the pleasant
ability to stuff his flesh with good things and bring it to that point
of soft warm fictile fattiness, and here I am already, by the grace of
God, a worthy mother of children—Boria! Borichka!

Do you yearn again for the rods of yesterday? Return, I say,
return! Do not be rash! Hmm…weaving, with a recognition of the
responsibility befitting that matter, the exalted weave of the generations; turning—and sitting there with arms folded, chattering in
soulful tranquility, and, on the contrary—let someone come and
tell us something. Let someone come and tell us, for example—for
example—let him tell us that the life of people in general is a matter which is not very nice, or…or…let us even suppose that he say,
for example, that maybe it would be worthwhile for people to live,
at least, differently, improving their lives where possible and giving
them, at least, another more decent form…

"Done with! *Skakoi, eto stati, skazhiti pozhalsta*? I don't want
to—and that's it! I do not want to and it is all over!"

Thus Ephraim found himself reflecting not for any purpose
or due to any cause but as one will reflect out of idleness upon matters he has gotten by circumstance, and suddenly he was concerned.
Evidently that odd tranquility which had come to dwell within him
together with his previous reflections had from the start been merely
that very concern, then frozen. He was concerned at first as one will
be by a vague dream, at once perceiving that it was his own soul
weeping secretly and his aching chest moaning on for the other—for
that one who had gone. He lowered his face and found on his lapel
a long huddled thread that had fallen here from her scattered locks,
and winding it about his face he dreamed again of the scent of her
distant oils that moved the heart with the pain of childhood, and
again his ear caught those ringing words with their stifled bursting
melancholy while his temples suddenly began moaning and he rose
as one rises neither willingly nor consciously.

He wanted to look at her face—he wanted to look again at
her face. The devil take it, this was the moan of the soul…this was
the moan of the soul!…*Pfui*! Yet…here, it seemed, his coat was
hanging. Ah, that melancholy—that melancholy! For man shall not
see it—and live as he lives. Here is the coat. Fine. Ha…It has been
said: And it came to pass that when the cords of death encompassed
him—he prayed mightily. When the cords of death encompassed
him…and when the cords of love encompassed him?…Of course! Of
course! You find in the gloomy stifled grief of this love something of
that yearning lamentation of the soul before its departure…the devil
take it! The devil take it! Possibly—there is something in it? For that
yearning melancholy—no. He ought to see her. He…ah, this filthy
sleeve—the devil take it! He will see her…He…ah? No—at the very
least there is something in it…at the very least! Cords of death—cords
of love…for dismal, dismal is the soul, as death, love…

Suddenly he stooped, as one whose knees had buckled, and sat
frozen on the edge of the bed. His coat had been put on only over
his left arm, his right arm remaining frozen hanging at the opening
of its sleeve as his face was pale as if listening, pointed toward some
orange spot hovering and hovering and troubling him somewhat. This
was that orange spot cast by the descending sun upon the coppice
of coated pines in the picture on the opposite wall, and there was
something else there as well—both of these troubled him, as if from
a distance not allowing him to collect the threads of some reflections which were most important, so it had seemed to him, now cut
away from him by some antic such as you find in flighty sunbeams.
Agony! Agony! Suddenly his soul groaned within him and his face
again looked across at her. He whispered, "Ruchama…."

She was discovered standing not far from the doorway, her
pale dismal face pointed with no confidence at his and her hands
ever busy with the tassels of her shawl which was folded as previously from her shoulder to her armpit, she being frozen and as if
retreating without commotion, as a stealthy shadow retreating in the
night. Apparently she had stolen in to him some while past. Finally
hearing his groaning whisper, she too groaned and burst over to him,
sitting out of habit upon his knees and embracing him with one of

270

her hands upon his neck as she begged him: "Ephraim, tell me what is the matter. Why did he begin putting on his coat and then stop? Why his face is full of such great anxiety—what…Ephraim, what did that one have to say, eh?"

At once she jumped up covering her face in her hands and complaining to her soul, "Ah, how foolish I am…God, how foolish I am!"

Ephraim, who had not moved at first and had sat and looked in puzzled wonderment, suddenly got up and began laughing again with that short fragmented laugh—that laugh as hard as rock which a person does not finish unless his chest begins to ache and ache, as if he had fallen from the roof and crushed it. When he finished his face was quite pale and he breathed heavily with noticeable weakness, patting the other upon her head as the empty half of his coat dropped and fell to his feet, and he asked her with that warm softness: "Could it be…that the reading is already finished there, Ruchamka?"

However the other was already provoked and in protest—she turned silently to the window and began drawing upon the pane with her fingernail.

A late bird dwelling in the nearby swamp below suddenly recalled the age of its distant spring and began laughing a filthy laugh which grated upon the hush of night as the scream of a wild kid lost and giving up the ghost in the far mountains—and Ephraim suddenly quivered out of his freeze, hurrying in a stifled seething breath to take the muzzle of the loaded pistol from his temple, which had already ceased sensing its chilliness, and pointing it down with a firm arm toward that black abyss upon whose edge he was sitting, he began in feverish haste to squeeze the trigger squeezing and squeezing and idly discharging one by one all six of the bullets which were in it, and the great melancholy of some late regret entered and gripped his heart, "Ah, this misplaced flightiness—how had it come to him?"

He fell at full length, smothering his face in the chilly grass that covered the mountain ridge by the edge of that black opening, and with his two extended hands he probed and probed in the hard ground round about, as if intending to embrace it. A wild fragmented sound burst suddenly from his throat—and owing to the searing pain it caused in his chest, it seemed to him that it was not the voice of a living man which had been so discharged, but some hard pointed rock thrown out together with phlegm, and he suddenly raised his face and looked before him with that usual tranquility of his. As previously the surrounding night was black with a great hush sprawling upon its blackness, and the breath was heavy. There was a blazing heat in secret places. From a distance—apparently from the far coppices that belonged to the duke, whose castle bestraddles the village in the plain—a sharp fragrant scent had been drawn up and coming from the start of night, such as that of scorched twigs, and it no longer passed on completely. Far at the edge of the sky in the distance silent rays of light ascended heavily from time to time and fell back to the tips of gardens. It was hot—and in the weakness of twilight, as a sprawling beast that has eaten its fill, the black night writhed.

"Evidently, it is Ephraim again?" Ephraim asked himself, with desolate feeling suddenly grown heavy beneath his chest.

"Apparently, *istig—ergo sum…. Cogito* now…already this is a new living he…putrid!"

Yet he suddenly sensed some odd weariness, which had burst out of his spent joints and had begun flooding and subduing all his limbs so that he fell back down and remained lying, sleeping the sleep of heroes with his arms and legs outstretched. Nevertheless, he was unable to sense anything until his slumber was suddenly gone and he raised his head again; but then a pure sun was already laughing at the clear renewed sky from the many metal roofs that were landing scattered and crowded in the lowland beyond the twisted chain of mountains before him, and gold cupolas of blue mosques sparkled with potbellied towers glistening here and there in their midst, and the tall brick chimney jutting up alone from the solitary broad yard, which was removed from the edge of the settlement and fenced in with stones, was already slicing up and emitting its black tail.

Below—apparently from the ruined yards of the teamsters at this edge of the settlement—a horse neighed on high while the ears caught the dull voices of men and a distant fragmentary commotion. Suddenly borne from the distance and beginning merrily was the hurried whistle of a train, a distant whistle faithfully subduing roads, and far away, by those distant red tents scattered upon the flat sands that enclosed the camp at its further edge, a squat column, white as immaculate wool, was discharged heavenward and began creeping and spreading there ever onward, the black tail behind it growing and growing, thinning out at its tip and fading amidst laughing brilliancies. Apparently day was already clamoring in the lowland.

However, that vacant distant stretch which began immediately beyond those distant red tents on the sands was stretched out there in the tranquility of morning, whitening itself with path after narrow twisting path, abandoned by man, and as could be seen from the many various brilliancies playing there below, it was sparkling with the nocturnal dew, while the great wail of treetops at its border beside the distant horizon was steaming away in holy tranquility at the sun in its majesty, and its blurred vapor was airy and bluish. There a new truth began. As Ephraim raised his hand that had been for some reason clenched and aching a little, and as he suddenly saw the still pistol it had apparently been holding since yesterday quite tightly, he laughed in his heart in grief. This pistol suddenly seemed to him a thing whose spirit had taken flight, and it seemed to him for some reason that it was also light as a feather, and he mocked: "Ah! And you, you dried fig, said no—eh? Ha, ha."

As one whose heart had begun reproaching him secretly he put it with affectionate care into his pocket beside his chest, while he made as if to wheedle: "So much for it...this is—another aspect of truth. Ha, ha. Yet it is just a little not nice that every truth has its way of throwing a man over to its companion, so that he bounds off as a balloon in the hands of playing children, passed from hand to hand. Ah, the devil take it! After such a discourse in philosophy that lady from Chernikov is in the habit of sighing wistfully and later paying for it with the good *rissoles* from that cookhouse of hers...too bad!"

Grasping the black raspberry bushes that grew in various places toward the bottom of that mountain, and descending carefully along the narrow winding path that led to the grassy cool lowland hiding below between the mountains, he noticed for some reason that while walking he was selecting certain ripe tart berries and throwing them into his mouth with great pleasure. At first he laughed tranquilly, through his nostrils, as it were. Ha! Here was the height of illusion. The bush of the field gave him to eat, and the waves of the brook moaning the foot of the tall mountains quieted his thirst. Ha, ha.

Just as we have found written in many books and repeated in ancient legends. Was it such a trifle—a man goes out alone and wanders for eight straight days in the fields and distant mountains. The dainties of village taverns are his food and hidden in the dark coppices he spends his nights. In short—a man who created a legend, ha, ha. As the sages said—a man who withdraws from life etc. etc. At least in form it was like this, my fine fellow. However at once he was struck again by that desolate resolute feeling which had weighed upon him yesterday beneath his chest, that feeling of filthiness which had risen of late with all that abyss of its nature against every single flicker of his soul and mind, because it was already well-acquainted with them and already fed up with them, and his temples began moaning and shrinking. He suddenly sensed his feverish breath—and his breath was loathsome to him as his blood streamed to his head in the form of a black tempest spotted with spots of fire, and he suddenly cried wildly, plucked from his place below as a mountain rock, which the tempest had come to overturn, and a number of stones along the narrow path tumbled after him raising light dust.

In the grassy lowland below he revived a bit. There was much shade, and solitary patches of sun as a cool morning wind blew tapping upon his shrinking face, and he breathed mightily. Round about was a hush of tranquility. In one of the nearby bushes some bird was merrily occupied, and it suddenly tumbled through the branches and flew off, beginning attend to another bush, and in the brilliancies of gold beneath the clear sky a distant woodlark was washing itself and showering down its song of morning. Again Ephraim breathed mightily and it was easy—it was suddenly so easy for him to wander languorously twisting through the narrow clefts, those that were dim and twisting and padded with grass to the sides of that tranquil lowland, and to nibble at the green moist branch that was suddenly discovered plucked in his hand. Easy—as it was easy for that sprig of birch, which was suddenly revealed alone in a padded tranquil cleft, to rustle its many light eternally moving leaves, as it was easy for this sparrow, hiding among the branches, to chatter merrily and hop from branch to branch—for that boisterous wind blowing and swirling in the grass round about.

There was one easy existence...ha. Could it be that there was a limit here, which would divide life from that "departure" from life? The devil take it! That pandemonium in the mind...the departure from life. There was of course a departure from life and one alone—this was the secret of that notorious rod in his pocket. However this, as the sages have taught, ha, ha...this, to all appearances a "departure" which the sages had established as a "preparation" for life, as it were, had already become—the chronicles of mankind, ha, ha. It was no longer vital air, but it was already—a philosophy. For an utter departure from life, that which perhaps gave refuge to a deliverance of the soul, what was it?

Let us say, that which has desisted from the life of man. Not life—but existence. As the beasts of the field and the birds of the air, at least. But the departure from life, when all the unrequired adjectives attributed to that Almighty Creator have been accounted for, seeing that the freedom of the soul is one of the most solid principles in his blood, in spite of the contemptible moral creeds which jeer at him as at one of the lowly, seeing that his free will suffers no command, absolute or not, in spite of his always being hitched to the tortoises and wagons of whoever is stronger or weaker than he, seeing that his talent for deliberating and troubling over the matters before him and at times, in spite of his constant groping in darkness, even for penetrating more or less to their essence, has not left him—and all in all, all in all: this departure from life when thought is on the whole alive—that thought which even when more original than the origin of originality is essentially a mere cliché, a broken-winged cliché stifling its breath in filth—pardon me, what is it if not just doubletalk, the fear of that notorious rod, the usual common denial of anticipated danger, in short—the chronicles of mankind? They come to one seized by weakness in the face of that "life," and say to him: is it deliverance you want? Fine.

Go, my son, lie down bound, as a steer thrust down, for the slaughter, and do not bellow—or, if you will, bellow, because it is all the same as long as you most lovingly accept all those things from which the soul has already shrunk, being vile, and you shall finally achieve, you, the sinner, those which are essentially none other than the grace of almighty God. Absolutely! For—oh, consider the years of a generation and tremble! We have had Moses and we have had Buddha and we have had Socrates and we have had prophets and we have had…we had a gray cat that used to chase her tail, ha, ha…the devil take it!

Meanwhile his legs led him from one cleft to another and soon he had left the twisted chain of mountains, remaining by the broad paved road with the mountains on one side and the great fertile plain, whose standing grain, lost on the horizon beside the spread wings of that distant mill, was already whitening and had also been cut and felled in places, on the other. Far to his rear remained that congregation of houses and roofs which he had previously seen from the mountain top, and from here nothing could be seen in that corner but the tall slanted hoist of that well beside the fenced graveyard by this road, while of that distant fragmented commotion not a thing remained.

There was a great hush here as the sun blazed powerfully while beside the horse dung on the road starlings hopped, and far off, in the lost fields of the harvest, the heads of reapers were seen, a scythe occasionally flashing up at the sun, and suddenly melancholy descended upon the heart, that melancholy which gnaws at one's heart on a dark wet day, when rain knocks upon the windows and the gloomy heart moans that loneliness alone was not the axis of its awful disaster, that even if on this gloomy day his little girl were sitting beside him, beautiful and feverish and seeking his protection, and if she were to snuggle up to him like a mute dove, neither of them would escape the awful storm which would wipe out their love and the flashes of their hearts from under heaven. Ah, that beautiful blazing snuggling girl, why she was miserable—as miserable and weak as he!

Melancholy descended upon the heart, gently stifling the breath, and the soul hid itself from the nearness of resolute fear. How does one begin? Where does one find a shelter? That riding-trap, hitched to a single horse, which for some while now had been blackening and racing at the start of the road, circling and turning behind the mountains where they started, had come nearer in the meantime, and the one sitting and riding in it began regarding Ephraim from afar and seemingly swerving the horse his way. Evidently this was Nachum Barbash, cousin of that Dina Barbash, Ephraim's companion of long ago who had begun drawing away from him during the days of their residence together with Dina in Petersburg, this Nachum having attended the university there, while Ephraim had not been disturbed by this aloofness, because the other had had from time immemorial a little weakness for Dina, and Ephraim had suspected at the time that he had divined his own relationship to her and because of this had drawn away from him.

Matters and their reverberations, distant and a bit wonderful. Much water had gone by since. When Ephraim departed from Petersburg to roam abroad, he left the other there, yet when he returned one morning from his passages to take up his abode for the summer months in this remote spot, he was told that after Dina's father had died, he having been in partnership with Nachum and his elder brother, the other had quit his college, for more than two years now, and taken his uncle's place. Ephraim had even seen him from time to time, yet they were already so distant that neither of them felt it was imperative even to greet his companion. Suddenly here was the other coming, intentionally swerving his horse toward Ephraim—and Ephraim raised his wondering face directly at him. The other was for some reason quite pale and his face, always shaved, the prominent somewhat noble lines of which suggested Dina's face, had become rather wrinkled since he had seen it, and Ephraim suddenly felt for him some odd hearty warmth.

Suddenly a warming desire was born warmly to embrace this person and to ask his forgiveness and to hug him tightly and to weep together with him for both their fates. He was quite spent, and the sun was blazing powerfully while that reluctant moaning melancholy never let him go. The black pampered horse stood, and the other was discovered sitting looking at Ephraim, for some reason seemingly guilty. "Ephraim?...but how pale you are...hmm!"

His voice was subdued and hoarse and he quivered inwardly

a little. It was obvious that he was very very spent and it was hard
for him to speak owing to some hardness, which would not melt in
the chest. Suddenly—as one who had toughened his forces, "Sit here,
brother, and come to the office with me."

And after having raised his face directly at him, his cheeks
blushing—in a voice that quivered again: "Why I…it is so hard for
me now to be alone!"

Some great gloomy melancholy of the soul sprouted from
every word of his, blowing from his whole being as he most heavily
said what he said and with the very same heaviness silenced as well.
Ephraim began to wonder. He quietly lit a cigarette and extended
one to his companion as well.

"It is a bit puzzling, Nachum. Since when have you been so
spoiled?"

The other—at first his forehead darkened apparently owing to
mute agonies which had shaken him; however at once he looked at
him quietly and for some reason there was in that look so much mute
remonstration of a pining soul that Ephraim was visibly embarrassed,
chattering and not sensing what he chattered: "Excuse me, good
Nachum, I…I shall go with you!"

He sat down in the trap behind the other, and his heart within
him was already hesitant about what he had said, as some desolate
feeling began nibbling at him beneath his chest; but the other made
room for him with some suppressed, warm excitement, turning to
him with that gust of deep spent melancholy in his subdued voice:
"Ah, fine. How nice, Ephraim. You too, apparently, are in need of
rest—and you shall rest at my place."

Then, looking at him warmly with some defeated softness, "You
are not sick, Ephraim? So pale, hmm…forward!"

The horse moved off hurriedly and the light trap began racing
again on the paved road. The other sat with this head hidden, as if
helplessly, upon his chest, while Ephraim sat bouncing behind him,
a bit chagrined at his companion's warm words and that decent concern he had expressed for him with that odd softness in his heart. He
sucked and sucked upon his cigarette with some frozen guardedness
as his spent, hesitant heart wondered and wondered at the meaning

of it all. The odd change he suddenly saw in the fellow, of what did it consist? A person has been proud and cold and silent for not a few years now—then he suddenly began speaking, and what he said was so dismal. Nachum—his good Nachum. Not apparently due to any great goodness was the other silent. When he was. Peering across at him, Ephraim suddenly saw the squat reddish nape of the other, suntanned with thin odd wrinkles settled in it, and his heart quivered. It suddenly seemed to him that he had discovered some guarded secret. In that wrinkled slightly crude reddishness was the hardness of rock—and it appeared that this had buried a great many awful agonies of the soul which had perhaps been mended with a stifled grunt in the solitary silence of a night without sleep…they conversing not even with the stones of the walls. That hot wave which had risen in Ephraim's heart for him the moment he had seen him came near again under the chest, soulfully pleased that he had gone along with him. Suddenly the other chattered and it was obvious that the words were said in a single breath and with a secret apprehension that he would not complete them—it was heavy, apparently, that melancholy in the heart which oppressed him, "So…so when did you come back?"

Ephraim did not respond at first, because at first that question was not adequately understood; the other began explaining and it seemed as if he were chopping piece after bleeding piece out of a complete discourse grown loud within him, ejecting, "Because I was told…I was told that you had gone to Kiev some days ago…yesterday, when I was there…"

"Ah! At my place—you were at my place?"

Ephraim remembered, and he was already put at ease. Before the last Sabbath, not yet having left home, he had said there that he was going to Kiev for a few days. Yet it was possible that the other had been at this place. Suddenly his heart demurred—why had he asked him about his? Now the other was silent…this common grossness of the soul!

The other was still silent, suddenly wringing out, "I dropped in."

Ephraim felt himself penned in here. If not for the trap's racing so, he would have gotten down and strolled a bit by himself. Apparently there was something in it. Certainly there was something in it. He began regarding with some thirsty perseverance of the heart that reddish taciturn nape of his companion. In vain. But he did not ask. No. He did not ask. He saw how hard it was for the other to speak at all. Moreover, for some reason he sensed as well some secret dread in the face of that approaching solution. Previously it had been so easy for him to sit, as he was now, beside the other...and he was afraid. Hmm...I pine away! I pine away! What cause could have urged him suddenly to drop over intentionally even to his dwelling? Nachum? His Nachum, ever a bit odd...He murmured: "I came back...last night I came back. I...I was not in Kiev."

In the meantime they came to the potbellied log bridge lying at the end of the road in the plain, and spanning the tongue of the distant stream, the water of which was in this place as if frozen, seeing that it was always hidden by the high tangled shoots of the stream next to the irrigated fields on this side, and by the many shadows of dusky poplars and bent wild—grown elms leaning over to it from the slope of the grassy tall mountain further on. On the top of that mountain the crowded upright pines were already flying over the large coppices of the Duke, those which from a distance would blacken upon the horizon and encompass half the surroundings round about—they were leased annually to the Barbash family.

At first a pattering cool wind blew upon their faces and the smell of silt struck their noses as the trap ceased racing and began tossing from log to log; however, the moment they had passed the bridge the grassy mountain began, and the road climbed slantingly to where it was already padded with needles and dry branches flattened under the blazing sun while the smell of the pines scattered here and there gave warmth as it seemingly groped to overcome the breath in the end. All at once it was twice as hot as it had been and before long the provoked temples were ignited and the spent flesh seethed as breathing proceeded heavily and the last remaining lucid thought was lost, wholly leaving only that hard, oppressive gloominess beneath the aching chest, that which suddenly reinforced, placed a stranglehold on the rest of the breath searing the eyelashes beneath the forehead.

Blazing heat and a choking hush and this gloomy spirit in the heart. You wanted to weep for relief. With seemingly such pleasure you would wallow in those healthy fragrant needles, weeping for relief. But weep you would not. You sat crushed and desperate and lost with only that hard silent rock still oppressing your chest. It was hard to breath and hard to weep and hard even to grunt brokenly—hard to live at all. A person lost and crushed—because everything round about was so healthy. A person foolishly lost and foolishly crushed. From whom should he hide it? What ever had been was so foolish and so unimportant and hence also unlovely so that no one would have lacked a thing if it had not been. And whatever was…whatever would be—if it would be…it would have been fine perhaps to have wept a bit; but weep you would not.

But now the trap swerved all at once to the right, entering the shade of two rows of tall dusky trees and beginning to speed along the straight soft road. The smell of the pines was strong here too; but it was already less hot and the wind revived a bit. The secret places of the coppice began emitting hissing prolonged groans—in the distant sawmill built alongside the office, logs were being cut and at the beginning of the dusky empty road appeared a column of horses harnessed to wagons transporting long boards to the station, apparently, and peasants dressed in white proceeded beside them rapping them from time to time. Suddenly, a dog began barking in the distance—and it seemed his many companions were barking an answer to him from the other ends of the coppice, while Ephraim looked about him again, breathing in relief. Suddenly, some great desire for liberation swelled in his chest and he called in subdued excitement, "Good Nachum! Come, let us breathe in relief—eh? Now this cursed heaviness…the devil take it! One cannot live with it…"

The other made no reply. Yet his own heart had become so heavy with that swelling within him of the bound lust for liberation secretly recovering its forces—that he did not sense the other's silence. Neither did he sense that the other had hidden his head even more. He set his two hands on his shoulders as words of admonition burst from his lips, "Do you remember—when we were children? God! Those awful dreams these coppices aroused in us…good Nachum, we are no longer children. And once more we are together here. Old? No. Yet—would that we were old. Why all this anxiety? The dreams have proven false…ah, but could it be they that we lack? Air…a bit of air to breathe, good Nachum…always…the devil take it! This eternal heaviness in the heart…"

However, he suddenly was still. Suddenly the reins which the other had been holding were discovered dragging in the sand beside the trap and the shoulders beneath his hands quivered while the lowered head of this companion was hidden in his two palms as he wept in a strangled fragmented weak voice, as one weeping in his difficult sleep.

Ephraim was embarrassed. He began jogging the other by his shoulders and chattering, "Nachum…but, Nachum!"

The other ceased at once. He suddenly groaned oddly and ceased at once. However he did not turn to his companion. He bowed and raised the reins, and eventually—wrung out his words, "Odd…but—you see…on the face of it, what was she to me? But, apparently…"

He did not finish. He only emitted a long sigh—seething with stifled sobs and quivering, "Ah, Dina, Dina…"

Ephraim remained seated, astounded. Dina—he said: Dina? Suddenly the palms of his two hands grasped the sides of the chariot beside his knees and he groped it mightily. Dina…Dina…now this was the meaning of it…what—Dina? What had happened to Dina?

"Nachum…"

His voice was choked in his throat and broke off. He was suddenly spent. He wanted to ask with a soulful alarm: Nachum—what has happened to Dina, Nachum? And suddenly he was spent. He was spent. He was spent, not feeling the heavy weight of the anticipated lie. The question had been asked. What would the other tell him? Dina was dead. And then? Then the other would be watching, regarding him—and waiting. And he—how would he "reward" him? He was spent. Ah, but Dina—what had befallen Dina? His voice fell. He recovered the last of his forces and chattered as if in a dream, "Tell me…talk of Dina, Nachum—if you can…"

Before long Ephraim was sitting in the padded chaise lounge which had been moved out of one of the Barbash family's dwelling to find its repose before the green desk in Nachum's spacious room in the office building, and his head was lying helplessly in the soft corner of its tall support, and Dina was standing across from him dressed in her gray broad coat with her white shawl wrapped about her head. The coppice of coated pines in the picture on the opposite wall was orange with the brilliancies of the spent sunbeams of afternoon as she went on drawing her glove over her hand with her slightly excited face grinning at him just as it had grinned awhile ago at Vera and Ruchama, and suddenly she uttered, putting out her hand to him in farewell, "Why...why death in its fundamental essence is so foreign to me...Ephraim! Why I am so healthy..."

And indeed all was put at ease—but a bit strange.

"Strange...strange...strange...eh?"

This was the groaning voice of Nachum who had suddenly woken to the moaning, slightly blurred ring rising up, as the creeping mist of night in the fields, in the cramped visioning soul of Ephraim who, spent, now quivered and returned to the absolute consciousness of the matter, choking some odd sigh in his throat. There was a hush in the room and, in front of the open windows, dismal brilliancies at play were frozen in the green atmosphere, while a bit further away crowded trees drowsed in the blazing heat of noon. Despair! Nachum was discovered supine upon the low wide bed nearby, the posts of which were tall with sparkling frozen knobs, and from time to time he reached the supple mattress below. He put his hands beneath his head and looked without desire at the ceiling and groaned brokenly, "I ask: how does it all tie together? The logical necessity of it all? I perceive nothing! That ridiculous doctor said: Typhus...that the patient's typhus was contagious and she did not take care...did not take care! But could it be that this is the necessary proof of it? Ha! It was...what it was: beauty...pureness...or what? Let us say: something not generally found in life, in consequence of which that life could be nursed by it...and in a moment you looked and it was no more. Because...some Pirtruk or Michai had Typhus! And he grasped nothing!"

Ephraim thrust his spent head back into the corner of the padded chaise lounge. Those vanities! Why now—the grave had apparently opened its mouth, and he was probing and searching for the necessity of it all...was it not a wonder— how those animals everyone called people could adapt themselves to life! The necessity of it...that "ridiculous doctor"—he had found him at once. It stands to reason: surely he had a wife and children and of necessity went back home to rest a bit—so as to go on supporting them. And the other? It was very possible that if he were a bit more aware than he had been of the situation he too would have found him and no longer would be groaning in that bed.

For essentially it is always enough for a person to have some hold upon life and that beauty and the like might very well be lying degenerating in the damp ground, with all due respect. While those are groaning: necessity of it! For he—Ephraim, who only by an unimportant ridiculous chance had not last night himself provided a repast for such a "logical necessity," he who in this case was perhaps a bit more aware than the other, was already furnishing—the "necessity" of it, ha, ha? And the other—the other in his place would have found! No. If the truth be told, one might think that life was rather easy. By no means!

Since the one responsible was not man himself but something outside of him, even if it be the logical necessity of it all—it was then possible to live. Ha, ha. Possible to live. For even the "direct result of life," its "other side"—death was then not so awful. What! For the necessity of it...ha! It is not nice, you see, good friends, only then, when one senses the absolute degrading circumstantiality of life and death as well, sensing it with his entire nature, even when the inner necessity of them is so understandable and "logical." Ha, ha...the devil take it! Should he offer the straw, the saving straw, to the other groaning there, praying in essence for this and this alone—this foolish straw? He began laughing suddenly coldheartedly, as it were: "Ha, ha, do you see—I have grasped it! I have grasped it as it is, Nachum! The 'necessity' of it—why this is every man's secret, ha, ha. And with Dina too..."

Suddenly he stilled, very spent—that was one thing. And

secondly, matters of that sort always were superfluous nonsense and here, it seemed, they were capable of assuming a special form of nonsense. These people—courting any hold at all upon life! No. Better to be silent and rest a little. With never a thought. With never a single reflection in the mind full of mist. As the twilight increased the visioning being in the soul would moan. All was over. Rest, rest, rest…fine! As the light mail-carriage hitched to one horse ran racing, clanking in the distant fields and motherless roads, in the quivering soul a concern began clanking far off. What was this concern? Now Dina had lit tonight for some reason the tall lamp in the corner beside the reddish curtains in the doorway, and its potbellied globe slightly blurred the lights of the room, while in the corner of the sofa it was so nice and easy to sit. When had it been like this? For it had been like this.

Now Dina whitened beside the piano and moaning voices imbued with much emotion penetrated to the visioning soul. She and her melody of death. A moaning melancholy penetrating to dark depths, and a whirling dream roaring for distant deliverance, and a vision cast in a hush caressing the broken soul. Beside the airy curtains to the rear of the tall shady flower in the corner, pale Vera was hiding—and as a white flower among the iridescent dark flowers of the wallpaper, her head dropped upon the wall and froze there. In the center of the room that whitish fellow was bunched up in one of the chaise lounges by the table with its red cloth, and his head fell lying in his outstretched palm. Little Ruchamka, sitting at first at the other end of the sofa, thrust her head back and was discovered supine in that corner, reclining with her hands dangling beneath her scattered curls and her breast rising over and over. When had it been like this—now when had it been like this? Days ago, it seemed. Not many days ago, one might say. He even remembered how when the last notes had been hushed with their sonorous moaning, Zina, who was apparently recumbent on that bed in the dark bedroom, began begging her from there not to stop, but to go back and repeat that very song—while little Ruchamka suddenly jumped up with her face blazing wildly and she cried feverishly with a sudden passion: "No! No! Ladies and gentlemen, first I want to read a poem to you. A wonderful poem, ladies and gentlemen! Dina! Darling! Come close to me, sit here. Beside Ephraim—there. Listen now, ladies and gentlemen."

She began—and Dina paled at once and her feverish hand grasped the astounded Ephraim's shoulder. That little one read:

> "If it be that he return from wandering and come to
> my land,
> I shall be tranquil.
> And if he visit my mother's home and I look upon his
> face—
> I shall look again upon his face,
> I shall be tranquil."

Zina darted out of the dusk of that room to stand beside the doorpost—white and lost upon the redness of the falling curtains with the great whites of her eyes fixed upon that little one's blazing face. Dina was breathing like a fish on dry land, and her feverish hand was squeezing Ephraim's shoulder more and more, as if it had never found the hold it wanted there. And that little one was standing just across from her and becoming more and more impassioned in her reading, until it seemed as if she were hurling straight into the other's face every word that left her mouth, singly. Before long her voice began quivering, filled with fresh tones and half-tones, and Zina darted entirely out of that redness of the falling curtains while that Vera was discovered standing holding the corners of the piano and the whitish fellow took his hand from his face which he turned with some wonderment to that little one. She was already whispering on:

> "And that blood will be mine, to quiet my thirst,
> And it will be my medicine,
> to quiet the desire of a lonesome sick soul,
> Wailing,
> Like a she-wolf in her hole,
> in agony for love
> Embracing still stones…"

Suddenly, she stooped, as if her knees had buckled, and burst into odd tears. A quivering hush rose round about and Dina burst into a little roar hastily drawing her close to her and hiding her head in her bosom, hiding it as if she meant to hide her precious secret and beginning to caress and kiss her silently, with pale quivering hands. Now Zina came up and sat in the chaise lounge nearby lighting a cigarette and beginning to look and look at Ephraim...no. When had it been like this—now when had it been like this? Ah, possibly—it was the same thing being repeated? No—how? Why? Let that twilight go on increasing and let that visioning being in the soul moan and moan. Thus. With never a thought. With never the slightest reflection in the mind. With never that constant pain. Rest...rest...rest...

"Ephraim...Ephraim!"

Nachum was standing beside him shaking his shoulder.

"Something...what?"

"Nothing...but...but a sudden fear gripped me. Maybe you should lie down and rest a bit—eh? You are so pale...ah! Now the days will come. Ha! Wet gray rainy days consuming the last remaining hope of the heart...autumn...the day is done—night has come...ha, ha, those great black nights mute as these walls baring to the lonely man terrible teeth colder than the black panes—this is the anticipation...that cowardly anticipation nibbling at the sick heart as you anticipate morning again—that sickly morning extinguished like the pupils of a slaughtered hen, wet, filthy, outliving the last remaining hope of the heart...ah, perhaps you will tell me, Ephraim, for what and for whom should I remain stuck here henceforth—eh? Ephraim...Ephraim!"

"Something...what?"

"Nothing...you might have some tea—let us have some tea, eh?"

To the full—Ephraim remembered those matters only at night as he stood in little Ruchamka's dark room and regarded, by the meager light of the lamp in the other room, the picture of Dina that he had found standing there in its slight frame. This was after Nachum at the close of day had been visited by his elder brother and that shortish fellow whose speech was reckless and who would spit on high and when speaking of Vera and Ruchama would say no less than: my Vera, my Ruchama. That elder brother was a fellow of stature and proportions not excluding a bit of girth, and his lush cheeks were shaven, while below his beard emerged as a decorated wedge, and he had a way of dangling his hands behind him beneath the tails of his light coat and strolling to and fro in the room, at times taking note of his taciturn brother with a glance from beneath his forehead, and when the other would turn and go out, this one would raise his head and the gold chain on his chest would suddenly hang about as he began singing, looking contentedly all around.

That reckless fellow came and removed the long white prayer shawl in which he had covered his head against the dust of the roads, and revealing his clipped graying hair drank tea with them and spoke incorrect Russian. They were talking of *dublikats* and his Vera and his Ruchama and numerators and denominators till after finishing his drink rapidly he went up to the desk picking through the bundles of *dublikats* and lists which hung beside it on the wall and returning to put on the white prayer shawl and take his leave of them—and Ephraim went out with him as well. As they walked, the other began talking again, talking much of his Vera and his Ruchama and of that whitish fellow from Poltava or America who apparently, why this was an "important person"—eh? He had of late seen some…and he resumed his talk of his Vera and his Ruchama and this very Nachum—and of that…of that Dina of "theirs," of whom it had been said that the matter of her death was not entirely simple; for…for were it not for this, it would really be difficult—how does a person suddenly get up and die! However, it was said…people were gossiping…gossiping…too much already…ha, they had a tale about…about that other doctor in the hospital—the one…the bachelor…so much for it. Not the wails of Ruchama, his little one—if he had seen! If he had seen!

When Ephraim thought and suddenly discovered that he by no means wanted to return home, without making much of a refusal he went home with the other and was very pleased not to find anyone there. That fellow left him before long and began busying himself putting on the light in his room as Ephraim, intending to sit alone a bit, entered Ruchama's dark room, the door of which opened upon the darkly lighted hall.

However before long he came across that picture standing alone on the little table in the corner, and, looking more closely, he recognized it. That was the only picture Dina had kept from former days—from those distant days whose brilliancies were so tranquil and whose shadows were so easy, this Dina wearing a short dress and flitting like a baby about the great chambers of her father's home, her fresh laughter ringing from the many windows full of great echoing; then she would capriciously tease Ephraim, who would visit them at times, laughing to his face about his capriciousness and weeping in secret once he had taken his leave and gone. So she told him years later when he met her abroad and she showed him this very picture. Here were those tall swells of curls which were then always scattered and rebellious, that pure attentive pallor, so that you were at your wits' end trying to grasp the impudent hidden smile hovering and vanishing here and sprouting there, for it would always burst out precisely where it was least suspected of being, tapping you, as a blow upon the cheek, right on your embarrassed face. Suddenly for some reason he recalled Nachum and the words he had said to him that day—in full.

Ah, in those days they used to greet the days of autumn with other spirits and other words…how that fellow wallowed there in his many pains—so much for it! And this picture had been bequeathed to—of all people—Ruchama. Was there something in it? Beginning to search, he came upon that little inscription beneath it and concealed, it seemed intentionally, by the edges of the plush frame. There written in the slightly fleecy script of Dina was "*Morituri te salutant*, my sister Ruchama, my little sister, somewhat hated indeed, but beloved—very, very much." The date below was recent. Ephraim suddenly got up and faced the door.

"*Morituri te salutant*…here is that 'logical necessity' of it all, ha, ha, ha."

He went out.

That day was apparently a *jour de fête* for the citizens, the rows

of closed shops having been decorated with little flags that rustled
in the wind, and in the tree garden in the square, the approach to
which was decorated with a great arc of red and blue lamps sparkling
in the black darkness round about, and with two big long flags, there
was apparently some celebration as the laughter of strolling men and
women rang out while the band thumped and roaring rockets were
hurled from time to time into that black darkness of the heavens and
Ephraim, turning away, went off to wander through the desolate side
streets of the town. In the landscaped streets where the darkness was
blackest owing to the many huge trees that concealed the visioning
houses, it suddenly seemed to him that his name had been called in
a whisper, and he turned to discover a little window open beneath
huge black boughs, and in this window some image whitened. He
went up to regard it closely, suddenly blurting out, "Alone...in the
darkness...Vera!"

Vera apparently already had regretful thoughts about the
matter. Her pale face, markedly obscure in the dusk of night, was a
bit dismal and introspective, and her pose was a bit strange as she
looked at him, as if by chance. However, she suddenly hurried to
call with a certain choked laugh, "Is it not, in truth, a very favorable
neighborhood for poets, eh?"

Evidently this was Zina's room. What had she wanted to tell
him? She—Vera—had had to see her and had not found her at home;
and since it had seemed to her, on the face of it, that it would be
nice to sit here a bit and dream, she had remained to wait for her.
It was even possible that she would have found her if she had gone
over to...that Kalmar's place—at Kalmar's...she would perhaps have
found her...what had she wanted to tell him? Ah, this. Did he see
that man of late has been busy writing a drama, a summary of which
he has read to several of us who found it really quite important. It
had some rather fine passages...why this is—*un homme de talent*!
It was apparent that he wanted to put in it several personages from
among...from among those who were living with us here...and
Zina—she remembered former days, ha, ha. In particular it was
she who for some reason had taken great interest in the matter. She
was so engrossed in it and enthusiastic. It was apparent that she had

again begun dreaming her dreams of the stage—did he remember those, of former days? She was an odd person, this Zina…with such a grand spirit…at times she would think of her as one not of this world…what had she wanted to tell him? This. Did he—Ephraim, she meant—did he want to come along with her, perhaps she would stop in there…how did he feel about it?

The words were in the end so dismal having been said as if with a secret complaint, a resonant moan alarming the attentive soul—and it was simply a shame to look at the face, the whitish always soft face of a woman being altered as the face of an old ill woman, owing to a mortal pain in secret places, while she, as if not sensing this, aimed it with visioning tranquility as it were, precisely at that lost horizon further on. And it was as if Ephraim had stooped suddenly beneath the suffering of that great melancholy which descended, pressing all at once upon his moaning heart. He took up Vera's little hand which was discovered to be somewhat cold, and cried with a moaning spirit, "How do I feel about it? Perhaps it is ridiculous, Vera, for me to say these things at all and especially for me to say them to you—of all people. But…ha, ha. It happens that one is willing even to be ridiculous—if only to see that he is capable, at least, of such a thing. Ah! I feel good, Vera, that all that incidental and essentially unlovely 'happiness'—and even if we allow that it is not imaginary—to which miserable people lift up their thirsty souls, is not at all worth their while, since it can be a cause even if only for a fleeting moment, of those filthy agonies that so degrade and disfigure the soul. How they detract from the splendor, which is in any case limited, of man…"

However Vera suddenly took her hand from his. It was obvious that she was straightening up as she sat, and her words were chilly and seemingly mocking, "What is this—philosophy?"

Ephraim was vexed at first and cast too hard a venom, "Ah! And I had entirely forgotten that she demands bread—and a male, ha, ha! And here am I, the ridiculous one, with my philosophy…"

However, suddenly that heart-piercing melancholy in him increased and he was disgusted with himself, some strong inner regret quivering in his voice, "No. Forgive me, good Vera. However that foolish greeting—what was it for? As if things of that sort were important to us…why…why to me, at least, only this is important, that you are suffering, apparently, great agonies, and for this I am sorry, too sorry, Vera. Ah—so much for it! You are staying here? Goodbye!"

But Vera, who had been looking at him as he spoke and grinning a broken fragmented grin, suddenly groaned and grasped him by the hand. She squeezed and squeezed it in those little dismal hands of hers while her face, pale in the dusk and soft, was suddenly changed, openly suffering and frank and lifted silently to him as her lip quivered and quivered. It was obvious that it was hard for her to speak, and her breast beneath that light quivering blouse gave rise, apparently, to heavy waves. Suddenly she leaned over and kissed him seethingly with fluttering lips upon the hand, then dropped with a weak groan back into the dark room. Was this not a dream, Ephraim—a dismal dream of the soul, that choked motherless weeping that quivered and vanished in the dusk round about?

It was a dream, the dark silent night and the whispering tranquil streets and the moan of the many boisterous waters coming from beside the distant mill that dreamed alone beside the tongues of the stream in the irrigated fields in the mist and flowing into the great hush to give it a special form. A legend was told about life and its tumult—a distant legend about people alive and bothersome and foolish and miserable who loved one another and caused one another agony and hated one another and were distant one from the other and caused one another agony. An odd disfigured legend so removed from reason and visioning reality. Agony—what was this agony? If it were as distant as utter rest was distant, it would be possible and even easy to live. The night was dark and the streets were whispering, and the moan of the distant waters went on putting the great hush to sleep.

Here was a rustle in the stalks. Who had rustled in the stalks and cast a quivering upon the slumbering leaves? A soft wind blew and nestling in its wings was a light scent—the somewhat sweet and somewhat oily scent of *kutba*. All is well in autumn, Ephraim. Here is the fragrant *kutba* already. This *kutba* was one of the first dismal flowers of autumn in these remote spots. When in the streets the scent of the oily *kutba* began, the scent of apples was already near as well, stored in the low sheds and barns beside the stream upon the slope, and the many camps of golden webs were near, drawn out over the fields of after-growth in the dismal days, and the many crowded stars, falling down profusely over the chilly nights and remaining many and crowded as they were at first.

All is well in autumn, Ephraim. Without a doubt, one no longer moaned dejectedly at the dismal coming of autumn, just as he no more celebrated in his soul the merry holiday of spring. But there was also the present, in the gloomy days of which one stored up the concealed forces of this soul, closing them in the silent breast—and he was his own man and his thought was a clear thought and his breath was direct. The trees were roaring dryly and the low sky was as gloomy as a few breaths of one who was given dismal life—and he was his own man and his muscles were strong muscles and his melancholy was a fertile melancholy…a fertile melancholy! He remembered a woman, a lovely soul moaning in secret places, who would weep at times at the smell of the first *kutba*. How that one would rage then quake silently! Her voice would quiver with every sound she made and night after night she would sit then beside the piano, infatuated with the melody she loved the best, a dismal dreaming melody that they had called the melody of death. This woman always used to tell him wordlessly that she loved him and that love, because it was love, always used to weigh upon his soul; but on the day she was suddenly unfaithful to him preferring—death, that enemy of his always greater and always stronger than he, the matter caused him that pain of bitter disappointment in consequence of which he had in the raging days of his childhood wept much at night…it was a bit odd, that feeling—without a doubt; a mature person would surely have laughed at it—or even risen up against it; for…so many things are sacred to people!

Ephraim suddenly sensed his hand clasping something cold and hard, and looking about him he saw that his legs had taken him beneath the jutting dome covered with sheets of green metal which emerged from the hall of that splendid house glittering behind the big bridge, and his hand was holding the sparkling doorknob. To his left, lost in the distance, were the lights of the feeble solitary lamps that were scattered, as if they had accidentally fallen from someone's hand, on either side of the corpulent roadway, while to his right in the little garden drowsed whitish and reddish cups of fragrant *kutba*, and leaves rustled in the dream of the low bushes and the panes sparkled blackly in their dusky abandoned windows. Far away was a hush as the nearby stream breathed boisterous and black and the wings of a little fear beat—the foreign awful wings of death which were already here.

Suddenly the hush quivered and his breath ceased. At first it seemed to him that he had been dreaming. From within the abandoned dark house his ears had caught some moaning visioning chord of a piano. However, the next sound to come was already as clear as the reality of death, and it was as if Ephraim's heart had been plucked from his chest while his knees buckled, and he stooped and sat down on the bench to the side. Suddenly the chords inside began moaning, lifted up one after the other, and every single moan penetrated to the soul, chilling him as a breeze bursting out of the dark crypts of cemeteries sunken in oblivion and clasping with a foreign chill the knees of a solitary wanderer. There was no doubt about it. Inside the house, dark and abandoned by man, a piano was playing, playing with inspiration and boisterous *esprit* as one would play in these days, playing the dismal dreaming melody with which that woman had been infatuated night after night—those big gloomy nights with the difficult secret of life stirring in their silence, as the dusky corners peeped out dismal and hushed and one's voice, whenever he made a sound, would quiver with the splitting cry of the cramped soul.

This was the melody that they had called the "melody of death." A dismal melody penetrating to moaning depths and fraught with the tones of a distant dream driving on up alone through the black breakers and coming near—that whirling dream full of yearning lament to which great despair always makes haste to find its shelter at every coming of its black end. It played—and Ephraim remained sitting there like a pillar of marble, his chest and mind suddenly mute as the astounded bird became suddenly mute, finding itself closed in the strong paws of its predator, seeing that it now feels nothing but those cold hard claws which will leave it alone no more. Yet, before long, he discovered that the matter was a bit puzzling—why was he sitting here? It was night, apparently, and he was wandering alone in the streets and that woman, apparently, was not asleep, for the piano was playing inside—and why did he not drop in? Those dreams! He got up, and with no forethought and with weary feet and as if only because he had already thrashed out the matter, he went up and began knocking without desire upon the door, as was his way here year after year. Once. Twice. Thrice…but the melody did not cease, and beginning to doubt, he looked around him. Perhaps it would be better for him to move on?

The streets were whispering and the night was so quiet. However, his gaze suddenly chanced again upon the dusky windows, sparkling blackly across from the low bushes and slumbering cups of *kutba*, and beginning to recall something not clear he went down and climbed leisurely up to one of the windows and looked inside. Darkness was in the house and the lowered curtains allowed no reasonable penetration so that nothing was recognized. However, pressing his face tightly to the cold pane, he suddenly heard from within some roar of fear and the moaning song ceased all at once. Then Ephraim suddenly returned to the strange consciousness of the matter and nearly fell; however, he recovered at once and hurried to return to the door. Inspecting it, he found that it had from the first not been closed, and he entered.

Lighting a match and looking at the open piano, he breathed in relief and fell, completely spent, upon the padded chaise lounge nearby. As a shot bird whose wing was lowered and bleeding as it pushed and squeezed itself into the corner where it had fallen from the heavens, looking with frozen quivering at its hunter drawing near with his crude hands, so from beside the open piano little Ruchama looked at him, pale and frightened and bunched up entirely on the little edge of her spacious chair. Suddenly her head fell to her elbow, and she threw herself upon the projecting corner of the piano, beginning to weep aloud as her shoulders quivered. Apparently her fear had begun to fade and fail.

When the dusk in the windows began graying a little and in the garden beyond it a solitary, mute bird cheeped, Ruchama was sitting on an arm of the padded chaise lounge in which Ephraim sat, and embracing his neck she complained, "Ah, where were you in all these bitter days, Ephraim? I was so lonesome here…"

As she embraced him, her flesh was quite warm and her limbs trembled beside him, as with a captured bird you take up under its wing, and Ephraim's head was lying back as he uttered, as if from afar, "Ha! And if I had been here, Ruchamka?"

"If you had been here! You see, the others all round—why they are all so far from me…always—and even thought lately…this Vera, who for some reason never sleeps at night; this whitish fellow who speaks night and day of his new 'creation'—and even Zina, whom I do not love very much at all…"

"And I?"

The other's lips puffed out as she tossed him a cry of complaining remonstration, "Ephraim!" Suddenly with some craving aspiration of the soul, "Ah! If you had been here, you would have sat and kept silent—and listened. Why I love it so much when you sit and keep silent and listen. It seems to me then that I and my thoughts and words as well are much more to be considered. And if you should happen to utter a certain word, I would ponder it later in the nights…"

Ephraim was suddenly disgusted with himself, as if he had been discovered sinning in secret, or as if he had been told he was a fool. He suddenly sensed that he was quite hot, and he carefully liberated his seething neck and got up and uttered at the other's wondering face, "This is unnecessary, Ruchamka. Do not love me."

The other suddenly began laughing out loud, and her laugh was a bit odd with its contorted cascades so that it rather resembled fragmented weeping, and he was disgusted with himself on account of this superfluous nonsense as well and turned, growling into his mustache, "Fool! Eminent bald fool—the devil take it!"

And before long the distant days were moaning again and moaning and the surrounding existence was again visioning and still; however that existence was already visioning somewhat grayishly, and the sleeping streets were as if sprawling while at the approaches to the closed doorways dogs sprawled and drowsed. No more was this a legend which had been told about life and its tumult, no more was this a distant legend told in a dream about people alive and bothersome and foolish and miserable, while that eternal searing pain closing the silent soul was not distant, just as that life was not distant nor what was beside that life.

Paler and paler grew the gray dream. Meager was the eternal light, burning orphan-like beside the house of prayer while in the adjacent street the celebrators had called it a day and the wide-open tree garden was abandoned and silent as the treetops blackened together; the lights of the arc in the decorated approach were put out and the two long flags lowered, while in the middle of the sprawling graying square nearby one of the musicians of the band, a drunken Swede who had lost track of the others of his company, was stooping in the dewy dust as his flute played a dismal half-wild song, one of those of his distant homeland. Now a treetop was quivering in the heavens and a napping bird leaped from a branch and cheeped and a light wind was blowing tapping upon the face and the rooster was crowing in the distance. How will it be when the edges of those bright spots redden in the sky?

Translated by Reuven and Judith Ben-Yosef

Rachel Albeck-Gidron is a senior lecturer in the Department of the Literature of the Jewish People, Bar-Ilan University. Dr. Albeck-Gidron's current research is on the works of Uri Nissan Gnessin and Yoel Hoffman. Her forthcoming book, *Leibnitz's Metaphysics and 20th Century Modernity,* is about to be published in Hebrew by Bar-Ilan University Press.

The fonts used in this book are from the Garamond family

Other works in the Hebrew Classics series
may be seen at www.tobypress.com

The Toby Press publishes fine writing,
available at leading bookstores everywhere. For more
information, please visit www.tobypress.com